A More
Perfect
Union

Other books by Jodi Daynard

The Midwife's Revolt

Our Own Country

A MORE PERFECT UNION

Jodi Daynard

LAKE UNION
PUBLISHING

Published by Lake Union Publishing, Seattle

www.apub.com

Amazon, the Amazon logo, and Lake Union Publishing are trademarks of Amazon.com, Inc., or its affiliates.

ISBN-13: 9781477823798
ISBN-10: 1477823794

Cover design by Laura Klynstra

Printed in the United States of America

For my father, in memory

Part I

1

July 1, 1794

IF PURGATORY WERE A REAL PLACE, JOHNNY thought, *it would be a ship sailing the Atlantic.* And if their ship, the *Castle Eden,* were purgatory, then he and his mother, Eliza Boylston, were being well and truly purged. By day, the smell of rotten meat and bilgewater, of unwashed bodies and human waste, had more than once sent them running to the gunwale. Johnny rarely reached it in time, but his mother nearly always managed to wait until her bosom overhung the ship's side.

They had left Bridgetown, Barbados, at the end of May, and it was now July. God willing, they would reach Boston on or about July fifteenth. Twice, gales had raged, forcing crew and passengers onto their knees in supplication. But Johnny knew how boats were built, and he sensed that this one was likely to withstand the wind's punishment.

In their first week at sea, a young seaman working on the foretop mast fell into the ocean and drowned. Johnny and his mother heard other splashes, but whether these were man, beast, or garbage, they knew not; they had learned not to inquire too thoroughly.

Johnny had been stashed like cargo in a room below the round-house, suspended in darkness in a hammock that swung from ceiling ropes. Mama had fared better: She was in the roundhouse above him, with the other ladies. Day and night she suffered the seamen's heavy treads, but at least she had her own porthole, which gave fresh air and light. Some of the women, needing to dry their washing, hung their undergarments from these portholes. But Elizabeth Boylston, originally of Brattle Street, Cambridge, would sooner wear damp and moldy undergarments than display them in such a shameless manner. Now, four weeks into their voyage, Johnny suspected that she had dispensed with her undergarments altogether, for she no longer complained about them.

They were sitting together in the messroom after endeavoring to eat a foul-smelling stew. Eliza suddenly put a hand up to her throat, a telltale sign that she would soon puke.

"Let us go up, John," she said. "Quickly."

They ran up the ladder to the deck; Johnny aided his mother as best he could. Afterward, wiping her mouth and placing a hand on her damp forehead, Eliza finally turned back to her son and cried, "Oh, Johnny!" On her face was a look he knew well.

In purgatory, after the physical suffering came moral doubt. He himself felt as if he might soon fly and was weighed down only by the sadness of memory. But his mother's soul was heavy with fear.

Johnny observed her now. At thirty-seven, Eliza Boylston was still fair and tall, still the very portrait of a Cambridge lady, even without undergarments.

"Do you really think we do the right thing?" she was asking. "Leaving Grand-mama and Cassie and Isaac and all our friends? You could return, work at the shipyard. Remain at the plantation."

Cassie had been his grandparents' house slave, but she was now a freewoman and his mother's close friend. Isaac was her adopted son, once a runaway slave.

"We are doing the right thing," Johnny replied, for the fourth time in as many weeks. There was no reason to turn back and every reason to keep going. "If you recall, it was Papa's particular wish that I go. And mine, too."

"Yes." She smiled. "Ever since your papa read to you your precious Constitution of the United States." Eliza referred to the fact that, by the age of ten, her son was a patriot in love with an America he did not know at all.

"Is it not yours, too, Mama?"

"I don't know anymore." She shrugged. In the fresh air, some color returned to her face. Then she brightened. "I know I shall be happy to see my friends after all this time. But for you, my love, there shall be no turning back once we arrive. Are you ready?"

"Of course I am. I shall try to be a good white boy."

Eliza looked with unabashed adoration at her child. Standing at near six feet, Johnny was very tall for his fifteen years. He had golden-brown hair that fell in curls to his shoulders. But in the sea dampness, his hair became a kinky halo about his round head, like a child's drawing of the sun. His facial features were Caucasian in the main, but a slight broadness in the nose, a slight fullness of the lips, might imbue in certain Americans a dangerous doubt. In Barbados, everyone thought of him as black, as he himself did. His blouse and trousers were well cut, though stiff with salt, and only the African *warri* beads that adorned his limbs betrayed him as a foreigner. These were love tokens from the slaves and hucksters who sought to anchor him in place with their charms. His necklace was especially precious to him, composed as it was of talismans: painted nicker nuts, dogs' teeth, fish vertebrae, and a magnificent red carnelian in the center.

But all the charms in the world could not keep Johnny from going to America. He would take the Harvard entrance exams and attend Harvard University. He would become a great statesman like his heroes John Adams and Thomas Jefferson. He would further the most excellent cause of democracy.

Johnny's father had known his son's wishes. John Watkins owned a lucrative shipyard, but he could feel his son's dreams in his own bones. Had Johnny, whether from guilt or grief, chosen to remain in Bridgetown as proprietor of the yard, his father would have done what he could to dissuade him. But no persuasion was necessary.

They had lost John Watkins six months previously to a putrid fever. He had always been so strong, so full of life, that even now it was hard for Johnny to believe he was really gone. But the fever took hold of him, locked its death jaws, and would not let him go.

In that last week, Eliza would not leave her husband's side. Toward the end, she called Johnny into their chamber. All week, he had sat just beyond the chamber door, waiting.

"Johnny!"

He started, and then rose from the chair and stood in the doorway.

John Watkins endeavored to sit up to see his son. "Come, sit by me, child," he said.

Johnny sat in a chair by the side of the bed. His father looked up from his pillow. Though ill, he was yet a very handsome man, with taupy skin and clear sea-blue eyes. John Watkins's father had been the governor of New Hampshire, his mother, a pretty house slave, not sixteen. Eliza always liked to say that she had fallen in love with his father's outward beauty first and that it was mere luck his soul was not a disappointment. Johnny knew she spoke in jest. His father was uneducated, yet he was the best of men: the kindest, and the most honorable.

John Watkins reached for his son's hand. Johnny took it. His father's hand was very rough, like sand-paper. This hand had once been crushed, but his father never told him how it had come to be so. He regained the use of it, but never the strength. The feeling of his father's ruined hand in his own strong one made Johnny burst into tears.

"You see, Eliza." John Watkins smiled and patted his son on the head. "The very thought of shipyard work revolts him."

"No," Johnny objected. "It's not that, Papa."

"Are you certain, son? You're very fair, Johnny. You might parlay my wealth into even greater wealth and comfort for yourself and your family."

His father referred to a fact they all knew: in Barbados, a free black man could rise far up the social ladder. Many free blacks even owned slaves.

"Thank you, Papa. But I feel as if something calls me." Johnny's voice broke.

"Well, I must leave it to someone."

"Leave it to Isaac. He has been your loyal apprentice these many years. I hardly know bow from stern."

"That's not true." His father frowned.

"I worked at the yard to be close to you, no more. Oh, Papa, you well know I could never keep my mind on the task at hand. Isaac is far worthier."

His father looked up feverishly at Eliza. "It's hopeless. Isaac shall have the business, and this high-minded pauper shall go to America to become its next president. God protect him."

John Watkins struggled to catch his breath. Then he looked up at his wife. "Shall ten pounds per annum suffice for his tuition?"

She glanced fearfully at Johnny, but Watkins was shrewd. "What, more?" he asked.

Eliza knew the sum to be far more but said only, "Leave what you can, my love. All shall be well."

"I pray 'tis true," he replied. Then he sighed and shut his eyes.

"Oh, Pa!" Johnny kissed his father and fled the room, blinded by his own tears of shame. His father knew him too well. He *did* have wild dreams!

When next Johnny saw his father, John Watkins was lying in his best suit with his rough hands crossed over his chest. Someone, probably Cassie, had lovingly rubbed them with oil, smoothing out their roughness. His aqua-blue eyes, which Johnny's mama had so loved, were closed forever.

. . .

Having succeeded in calming his mother somewhat, Johnny took his leave and returned to his hammock, where he read by a reeking oil lamp. His mother played a game of whist with the other ladies and did not see her son again until morning.

When Johnny met his mother at breakfast, her crisis seemed to have passed. She smiled affectionately at him.

"Did you sleep well, Mama?" Johnny asked.

"Oh, well enough. I've grown used to the stomping about above me. But I had strange dreams."

Johnny didn't ask what they were. Instead, he wished to know more about where they would stay in America.

"We shall stay first with the Lees in Cambridge. They live but a few steps from where I grew up. After your exams, we head to Quincy, to stay with the Millers. Lizzie Miller is the midwife who brought you into this world. But I suppose I should give you fair warning." His mother paused. "The cottage is, well, it is—cozy. I fear you shall have to sleep in the parlor."

"It can't be worse than the hammock on this ship," Johnny replied.

"God forbid! But in any case, you shan't be there more than a few weeks. School starts in the middle of August."

"Will Mr. Adams be in Quincy when we are there?"

"I should think so. He hates to be away and hies it home the moment he can escape his duties in Philadelphia. In fact, I wouldn't be surprised if Abby—Mrs. Adams—suggests we lodge with them. Peacefield is large and has many empty chambers."

"Lodge at Peacefield! Oh, Mama—can it truly be?"

"I'm not certain we will, Johnny. But it is possible."

Johnny's heart thumped at the very idea, and he wondered at his mother's own calm demeanor. "But is he very impressive? Oh, I know his accomplishments. But the man himself, I mean?"

Eliza bit her lips to keep from giggling. She would never speak an ill word about the man who had once risked a great deal to help her and John. "He is—unusual. I'll leave you to judge." A sudden bump beneath them knocked over a saltcellar that had stood in the middle of the table, and his mother jumped. Johnny had never known her to be particularly superstitious, but now she looked stricken once more by doubt. "But, oh, do you not miss Grand-mama, and Cassie? Is it not a great cruelty to tear their favorite child from them? I'm sorry, I'm sorry . . ." She burst into tears.

Johnny did miss them. When he thought that he might never see them again, he could hardly bear it. Grand-mama was a dour woman, who had been quite cruel to his mother when she found herself with child, out of wedlock. But she had been an affectionate grandmother and thereby atoned somewhat for her sins. He loved Cassie even more: she had raised him as much as his own parents had. But he could not be both there and in America. He had to choose.

Back and forth they went, between terror and expectation, grief and joy, memories and visions, like the ship's own constant rocking.

Twelve days later, they saw their first sliver of land and put in at New York. Then, two days after that, Johnny was looking at the sunrise through a porthole when he heard someone shout, "Boston! Boston ahead!" Everyone raced like sheep up the ladders to the main deck. Several dozen passengers jostled each other for a good spot at the gunwales in order to watch their slow approach into the busy harbor.

Eliza turned to her son anxiously. He knew what was coming.

"Johnny, oh—is this not a terrible mistake?"

Johnny's heart was pounding so hard he could hardly breathe. He could no longer console his mother for her fears.

"Oh, Mama, I really don't know. But in any case, we're here!"

2

July 14, 1794

THE FIRST THING JOHNNY NOTICED, STEPPING ONTO Boston's Long Wharf, was the whiteness. White faces, white bonnets, and a cool white light that made the ships in the harbor look cleaner than they actually were. The second thing was the wharf itself: a long, even row of new shops and warehouses, so unlike the rank warrens of Bridgetown, Barbados.

He saw but three black men. They were readying a ship for departure. Great beads of sweat rolled down from their hairlines as if it were quite hot. But the sun on this day, his first day in America, was eclipsed by hazy clouds, and it was not really very hot, not by Barbadian standards.

Disembarking alongside him, his mother wept. "Oh, Johnny, Johnny—regard Boston. It has been so long!" Johnny did not regard Boston but rather his mother. In the morning sunlight, in this new country, she appeared quite beautiful. Her sudden joy moved him, too. It was a welcome change from her attacks of anguish on the ship.

Down the wharf, a coach awaited them. Before it stood a small dark-haired woman dressed in a high-waisted cotton gown that shivered in the breeze. The woman was his mother's age, perhaps slightly younger. Her dark eyes searched the wharf in a steady arc, like lighthouse beacons. Then they lit upon his mother.

"Eliza!" she cried and came running—quite spryly, Johnny thought, for a woman of her years. After squeezing his mother tight for several long seconds, the woman gazed up into Johnny's face and remarked, "Why, you're nearly a man! My dear little Johnny!" Here, she burrowed a tearful cheek into his shirt.

This must be Martha Miller, he thought. Martha Lee, now. This woman had helped to deliver him, had watched him take his first steps. But he could recall nothing of those days, and this fact irked him.

Johnny remembered everything, a gift of which he was almost vainly proud. He first noticed it as a very young child, not four years old. He could stare at something, then shut his eyes, and the image would remain before him in its every minute particular before fading away. He learned to cheat his friends out of their money by betting he could describe something with his eyes closed. They might ask him to say the number of windows in a warehouse or the color of the carriages in the market square. With his eyes closed, it was easy to describe the things at his leisure before the image faded. He hoped to impress Mr. Adams with his skill when he met him.

Johnny shut his eyes. How many white faces had he seen upon arriving at Long Wharf? Twenty-nine, among them seven ladies. How many buildings were there? Forty-three. What was for sale in the shops? Everything one could want: tobacco, sugar, linens, a haircut. There was even a tavern at the head of the wharf. One might have made a tidy sum wagering whether Johnny, eyes yet closed, could recall how many windows were visible along the wharf.

Two hundred and sixteen.

At last, trunks loaded onto the carriage, they set off for Cambridge. Eliza looked back once, wistfully. They had been obliged to sell the furniture they had brought along to use on the ship: a mahogany chest of drawers, two chairs, a bookcase, and one small writing desk. Although they had needed these items on the voyage, Eliza decided that it would be useful to procure the money. In the end, John had been able to leave them a fair sum, but to economize was essential. The rest of their things were now packed up in two heavy trunks.

His mother and Mrs. Lee were soon locked in conversation as Johnny observed the cool cobbled streets of Boston and the simple, stately homes. These homes, in their upright primness, reminded him of the Negro grannies who sat so erectly in St. Michael's Church, eager to hear the reverend's every word. Where *were* all the Negroes, anyway? Passing from Boston to Cambridge, he saw not a one. Then Johnny reminded himself that he was white now. He wasn't supposed to care about how many Negroes there were.

They traveled through Boston Common, a vast pasture dotted with cows and strolling couples; its far end declined gradually to the sea. The carriage soon crossed a bright new bridge of impressive dimensions. Johnny estimated that it was at least one quarter of a mile long. Seagulls squawked overhead, and the marsh soon gave way to hilly farmland. From these hilltops Johnny could see the Charles River, wending gracefully eastward.

Somewhere just before reaching Cambridge, lulled by the rocking carriage, Johnny fell asleep. He slept deeply as they rode past the university, the busy market, and the stately homes of Brattle Street, until the carriage finally lurched to a stop. He awoke but allowed his eyes to remain closed.

He had been dreaming: It was early morning, and the air was cool over Carlisle Bay. A gentle breeze blew in from the east. He was riding down the beach upon the back of a green turtle. Soon he would hear Cassie call him to breakfast. Cassie would stand at the edge of the hill and call down, her wrinkled brown hands cupped around her mouth: "John-eee! I hope you not be swimmin' down dere where nobody know if you drown yah'self!"

His mother shook him gently. "Johnny, we're here."

"All right, Mama," he muttered. But Johnny kept his eyes closed a moment longer. He knew that when he opened them, he would see an entirely new world, and the old one behind his eyelids would be just another memory.

3

MRS. ELIZABETH LEE BOYLSTON MILLER, OR "LIZZIE," was already within, having traveled from Quincy for Eliza and Johnny's homecoming. Johnny thought Lizzie a handsome woman. She had rich auburn hair through which snaked a single thick streak of gray. Though also in her late thirties, she appeared in robust good health. She wore a cotton summer gown of a cerulean blue that suited her fair complexion and made her hair glow like embers. But Johnny also gleaned that Lizzie was indifferent to her appearance: Her gown was several years out of date, and her shoes betrayed a recent trek through a muddy field. How plain she was compared to the fine Barbadian ladies, so keen to keep abreast of London fashion!

Suddenly the object of his study came flying toward him. She engulfed him in her arms, crying, "Is it really you, Johnny? Goodness, but what a fine fellow you've become!" Turning to his mother, she exclaimed, "Eliza, I can hardly believe it. Oh, but what a great difference fifteen years makes. He's every bit a man—and so very handsome!"

"Yes." Eliza beamed. "Very like his father."

"But I do wish Tom were here to greet you, Johnny. He's in New Hampshire just now and shan't be home for several weeks." Shifting excitedly back to Eliza, Lizzie said, "Just wait till the children see him! They will eat him alive!"

JODI DAYNARD

Where were the children, anyway? He had heard that, between Lizzie and Martha, there were ten of them. But he saw not a one as Aunt Martha fairly dragged him into the kitchen, where she commanded him to strip out of his filthy garments and step into a tub of hot water.

Johnny stood in his salt-crusted clothing, defiant. He was bone-weary and eager to get into a real bed, but it had been years since he had allowed any woman to see him naked, and he would not do so now. After a standoff of some minutes, Aunt Martha said, "Well, suit yourself!"

"You must mean 'unsuit,' Aunt Martha." Johnny smiled.

"Oh!" She left him with an annoyed little huff.

Then, just as he had settled into the bath, he heard the door bang open. It was Lizzie. She strode toward him and took up his necklace in one hand. "What on earth is *this*, pray? It looks quite savage."

"It brings good luck. Especially the carnelian."

"And your hair!" she went on, placing a hand upon his head. "It's so very curly!" Then Lizzie did something Johnny did not see coming: she pulled a pitcher of water from behind her back and poured it over his head.

Johnny cried and belatedly fended off the water.

Lizzie laughed.

Eliza heard her son's spluttering cry and entered the kitchen. Seeing Lizzie standing over him with the empty pitcher, she turned to her friend: "He *detests* such ministrations, you know. It's best to let him get on with it himself."

"Oh, so sorry," Lizzie said. But neither woman seemed very contrite when, giggling, they finally left him in peace.

Soon, clean and dry and swaddled in a thick cotton dressing gown, Johnny was led by his aunt up a carved staircase and into a handsome chamber, wherein stood a heavy mahogany bed.

"Sleep well, dear boy," she said. Then she closed the window curtains and shut the door behind her. Johnny sank gratefully into a real bed at last. Oh, luxury! He was asleep within a minute and did not stir until late the following morning.

In his sleep, he still felt the rocking. Rolling one way and then back the other: fear and anticipation, back and forth. As the sun began to filter through the gauzy curtains, the trees beyond, unmoving, Johnny realized that he was no longer on a ship. He rose from the bed and opened the curtains. The blazing sun made him squint.

After washing and dressing, Johnny soon emerged into a cool and silent hallway. He was fully dressed, save for his bare feet, and eager for coffee. He had begun drinking coffee in Cassie's kitchen before he could reach the table. Cassie would hand it to him, steaming hot, in a child's dish. *What was dear Cassie doing at that moment,* he wondered, *without them?*

Descending the stairs, Johnny was met with more silence. Now the strangeness of this new place came upon him. The house seemed a familiar-enough dwelling. With its double parlor and fine staircase, it was much like his plantation home. But the smells were different, and the light that came in from the window was a far whiter light than he had known in Barbados, a blue-white diamond light.

Johnny drifted toward the kitchen and saw an old woman napping by the hearth, head bent into her chest. She had on a well-worn lace cap that partially concealed a florid white face. Beside her, sitting upon a tall ladder-back chair, snoozed a grizzled old Negro. He was dressed in a worn linen suit. His old head was bent onto his chest, and a pair of hexagonal-shaped spectacles dangled at the end of a broad nose. These must be Bessie and Giles, old servants of Lizzie's family. Giles had once been a family slave. He was something of an inventor, Johnny's mother told him.

Bessie, hearing him approach, lurched upright and exclaimed, "Oh! Heavens! Everyone's at meeting. Why, you must be Johnny. I knew you when you was the size of a Sunday roast. And near as dark, too.

Goodness, but you've whitened up considerable. Yes, a handsome white lad you are now."

Johnny laughed good-naturedly.

"You can call me Bessie. But Lord, it's past ten! You must be starved!" At this worrisome thought, Bessie hastened to prepare him a breakfast. Her shouts finally woke Giles, who stood with some difficulty and bowed to Johnny in a most dignified manner. Johnny bowed in return and then retreated into the parlor, where he sat at the dining table and waited, his bare toes snuggling into the fine Turkey carpet.

Soon Bessie brought Johnny a plate of eggs, ham, and a warm biscuit. He dug in. Just as he was finishing his last mouthful, the entire Lee clan burst through the front door. Mrs. Lee was first, followed by three girls, one about his age and two young ones, perhaps five and seven, both in calico frocks and pink ribbons. Next came two boys who, by contrast, appeared rough and hardy. Hands shoved deeply in their pockets, they affected boredom with their sisters and with domestic life generally. The older one, perhaps twelve, kept glancing toward the front door, as if everything exciting lay beyond it. This lad, Johnny later learned, was Ben. The younger boy was Harry, and he was ten.

Finally, Johnny's eye was drawn to the eldest girl. Her dun-brown hair was pinned atop her head in a sloppy bun, and her eyes, though a pretty amber color, were obscured by a pair of metal spectacles much like those old Giles wore.

The youngest children swarmed about him as if they had discovered a great wild beast.

"Oh, but look at his hair!" cried the older little girl. "Regard how very curly it is! May I touch it, Mama?" she asked, sticking her hand into the soft fuzz.

"Certainly not, Elizabeth." Martha Lee pulled the child back.

At the sight of the strange beads, the little one exclaimed, "What are *these*, pray?" She reached out to touch Johnny's bracelet, but Aunt

Martha steered her away as well. "Hannah! Elizabeth! Where are your manners? Let the poor boy finish his breakfast."

Hannah began to cry, and Johnny gratefully swallowed the last mouthful of food that had sat in his cheek since the family had arrived.

Mr. Lee, the children's father, was the last one to make an appearance, having been detained at meeting. "The devil take Mrs. Appleton," he cried upon entering the foyer and removing his hat. "She held me back with a long-winded tale of her husband's gout!"

"That's uncharitable," Aunt Martha said sternly.

"Oh, well, I suppose you're right," said Mr. Lee, suddenly chuckling boyishly. Though now domesticated by a wife and five children, Harry Lee still bore the telltale signs of the roguish privateer he once had been. He had muscular arms, a rakish stance, and a careless mop of graying blond hair that fell to one side of his face.

Espying Johnny, Mr. Lee let out a snort of delight. Then, though a good head shorter than the boy, he proceeded to lift him off the floor.

"Daddy! Daddy!" Elizabeth and Hannah protested, finding it unfair that he should be able to touch the exotic stranger. Mr. Lee set Johnny down. "All right, children. You may devour him." He then turned to his wife. "Speaking of which, I'm starved!"

The children were upon Johnny at once. Even the two boys could no longer feign disinterest. Grasping Johnny's bead necklace, Ben asked, "What are these long things?"

"Those are dogs' teeth."

"And these round ones?"

"Fish vertebrae."

"Ew!" cried Hannah.

"Can you eat them?" inquired Elizabeth.

"They're probably poisonous, you idiot," young Harry replied.

"I wouldn't," said Johnny. "They're not poisonous, but I doubt they're very tasty."

"Mama! Harry called me an idiot!" Elizabeth cried.

But her mother had gone to see about dinner, and Elizabeth, seeing that her complaint fell on deaf ears, turned back to Johnny and asked if she could try the necklace on.

"Oh, but *I* should like to wear it," Hannah whimpered, her little chin wobbling.

The children all clamored at once, and Johnny offered up the necklace and the two bracelets, much to their delight. He kept only a gold ring set with a large ruby, which he feared to lose. This ring had been given to him by a certain Madame Pringle, tavern owner, as payment for Johnny's help with her accounts.

Martha whispered to Lizzie, "I fear we are in danger of falling as much in love with Johnny as we did when he was an infant."

Lizzie nodded. "Indeed. Regard how natural he is with them."

"And so patient," added Martha. "Not the way some youths are, who feel they *should* like children and make a sickly sweet show of it."

Once the family had dined, Johnny found himself on all fours pretending to be a pony. Little Hannah climbed upon his back and the others cried for their turn. Only the eldest girl, whose name was Kate, sat apart, reading upon a book. For this activity, the poor girl was obliged to raise her spectacles and hold the book so close to her face it almost touched her nose. Occasionally she ceased reading long enough to scold one or another of her siblings for grabbing Johnny too harshly or yelling in his ear.

Without, the day was sunny and fine, and not too humid. His mother had opened the front door. As the children finally moved off to other pursuits, Eliza glanced at the door.

"Johnny, do you—would you like to see the house in which your mother grew up? It's just down the road."

"Oh, yes, Mama!"

His mother did not say that her memories of that place were painful, but Johnny knew they were. She had told him how her father had sold Cassie's husband, Cato, and their child, Toby. Toby had been a great favorite of Eliza's. She had only just taught him to read when he fell victim to her father's financial "retrenchment." It was the first time, Eliza said, that she understood what slavery was. Then, the following year, a beloved younger sister, Maria, had died in that house, of the throat distemper.

They strolled down Brattle Street, Johnny admiring the great estates along the way. Stands of hawthorn, maple, and ripening apple trees flourished all the way down to the river. He had somehow imagined America as being stark and arid, and was surprised to discover its lush vegetation and tall trees.

After walking for five minutes, his mother stopped before a large, stately home. It was painted a bright yellow with cream trim. Roses, having already bloomed, flanked the path leading up to the stone stoop and a dark-green door.

"This is it," she said. "This was my home."

Johnny found no words for what he saw.

"Of course," she continued, "it has changed. We owned the land behind the house, too, all the way down to the river. There are other houses there now. But we used to play in the apple orchards just there—" she pointed into the distance. Johnny strained to see what his mother saw, but he realized that it was a vision from before he was born. "Oh, I would love to peek inside!" She giggled.

"Shall I do it?" he offered.

"Nay, Johnny! Someone is certainly within!"

But Johnny had already run off without waiting for permission. At the front door, he crouched down and peeked in a sidelight, gazed about for a moment, and then ran back to his mother, laughing.

"Johnny! How could you?" she began. She pulled him away from the house by his elbow. "You are very wicked!" she said. But Johnny saw that she stifled an urge to laugh.

Once they were safely down the road he said, "Mama, would you like to know what I saw?"

"Indeed not," she said, chin in the air.

"Very well." Johnny walked along in silence. His mother stopped.

"Oh, well, since the deed is done, you may as well tell me what you saw."

He smiled and lightly shut his eyes. "It is very beautiful. The floors are polished, and there is a green carpet in the foyer. An impressive staircase winds its way by means of four differently carved turnings, painted bright white. Instead of a newel post, there are seven—no, eight carved spirals."

"And people? Did you see any?"

"Nay. But I did have a glimpse of sorts off the foyer on the right."

"That was Papa's library. That was where he sat, reading upon a broadside, when I asked him what he'd done with Cato and Toby. He told me that we needed to 'retrench and consolidate.'" Tears sprang at once to his mother's eyes. "Oh, let us go and leave the ghosts to rest in peace!"

4

ON THE FOLLOWING MORNING, JOHNNY BREAKFASTED EARLY with the children. He had not yet fully dressed, and his feet, as always, were bare. The adults were nowhere in sight. But after he had played for near half an hour with the children, Johnny heard his mother calling to him. Her voice was syrupy.

"*Johnny*, would you kindly join us? We're just here, in the library."

The children clung to him like barnacles as he rose and moved off to Mr. Lee's study. Entering the room, Johnny saw a tall glass-fronted case containing an annotated chart of the West Indies, a fragment of a China bowl, and an old sextant. His mother, Aunt Martha, Harry, Lizzie, Bessie, and Giles sat in a single row upon a red damask sofa. The late morning sun cast them in silhouette. Johnny squinted. What was it they wished to speak to him about, so inquisition-like?

"Aunt Martha has something to say," his mother began.

That was ominous. People rarely prepared one to hear *good* news, he thought. From her pocket, Aunt Martha took a piece of paper and handed it to Johnny. Then, noticing that the door was ajar, Eliza rose to close it.

"What is this, pray?" he asked.

"It's an oath, sworn to and sealed by all of us in this room and three who aren't. We've sworn to remain silent regarding your lineage. No one else must know, not even our children. It would be very dangerous for you."

"Yes, I understand. Mama and I have discussed it."

Johnny glanced down at the document. In addition to those in the room, it was signed by Thomas Miller, John Adams, and Abigail Adams. Indeed, Johnny thought, there were so many signatures, and such illustrious ones, that it might have been the Declaration of Independence.

"Do you truly, Johnny?" Aunt Martha continued. "Think about it. Think about the very grave dangers, not only to yourself, but to all those who know you. Lizzie could no longer procure work as a midwife. My husband would lose his job at Boston Harbor. Even Mr. Adams—"

Suddenly, Johnny heard giggling beyond the door. He opened it, stuck his tongue out at the expectant children, then slammed the door shut. He burst out laughing.

"Johnny!" Eliza scolded him. "Listen to your aunt."

"Yes, child. This is serious. Do you hear what we say?"

But Johnny already knew what they told him. He'd had many weeks to think of little else. He replied gravely, "I understand full well, Aunt Martha. The very taint of knowing me would spell death. The Black Death."

Eliza scowled at her son, who had a terrible way of growing more antic the more one fretted over him.

Aunt Martha sighed. Then, with an effort at cheer, she said, "Well, but now that's done, our dear friends beg leave to impart some gentle advice to you, in preparation for your exams."

"Indeed?" All this, too, he knew already. But he crossed his long legs and placed his hands in his lap.

"The beads must go," Harry said regretfully.

Everyone nodded his assent.

"Something must be done about the hair," added Giles. "Pomaded, I should think. And neatly plaited by someone who knows what they're about. With such—colored—hair."

"Powdered?" his mother inquired.

"Nay," objected Harry. "No one powders his hair these days."

Bessie added, "He'll be needing some proper clothing, too. A blue coat, at least."

"Oh, heavens," Eliza breathed. "It has been too long. I know not what the American lads wear these days."

"Simple calico will do for now, madam," Giles assured her. "But he shall need a blue coat come autumn."

Johnny knew it all already. He'd had an excellent tutor in Bridgetown, the abolitionist Reverend Nicholls of St. Michael's Church. From Reverend Nicholls he had learned Latin and Greek and some Hebrew and French. Reverend Nicholls had also taught him about white attitudes. He must keep his bearing tall and erect, and look men directly in the eye, unashamed. He must be clean-shaven. And above all, he must never voice any objection to slavery or to those who favor it.

For half an hour, Johnny had listened with gentle forbearance to his concerned friends, but now it was time to shatter their earnestness. He suddenly stood up, shook his curly head, and in his best Bajan creole, exclaimed, "Ooh, nay, nay! I not be wearin' a blue *jack*-ette fuh *noh*-body. Da pompassettin' do nobody no good in dis' worl'."

"*John*-ny." Eliza frowned.

Bessie's eyes nearly sprang from her head. She turned to the others with an air of desperation and announced in her own East London dialect, "But the child don't even speak English! However shall 'e pass muster? Don't 'e have to speak proper English and Greek and Latin and I don't know what else? And here we have but a day to learn 'im!"

Aunt Martha placed a steadying hand on the poor old woman's arm, while the others sucked on their lips. "It's all right, Bessie. I fear the child teases us all rather cruelly."

"Teases, Mrs. Lee?"

"Yes. I suspect he speaks better English than you or I, should he wish to. Can't you, Johnny?"

"'e do? I don't believe it. Let's 'ear it, then." Bessie set one old, able hand upon her hip. Johnny fell dramatically to one knee, and in the King's English, declaimed,

> In the corrupted currents of this world,
> Offense's gilded hand may shove by justice,
> And oft 'tis seen the wicked prize itself
> Buys out the law. But 'tis not so above:
> There—

"Imposter!" Bessie interrupted him. "A right fraud 'e is, pullin' our leg so! Ooh, I've a mind to beat 'im right good!" She wagged a finger in his direction.

"Oh, dear Bessie," Johnny said. "Forgive me. I couldn't resist." He grasped her rough hands and gazed into her watery eyes with his contrite sea-blue ones.

She forgave him at once, like women everywhere.

• • •

That afternoon, in the sweltering parlor of Harvard President Joseph Willard's house, Johnny counted twenty-nine boys, all shifting anxiously from foot to foot. Johnny stood in his pressed shirt and breeches, his hair shorn and pomaded, his limbs denuded of trinkets. Aunt Martha had given him a small papered box for their safekeeping. Four at a time were called in for their exams, and Johnny was in the second group of boys. The exams were absurdly easy: simple translations from and to Greek and Latin. Then, one by one, they met briefly with President Willard. The president of Harvard University asked Johnny to do a simple mathematical problem, but when Johnny gave the answer, President Willard bellowed, "Incorrect!"

"I'm right, sir," Johnny replied. "Respectfully, I mean."

"I'm wrong, am I?"

Johnny did the sum on a piece of paper, itemized the steps, and handed the paper to President Willard. Willard studied the paper, looked up at Johnny, then waved him away in mock anger.

"Go on, get out of here." But he was smiling, and when the president emerged into the foyer, he pulled Eliza aside.

"Your son is most remarkable. He has a very bright future ahead of him, God willing."

Eliza curtsied and thanked him, hiding a smile. It was nothing she didn't already know.

They walked back to the Lecs' house in companionable silence. Within, the children did not recognize this sad, plain boy with the short, pomaded hair. They wanted their exotic stranger back.

"He looks so boring!" Ben exclaimed.

"I'll get his beads!" Elizabeth raced off to find the box Johnny had put them in.

Once they had restored Johnny to a semblance of his former self, they fell upon him for their pony rides.

5

THE FOLLOWING DAY, PREPARATIONS FOR COMMENCEMENT
BEGAN early for the class of '94. Over breakfast, Johnny asked if anyone
would like to accompany him to it. Harry Lee, munching on a piece of
toast before heading off to Boston, frowned and said, "Commencement?
I wouldn't be caught dead in the village just now. Pomp, circumstance,
and inebriation, if you ask me."

"Well, then, if I may excuse myself, I should like to walk into
town."

No one wishing to join him, Johnny strolled down the grassy hill
to the banks of the river alone. For some time, he watched the white
canvas sails drift lazily eastward, toward Boston. Families sat upon blankets or walked the path as children and dogs hurled forward and were
repeatedly called back, like bandalores.

Johnny turned his sights toward town and saw a great impress of
activity. Sailcloth tents had been pitched, and vendors worked the gathering crowd, selling all manner of goods, from bottles of eternal youth
to Oriental fans. Graduates swayed about in their calico gowns, arm in
arm, already tipsy with drink.

The lively scene reminded Johnny of preparations for Crop Over, a
festival that took place in July back home. It was for the slaves, mainly,
but Johnny always ran wild through it with his friends. For some of

the slave boys, it was their one chance each year to stretch their limbs, dance, and feel alive after deadening months of picking sugar cane.

The sun was high in the sky when Johnny approached the meetinghouse. Many people were already within, listening to an oration. Johnny peeked in and once more noticed the whiteness of all the faces. There were no gradations of color at all. Their dress was far plainer, too. *They all look related*, he thought.

Johnny moved up the road toward the college. He passed a merchant selling enormous pink peaches beside a cage of moistly slithering reptiles. He bought a peach, bit into it, scowled, and threw it to the side of the road: it was mealy and flavorless. Next he passed a rapt crowd who listened to a gray-bearded man in a dusty suit, selling brown bottles of oil. Another man declaimed, "Fat baby here! Come and touch the fat baby!" He pointed to a pyramid of heaving pink flesh upon a three-legged stool; that it was human could barely be discerned. With a shiver of disgust, Johnny moved on.

At last, just beyond the vendors, the object of his childhood dreams came into view: Harvard University.

Two buildings presented their flanks to the road. They were made of brick and were simple yet classical in design. Johnny was pleased with their symmetry. The building on the right, he knew, was called Massachusetts Hall. His mother told him that it had been a barracks during the war. The building on the left, Harvard Hall, was nearly identical save for a cupola atop it. This hall housed the commons, a prayer room, and John Harvard's famous library.

Moving down the grassy path between them, Johnny found himself in a vast yard. To the left he noticed a very small chapel and a fenced field. To the east was gently rolling farmland dotted with russet-brown cows.

The children had adorned him with his trinkets after the exams, and he wore them now; but soon, he knew, he would need to remove them for good. He thought with sadness of all those who had given him these trinkets: the old hucksters and fruit sellers and slaves with baskets on their heads. He thought of the slaves in the cane fields, some missing fingers and eyes, or shoes, who always smiled and waved at him as he skipped by. He thought of Madame Pringle's tavern, which he now knew to be a whorehouse, the ladies who sat about in their finery, whores. Perhaps the women who had given him these gifts were not very good. But on the other hand, he did not see how they were very bad, either. All of them had been kind to him.

From behind him, Johnny heard a familiar cry. It was fractious, miserable, and nearly human. Facing the entrance to the college stood a tall cage filled with half a dozen crazed gray monkeys. They jumped from post to post, crashing heedlessly into one another.

These were not the green monkeys of his homeland, the ones that flew across the treetops in great squawking packs. Yet they had the same worried look. For a moment, Johnny thought he would come back under cover of night to set them free. But he could not risk such trouble. He would have liked to, though. It was cruel to keep them caged so.

Johnny walked back down the street toward the meetinghouse, where commencement was now underway. Before the meetinghouse sat two tutors offering the day's Order of Exercises.

"Thank you," he said as one of them handed him the leaflet. The young man gave him a quizzical stare, and Johnny realized that with his beads and kinky hair, he must have cut a bizarre figure.

He entered the meetinghouse and looked down at the program. At that moment, a boy named Joseph Perkins was giving his valedictory speech, "On Eloquence." There would be several poetic verses, and the pageant would close with a discourse upon the topic of "Whether the Discovery of America by the Europeans Has Contributed to the Increase of Human Happiness." Now that would be interesting to hear. Johnny himself didn't know the answer, but he thought that in due course he would probably find out.

6

July 30, 1794

THE OLD MAN INSISTED ON PUSHING THE cart uphill himself. He muttered curses under his breath and perspired profusely, wiping the sweat from his forehead with a dirty cuff. Yet his refusal of aid was absolute. This was John Adams, vice president of the United States.

Johnny recalled how, on the ship, he'd asked his mother if Mr. Adams were very impressive. "I'll leave you to judge," she had said. Well, Johnny had been in Quincy for two weeks now, most of that time residing at Peacefield, the Adamses' residence, and he still had not made up his mind. On the one hand, this was the man who first recognized the need to break from England and whose profound insights into democracy helped to shape the American Constitution. On the other, this stubborn old man urinated on tree stumps and was far too proud to admit when his energy flagged.

"Why do you stop here, Johnny? You slept till near noon. Surely you can't be more tired than an old man. Move along now."

They resumed their course up the hill, where Adams had long wished to repair a stone wall. A man named Billings and another by the name of Sullivan usually helped them. Two young black boys sometimes helped as well, but today they were alone.

They worked until the sun was high in the sky. Abigail had packed them a canteen of cider, though Johnny would have preferred tea. He had never acquired a taste for strong drink, though on their crossing that was all he dared to imbibe. Then, seeing that Adams was red in the face and breathing heavily, he stopped once more. This time, Johnny was respectful but firm.

"Mr. Adams, sir. I should not like to be the cause of the sudden death of the vice president."

Adams laughed. "It will take more than a few trips up this hill to dispatch me—a fact that has greatly dismayed my enemies for many a year."

"Have you enemies, then?" Johnny asked.

"Naturally."

Johnny asked nothing further, and when he returned with one last barrel of stone, he found the vice president urinating indecorously upon a tuft of blue harebell.

"Natural weed killing," Adams said, as he always did, and chuckled. He buttoned his breeches. "Franklin and I often discussed the use of urine in farming, although if I recall, the good doctor was more interested in the relation of the—"

"Should the rock go just *here*, sir?" Johnny interrupted. Mrs. Adams would have scolded her husband roundly for such talk. But Johnny suspected that the old man enjoyed these excursions, in part because they released him from the conjugal constraints upon his free speech.

A bell clanged below. Johnny could almost hear the impatience in its rushing arrhythmia. That was Abigail, calling them to dinner. She had spent many years apart from John and would not countenance an extra five minutes now. Mr. Adams wiped his hands on his worn breeches.

"I count this a good day's work, Johnny. Shall we continue tomorrow? I shall get Sullivan and Bass to help."

"If you wish it."

Before descending, Johnny paused to gaze out over the rocky hills. Directly below him was Peacefield. It was a fine gray clapboard manse with black shutters. To Johnny's eye, however, it looked quaint and even somewhat rustic. He had not yet grown used to New England's wooden houses. All the fine homes in Barbados were built of stone.

Surrounding the main house were a barn, several sheds, and Abigail's garden, whose brilliantly colored roses prepared to bloom a second time that year. Beyond the farm, due northeast, stood Lizzie's cottage, where they had stayed but two nights before Mr. Adams insisted that Johnny lodge with them.

Johnny refused at first, being too intimidated, but his mother said, "Don't be. He invites you the better to work you to the bone."

In the main, it was true, though Johnny would not have traded these past two weeks for anything.

As they descended the hill, he realized that Mr. Adams had not tested him upon any topic that day, as had been his wont ever since Eliza had boasted, on one of their first evenings in Quincy, that President Willard called Johnny's exam "an example of profound intuitive intelligence."

"Indeed?" Adams had pressed her for more details.

Eliza was happy to oblige. "Johnny even corrected a mathematical error on the part of Mr. Willard."

"*Mama*," Johnny objected.

Almost immediately, Adams had taken it upon himself to continue to examine Johnny, as if he did not entirely trust the opinion of President Willard and would sound the boy himself.

Now, however, the time for questions had passed; Abigail stood on the porch beside his mother, tapping her right foot impatiently. Johnny was relieved, as Mr. Adams's questions were more difficult than President Willard's had been.

Suddenly Adams stopped and turned to Johnny. He asked, "Tell me, lad, if you would. Ought we to treat with the British?"

Johnny smiled with relief. This was easy. "Of course," he said. "Why say you so?"

"No doubt, sir, it is as obvious to you as it is to me. We can't afford another war with Britain. The Union will not hold. Those who think otherwise are fools." Johnny then proudly recited a letter, signed by John Adams and addressed to his wife, which he had read that past spring. It had been published in a local Bridgetown paper.

You cannot imagine what horror Some Persons are in, lest Peace Should continue. The Prospect of Peace throws them into Distress. Their Countenances lengthen at the least opening of an Appearance of It. Glancing Gleams of Joy beam from their Faces whenever all Possibility of it seems to be cut off. You can divine the Secret source of those Feelings as well as I.

Johnny had been waiting for just such an opportunity to display his gift to Mr. Adams. But instead of being impressed, the old man frowned deeply and moved toward the porch. He kissed his wife, nodded distractedly to Eliza, and scurried on his pudgy legs into the house. He emerged a few minutes later wagging a copy of a letter.

"Johnny!" Eliza turned to her son. "Whatever have you done to annoy Mr. Adams?"

"Why, nothing, Mama. He asked me a question, and I answered it."

Donning his spectacles, Adams explained, "I have before me a letter I wrote in confidence to my wife, of which I made a single fair copy."

Adams read, "You cannot imagine what horror Some Persons are in, lest Peace Should continue . . ."

Johnny stood before Mr. Adams, head bowed. He felt ashamed, but he didn't know why.

Mr. Adams removed his spectacles and folded them. He shook the letter at Johnny. "How came you to know of this letter, son?"

"It was published in our paper, sir."

"Which paper?"

"The *Barbados Mercury*. Dated"—he closed his eyes in order better to see the date upon the broadside—"May fourth."

"I see. And how came you to know it so *to* the letter?"

Now Johnny felt like crying. "I know not how, exactly, sir. I—*see* it."

"You *see* it," the old man muttered.

Eliza intervened. "He has always possessed this talent, Mr. Adams. Since he was quite small."

Johnny glanced gratefully at his mother. "Yes, sir. Often, the image fades rather quickly, but not always."

Mr. Adams approached the boy and whispered into his ear: "Well, your preternatural memory has just exposed an old friend for a spy. I'm most grateful, child, though it pains me, as must be very plain to you."

Johnny didn't understand. Not entirely. "But sir. How can it be harmful for the British to know you favor a treaty with them?"

Mr. Adams took the boy by the sleeve and pulled him close. He whispered so that the ladies could not hear, "I don't give a damn what the British think or suspect. But the *Jacobins*, I dare say, shall make much of it."

"Jacobins, sir?"

Johnny had not yet heard that current derogatory term for Thomas Jefferson's new party. He realized he knew almost nothing about the current state of American politics. He would need to study up on it so as not appear a fool before Mr. Adams.

Seeing the boy's crestfallen expression, Adams said, "Never mind, lad. There's time for you to learn what has become of us in your absence. Indeed, I fear, given your quick mind, you shall learn all too soon. Mrs. Adams!" he called suddenly. "We're starved. What have you for us?"

"A tub of hot water, John," she said. "For you both smell."

7

AT PEACEFIELD, SUMMER WAS A TIME FOR farming and for the consoling rituals of the season: a morning project, followed by a bath, and then dinner with the Millers. After dinner, Mr. Adams took a nap while Johnny wrote letters. He wrote to his grandmother and to Cassie, asking how they fared. If the winds and fate obliged, he would hear back from them in about four months' time.

Before bed, Johnny read for several hours. Mr. Adams's library was vast, and Johnny spent many happy hours burning the Adamses' candles. To challenge himself, he decided he would commit a book to memory. He chose *Common Sense*, by Thomas Paine. After a week of practicing, he felt confident that he knew it by heart.

One night, as he approached his chamber after taking a light supper, he found the door ajar. Johnny bent down to find a tall stack of broadsides holding his chamber door open. A note had been placed on the top, held down with a small stone. It read:

> So that you may better understand the mad goings-
> on of the Brobdingnags —J. A.

Johnny laughed and shook his head. He began to read the broadsides that same night, and by the end of the week he thought he had begun to understand the current American situation. From all he could glean, a bifurcation had begun to separate those citizens who favored France and those others who favored Britain. However, the different positions went deeper, Johnny sensed, than merely attitudes toward these foreign powers. The country suffered from increasingly wild and divergent fears. Federalists such as Adams feared mob rule and the establishment of a despotic "people's government," as was occurring in France.

Jeffersonians—or Jacobins—feared power vested in any single person or place. They worried that the Federalists secretly wished to establish another monarchy, along the British model. But it seemed to Johnny that certain Jacobins, in fighting for states' rights, actually worked to preserve the institution of slavery.

Johnny's new knowledge about the state of the Union unsettled him. Washington, he knew, fervently rejected the notion of political parties. Hamilton and Madison, too, had written about the dangers of political factions. To Johnny, such opposing parties could but hinder the pursuit of a unified America. But then, perhaps there was something in all this he didn't understand. He would have to ask Mr. Adams about it.

When not reading or helping Mr. Adams with his chores, Johnny spent his time playing with the children. These were the times he loved most. After working on the hill, he would sprint the mile and a half to Lizzie's cottage. Seeing Johnny running down the lane, the children would race after him crying, "Wait! Wait for us!" But Johnny always continued on down to the water, where he would leap in with a great whooping cry.

Only Tom, the eldest Miller child, refused to join them. A serious lad, he preferred to work in the fields and frowned at Johnny's frivolity. Miriam, on the other hand, a bright, bold girl of twelve, loved nothing better than to follow Johnny wherever he led.

One afternoon, her younger brother Will taunted her, "Miriam loves Johnny! Miriam loves Johnny!"

"I do not!"

"Do, too!"

Miriam punched him in the neck, and he tackled her. She fell back onto a stone. Rising and holding the back of her head, she cried, "I'm going to tell Mama!"

Will sang as she scrambled up the dunes,

Tell Tale Tit,
Your tongue shall be slit;
And all the dogs in the town
Shall have a little bit!

Lizzie ministered to her sobbing child, but within moments the girl had dried her tears and struggled to free herself from her mother's arms.

"Oh, I'm all right, Mama," she said. "Let me go."

Johnny smiled at the recollection of his own Barbadian games. One game he and his friends loved to play was called "stick-licking." This was essentially sword fighting using homemade wooden swords. The last time Johnny played that game, he accidentally smacked his good friend in the mouth. The child's mouth bloomed blood, and he ran home screaming that Johnny had hit him on purpose.

Cassie did not approve of stick-licking or most of the other games that he played down by the shore. "You wit' dose ruffians again?" she would ask, not guessing that Johnny was the worst of the lot. She would sniff him and rub her finger behind his ear. Then she would lick her finger, tasting for salt. Heaven help him if her lips puckered!

There were knife fights, too. All the boys owned knives. Some were rustic paring knives filched from kitchens; others were slim, elegant daggers. Johnny's was a small pocketknife with a bone handle, which his father had given to him one day. They were at the shipyard, and it was just growing dark. Soon, his father would head home.

"Don't use it for fighting," his father said. Then he added with a smile, "And don't tell your mother."

They both knew that if his mother caught him with the knife, she would make him toss it into the sea.

Observing Lizzie's children, Johnny could not help but admire their honesty and directness. He admired their lack of airs, too. They worked hard and played with abandon. Then they sat ramrod straight when dining, their manners refined. No one here found contradiction in this. In Barbados, one was either a nobleman or a farmer. In America, Johnny marveled, one could be a farmer in the morning and vice president by dinnertime.

·   ·   ·

On the day before his departure for Harvard, Johnny walked to the cottage after breakfast and met his mother in the kitchen garden. She was picking herbs for their dinner.

"Oh, hello, Johnny," she said, kissing him. "Well, your time in Eden is almost up."

"This *is* Eden," he replied. "Unlike our ship. I admit I'm sad to leave."

"Does it remind you of home?" Eliza asked. Since their arrival in America, they had spoken only rarely of home.

"In some ways," he said carefully, not wishing to open any wounds.

"Well"—Eliza tapped her thigh—"I shall go help Lizzie. You know she plans a farewell dinner for you?"

"I didn't."

Eliza opened the door, and as she did so, the children leapt from their hiding places, giggling.

"Surprise!" they shouted and tumbled into Johnny, endeavoring to climb him like a tree.

Miriam was fretful. "Johnny. I thought you'd *never* arrive!"

"Yes, we want to play! We've worked *all morning*!" Will complained.

Lizzie called to them from the kitchen, "Don't go far. The Lees arrive any time now."

The children began to groan just as carriage wheels could be heard crunching over the stones in the lane.

"They arrive!"

Another two minutes found everyone happily greeting one another. Johnny knelt among the eager Lee children, while Aunt Martha and her eldest daughter, Kate, moved into the kitchen to help Lizzie and Eliza. Johnny thought that, with her spectacles and sloppily pinned bun, Kate looked as plain as ever, though he did notice her comely figure.

Johnny rallied the children. "All right," he said. "Why don't you all head down to the beach and wait for me there. I must fetch some pails."

"Pails?" asked Ben derisively. "Whatever for? Pails are for little children."

"Not at all. You'll see."

At once, Johnny ran off to the barn, picked up a number of pails, and ran to the shore, where he was soon joined by Kate. She strolled toward him, one hand shielding her eyes from the sun.

Johnny nodded to her, then spoke to the impatient children.

"As there are only four pails and nine of us, I shall have to make teams, and one of us shall be on his own. Will and Ben, you find black shells. Miriam and Sara, you can find yellow ones."

"But I want to be with Hannah!" Sara cried, pointing to the littlest Lee girl.

"Hannah shall go with Will," Johnny said.

"Ew! I don't want to go with *her*," Will complained.

Hearing this, Hannah cried, and Kate moved to console her, glancing balefully at Will.

Eventually, the pairings were sorted out to everyone's satisfaction, except for Kate, who made nine.

"Kate, you're the odd number," said Johnny.

"Oh," she said, "I don't mind."

"Well, you can search for pink shells. You know the ones I mean. I believe they are scallop shells. Let's give ourselves half an hour."

"An hour!" Miriam objected.

"All right, an hour, unless we are called to dinner. Then we'll count and see who has the most."

"But black shells are not common. We shall lose!" whined Will.

"Nonsense, Will," said Miriam. "They're as common as pink or yellow. Mussel shells are black. Johnny has chosen quite equitably. Now let's go!"

"A moment." Johnny held his arm in the air. He knew how to whip his young audience into a froth of suspense. "I shall count it down. On your marks." They gripped the pails. "Get set." They crouched and leaned forward. "And go!"

All the children save Kate shot forward and scattered across the shore. She and Johnny ambled up the beach, their backs to the sun. Kate seemed in no rush, either to hunt for shells or to speak. It occurred to Johnny that her one sentence, consisting of four words, was nearly all he'd ever heard her say. Perhaps she was one of those shy, simple women who remained with their families all their lives. An old maid.

Sara, meanwhile, had abandoned Miriam in favor of her new relative. She clutched Johnny's hand as if they walked on jagged rocks, though the beach was pebbly and even sandy in places.

As Johnny and Sara looked for yellow shells, the water, the children, and even Quincy gradually disappeared, and in his mind's eye, Johnny found himself wading in the clear blue water of Carlisle Bay. It was so clear that he could see his feet, like pink coral, in the white sand below. Tiny fish swam between his toes. He saw the slender rowboats as they traveled back and forth from ship to shore with supplies of every imaginable kind, and the red-turbaned women walking barefoot from the hills with live turkeys riding on their heads. He saw Cassie waiting by the gate with her stern judgment, and he ran to her, skipping in rhythm to distant kettledrums.

Kate coughed once, returning him to Quincy and the shell hunt.

After an hour, the children all gathered in one spot on the beach, each group excited by their haul. A cursory glance in the pails told them that the count would be close.

By the time they returned to the cottage, the dining table and chairs had been taken out into the garden.

Lizzie appeared at the door. "Children, dinner's nearly ready. Go and wash up. There's a bowl and pitcher in the kitchen."

Just then, Mr. Miller, whom Johnny had not yet met, came riding down the lane on a noble-looking black horse. He appeared hot and weary from his travels, but the moment he espied Lizzie and his children, he grinned and quickly dismounted.

Johnny thought him a striking-looking man: His bearing was erect, his forehead tall. But, with his large nose and wide-set eyes, one could not quite call him handsome.

Lizzie's face lit with joy. "It's Thomas, at *last*!"

A sudden motion made Johnny turn to discover Mr. Adams, reading upon a broadside at the far end of the table. He had been sitting so quietly that Johnny had not noticed him until that moment. Seeing Mr. Miller, Adams stood. "Thomas! Excellent timing! How did you fare?"

"Well in some ways, galling in others," Mr. Miller remarked, referring to his tour in New Hampshire as a circuit judge.

"Well, let us share our gall after dinner."

Mr. Miller then turned to Johnny and bowed. "Hello. Allow me to introduce myself. I'm Thomas—*Johnny*?" he cried, suddenly realizing who this tall child was.

"The same." Johnny bowed.

Mr. Miller wiped his brow and then pumped the boy's hand vigorously. "I didn't know you! Well, but I hear you're off tomorrow to that great castle of learning in Cambridge."

"Yes, sir."

"He's off to the kitchen, Tom, to wash the sand off," Eliza corrected, wiping her hands on her apron. She smiled at Mr. Miller warmly and approached him. Then she took his hands in hers as if he were her brother. Johnny knew that Mr. Miller had been the one to bring Mama to Quincy when she was big with child. He had withheld his judgment when her own family had condemned her. Indeed, Cassie and his mother had so often shared how Mr. Miller saved mother and child that it had acquired a certain biblical grandeur, like the story of Moses in the bulrushes.

•   •   •

Dinner began cheerfully, with a toast to Johnny's success. Miriam, eager for attention, said, "Well, Ben and I *nearly* won our game. We got more shells than Johnny and Sara, but Cousin Kate got the most shells of all."

"The most what, child?" Mr. Adams asked. Though often distracted, he was fond of children in general and had indulged his own far beyond Abigail's stricter sense of child-rearing.

"Kate found more pink shells than we did black or yellow," Miriam replied.

"Indeed." Mr. Adams nodded and took another sip of his cider. "But you know, Kate," he drawled out. "One must question, 'What *is* pink?' For I do believe that 'pink' might cover all manner of reds and ivories and indeed even some yellows. You might have had an advantage." Here, Johnny saw Mrs. Adams's eyes roll.

Kate turned to the old man. "Advantage, Mr. Adams? In what sense?" The Lees' eldest daughter had been so quiet during dinner that everyone had nearly forgotten about her, including Johnny.

"Oh, John," complained Abigail, "why must you ruin the children's fun with a philosophical discourse?"

"Fairness, Abigail. Fairness."

There were stifled giggles about the table. But Kate continued with some heat, "Fairness, Mr. Adams? Is it fair to condemn a person to the ignominy of having cheated without so much as a shred of proof?"

Johnny nearly fell off his chair. The girl could not only speak but now did so quite powerfully—and to the vice president!

"Katherine," scolded Aunt Martha. "Pray, do not speak to Mr. Adams like that."

Kate stood up and moved off to the house without a word. She returned with her pail, sandy and reeking of dead mollusks. She set it down upon the great man's lap.

"Have a look, Mr. Adams. Do." The vice president had been about to bite into a juicy scallop. But he set fork and scallop aside in order to consider the smelly bucket of shells.

"Hmm—let us see." He poked a pudgy finger into the pail. Johnny heard the shells scrape against one another.

"Pink. Pink. And—pink." He cleared his throat and gazed up at the proud girl. The he reached for her hand, which she proffered reluctantly.

"Well, child. You're your mother's daughter, all right. I'm most humbly apologetic and do beg your forgiveness. The pail is a veritable *sea of pink*. As usual, my reach has exceeded my grasp."

Abigail raised her eyebrows.

Suddenly, Kate said, "Oh, I forgive you, Uncle John. For you do seem truly remorseful. What's more, though you were not correct, it was nonetheless a reasonable *theory*. For many shells are indeed a remarkable combination of shades." Here, Kate drove home her point. "But I was careful to choose the pinkest ones."

The entire table was silent at this speech. But instead of gloating over her decisive victory, Kate emitted a sudden giggle and gave Mr. Adams a fond peck upon his cheek. Adams's hand rose to touch the place she had kissed. The rest of the table began to titter, and Mr. Adams himself finally burst into loud guffaws.

8

"WHAT AN EVENING!" ELIZA EXCLAIMED AS SHE and Johnny traveled toward Cambridge the following morning.

"Most astonishing," Johnny agreed. "I must say, I had thought the eldest Miss Lee either shy or simpleminded. But she is neither. Not at all."

"She's her mother's daughter," said Eliza.

Johnny glanced at his mother. "What mean you, Mama?"

"Oh, nothing."

This was not the first time that Johnny's mother had alluded to Aunt Martha's mysterious past. It was as if she wanted to tell Johnny but dared not do so. Often, at home, his mother had called Martha an "unsung hero" of the Revolution. But she had never revealed her meaning.

When the chaise crossed the bridge into Cambridge, Johnny saw tears come to his mother's eyes.

"Mama, why the tears? Is this not fairly near Quincy?"

It was not the distance that had made Eliza cry.

"Oh, Johnny. I want everything good for you. I want—I *hope*—there will be no limits placed upon what happiness and honor you find."

"Why should there be limits, Mama?"

"You know why."

The secret of my blood, he thought. But his kinky hair had been pomaded, and the beads removed.

"I shall bear it. Do you think me so weak?"

"Nay, John."

"Then what?"

Eliza sighed. "It's others I fear. It's always others."

As they made their way along the river and finally arrived at the Great Bridge, Eliza recalled how, twenty years earlier, the rebels had removed its planks to keep the British soldiers from crossing over, and how the British army had found the planks and restored them. Then she remembered how Papa and the stable boys had nailed planks across their home's doors and windows, fearful less of the British than of the rebels themselves. As she crossed that same bridge now, Eliza shivered with the same fear—not of the British, but of Americans. Of those who would harm her son.

Cambridge was crowded with carriages bringing new and returning students to their lodgings. Coachmen hoisted trunks down from the carriages and brought them to and from Harvard and Massachusetts Halls. Their chaise could not approach the curb, and Johnny was obliged to descend in the middle of the street. Eliza could not go with her son to see his chamber, which was vastly disappointing. She knew Johnny was to have a roommate but wished to know: What sort of boy was he? Would he be kind and studious or wild and troublemaking?

The coachman tethered the horse by means of a long rope and followed Johnny into the building with Johnny's trunk. When the pair had returned, and the coachman had mounted his seat once more, Johnny grinned up at his mother.

Then Eliza spoke so commandingly that anyone overhearing her would have thought she was made of stone. "You must write at once and say whether the accommodations are acceptable."

"I shall." He laughed. He knew that his mother sounded far worse than she was. Johnny reached up and kissed her as she bent down to meet his face.

"Good-bye for now, Mama!" he called as the carriage pulled away.

He waved until his mother was out of sight. Then, as he turned to face the college, a thrill of anticipation ran through him. He willed himself not to mourn. So much lay ahead of him. He was almost sixteen. He would unlock the mysteries of the universe.

9

THE DOOR TO NUMBER 32 MASSACHUSETTS HALL was already open. Johnny pushed his way in with one shoulder, dragging the trunk behind him. Once inside, he was startled to find a great blond fellow stretched out upon one of the room's two narrow beds. The boy had taken the one nearest the window, facing Harvard Hall, leaving Johnny the other near the fireplace. The boy's long bare feet extended beyond the pallet by several inches, and his silvery head rested upon his hands in an odd semi-reclining position. This, Johnny realized, was caused by a pile of books beneath his pillow.

The rest of him was entirely naked.

Seeing Johnny enter, the boy opened his eyes and said, drowsily, "Oh, hello."

"Hello, yourself," Johnny replied. "What do you do with all those books beneath your head? And where are your clothes?"

Here, the boy chuckled and finally sat up. Of all the white people Johnny had ever met, this boy had to be the whitest of all. His eyes were so light blue they were nearly translucent.

"Oh, I brought not my manservant. Who shall clean my clothes if I sully them? And it's awfully hot. As for the books, I was hoping they would penetrate my brain. I've heard tell that, sleeping in such a way, the mind draws the information in—unconsciously, as it were."

"By what, pray?" Johnny laughed. "A magnet?"

Johnny noticed that the boy pronounced his *i*'s differently from how his New England friends did. He made them sound like "ah." It was a pleasing, genteel accent.

The boy grinned and rose at last to his full height. He bowed. "Peter Fray, at your service."

"John Boylston." Johnny bowed as well.

"Say," Peter said, reaching for a fine linen shirt upon the back of his desk chair, "where're you from?" He raised a hand to his ear. "Your voice has a foreign ring."

Johnny replied, "You have a good ear. I am from a distant place, though I was born here. I'm from Barbados."

"Barbados!" The boy stepped into a pair of neatly pressed silk breeches. "And I thought I'd come a long way."

"Where came you from?" asked Johnny. "You sound foreign, too."

Peter laughed. "Virginia. Near Fredericksburg. Arrived nearly a week ago, before anyone else. Boring sea journey. Infernally hot, too." The boy frowned. "But never mind. We're here now. It's a cozy little school. Shall I show you around?"

"I'd be greatly obliged." Johnny nodded. "Allow me to unpack first."

"Say, are you hungry?" Fray suddenly asked. "I stole some bread from the commons this morning." Here again, Johnny noticed that the boy pronounced *hungry* as "hung-reh." He decided this was a very beautiful manner of speaking English. It sounded soft and lazy, unlike the clipped Barbadian English he had always known.

Johnny smiled. "No, thanks. I'm not very hungry. You haven't got anything to drink, though, have you? I'm parched."

From beneath his bed, the boy produced a leather flask. "Kentuck-eh whisk-eh." He offered it to Johnny.

"Nay, I don't drink spirits. I meant cider or tea." Johnny knew that keeping spirits in one's chamber was forbidden, but he said nothing.

Fray made a face. "Never touch the stuff. But we'll stop at the buttery on our way out, if you like."

Johnny nodded and began to unpack his things. On his side of the chamber stood a small chest of drawers and a built-in bookcase containing three shelves. These would not do. He wished he had kept his fine bookcase, the one they had left behind on the ship. Suddenly he felt hands reach over his shoulders and take hold of his belongings.

"For goodness' sake, man. Just put them *any-wayah* for now. Otherwise, it shall be dark before you finish."

Here, his new roommate tossed Johnny's things, so lovingly folded by his mother, onto the bed. "Come on, man, it's time to *vini* and *vici*."

Without, the air was still quite hot, but a cooling breeze came off the river. Gulls circled overhead. Johnny cast his eyes upon the scholars passing across the yard, gowns flowing, and thought, *Oh, if only Papa could see!*

The boy led Johnny across the narrow grassy strip to Harvard Hall, where they descended into the basement. It was cool there, and the buttery was open. The top panel of a two-part door hung ajar, and behind it stood an ancient white-haired fellow.

"That's Mr. Painy," Peter whispered to Johnny. "I call him Mr. Pained. You'll soon see why."

Johnny asked Mr. Painy for a mug of cider. "Can you put it on my bill?"

The old man reached for a mug and poured the cider from a large stoneware jug. At the effort, he cringed in pain. *The poor fellow must have rheumatism,* Johnny thought. He now saw why Peter had renamed the man but he didn't find the sobriquet amusing.

"First day, sir?" Painy asked, handing Johnny the mug in a shaking hand.

"Yes, sir."

Johnny gratefully drank the cool, fermented cider.

"It's gratis, then, my boy. Good luck to ye—"

"Oh, never mind the niceties," Fray cut in, leading Johnny up the stairs.

"Thank you, sir!" Johnny called back over his shoulder.

Once they had left, Johnny turned to Fray.

"Seems an excellent fellow, actually."

"Oh, yes. I expect we shall take terrible advantage of him," his new roommate replied.

Although flanked on two sides by commerce, Harvard had an appealingly cloistered feel. It was sunny and hot without, but in the yard the air beneath the elm trees was cool and still. Johnny had never seen an elm tree before and thought them very beautiful. The word *elegiac* came to mind. He stared up at them until Peter pushed him to move along. They came to a small chapel, which was open. Johnny entered it. Within, the air was cool, the light dim. A tutor sat in a pew with his head bent.

Johnny would have liked to linger, but after a few moments, Fray said, "Come on. There's more to see."

From Holden Chapel it was but a short stroll to the northern edge of the campus, where they came upon a vast field encircled by a fence, to keep the cattle out. Within, boys chased one another or wrestled. As they stood watching the other boys, Fray said, "Papa's a planter, you know. We live not far from Mr. Jefferson; he's a personal friend. Though we have not nearly so many slaves as he does. Only a few dozen."

Seeing Johnny's blue eyes widen, Peter added, "I don't hold with slavery, of course. But I don't see how we rid ourselves of it, either."

"Free them," Johnny said. Fray cast his roommate a sudden, wary glance. Then, believing him to have spoken in jest, he laughed.

"Free them. Of course! Then we shall have to use the Irish to work the land. Hey," he cried suddenly, "let's wrestle."

Peter was at Johnny's feet. He pulled on them and Johnny crashed to the ground. The two boys rolled around on the grass grabbing at one another and laughing.

Johnny had often wrestled with boys at home. It could get rough, but the rules were clear: biting, pinching, scratching, locking with the arms or legs, and grabbing the groin were all prohibited. Fray, however, did not play by the rules. He pulled at Johnny's clothing and struck him about the body. Johnny was going to stand up when suddenly Fray grabbed him by the throat and squeezed.

For a terrifying moment, he couldn't breathe. It felt as if his lungs would burst, and he reached for the knife in his pocket. Fortunately, Fray loosened his grip just then. Johnny cried, "Leave off!" Roused to anger, he took his advantage. He used his full force to flip his roommate onto his stomach and pin him in an iron grapple hold. Johnny thought he might be hurting Peter, but at that moment he didn't care.

Fray went limp and ceased to struggle. Johnny released him, panting with the effort. In the distance, a bell clanged. The other boys fled the field, and the roommates were alone.

"Did you hear that?" Peter suddenly sat up, pretending not to notice his defeat.

"Why'd you do that?" asked Johnny, still breathing hard.

"Do what?" the boy asked, getting to his feet.

"Strangle me almost to death. I couldn't breathe."

"Oh, I was only fooling. Well, we should go. They fine you if you're not in your chamber at the appointed hour."

Here, Peter laughed and extended his hand. After hesitating a moment, Johnny took it. They walked back to their chamber in awkward silence, Johnny feeling confused. Did all the American boys here fight so wildly, with so little respect for the rules? The thought crossed his mind that perhaps he needed to be on his guard, if that's how the boys played their games in America.

10

THE FOLLOWING MORNING, A SHRILL BELL WOKE Johnny. It was so loud that he felt his teeth vibrate. The sun had not yet risen, but it was time for prayers. Peter slept through the bell, and Johnny considered leaving him behind. Then he sighed and shook his roommate on the shoulder.

"C'mon. We'll be late."

Peter opened his eyes and cried, "Oh, damn!"

He rose and threw on his clothing, and they soon made their way to Harvard Hall and the chapel room. They knelt on a long, low bench until their knees ached. After prayers, they moved into the commons, where many students already sat in groups. Wait-boys toured the tables offering cider and setting down jugs of steaming coffee. Some boys sat on raised platforms, and Johnny made his way toward an empty space among one of these. But Peter pulled him back.

"Oh, no, man. Those are for the upperclassmen. We peons must sit below."

They found an empty table and sat down. Soon they were joined by several fresh-faced lads, a few of whom looked to be no more than twelve or thirteen years of age. Their names, they offered, were Selfridge, Shattuck, Farquez, and Wales. Another boy named William Shaw, older and taciturn, sat with them at first. But he soon thought better of it and, with a slight bow, moved off to another table.

"Good riddance," Peter said loudly when he'd left. "Looks too studious for us anyway."

Everyone laughed. Johnny did, too, not wanting to stand out.

Shattuck was a hulking boy of fourteen who hailed from Worcester. Farquez, small and freckled, was the son of a farmer in Shrewsbury. Wales, the youngest, had come from Boston. Finally, Selfridge shared that his family lived in Portsmouth, New Hampshire.

"Indeed?" Johnny asked excitedly. "My family lived there, too, during the—"

"I thought you said you were from Barbados?" Peter interrupted.

"Oh, yes, we are." Johnny cursed himself. He had not been in the commons five minutes before he had broken a solemn oath!

"When did your family live in Portsmouth?" asked Selfridge.

"Oh, just for a short while, during the war."

"What were their names?" he pursued.

Just then, Peter threw salt at Farquez, and the ensuing food fight made them all thankfully lose interest in Johnny's forebears.

•　•　•

That fall, Johnny's days fell into a consolingly ascetic rhythm: up at five for prayers, breakfast, recitation, study time, dinner, more study, supper from the buttery, and candles out at nine. One night, Peter noticed Johnny moving his lips as he held a book half-open in one hand.

"What is that you do?"

"Committing something to memory. It's sort of a game."

"A game? Sounds jolly. I've not managed to commit my own name to memory. How do you get on?"

"Very well." Johnny smiled. Then, he could not help but say, "Last summer, I actually managed to memorize *Common Sense*."

"The entire essay?"

"Yes. It took about a week but wasn't terribly difficult."

"Goodness! Well, carry on!" Peter exclaimed cheerfully and headed off to a tavern. Then he turned and looked over his shoulder and said, "Whilst you commit to memory, I shall commit to forgetting!"

Peter left then. Later he bounded in noisily after Johnny was already asleep. He cried, "Oh, what a jolly time we had at Porter's! A pity you didn't join us." Johnny put a pillow over his head and grunted.

While Peter joined his friends at night in the taverns, Johnny engaged in more salubrious activities. He joined several other freshman boys to form a wrestling team. They were sweet, unworldly children who, Johnny thought, would do well with a little prodding. Then there were Selfridge, Shattuck, Wales, and Farquez, whose humor Johnny enjoyed. They loved a good prank, and at first Johnny went along with them. One night, they stole the bell from atop Harvard Hall. Its absence was noticed when no one woke for prayers or breakfast. The bell was subsequently discovered by a tutor in Selfridge and Shattuck's chamber, and cost them three dollars apiece in fines.

· · ·

Sometime just before his sixteenth birthday, returning to his chamber from dinner, Johnny found a letter from his mother beneath the door.

Dear son,

Mr. Adams has set off with some reluctance for Philadelphia, Lizzie and Company are well tho very busy at the moment. Miriam took sick but it was just a cold, a bad cough remains. Thankfully, we none of us caught it. I should very much like to come to Cambridge for your birthday, if you're not too occupied with your studies to visit with your old mother at the Lees'.

Johnny was pleased at the thought that he would soon see his mother again. He set the letter aside and removed his clothing, having decided to bathe before classes. As he unbuttoned and removed his breeches, his pocketknife fell out, and he reached down to take it up.

At that moment, Peter entered the chamber.

"Whoa!" the boy shielded his eyes. "There's a very ugly naked boy in my chamber, and with a knife, too. What are you about?"

"I've had no chance to bathe," said Johnny. He quickly placed the knife on top of his chest of drawers. Then he smiled, abashed. Peter looked about the chamber. He approached Johnny's end of the room. Suddenly he espied the carved handle of the pocketknife and reached for it.

"Say, what's this, old mole?" Peter took up the knife. Then he opened it. "This could do a bit of damage, what!"

"Leave that alone," said Johnny.

"Only if you tell me what it's for. Killed many people with it?"

"Not yet," he said.

Johnny made to grab the knife from Peter's hand but Peter pulled back just in time, laughing. "All right, don't be touchy." He shut the knife and placed it back on the dresser.

"It was a gift from my father."

"Ah, I see. For what, pray?"

"All the boys have knives in Barbados."

Peter widened his eyes in mock fear. "I suppose I should be careful around you, then."

"Funny," Johnny said. "I was thinking the same about you."

$$\bullet \quad \bullet \quad \bullet$$

Several days later, as Johnny prepared to go to meet his mother, he noticed that Peter had a small looking glass upon his bedside table. He made free to pick it up and look at himself. He was reminded of the good Reverend Nicholls's words about Americans always being clean-shaven and was just thinking he needed to find a barber when a voice jolted him from behind:

"Admiring your good looks, eh?"

Johnny blushed at being caught out. "Nay, I begin to grow a beard. Know you a barber?"

"Why don't you use that pocketknife of yours?" quipped Peter. "Careful you don't slit your own throat, though. Ha ha."

"I'll leave my neck in the hands of a proficient, thanks all the same."

Peter gave him the name of a fellow just down the street, near the market.

"But I dare say he won't be open now."

Johnny frowned. The dark growth made him look blacker, he thought. But it would have to wait.

. . .

He expected his mother, but to Johnny's great surprise and delight all the Millers were there as well. Everyone hugged and squeezed him near to death. For his birthday dinner, Aunt Martha had reaped the fruits of her gardens, and accompanying the ham and duck there were green beans, Brussels sprouts, breads, pies, and several cakes.

"We've been baking for several days," said Kate proudly. Then she blushed. Johnny glanced at his mother, recalling her stories of their privation during the war, when food was so scarce that Cassie resorted to dressing squirrels and voles.

At the end of the meal Johnny groaned, excused himself, and lay down face-up upon the parlor floor, which put the children in a frenzy of glee as they ran from the table to jump upon him.

"Children, don't crush him!" said Aunt Martha.

But Johnny, protecting his tender, distended belly, had already flipped onto his hands and knees and galloped away from them with a whinny. The children laughed and chased him.

Later, as Johnny was about to take his leave, Kate approached. She had hardly said a word all evening.

"Your roommate has asked me to go on a boat ride with him."

"Peter Fray? Do you know him?" Johnny asked. For some reason, the idea gave him an uncomfortable feeling.

"I was in the library borrowing a book when he came in. We got to talking, and we soon realized that we both knew you. Then he asked me if I would join him this Thursday. I saw no reason to decline."

Johnny didn't know that people from the town could borrow books from Harvard's library. He wondered why it was that Peter had mentioned nothing to him about it.

"And what did you say?"

"I said I would go. The weather has been fine, and the river looks inviting. I go abroad so rarely."

"Have your parents approved?"

"Certainly. Elizabeth shall join us."

"Sounds jolly."

Kate suddenly asked, "How go your studies?" Behind her thick spectacles were bright, inquiring eyes.

Johnny grinned and led her to the sofa, only too ready to tell someone. "Oh, Cousin, it's a dream come true! All those books! I never imagined I'd have such a quiet, gloomy library all to myself. Mr. Shipley, the librarian, takes no notice of me."

Kate blushed.

"What is it?" Johnny asked.

"From *me*, on the other hand, Mr. Shipley demands a rather loathsome kiss in exchange for a book."

"A kiss?" Johnny stood up from the sofa. "I shall punch his face! Indeed I shall!"

"No." Kate smiled and urged him to sit down. "He's harmless enough, I suppose."

"When next you go, tell me, and I shall accompany you," he said earnestly. "But oh, I read and read until my eyes water and I feel my head will explode. My world expands exponentially. Rome, Carthage, Athens—I begin to *see* them. I should so much like to *discuss* what I read!"

This last plaintive note caught Kate's attention. "But you are at the finest college in the land. Is there no one there interested in sharing these worlds with you, in discussing them?"

Johnny laughed, suddenly realizing that he had revealed more about his loneliness than he'd meant to. "There must be, though I've not met such a one as yet. It's early days, I suppose. Alas, those I am closest to care more for sport or taverns than the library. No one enjoys reading, as I do. No one seems—*curious.*"

"Oh, but I am!" Kate suddenly blurted, then blushed deeply.

Johnny looked at her, his head cocked. "Is it true? Would you really like to discuss such things? Cicero, Socrates, Locke?"

"I would love to," Kate said quietly, but her tremulous voice betrayed her emotions. "I'm sorry." She let out a laugh and wiped her eyes behind her spectacles.

"Don't be," Johnny assured her. "I'm delighted. It's a rare thing to come upon anyone—much less a girl—who wishes so fervently to study. Not many girls of my acquaintance want to read difficult books."

"Apparently not many boys do, either."

At Kate's quick wit, Johnny grinned. "Very well, then. When next we meet, let us discuss Locke's *Essay Concerning Human Understanding.*"

Kate stood up and curtsied once more. Johnny suddenly noticed, with a blush of his own, that she had a fine figure. "Until next Sunday, then," she said.

Several days later, as he lay on his stomach reading upon Locke's *Essay*, Peter burst noisily through their door. It was just after supper, and he was deeply engaged.

"What do you know but I've lost it! Hell and damnation!"

"Lost what?" Johnny looked up at Peter dreamily.

"*Common Sense*! I had it in the boat, but when I went to disembark, it was gone."

"Oh, I very much doubt you had common sense in the boat," said Johnny.

Peter didn't catch the joke. He frowned in consternation. "But I *did*—I'm sure of it. I thought to read bits to—to the ladies. I need to know it for Monday, for a recitation. And now it's gone. They shall fine me for sure, but that's not so concerning. The fact is, I must *know* it, man."

Johnny thought it odd that his roommate had lost the very book he himself had memorized the previous summer. "Do they not have another copy in the library?"

"Remarkably not. Or, well, perhaps another student has borrowed one. Oh, I shall fail utterly, and the governors will write to my parents."

Johnny doubted that any such thing would happen, not for a lost book alone. He wished to finish Locke's *Essay* just then and was about to turn a deaf ear when he thought, *Here might be an excellent chance to impress the other boys without appearing to do so.* But could he remember *Common Sense* after these many months? It would be a chance to find out. Johnny sat up and said, "I can probably help you, though it *is* inconvenient."

Peter, hearing only the part he wished to, smiled most winningly. "Oh, could you? Could you really?"

"I don't know. We'll see," Johnny replied. Then he added, "I did happen to study it most particularly last summer."

"Why, your memory is nearly preternatural," Peter flattered. "Even our tutors have remarked upon it. Oh, if only you could, I'd be eternally grateful."

"Well, procure me a great stack of paper and several bottles of ink. Until then, leave me in peace, if you will."

Without another word, Peter left for the buttery, which would have the items he sought, though so much paper would cost Peter dearly.

When Johnny returned to Locke's essay, he cursed Peter, for the deep communion he had felt with the philosopher was gone.

Peter returned with the requested items. Johnny took them, rose from his bed, and moved into his small study on the other side of the fireplace.

"I shouldn't like to be disturbed till I'm finished," he said.

Peter put a finger to his own lips, grinned, and next Johnny looked up, the boy was gone.

Johnny worked well into the night. Peter headed to Porter's Tavern and did not return until after his roommate had gone to bed, at around two. In that time, Johnny had been able to recall about one-third of the treatise. His fingers were black with ink and cramped.

There had been moments when he drew a blank, and these moments frightened him. He had no wish to fail and suffer humiliation. Fortunately, the moment Johnny was able to see one word, the whole paragraph came into view. And with the paragraph came the margins, the page number and heading, and then the full page itself, blossoming open like a newly hatched leaf.

Johnny missed prayers the following morning, for which he knew he'd be fined. At breakfast, he sat apart from the other scholars, not wishing to break the spell. Peter glanced at him once or twice but was wise enough not to intrude. The boys whispered among one another with hunched shoulders, as if speaking about him.

Well, what of it? He had been lying low since his arrival at college, endeavoring to fit in, playing with the wrestlers, even going so far as to make the odd mistake in French or Latin. It was time to lift his head up and fly his intellectual colors.

Johnny finished the transcription late that Thursday afternoon. He placed the cap on his ink bottle, gathered his sheets of paper in a neat pile, and washed his ink-stained hands. His fingers ached, but he was satisfied. He had not known whether he could remember the entire essay and was gratified to know that he could, give or take a phrase here and there.

Johnny had just blown out his candle when Peter came banging through their door, the worse for drink.

"Johnny-boy, r' you awake?"

"Barely," Johnny replied. He was tired and wanted to go to bed.

"Well, do you have it? If I'm to study, I s'pose it mus' be now or never."

Johnny fumbled for a straw spill with which to light his candle. After kneeling for some time by the coals, he finally succeeded. "It's just there." He pointed. "Upon your desk."

"I can' bleeve it," Peter slurred as he looked down at the manuscript. "You've actually done it. I didn' think you could."

"I said I could, didn't I?"

"People say all kinds of rubbish."

"True enough. Well, go study, Peter—elsewhere. I've no need to hear Paine again. *I've* spent all week with him. Now it's your turn."

Peter laughed loudly. "Yes, sir!" He took up the manuscript and his candlestick and was just about to go to his own study, when he said, a look of sincere affection in his bleary eyes, "Thank you, Johnny. I'm greatly admiring and indebted. I shall find a way to repay you somehow."

"Go," said Johnny, whose own eyes were closing. "Let me sleep. That shall be payment enough."

By breakfast the following morning, word of Johnny's accomplishment had spread throughout the college. He had imagined the handshakes, the smiles, the general approbation. But when he entered the commons, he was met with silent stares. The boys began to giggle and whisper. Rather than impress everyone, it seemed his feat had caused the boys to consider him a freak of nature, like someone with a six-fingered hand.

No one at his usual table had saved him a seat, and Johnny was obliged to sit elsewhere. He turned away and caught the eye of a sickly boy who sat at the adjacent table. Several times he had heard Peter and the rest of them ridiculing this boy. He was fair-haired, with a long, aquiline nose, broad forehead, and a wry pale mouth. Had he not been so terribly thin, he might have cut a dashing figure. But his back was hunched, and his blue coat swallowed him; it was hard to discern the contours of body in the bulk of fabric.

The boy extended his hand without rising. "I'm Eliot. Delighted."

"I'm Johnny. Johnny Boylston."

"I know your name already. Your fame precedes you."

"My fame? You must mean my notoriety. For behold how they behave. My roommate lost his book, and I copied it for him, from memory."

Eliot's eyes flared. "Lost it? Is that what he told you?"

"Indeed. Why?"

"Oh, never mind." Eliot shrugged. Then he said, "But they never shall admit that they are impressed, you know. They're too envious. All the boys here fashion themselves geniuses."

"And you don't?"

"It depends upon your definition."

Johnny considered this statement. "Now, that's an interesting question."

The boy coughed slightly. He removed a linen handkerchief from a breeches pocket and placed it to his mouth.

"I heartily agree. Shall we discuss it?"

"Ye-es." Johnny was not in the mood to discuss anything regarding Thomas Paine or the epic feat that had now been ridiculed by all. "But perhaps we should fortify ourselves first with some of this excellent—uh, what is this, do you think?" Johnny poked at the meat upon his plate.

"Not sure." Eliot shrugged, stabbing uncertainly at his own plate. "A truant student, perhaps. They are certainly plentiful this time of year."

Johnny laughed, realizing he had not done so in quite some time.

• • •

When he and Eliot parted at the entrance to the commons, the sky was an ominous iron gray. Eliot donned his hat and tipped it toward Johnny. Then he walked off with his cane, hunched as an old man. Johnny was not ready to return to his chamber. He looked up at the sky; in Barbados, such a sky might signify an oncoming hurricane. But here, Johnny knew not what it meant. He was filled with difficult emotions. The boys' derision and meeting Eliot seemed an odd correspondence. Would the boys now label him a freak, as they had Eliot?

Suddenly, white flakes began to fall from the sky.

The snow soon covered everything: the roofs of Harvard and Massachusetts Halls, the walkways and fences, the trees and their branches, and the steeple of Christ Church.

Johnny walked to the center of the yard and turned a slow full circle. Soon the bell would send him to class. His toes were numb, and he cursed his flimsy leather shoes. He would need to ask Mama to procure him a pair of boots.

Johnny looked up one last time to watch the white flakes as they descended upon him. They caught on his eyelashes and melted in his eyes, blurring them. He stuck out his hands and tongue, and felt the snowflakes alight upon his warm skin, stinging slightly as they melted.

He had seen this thing called *snow* in paintings. But no art could capture the way the lamplights magically illuminated the invisible flakes, or how the whiteness imbued the soul with such cleansing calm.

I must tell Mama, he thought. And then he realized that it would be snowing in Quincy, too, and that snow was nothing new to his mother.

He felt alone, but not lonely. His soul opened to the great possibilities of life in this beautiful country, with its cleansing snow. He even forgave his fellow students for laughing at him. He felt certain, standing alone in the yard in the snow, that he was destined to achieve great things. There were no limits to what a man bent on success could accomplish. Had not his heroes taught him this?

11

ON SUNDAY, NOVEMBER 23, JOHNNY DINED AT the Lees'. After dinner, he and Ben had a snowball fight until Aunt Martha, concerned that they would catch their deaths, called them in. Johnny had dutifully brought Locke's *Essay* to discuss with Kate, although he was by no means confident that she had read it. Nonetheless, after he had dried himself off and removed his shoes and combed his fingers through his damp, curly hair, he wagged the book before her weak eyes, whereupon she grinned and scrambled up to her chamber to retrieve her copy. Kate then hastened to the parlor, where she fairly leapt upon the sofa with a girlish giggle.

"Where shall we begin, Johnny?"

"Well." He blushed. He had never conversed at length with a girl before and hid his discomfort behind a pedantic manner. "It's always helpful to summarize a work. It brings everything to the fore of one's mind, as it were." Kate stifled a smile, for to her, Johnny's discomfort was perfectly discernible. Then, feeling Kate's leg next to his on the sofa, Johnny stood and moved to a wing chair, which he pulled up close to her. He still felt uncomfortable but didn't dare move again. He crossed his legs.

"Shall I begin?" she asked demurely.

"Yes, by all means."

Just then, Hannah and Elizabeth popped their heads into the parlor. Seeing their sister with Johnny, they giggled.

"Scoot!" Kate cried harshly. Then she looked down at her open book and began. "First of all, perhaps it's wise to describe the context in which Locke wrote the work." Kate paused and looked at Johnny for approval.

He said merely, "Go on."

"The prevailing understanding at the time was, I believe, that a man—a person—" she fumbled to find her words.

Johnny encouraged her, "Yes? 'The prevailing understanding,' you were saying?"

Suddenly, Kate sat back on the sofa, pulled off her glasses, and burst out laughing. "I feel as if I am sitting an exam."

"Perhaps you are." Johnny grinned. "But you're doing excellently well." Johnny uncrossed his legs. "Do go on."

She continued, "From what I have been able to read, the prevailing notion in Europe at the time was that man's understanding is circumscribed, limited by innate—inborn, as it were—ideas."

She paused, and Johnny made free to reply. She responded. For a full hour, Johnny nearly forgot that Kate was a girl. She challenged his every move forward, and he challenged hers, until together they had navigated Locke's long and winding narrative.

When the conversation drew to a close, Johnny looked at Kate curiously. He asked, "But clearly this is not your first foray into philosophy. I know you've visited our library, but it is clear to me that you've also been educated. Who has educated you?"

Kate gave a tiny prideful smirk. "I have educated myself. Well, the Adamses have also proffered lists of books for me to read, since I was quite small."

Just then, Aunt Martha entered the room. "Johnny, it grows dark. You must head back before they fine you."

"Oh, yes." He rose and glanced at Kate. She returned her glasses to her face and, like Cinderella, changed back into a shy, plain girl. But this demeanor no longer fooled Johnny.

In parting, he said, "Kate, I don't know exactly how to say this, but I find you far more worthy of a place at the college than all the boys of my acquaintance. I thoroughly enjoyed our conversation, and I hope we have another again soon. You may choose the next work, if you wish."

"Oh, yes, let's! Next Sunday?" She clasped her hands together with delight. "But *you* choose, for I should go mad with indecision." Then she blushed, and was about to scurry from the room when she noticed a book upon her father's desk. She reached for it and handed it to Johnny.

"I nearly forgot! Would you kindly return this to Peter? He loaned it to me during our ride upon the Charles, as I had expressed an interest in reading it."

In her hand was *Common Sense*.

Johnny took the book from her without a word, bowed, and left. So, it had not fallen overboard, had not been lost in the Charles River, or left on the boat. Why had Peter lied? To what end, making Johnny work at a long, arduous, and unnecessary task?

When Johnny entered his chamber half an hour later, he found Peter stretched out upon his bed, reading a letter.

"Say, where've you been?" Peter sat up. "I've been wanting to talk to you."

"Oh? What about? I was at my cousins' house. You know Kate, I believe."

"Somewhat," Peter replied evasively.

"Oh? She seems to know you rather well. Well enough to ride out upon the Charles. Well enough for you to loan her a book. Here—she gave me this to return to you."

A smile appeared at the edges of Peter's lips as Johnny held out *Common Sense*. "I've been found out, then."

As Johnny said nothing, Peter continued, "It was just a silly bet. We were talking at dinner one day, and I said you had an unusual memory. The boys doubted my word, and one thing led to another." Peter approached Johnny and touched his shoulder. "Come on, man. It was just a joke. I won the bet as I knew I would, mind you. But I'm not interested in the money. You can have it."

Johnny said nothing.

"Forgive me, *please*?" Peter asked contritely, bending his knees and clasping his hands together.

"I trusted you," Johnny finally spoke. "It was mortifying to be laughed at like that by the whole table of boys."

"I won't do it again."

"Solemn promise?"

"Most solemn."

Johnny hesitated, but he was not one to hold a grudge. "Very well. I accept your apology."

"Excellent!" Peter cried. At once the whole event seemed in the distant past. "But look—I've just had a letter from Papa. Winter break is but two weeks away, and he says I might bring you home with me."

"Bring me with you?"

"It would be jolly fun! You will absolutely love Moorcock."

Johnny said, "Surely you won't be fool enough to attempt the roads at this time of year? You'll waste your entire holiday in travel—if you get there at all."

"Nonsense," said Peter. "I've made the trip twice before. It takes a week."

"You have a magic carpet, then."

"A *floating* carpet, actually. It's a tidy little packet, owned by a friend of Papa's. He's a fur trader who comes to Boston nearly every month. From Yorktown, we can board a smaller vessel. Papa has made inquiries, and the ship is set to leave Boston on December fourth. The winds are good this time of year, and Papa shall send a coach and four to meet us in Fredericksburg."

"You make it sound so simple," Johnny said skeptically. He had been looking forward to seeing his mother, Lizzie, and the children in Quincy. Six more weeks with Peter, two of them on a cramped vessel, was hardly recompense. And yet the idea of seeing Virginia and its inhabitants tempted him.

"Oh, but Mama shall be devastated," Johnny said. "And besides, I imagine the expense is prohibitive."

"Never mind the expense—I am in your debt. Doubly so, now that you've forgiven me." Peter grinned. "As for your mother, tell her you are very like to meet our good friend Thomas Jefferson."

The thought of meeting the great idol of his youth tipped the scales for Johnny.

Eliza Boylston, however, was far less pleased. It was the next day, and she was sitting upon his one chair, having arrived for a visit. She looked fretful.

"But Johnny, I—we—have so been looking forward to your return to Quincy. I've not been too overbearing, have I? Why, I've hardly even written. Twice a week at most."

"Nay, calm yourself, Mama. He has made me an offer I think wise to accept. I shall see a wholly different way of life from our beloved little Quincy."

"Different, yes."

Johnny cocked his head, puzzled. "That is hardly all! I shall see a grand plantation and meet Virginia society. Peter said I might even be so fortunate as to meet Mr. Jefferson. He's an old family friend."

Eliza continued to look quite vexed. She finally said, "I worry about the roads. They can be dangerous this time of year."

"We sail directly to Yorktown and thence to Fredericksburg, where a fine coach and four shall be waiting."

"But if there should be a storm at sea—"

Johnny wrapped an arm about his mother's narrow shoulders. "We shan't be 'at sea,' Mama. We hug the coast. If there's a storm, we'll put in somewhere."

Johnny thought he had worn down all her objections, and he expected her to acquiesce with one of her long-suffering sighs. But Eliza shook her head, to which Johnny replied wearily, "If you fear that I shall witness some nasty business, I say I've seen it all in Barbados already. How could things be worse?"

It was true: Nearly everyone in Barbados owned slaves, including the free Negroes. Johnny had grown up among them. He had witnessed their scars, seen them drop dead in the fields as if struck by invisible lightning. He had heard them bear the assault of violent words, humiliating words, in humble silence. What more could there be that he did not already know?

But Eliza continued warmly, "No, Johnny. It's not safe. There is an excellent trade in black men just now. The scoundrels kidnap free men and sell them into slavery. You're young and strong. You would fetch a pretty penny. And there are other things I daren't speak of."

Johnny had no wish to fight with his dear mama, whose opinion he always respected. But in this, he felt certain she was in the wrong.

"I'm a white boy, remember, Mama? Is this not why we've come to America? So that I could get an education and rise to my rightful station in life?"

"Yes, I believe it's your whiteness I fear most," she whispered mysteriously. She then placed a hand upon her heart.

But Johnny was determined. "I'm going, Mama. Whether you fear it or no."

12

THE WIND BLEW FIERCELY FROM THE NORTH when, at last, carrying just one small trunk apiece, Johnny and Peter found themselves on Long Wharf waiting to board the *Columbia*. Peter's father had written of its estimated arrival in Boston, but twice they'd traveled to the wharf only to find no ship waiting for them. The wind had been unobliging, and it was not until December 7 that they finally set off.

In the open air, away from books, taverns, and bells calling him to prayer, Peter was playful as a child. He kept jumping upon his friend and riding his back. Laughing, Johnny did the same to him. It kept them warm as they waited.

Peter said, "I don't believe anything on earth is more lovely than Moorcock. I shall never leave it, not even in death." He smiled wistfully, then suddenly asked, "Why'd your family leave America, anyway? They weren't Tories, were they? My family managed to avoid declaring themselves one way or another, but that was in Virginia. One could not fence-sit in these parts, I'm sure. Though you would know better than I."

"No, my parents weren't Tories, though my grandpapa and Uncle Robert certainly were."

"Uncle Robert? Who's that?"

"My mother's—"

Johnny bit his tongue. He shifted uneasily from foot to foot and blew upon his hands, affecting cold, though he was still warm from their rough play.

"Barbados is beautiful, too," he said abruptly. "But I grew up feeling more American than British. Those I hold in highest esteem are Americans. And I hold the American Constitution to be one of the greatest documents ever created. I always dreamed of coming here."

"So, why'd they leave, then?" Peter persisted. "You haven't really answered the question."

"Grandpapa left his estate in Bridgetown to my mother, and as they had no money, I suppose it seemed best."

"Curious," Peter concluded. "Come to think of it, we have excellent friends in Bridgetown. Papa can tell you their names."

Johnny felt a shiver of fear run through him. This was too close. Any family in Bridgetown could have told you to whom Eliza Boylston was married, even though in Barbados she was known as Elizabeth Watkins. Everyone knew the odd couple, though it took many years before they were accepted, and even then never by the highest echelons of society.

Thankfully, Peter was distracted just then by the sudden appearance in the outer harbor of the *Columbia*. The packet soon arrived, and they boarded it.

• • •

The ship was cramped and dirty. Johnny attempted to read in his berth, but it was impossible. The water was too rough, the air too close, and the smells too rank. The room in its entirety measured, he estimated, twelve feet by fourteen feet. Whenever possible, he strolled the poop deck and watched the constant industry of the seamen, which reminded him of home. Seamen were forever doing something: mending rope, adjusting the sails, or swabbing the decks with their bare red hands.

The captain was a plump, pink-cheeked man of perhaps forty-five. A grizzled beard hid his mouth, as did the tankard of beer from which he drank all day. But his eyes were clear, and he deftly managed his men.

The voyage took six nights and days. Johnny watched for whales and seabirds. He noticed how sometimes the water looked like slate—at other times, like veined marble. At night, as on their voyage from Barbados, the waves sparkled in the moonlight.

On the morning of the seventh day, having set sail once more and traveled up the narrow inlets of the Rappahannock, Johnny watched Fredericksburg grow ever more distinct, until he could make out the taverns and warehouses upon the wharf. How temperate the air was here, even in December! They finally anchored, and as they descended onto the dock, Johnny espied an elegant carriage waiting for them. A Negro coachman rode postilion on one of four fine white coursers, their tails flowing. Peter had not exaggerated the fineness of his carriage.

Once installed, they set off up the hill to the main road. Peter pointed off to the right and said, "That's Washington's childhood home, you know." Johnny peered out at the farm, which looked sadly abandoned. But the land was still fertile, the streams still flowing through verdant banks toward the river.

Peter had already told Johnny about his older brother, Frederick, and younger sister, Charlotte. Fred had gone to William & Mary for a year until some event in his sophomore year had sent him packing. The suspension was to be for six months, but Fred never returned.

Peter said, "Oh, and one more thing, Johnny. Whatever you do, don't bring up the treaty with Britain. I'd steer clear of anything along those lines."

"It would not occur to me to do so, but thanks for the warning."

"Papa is still quite angry that he has not been paid what he is owed."

"Paid for what?"

"Two dozen slaves. Bloody British took 'em and paid not a penny. Never will, now, thanks to Mr. Jay."

That past year, President Washington had sent John Jay, first chief justice of the United States, to Britain to negotiate a treaty. One of the American demands was for the British to reimburse slave owners for slaves seized during the Revolution. But the British had been intractable on this point.

Johnny was silent, as he'd been sternly instructed; perhaps he nodded his understanding.

Moorcock Manor was but five miles away from the harbor. Johnny looked out the carriage window at the gently rolling farmland. Although it was now winter, honeysuckle vines clung to the old stone walls, eagles flew overhead, and horses galloped through fields in the distance. He passed by creeks all flowing down gently to the Rappahannock, and thought, *This does not look at all like Barbados!* It was more fertile, more lyrical.

Suddenly, Peter touched his friend's shoulder. "You know, Johnny, they'll have begun the Christmas festivities already."

"So early?" His own family never made much ado about Christmas. Cassie always made them a good dinner, and then they sang a few songs, little more. Gifts were exchanged six days later, on New Year's Eve.

"Why, this isn't early. Our festivities go on for weeks. Nothing like you parsimonious Puritans. I'm sure there'll be a ball and a foxhunt or two as well. The locals are vastly fond of them. And, oh—have you ever attended a cockfight?"

"A cockfight?"

"So exciting. The cocks wear steel spurs. They positively tear each other to shreds."

Johnny made a face. That was not his idea of entertainment.

"Oh, but look—Moorcock!" Peter cried. "Let the fun begin!"

Johnny saw before them a long road flanked by massive oak trees wrapped in vines, which, bending, formed an archway overhead. The carriage turned in and proceeded down the private road. Along the way, they passed several outbuildings. In one, Negro men worked at a manufactory of some kind. They were very black, and their eyes shone as they glanced up from their work. Johnny looked away, toward the tobacco fields beyond, now fallow after their harvest.

The great house itself soon came into view. It was composed entirely of red brick. Johnny counted eight chimneys: four in the main house and two in each of the one-story wings. A semicircular double staircase and wrought-iron railing led up to a double portico. Sandstone columns flanked a broad red door. As a backdrop to this magnificent edifice, rolling hills gradually ascended to a bluish ridge of mountains.

The coachman pulled the carriage up to the base of the steps and stopped. Peter descended, raced up the steps, rang the bell, and shouted, "Mama! Papa! The prodigal returns!"

Impatient, Peter opened the door himself, and Johnny was able to see into a hall adorned with finely carved furniture covered in gold damask. Yards and yards of this same rich fabric festooned the windows.

Peter turned to his roommate and bowed. "Welcome to Moorcock Manor, Mr. Boylston!"

"Thank you, sir." Johnny bowed in return.

Peter's father soon arrived to greet them. He was a sandy-haired, affable man of about forty. "Welcome! Welcome!" he cried, leading them into the hall. There, Johnny had a better view of the room, which was at least eight hundred square feet in size. It had six windows, two skylights, and a pair of fine mahogany staircases leading up to a balcony.

After several minutes, neither the butler nor Mrs. Fray had materialized, so Mr. Fray, with some embarrassment, led Johnny to his chamber.

It was a large corner room, facing Fredericksburg and the river. As Johnny peered out at the view, he heard a flustered, feminine voice behind him:

"But why did no one tell me they had arrived? How awkward to greet the boy already in his chamber!"

Johnny turned to find a woman standing in his open doorway, in a splendid blue silk gown. She was comely and dark-haired, perhaps thirty-five years of age. A light-skinned Negro girl stood just behind her, head bowed and tied with a linen rag. Mrs. Fray curtsied and then offered Johnny a smile. Her pale, shrewd eyes looked him over carefully. But she seemed satisfied with what she saw and said, "You must be Mr. Boylston, Peter's roommate. I hope your journey wasn't too tedious."

"Oh, no. Nothing to compare with the journey from Barbados, anyway."

"That's right. Peter told us you're from Bridgetown. You must know many of our friends. My husband goes once a year on business there."

Mrs. Fray had the same beautiful lilt as her son. But the words themselves sent a chill through Johnny. He merely nodded.

"That's Harriet," Mrs. Fray continued. "I'm afraid she's been indisposed this morning. That's why Curtis and I—but never mind—" she broke off. "You may make free to call upon Harriet for anything you need. There is a bell, just here." Mrs. Fray pointed to a long needlepoint pull that hung to the left of the doorframe. "She can draw you a bath now, if you like, or bring you tea."

"Thank you." Johnny bowed. "I should first of all like to write my mother and tell her I am safe arrived."

"Of course." Peter's mother nodded briskly. "Harriet, bring Mr. Boylston some *pay*-puh and ink. Oh, and a pen, of course." Mrs. Fray turned to Johnny. "One has to spell these things out, you know." She smiled.

Johnny bowed slightly, but he could not return the smile. Harriet curtsied and left at once to fetch the items. These items duly brought and the door of his chamber closed, Johnny sighed with relief. He then took up his pen:

> Dear Mama
> I am just arrived at Moorcock Manor, Peter's home. My chamber has an excellent view over the Rappahannock River and all of Fredericksburg. Though I have been

here but five minutes, I can already tell that these people live very different lives from our humble Boston
brethren. I shall keep a faithful diary in my mind to
share with you when I return. I am glad I am come,
but beg forgiveness for my ill-mannered insistence
upon it.

After sealing his letter, Johnny took the proffered bath and then
had a dish of tea. He lay down upon the bed, intending to rest a few
moments. But it was very soft and comfortable. He fell asleep and slept
dreamlessly until late afternoon. It was nearly dark when he finally rose,
dressed in the blue coat he purchased for school, and descended.

In the great hall, a large gay party was in full swing. Johnny knew
at once that his coat, though fine enough by Boston standards, was
entirely unsuitable here. Next to the brilliant imported silk costumes
all about him, he felt like a field hand in his Sunday best.

Ladies stood in groups, their large rumps touching one another.
From across the room, one such group appeared to be a sort of Scylla
with half a dozen heads. In New England, hoops had already been done
away with, the Northern ladies preferring to look like Greek statues
come to life in flowing empire-waist muslin frocks. But these Southern
women clung to the European court style of yore.

At the wassail bowl, Johnny made the acquaintance of Peter's little
sister, Charlotte. She had pale-blonde hair and wary eyes. She ran off
within moments of curtsying. Peter had already helped himself to a
glass of wassail, and when he saw Johnny he grinned and patted him
on the back. "I feared you'd never descend," he said. "But look—here's
Frederick."

A handsome burly young man approached them. He had a ready grin
and very pale-blue eyes, like his brother's. But his hair was darker than
Peter's, more brown than blond, and he was not nearly as tall. When he
smiled, his jaw clenched, as if the affability cost him some effort.

Johnny bowed, and Frederick returned the bow.

"Johnny's from Barbados, and he's at the top of our class," said Peter by way of introduction.

"Save one," Johnny corrected him.

"Oh yes, one freak of no account."

At the news that Johnny was from Barbados, Fred's pale eyes brightened with interest.

"Then you must know our dear friends the Cumberbatches. I hear their plantation, St. Nicholas Abby, is *very* fine. Excellent rum, too." Fred grinned his lockjawed grin.

"Yes," replied Johnny. "At least, I've heard so."

"Excellent. Well, we must have a long discussion about them sometime." Then Frederick leaned in to Johnny. "I've heard the native wenches rival the rum for their potency."

Johnny blushed at this comment. Thankfully, Frederick noticed a new party that had just then entered the room. "Excuse me," he said, bowing. He moved off to greet them.

Peter, steering Johnny off in a new direction, commented, "Never mind about him. Against a pretty girl, we shall always lose."

"Pretty girl? Who, pray?" asked Johnny, craning his neck to see above the crowd.

"Miss Burnes. Marcia Burnes. I'll introduce you by and by. But first, let's take a tour of the sweets."

Set out upon a long table, small cakes of every variety—pies with lattice tops, bonbons, and fruitcakes, all flanked by two stately sugarplum pyramids—made Johnny's mouth water.

"You've missed the entrée course, sleeping as you did. But if you like, we could fetch something from the kitchen."

"Nay. These look like they will do excellently well." Johnny had no wish to see the slaves working in the kitchen, though he knew they were there whether he saw them or not. He helped himself to several of the sweets and then looked about to find a chair.

While Johnny feasted on the sweet confections, Peter went off to speak to some of the guests. A servant came around with a tray of wine in glasses; Johnny took one and drank it quickly. It made him light-headed.

Suddenly he felt the presence of someone behind him. He turned to find the girl Frederick had left them to greet. Abruptly, he stood up, nearly emptying the contents of his plate onto the floor.

"Oh, sorry," he said, grasping at his sweets to keep them from falling off the plate.

The girl placed a gloved hand over her mouth to hide a smile. She was not very tall, but her posture was erect, her neck long. Soft warm-brown curls fell about a heart-shaped face, and a dimple in her chin lent a voluptuousness to the brilliant composition. Her eyes were intensely green, like emerald discs, and bemused. It was as if she found the party generally, and Johnny in particular, cause for laughter.

The girl, whom Johnny guessed to be perhaps sixteen, wore a lavender gown with white-lace trim. For her hair, she had procured fresh lavender, which had been woven into a coronet.

"Hello," she began. "You must be Peter's friend, from Cambridge."

Johnny might have said, "Yes, I am," but he could not be sure.

She curtsied. "Miss Burnes."

Johnny bowed, he was fairly certain.

"Our families have known one another—oh, as long as I can remember. Mama was a childhood friend of Mrs. Fray. We live up the Potomac, in the new capital city."

Johnny might have nodded.

"You're not very talkative, are you?" Miss Burnes laughed lightly.

Then Peter was beside them. He hooked an arm genially in Johnny's own.

"He is struck dumb by your beauty, Miss Burnes," he teased. She cocked her head charmingly, and Johnny unconsciously tilted his head at the same angle, as if wanting to stay in perfect alignment with her.

"Oh, that can hardly be true."

Johnny blushed.

"Johnny is from Barbados."

"Barbados! I should like to hear about that. Oh, I would love to visit Barbados someday."

"What Johnny won't tell you, since he can't find his tongue, is that he's an absolute genius."

"Nay," Johnny finally managed a syllable, his own voice sounding foreign to him.

"Try him yourself. Have him recite something from memory."

"Very well." Marcia clapped her hands together delightedly. "I shall." Here, the beautiful girl placed her fingers together as she paused to think.

"I'd love to try some of those other cakes," Johnny suddenly blurted. And, with a barely civil bow, he walked off toward the other side of the room.

Peter caught up with him.

"Say, what's the idea? You already took a plateful!"

"The desserts are excellent. I fancy another helping," Johnny replied, scanning the long table, though he had not finished the items on his plate.

"Why did you leave, and in such an insulting manner? One doesn't simply walk away from Marcia Burnes."

"Why not?" Johnny asked sourly. "You of all people know that I don't enjoy performing tricks for others to laugh at."

"Oh, you're too feeling," Peter concluded jovially, patting him on the back. "Why, I believe she liked you."

But Johnny was still feeling peevish. "Who is she, anyway?" Out of the corner of his eye, Johnny saw Frederick, who was endeavoring to impress Miss Burnes with ample smiles and glances, if not his wit.

"Miss Burnes?" Peter continued, "Why, apart from being beautiful, she is also the richest girl in all Maryland, or very soon shall be. Her father, David Burnes, sold his land to Washington to make the capital city. She shall receive *thirty thousand dollars*."

"Thirty thousand," Johnny mused. "Too bad I mortally offended her, then."

At this comment, both boys began to laugh, and Johnny's dark mood finally lightened.

Throughout the evening, Johnny caught Marcia glancing at him curiously from across the room.

"Why does she look at me like that?" he asked Peter, not once but several times.

"I suppose she cannot get over the enormity of your blunder."

"Ha!" Johnny said. He had taken another glass of wine and was now in excellent humor. The next time Marcia glanced at him, he met her eyes and grinned, which made her look away.

But at the end of the evening, Johnny saw Miss Burnes once more just as her family was leaving. She shot him an inquiring glance, tinged with something Johnny chose to interpret as regret.

13

A CEASELESS ARRAY OF ACTIVITIES LED UP to Christmas. There was a winter ball at a "nearby" plantation. It was ten miles of rough roads, and they were obliged to stop the night. There were shooting parties and bets upon quarter- or three-mile horse races at the Frays' private racetrack. There were cockfights and countless foxhunts. These Peter participated in with great alacrity, urging Johnny to come along. "There is nothing to it," he insisted. "Just keep your arse in the saddle."

Johnny had never ridden upon a saddle. "Mama would not be pleased to learn that I broke my neck chasing a fox," he said to Fray. It seemed to Johnny that these Southerners liked nothing better than to risk life and limb and then return to the manor, where they festively celebrated their continued existence.

"Well, suit yourself." Peter shrugged. "But you're missing a real thrill." He had just turned to leave when Johnny touched his shoulder. "All right. I suppose I should see what all the fuss is about."

Peter grinned. "Well then, let's go!" He wrapped an arm companionably about Johnny's back.

The race began upon a hill about a mile from the estate, where the hunt club had its meetinghouse and stables. An impressive crowd of men in red wool coats, reminding Johnny of British officers, adjusted their saddles and checked their bridles. A great joviality pervaded the crowd, and within the club, refreshments such as tea, cider, beer, and cakes were for the taking.

Eventually the gentlemen mounted their horses. They readied themselves. A horn was sounded and the horses charged as if into battle. Twice Johnny nearly tumbled headfirst off his steed, having no experience of going so quickly, much less leaping across streams and fallen tree limbs.

Mr. Fray's hounds, imported from England, were sleek and fast, but the red fox was faster and got away. This secretly pleased Johnny, who could not bear to see any living thing killed.

After the hunt, Peter could not stop laughing and patting him on the back. "That was close, my friend. Very close. But that's the Southern way."

Johnny smiled. He had greatly enjoyed it.

For near two weeks, Johnny spent his days abroad either hunting birds or chasing foxes. Then he retired within, accompanied by men of great good cheer. Frederick was particularly solicitous of Johnny's well-being. He made certain Johnny's saddle was tight beneath him and gave him advice on how to do better at the hunt. Once inside, Frederick was always the first to hand Johnny a warming toddy. And yet, there was something about Peter's brother that Johnny did not quite like. Some self-satisfied air, as if he were besotted with pride of place. As if he believed he was very nearly lord of Moorcock Manor already.

Gradually, Johnny began to understand the Southern way. Unlike the edgy bustle of the port cities, here, nothing moved quickly. The stone walls had not changed in generations; one bounded the brook as a boy of six and again as a man of sixty. Waking in the morning, Johnny thought, *Time stands still. To live in this world is to live forever.* At least he felt that it was so.

Within the great house, the rituals were equally indolent: for hours they played cribbage, dice, or charades, accompanied by a cheering toddy or in singing carols around the pianoforte.

And all about them, human shadows worked and worked and sacrificed themselves for their masters. Johnny managed to avoid them as best he could. But his indifference, he knew, was only skin-deep. He did not trust himself to keep his composure near them, so he stayed away. The only slave that Johnny found nearly impossible to ignore was Harriet. Mrs. Fray demanded the girl sleep on the floor in the hallway. How mortifying it must be to sleep like a dog by the mistress's chamber door!

Johnny had grown to like Harriet. She was bright and hardworking. He would have liked to speak to her, to ask her about her life at Moorcock. But to do so would be unthinkable. Once or twice he even approached her, but he saw the fear in her eyes at once and turned away. At such times, he felt such pain that he wanted to cry out, "But I'm not one of them! I'm not a white boy! I'm black, just like you."

•   •   •

The festivities reached their peak on Christmas Eve. A hog was slaughtered. A boar's head dressed with bay leaves sat upon the table, as did a peacock, adorned with a headdress of its own feathers. There was carp tongue, roast goose, mince pies, and cakes of every kind. The weather was cold but clear, and Mr. Fray proposed another foxhunt. Peter accepted, but this time he could not persuade his friend to join them.

"I think I'll write some letters home," Johnny said.

"How very dull of you!" Peter exclaimed, and went off to prepare for the hunt.

Within Johnny's chamber, a fire was lit. He sat at his desk. Through the window he could see the hunting party heading off down the footpath to the lodge. He took a pen, opened a bottle of ink, and endeavored to write his mother.

Dear Mama

I find myself

Johnny got no further. In truth, he didn't know how he found himself. How could he describe the lavishness of daily life, the warmth of the hospitality, or the beauty of the surrounding countryside? New England had its charms, but it was nothing compared to this. Then, how could he describe how he felt about Harriet? Not what he saw in her but rather what she saw in him? Johnny's pen dried as it remained poised above his paper.

Finally he set the pen down. Writing was hopeless. In the chamber's enrobing warmth Johnny grew drowsy and moved to his bed. He lay down for a brief moment and told himself he would doze for a few minutes. When he woke, he found himself in complete darkness. He rose, lit a candle, cleaned his teeth, dressed in his blue coat, and pomaded his hair. Then he descended with a long sigh.

The guests had already arrived. They stood in groups, magnificently attired. The rooms' windows, freshly washed, reflected the luxuriant fire's red glow. All the mantels and newel posts were festooned with fresh green holly branches, and bunches of mistletoe hung in the doorways.

For a brief moment, Johnny expected Miss Burnes to appear out of the crowd. But she did not. Instead, looking about, he saw Frederick, who stood among a group of other young men. When he saw Johnny, Fred smiled and winked conspiratorially.

"Finally!" Peter swaggered up to him, a glass of rum punch, clearly not his first, in his hand. "What have you been up to?"

"I fell asleep," Johnny admitted.

"Well, thankfully, you haven't missed Jefferson."

"Jefferson? Where?"

Peter placed his hands on his friend's shoulders and turned him about. "Just there." He pointed to the library on the other side of the hall. "He's with Papa. Go and introduce yourself."

"Introduce myself? Not on your life."

"Oh, very well." He sighed. "Come with me." Peter linked arms with his friend and led him to the library.

As a child, Johnny had imagined long conversations with Jefferson in which they discussed the new nation, states' rights, and the Constitution. What would they discuss now, now that it was no dream? His heart pounded with anticipation.

Within, the sound of voices was muted, as if the men discussed something of a sensitive nature. Hearing the boys approach, they fell silent. Johnny found himself standing before a very tall, slender man in his middle fifties. He had a full head of graying red hair. Careworn creases lined his long pale face.

"Mr. Jefferson." Peter bowed. "I'd like to introduce to you my good friend John Boylston. He rooms with me at school."

Johnny bowed deeply.

"Mr. Boylston, is it?" Jefferson bowed in return. "That school you speak of—that's over in Massachusetts, is it not?" His voice was remarkably soft, almost inaudible.

"That's right, sir."

"How do you enjoy it? The college, I mean?"

"Very much, sir," Peter replied for his friend. "Though it is very cold just now. We had a great storm last month. Nearly two feet of snow, I believe."

If Johnny had thought that Jefferson would launch upon a discourse concerning the French Revolution or Jay's Treaty, he was to be disappointed. The weary man merely said, "I wonder if Mr. Adams had more luck with his wheat this year than I did."

"Let's hope not, sir!" replied Peter, and they both laughed.

Johnny bowed and left the library. Mr. Jefferson sent him a bemused smile as he returned to his conversation with Mr. Fray.

"You were very dull," Peter said once they had met up in the hall.

"I know," said Johnny. "I couldn't manage a single syllable."

The rest of the evening passed in singing carols, making toasts to health, and lively conversation. But Johnny continued to brood upon all the things he might have said to Mr. Jefferson, and all the things he dared not say.

·   ·   ·

Late that night, he awoke with a start from a deep slumber. He had drunk two glasses of wine and a cup of punch as well. He thought he had heard a noise, though at the moment there was only silence. Johnny lit a candle, rose from his bed, and crept down to the place where Harriet slept. Her thin pallet and bedding were there, but the girl herself was not. Had Mrs. Fray sent her on an errand in the dead of night? It seemed unlikely.

Johnny retrieved his dressing gown and began to wander through the house, listening, ears keen. The hall below was silent. Beyond the windows, trees swayed in the moonlight. The moon was full, or nearly so. Johnny passed Mr. Fray's library and approached a green baize door. He heard nothing there, either, and nearly turned back. Then he made the decision to head to the kitchen. It was in a separate building, at the end of a long covered passageway.

Moving through the passageway, Johnny thought he heard a rustling sound as he approached the kitchen door. He opened it. Through the windows, bright moonlight shone upon the naked globes of a man's buttocks.

The man's trousers were pulled down to his ankles; his boots were still on. Beneath him was Harriet. Her gown had been hitched up to her waist. Her bare legs were splayed, and her body had gone limp as a rag doll. Her face was turned to the side, and her closed eyes leaked two steady streams of tears. But not a single sound came from her.

Hearing the door creak, the man turned and stopped his motions upon the girl.

"Bloody hell—who's there?"

It was Frederick. Johnny propelled himself into the kitchen but then just stood there, not two feet from Frederick.

"Oh, it's only you. Thank goodness. Go back to bed. If you're hungry, you may ring your chamber bell, and another servant will bring you something." Frederick lifted himself off the girl with a grunt and descended the table.

Johnny made no reply. He cast a final, pitying look at the girl, who sat up and tugged her petticoat down over her legs, and then fled the scene.

•   •   •

He stood in the middle of his chamber, breathing hard, heart pounding. The way she had looked at him! Her look displayed no relief at Johnny's appearance, no sense of having been rescued by a good and noble man. It said only, *Oh, God, another one.* Johnny thought he would never get those frightened eyes out of his mind as long as he lived.

Suddenly his stomach heaved, and with a loud, involuntary groan, he ran to the washbowl in time to hurl his sweet supper into it. He took the dirty bowl and pitcher of water and crept down the back stairs. He didn't want anyone knowing he'd been sick. He was able to exit by a back door, toss the bowl's foul contents, rinse it, and return to his chamber.

For the rest of the night, Johnny paced his room in a torment of indecision. Finally, after the sun had risen, he sought out Peter. His friend was enjoying breakfast at the dining table in the hall. Frederick, mercifully, was not present. Johnny had little appetite, but he took coffee and a sweet roll, alert and on edge, expecting Fred to enter at any moment.

"How'd you sleep, old mole?" Peter asked. "The sun shines—we should go for a ride."

"I didn't sleep. Or hardly."

"Why on earth not? Surely the bed is comfortable?"

Johnny nodded. Then he leaned across the table and whispered to his friend, "I must speak to you."

"About what?" Peter's pale eyes flinched. He disliked it when Johnny was intense about things.

Johnny leaned into him. "About your brother."

"Ah." Peter nodded. "I suspect I know the subject. Does he keep you awake with his *amours*?"

"Amours, you call them? I saw it with my own eyes."

"Saw what?"

Johnny inhaled, then let it out. "It was—beastly."

But instead of being shocked, Peter let out an amused laugh. "Serves you right for snooping about at that time of night!"

Then, reluctantly, Johnny remembered his solemn promise to his family.

"I'm sorry to bother you with it. It's just—their footsteps woke me."

"Oh." Peter smiled. "Well, why didn't you say so? I'll tell him to be quieter next time."

Peter and his family went off to church, but Johnny said he was indisposed and remained behind. For a few moments after they had left, he just stood there, unsure of what to do. His agitation grew the more he endeavored to suppress it. Finally, he retrieved his coat and stepped abroad. For nearly an hour, he wandered the estate, making his way through the beautiful arbors and down to the slave quarters. As he passed the rough, floorless huts, he held his shoulders high, as he'd been taught to do. But a cry threatened in his throat as eyes stared out at him from the huts' dark interiors. Before one of them, two small children in dirty white blouses stood holding hands. It was cold enough for Johnny to see his breath, but the children wore no more than the blouses. They watched him pass them by. Suddenly, Johnny turned back and moved toward them, bent on asking them their names. But at the sight of him approaching, they shrieked and scurried back into their noisome dwelling. Johnny made his way back to Moorcock in a state of great confusion.

. . .

The family returned from church at noon, and at one o'clock they gathered for Christmas dinner. Johnny had been quiet since their return, but Peter did not remark upon it. Johnny often went for hours without saying a word.

The first course was a delicious duck pâté, which had everyone murmuring approbation. Johnny took one bite of a round of toast before setting it discreetly to the side of his plate. The second course was a flavorful celery soup, and it was in the middle of this course that Johnny stood up from the table.

Alarmed, Mr. Fray looked up at him. "Are you ill, son?"

"Nay. Forgive me." Johnny bowed. "But I only just now realized that I must return home."

"What, now? Can it not wait till after dinner? What has happened?"

"I'm afraid it can't wait," Johnny replied, allowing the Frays to retain the mistaken notion that something very urgent called their guest away.

Frederick, who had managed to ignore Johnny since the incident in the kitchen, now looked at him through wary eyes. Johnny caught Fred's look but glanced quickly away.

Now it was Peter's turn to stand. "But it's Christmas!" he exclaimed. "You can't leave now. Besides, you can have no expectation of a ship's leaving Fredericksburg today or even this week."

"I know, and I'm very sorry. But while I endeavor to eat, my guilt eats at me."

"Well," Peter replied, sitting back down in a huff, "*I* plan to remain another week at least. And Mr. Jefferson remains until the New Year."

"He's *here*?"

"Not at the moment," Peter said coolly, turning back to his meal, "but he returns this evening."

"Yes," interjected Fred. "Perhaps you'll even be so fortunate as to meet his favorite slave, Sally." The brothers laughed.

"Frederick!" Mrs. Fray cried. "How appalling!"

"Oh, we're only fooling, Mama," Peter said, though Johnny observed a knowing look pass between the two brothers.

"What mean you by all this?" he asked Peter.

"Oh, nothing. Fred loves to joke about these things. How even the mighty fall and all that."

But as Johnny stood there trembling with mortification, he paid scant attention to the rest. His mind was bent on departure.

There followed an awkward silence during which Mr. Fray rose and scurried off to his study. He returned moments later with five shiny silver dollars. These he pressed into Johnny's hand. The coins felt hot; they burned him, and for a brief moment he resisted.

"Please, son, it comforts me to know you have them."

Johnny had no choice but to take the money.

"Thank you," he said. "Now I must pack."

Johnny bowed deeply and left the gathering; all, save perhaps Frederick, were astonished by their guest's behavior.

He returned to his chamber. As he reached for his trunk, Johnny noticed that his hands were trembling. When he had finished packing, he moved into the hallway and crouched down by the folded blanket before Mrs. Fray's chamber. There, he paused for a moment. Johnny was just removing something from his pocket when Harriet, carrying an armful of linens, emerged from Mrs. Fray's room. Seeing Johnny, she started.

"Sir, can I help you?"

He opened his palm and showed her his pocketknife.

Harriet's mouth opened as if she would object.

"Shh." Johnny put a finger to his lips, then tucked his knife into the blanket's folds. "There," he said. "Use it."

He descended at once, to find the carriage already waiting, ready to remove him from Moorcock.

"See you back at the college!" Peter called after him, now in great spirits after several glasses of wine. "Though I don't see why you suddenly bear a conscience!"

Johnny was off, and the enormous brick house and waving people soon retreated and then disappeared altogether.

The packet from Fredericksburg would not leave until the following day, and Johnny was only obliged to stop one night at the tavern, which provided him excellent accommodation. But he could not settle; he paced much of the night, examining and reexamining what had happened. He cursed himself for his impulsive gesture. To what use might a young chambermaid put a boy's knife? What a fool he was! That poor girl had no power. Even if she did, knives were plentiful on a plantation. She could have no earthly use for his. But he had needed to make *some* gesture, and so he had. Ah, well. Perhaps she would give the knife to a father or brother in need of it.

It was now nearly four in the morning, and Johnny finally lay down upon his bed and willed himself to think no more, though he knew that there remained a great deal to think about.

Later that morning, he boarded the ship. It had a good wind and made excellent time, arriving in Boston on New Year's Day, 1795. From Boston, Johnny hired a coach, with the last of Mr. Fray's silver dollars, to take him to Quincy. It was ten miles of straight road, though icy in places. When Johnny finally saw Lizzie's cottage, he leapt from the moving chaise and began to run. The door opened for him, and he fell into his mother's arms, so grateful to be home that he wept.

Part II

14

EVERYONE WISHED TO KNOW HOW JOHNNY FARED in Virginia. So he told them. He spoke of the beautiful light over the open hills, and his first foxhunt, and the hall with its many windows and skylights. He told them of the boar's head dressed in bay leaves, and the peacock adorned in its own feathers. He told of the wassail bowl and the men in their fine red coats sitting erect upon thoroughbred horses. And, finally, he told them how he met the great Jefferson.

Abigail muttered, "I suppose he pretended to be a simple farmer."

Johnny said, "Indeed, he wondered how Mr. Adams's wheat crops fared."

Abigail glanced cannily at Johnny, catching his drift. "Yes, all right," she admitted. "They both pretend to be much less interested in politics than they actually are."

Lizzie and Eliza soon excused themselves from the dinner table. A young woman of the parish was in travail with her first child, and both women would attend.

Eliza grasped her son's hand. "I'm so glad you're home," she said.

"As am I."

"I was wrong to forbid you to go. You're not a child any longer, though I sometimes wish you were."

"No, I'm not a child," Johnny agreed. "But I probably should have heeded you. There is much to admire and much that is beautiful. But in the absence of *true* aristocracy, they hold themselves to be aristocrats, Mama. Imagine that! They see themselves as paragons of all that is fine and jolly and good. They truly *believe* they are virtuous. Why, they out-British the British!"

Eliza had meant to change the subject, but as Johnny spoke these last words, she grew suspicious.

"Johnny, did something happen in Virginia? Were you harmed in some way or—did you speak out of turn?"

"I admitted that we knew the Cumberbatches. Apparently they are particular friends of the Frays."

"Oh, Johnny," said Eliza. She sighed. "That is too close for comfort. One word of inquiry shall tell them precisely who your father was."

"I don't think they were overly curious, Mama."

"Let's hope not."

Eliza sent her son a mournful glance and had nearly gone out the front door when she turned around, convinced that her son lied to her, by omission if nothing else. She could always tell.

She pulled him toward her, out of earshot of the others, and asked, "Was it very awful, Johnny?"

At her entreating look, Johnny broke down. "It was—oh, don't ask me to share with you what I saw! It was horrible, so horrible I shan't ever forget it. I had imagined such things happening. And the way it felt, to do nothing. To be silent—" he shivered. "I stood up from the Christmas dinner table and fled!"

But instead of being shocked, Eliza placed a hand on her son's arm. "I stood up from a Thanksgiving dinner table once. I refused to eat the meal because your father had been whipped for hunting the meat for us. He went hunting for our benefit, not his. He broke his curfew to do so, and because of that my uncle punished him. My family shunned me for two weeks."

Johnny smiled slightly, consoled to hear his mother's story. Then he said, "You feared for me, Mama, and you were right. Moorcock was nothing like our Barbadian plantations. It was worse. At once more beautiful and more villainous."

"How do you mean?" she asked.

"Ours is a small island. What cruelty there is, what travesties of common humanity, are apparent to all. There is no hiding. But Moorcock is so vast, and there are so few witnesses, that one might easily deny it all. The Frays *do* deny it, Mama. Even to themselves!"

Eliza had her own opinion, namely that the Frays had no need to deny anything. No one in the South would hold them accountable, even were the cruelties to become known. Yet she said only, "But Johnny, there is no need ever to venture South again, if you do not choose to."

Johnny hugged his mother to him and replied, "I sincerely hope I shall *never* go South again."

•   •   •

Several days later, when Johnny finally woke up in his own chamber at Cambridge, he had the sensation that the entire journey had been a lurid dream. His mother had tried to warn him. He had been annoyed with her and disobeyed her. But she had been right, and he had been wrong.

Through the haze of his unpleasant ruminations, Johnny thought he heard a ping against his window. He lay there for a moment. Then he heard another ping. The icy floor shocked him awake as he threw his dressing gown over a flimsy nightshirt. He looked out the window. Kate stood below, peering up toward him, unable to see beyond the sky's reflection in his window. As he bounded down the stairs, Johnny removed his nightcap, which sent his curly hair springing about his head.

A flood of icy air hit him as he opened the door. Kate's face was eclipsed by a bonnet, scarf, and eyeglasses, and she wore a full-length cape.

"How was your trip?" she spoke to him through the crack in the door. "Mama tells me you went to Virginia. Was it very beautiful? I've heard about plantations but have never seen one. But it's cold! Shan't you let me in—the hall, I mean?"

"Kate." He frowned. It was awkward to stand there in his dressing gown, the wind lifting his nightshirt.

"Oh, pardon me!" She blushed and put a hand to her mouth. "I've been up for hours and have forgotten my manners. I merely came— Mama wished to know—whether we shall have the pleasure of your company this afternoon. The little ones long to see you."

"Yes. It's been too long." Johnny bowed.

Kate curtsied. "By and by, then," she said, inwardly scolding herself for her awkwardness as she turned back to the road. Luckily, Johnny noticed only that she looked slightly cold.

•   •   •

After dressing, Johnny crossed the path to the commons. It was nearly empty. Few had yet returned from vacation. The boy whom everyone shunned, Eliot, sat at a table by himself. His thin blond hair touched his collar. He was hunched over, swimming in his large blue coat. With his hands upon the cane poised between his knees, he reminded Johnny of a great blue heron.

"May I?" Johnny asked, pointing to an empty seat.

"Of course." Eliot coughed slightly.

"Did you have a good vacation?"

Eliot nodded. "Tolerable. I remained here, actually."

"Oh? Did not your family insist upon your returning to Connecticut?"

Eliot glanced away. "Travel tires me. And let's just say that neither party was devastated."

"Indeed?"

"It's a long story. So, how was the venerable South?"

Eliot's tone was lighthearted, but Johnny could not joke about it. "It was very beautiful," he managed to say. "But I shan't be going back there anytime soon. Shall we finish our meal and head back to my room to discuss—what was it we had planned to discuss?" Johnny pretended not to remember.

"What is genius?"

"Well, shall we?"

"Yes, but let's go to my chamber instead."

Johnny walked beside Eliot as they moved slowly across the commons, down the steps, and across the path. Eliot lived one floor above Johnny and Peter.

"Voila," he said, finally opening his chamber door.

It was a capacious room, cozily decorated. On one wall stood a tall shelf full of books. On the floor was a fine Turkey carpet. There were several lamps, and a worn but comfortable-looking wing chair poised by the fire, complete with footstool and blanket.

"Aren't you lucky," Johnny said enviously.

"Lucky to have no one willing to room with me, do you mean, or to have no friends? I tried to befriend that fellow Shaw, but he was even more snobbish than I. And my roommate moved out when he perceived I was ill."

Johnny's eyes then lit upon a heap of blood-tinged cloths in a basket beside the bed. He looked away.

"But surely you have friends," Johnny said.

"As you know, the boys here consider me a freak."

Johnny said nothing, but Eliot chuckled.

"Sorry. That sounded like a lament. I'm actually rather contented. The unfortunate thing is, I'm a social creature by nature."

"From what do you suffer?" Johnny blurted.

"Consumption. Very romantic." Eliot adopted a classical pose of grief, wrist to forehead, eyes to sky. It made Johnny smile. "Yes, the scholarly life suits me, and my parents feel I must be educated on the slim chance that I survive, in which case I should be obliged to earn a living." Abruptly, he changed the subject. "But were we not going to talk about genius? They say you are one. Why do they say that?"

"I suppose it's because of my memory." Johnny shrugged. "My esteemed roommate made sure everyone at college knew. As you know, the response was not positive."

Upon the mention of the *Common Sense* debacle, Eliot looked sympathetically at his new friend.

"Well, perhaps there is a lesson in it for you."

"What is that?"

"You must be on your guard. Here, people are not always what they seem."

"And you believe them to be more so elsewhere?"

"I don't know. I've never been anywhere else. But nowhere could be more two-faced than our own beloved country just now." Eliot sat down in the wing chair and pulled the blanket over his legs. "Would you kindly put the kettle on? I—can't be bothered." He laughed, then coughed.

Johnny did as he was asked. While he waited for the water to boil, he thought: *Perhaps it is true, what Eliot suggested.* The treachery Johnny had known back home was rarely covert. The boys got angry and fought or pulled out their knives. They would never have suggested he record a book from memory for the sake of a wager—not in a million years!

Johnny made the tea and set a dish down on the table beside Eliot, who took a sip and sighed. He began, "I myself am possessed of an excellent memory, though not such a one as yours. However, even you must admit that the simple retention of information without deep understanding cannot be called genius."

"I wholly agree," Johnny replied.

"But let's take an example. You've read *Common Sense*. Memorized it to the letter, in fact. But were I to ask you whether *Common Sense* bears any relevance to our current state of affairs, what would you say?"

"I—well, yes, surely it does."

"Surely? Are you, in fact, sure? You haven't given it much thought."

Johnny turned a deep shade of red.

"You see. And the answer is that in fact it is *ir*relevant. A fossil from the antediluvian era."

"But—"

"Paine's a fool," Eliot concluded. "He happened to say the right thing at the right time, but he was wrong then and more so now."

"Why say you so?" Johnny, though wounded by Eliot's dismissiveness, remained curious.

"It's obvious. Paine's call for a single unified body to represent the people directly would have been catastrophic, had it been implemented. Thankfully, Adams saw the problem with direct democracy at once, which you would know for yourself had you read his *Thoughts on Government*."

Johnny cursed himself for not yet having read that work.

Eliot went on, "But even this, my excellent critique of one previously so revered, can hardly be called genius. Many have such a fine faculty. Yet in being critical, I do not create anything new. I merely tear down. A genius must go beyond memory or even critical understanding. A genius must create something new, or at least provide a new way of seeing the world."

Johnny felt brought down, but then he had a thought that made him laugh out loud.

"What is so funny?" Eliot asked.

"I must thank the ancient gods that I have found the antidote to hubris."

"Really?" Eliot looked interested. "And what is that?"

"His name is Eliot Mann."

"Oh, ha ha," Eliot said. "Very amusing." After a few moments, Eliot suddenly asked, "John, are you in love?"

"In love? Now, you mean?"

"Yes. You know, with someone. Some *female* or other," Eliot said the word with some distaste.

"Oh." Johnny understood the question. "Terribly so, in fact. With the most beautiful girl—she is absolutely heavenly. Alas, when we met I stood before her mute as the village idiot."

"What's the heavenly creature called?"

"Marcia. Marcia Burnes. She is entirely beyond my reach, though."

Johnny recalled Miss Burnes's parting glance at him. Then he sighed.

"John." Eliot suddenly yawned. "I grow tired . . ."

"Oh, I beg your pardon!" Johnny stood up. "I shall take my leave."

"Nonsense." Eliot lay back on his bed and indicated the other bed with a bony white finger. Then he stretched out and shut his eyes. "I meant simply that when I tire, I lose my breath. But I wish to listen. Tell me all about Barbados. Give me the grand tour."

"Very well." Johnny hopped onto the second bed and stretched out comfortably, his arms folded upon a pillow beneath his head. "I shall begin with the topography. Imagine mountains rising up from the bluest, clearest water you've ever seen . . ."

"Blue, clear . . . mountains." Eliot yawned again.

Johnny went on to describe the rolling hills, gentle by Carlisle Bay but becoming more dramatic as one traveled north. He spoke of the water, so clear one had only to look down to see the red and yellow fish and winnowing blue barracudas. He told of the merchant ships, large and small, and the neat rows of British soldiers enacting military exercises upon the parade by the garrison, and the green monkeys that flew through the branches of the trees, crying over their perceived losses. Johnny mimicked the deep drumming sound of the slaves on their Coromantee drums. There he stopped.

"Why do you stop, John? Your descriptions are excellent. But you've not said a word about your family. You make it sound as if you were shipwrecked upon that island. Where are the people?"

Johnny realized he could not continue without peril of revealing himself. "I probably should return to my chamber before I'm fined for my absence," Johnny said.

Eliot sat up. "What are you hiding, John? You're hiding something. I can always tell these things."

The boy's tone was teasing and Johnny smiled. Then he proffered his hand, which Eliot grasped with unexpected strength.

Johnny said, "I'm glad I thought to sit by you today."

•   •   •

They began meeting in Eliot's room after supper. At first, they mainly discussed books, and Johnny was careful to come prepared. Eliot tempered his searing insights with bursts of humor. Sometimes Johnny sang Barbadian songs, ones Cassie had sung to him as a child:

Aunt Nancy, open da door
Pater want de sarsop soup.
Aunt Nancy, open da door

Then, one evening, making certain that the door to Eliot's chamber was firmly closed, Johnny danced for his new friend. It was a gyrating African dance the slaves always performed at Crop Over. Seeing Johnny dance in such a scandalous manner, Eliot's eyes fairly started from his head. He cried, "Stop. Stop at once or I shall have to call the constable!"

But then Eliot rose from his bed and tried to copy Johnny's movements, until they fell down laughing.

Some nights, the conversations grew serious. On one such night, Eliot turned to Johnny and asked, "Johnny, may I ask you a question?"

"You may ask," replied Johnny.

"What do you most fear?"

Johnny thought about this. "I fear . . . to leave no mark upon this earth. To come and go as if I never were. I'm very—ambitious," Johnny admitted.

Eliot was silent, waiting for Johnny to continue.

Johnny went on, "My beloved papa was a good man. But he was barely literate. He knew nothing of government, or the Constitution, or the law." Johnny suddenly felt ashamed at his own words.

Eliot nodded his understanding. "You wish to be a great man. Like your heroes Adams and Jefferson."

Johnny looked down at his feet. "You mock me."

"Not at all."

Eliot recited:

> God doth not need
> Either man's work or his own gifts; who best
> Bear his mild yoke, they serve him best: his state
> Is kingly; thousands at his bidding speed,
> And post o'er land and ocean without rest;
> They also serve who only stand and wait.

"Milton?" Johnny asked.

"Yes."

"It's a beautiful poem. But I can't see how it relates to *me*."

"I feel it does—or shall. Be patient."

Johnny was not sure that he understood what Eliot meant. But instead of inquiring, he asked, "And what is *your* worst fear? Is it—illness?"

Eliot smiled. "Illness? You mean death, perhaps, for I'm already ill. No. The truth is, I fear going to my maker without having been truly loved."

It was the saddest statement Johnny had ever heard. He was about to object that surely Eliot was loved, when his friend said, hands and eyes raised in supplication, "Yes, loved with the kind of burning passion such as yours for Miss Burnes!"

"Oh, you die!" Johnny grabbed his pillow and threw it at his friend. There ensued a happy pillow fight, bird feathers flying about the room like snow.

•　　•　　•

As winter deepened, it became a challenge to keep fires going and candles lit. One snowy night in mid-January, as the two boys were locked in conversation in Eliot's chamber, Johnny realized that the coals had long since burned out. It was freezing. They both lay in bed fully clothed, in their coats and hats and mitts. They saw their breath float like puffs of smoke in the air.

It was too late to fetch more coals from the buttery, and this thought led Johnny to another.

"You know, Eliot, I have a cousin of sorts who lives nearby who would greatly enjoy our conversations."

"Invite him—do," Eliot replied. "But only if he can keep up with us and has a warm coat."

"She's a girl, and I'd rather invite ourselves *there*, as she lives in a fine, warm house."

"A *girl?*" Eliot looked at his friend with narrowed eyes.

"Oh, it's not like that." Johnny shook his head. "You'll see." Johnny promised he would discuss it with "the girl" the following day.

•　　•　　•

"A club?" Kate cried when Johnny had proposed it to her the following morning. "And *I* a member?"

"The other member is—singular," Johnny warned.

"How so?" Kate looked warily at Johnny.

"Oh, nothing untoward. He's a dear boy, really, and so funny he will have you on the floor. But—he's ill, Kate, a case of consumption. Though I've known him but a few weeks, I've already had the most amazing conversations with him. He's shunned by all the thick-headed college boys, naturally. But I think you will love him. If your mother agrees, I shall fly back to Eliot with the happy news."

Kate was not convinced, either then or when she first set her weak eyes upon the creature. When Eliot entered the foyer of the Lees' home, Kate saw a boy in a scandalously newfangled high hat and carrying a walking stick. He appeared to be a cross between a stork and a dandy. Seeing Kate for the first time, Eliot dropped the stick to the floor and extended his hands out from his body.

"This must be the extraordinary Katherine Lee." Eliot fell to one knee and tipped his hat to her.

"Why, he's mad as a hatter!" Kate exclaimed to Johnny.

15

THEY CALLED THEIR CLUB THE SLOTTED SPOON Society. It was a merciless reference to the intellectual dregs that Eliot and John believed floated atop the Harvard punch bowl. Their mission, they agreed, was to remove the dregs and savor the pure elixir of fine thought. They would discuss a different book each week; it was to be a very serious club. But each time one of them mentioned its name, they all burst out laughing.

Some days, and at certain angles, Johnny thought Miss Lee very comely despite her spectacles and carelessly pinned hair. But then, back in his cold chamber, as he lay alone on his cot, that lurid Virginia world returned to him, and he imagined Marcia Burnes's smile, her amused green eyes, and other attributes he dared not enumerate.

It was now February, and Peter had not yet returned. Johnny began to wonder what delayed him. Part of him hoped he would never see the boy again.

Then on a fair day in March, when the emboldened sun finally began to melt the mounds of dirty snow, Kate, Eliot, and Johnny gathered in Harry's study to discuss their latest topic. Eliot reclined upon a red damask sofa, while Kate and Johnny sat in two Puritanically rigid slat-back chairs. They looked at Eliot enviously.

He knew their thoughts. "Well, when *you* are dying, my lovelies, I'm certain your children shall let you have the sofa. But it's my turn now."

Kate blushed, but Johnny frowned and said, "You're not dying, Eliot."

"Not today," Eliot agreed.

"All right, friends," Johnny began. "Let us come to order."

Kate's eyes were bright; she clasped her hands together in anticipation.

"The topic I put before us today is, 'Whether a community can, in any sense, be justified in giving up one of its innocent members to death for the public good.'"

"What a gloomy question!" Kate cried. "I don't like it."

"It is a most excellent question," Eliot rejoindered, "of obvious theological as well as philosophical import." Just then, Aunt Martha stepped into the room. She always took a lively interest in their group, though was careful not to get in their way. Sometimes, after offering them tea and cakes, she remained to listen in silence.

"What is it you discuss?" she asked. Kate, her face stony, made no reply. It was Eliot who repeated the question.

"I see," Martha answered thoughtfully. "And what is your opinion?"

"We've not yet begun to discuss it. Would you like to join us?" Eliot asked.

"Yes, do you have an opinion to share, Aunt Martha?" Johnny added.

She nodded.

"*Mama*," Kate sighed, as if she would prevent her mother from speaking.

"I should *like* to hear her opinion, Cousin," objected Johnny. "Surely it cannot influence our discussion in any great way?"

Martha Lee said, "Convictions change, Johnny. I know mine did."

Poor Kate squirmed in her chair, but Johnny, eager for an explanation, urged Aunt Martha to continue. All his life Johnny had heard whispered intimations about his aunt—everything from her having been a spy for George Washington to having killed a man. Perhaps she would reveal her secret now.

"Mrs. Lee," Johnny pronounced formally. "On the topic of whether a community can, in any sense, be justified in giving up one of its innocent members to death for the public good, what say you?"

Mrs. Lee slowly shook her head. "I used to believe that ends justified means. But it led me to into a dark cul-de-sac, Johnny, and I realized my mistake too late. Harry and I—well, we atoned together." She did not explain what she meant, but merely added, "Did Christ not say that even the worst sinner may be saved?"

Kate's cheeks reddened, and Aunt Martha concluded, "I shall leave the rest for you young people to decide. It is a truism that each generation needs to make its own mistakes. But by my daughter's looks, I've intruded quite enough. I shall tell Bessie to bring you some tea."

Aunt Martha curtsied then and left the room.

"What an extraordinary woman," said Eliot. "Do you have an idea what she's talking about?"

"Not at all," Johnny replied.

Johnny stared at Kate, looking for an answer. But Kate burst into tears and ran from the room.

Johnny rose. "I shall go after her."

He caught up with Kate in the hall.

"I'm sorry," she said, once they had returned to the study. "It's not something we often discuss. She—no one knows save our family and the Adamses. But Mama—something happened during the war. The younger ones know nothing of it and must never know."

Eliot inhaled. "Did she *kill* someone?"

"Eliot!" Johnny cried.

Kate nodded slightly, and the boys' eyes widened.

"Is that why she's now a Quaker? Mama told me she had converted."

But Kate did not answer. She said, "Please, no more. Another time, perhaps."

The atmosphere in the room became awkward. Then a wicked gleam appeared in Eliot's eyes.

"We-ell," he drawled. "Johnny, I suggest, since Kate shared something of a very intimate nature, that we do the same. In solidarity, as it were. We may think of it as our little society's blood oath."

"That's not necessary." Kate frowned.

"I'll go first." Eliot ignored Kate's objection. He inhaled deeply, then let it out. "Well, ladies and gentlemen, I must admit to preferring the company of men to that of women, apart from my dear Kate here."

The friends knew at once what he meant but would never breathe their acknowledgment of it. They sealed their oath of silence by a solemn nodding of heads, which had the additional benefit of concealing their embarrassment. Finally, Eliot and Kate turned to Johnny.

"What could you possibly have to share with us?" Kate asked.

Johnny glanced at her, then took a deep breath. His mother would be horrified, but it was the only secret he had to share.

"I'm black," he said.

16

"WHAT STRANGE GAME IS THIS?" OBJECTED KATE, rising to her feet. "You are both merely trying to distract me from my own troubles. It's very sweet of you, really, but—"

"It's no game," Johnny assured her. "Sit down and I'll tell you all about it. Oh, you can have no idea of my relief in doing so!"

"Tell us absolutely *everything*," Eliot said, eyes shining.

"My father, as your own parents will attest, was a slave for the first twenty-six years of his life. A most excellent man he was, a shipwright at Colonel Langdon's yard in Portsmouth, a great aid to the Rebels during the war, and yes, Mama's lover."

"Mrs. *Boylston*? You can't be speaking the truth." Kate had met the tall, fair, imperious woman twice now. While personable, Eliza Boylston retained the superior and standoffish air of a wealthy merchant's daughter.

But Johnny confirmed it with a nod. "They were very happy together," he said, "when they finally could be. Not *here*, of course. In Barbados."

"But you were born here." Kate suddenly realized the significance of Johnny's admission and cried, "Oh, goodness!" Then she blushed.

"He's a bastard," Eliot affirmed rather too gleefully.

"Well, my parents *were* married on the ship that left America," Johnny said.

Johnny went on to recount his mother's story: her life as a spoiled girl who lived just up the road from where they now sat, and the terrible death of her brother Jeb at the battle of Breed's Hill.

Kate and Eliot hardly breathed. Johnny went on, "After Jeb's death, my family fled to Portsmouth, where they remained for three years. Soon after their arrival, Mama, nearly dead with grief, became drawn to John Watkins, her uncle's slave. He was an able shipwright hired out to Colonel Langdon at his shipyard on Badger's Island. Papa was rather fair-skinned. His own father was a white man. Anyway, they fell in love, although I believe they tried hard to break it off. When Mama came to be with child, Grand-mama's rejection was total. Only her papa eventually forgave her before his death. Then Tom Miller, Aunt Martha's brother, brought her to Quincy, where Lizzie and my Aunt Martha delivered her of a child. Me, that is. The rest I believe you know."

When Johnny had finished his story, his friends were quiet for a moment. Finally, Kate asked, "Who else knows?"

"The Adamses. Your parents. The Millers. And now you. It must remain our secret."

"Obviously," said Eliot. Then he clasped his hands together in triumph. "Oh, but I knew it!"

"You did not." Johnny frowned.

"I knew there was *something*. All those Barbadian songs and dances—"

"Dances?" Kate asked.

"You must ask him to show you sometime."

Johnny blushed. "Never," he said.

Just then, Bessie brought in their tea, and the gathering fell silent. She looked at the three friends with suspicion, as if they were up to no good. Once Bessie had left and they'd finished their refreshments, they spoke earnestly, as friends. Eliot spoke of having always felt different, of being shunned and ridiculed by other boys.

Johnny shared his experience of Virginia, of how helpless he'd felt pretending indifference to the suffering he witnessed. He did not mention Harriet's rape in front of Kate. But he did tell his friends about the seduction of that place, the timeless feel of the hills and stone walls, and the brooks wending through grassy pastures, of waking up in his chamber imbued with a precious sense of privilege. Most of all, he endeavored to express how he felt when he woke up in the morning surrounded by such beauty and comfort, and that very nearly made him wish he were a Southern white boy.

Johnny concluded sadly, "There was much I loved about the place."

"Well, who *wouldn't*?" Eliot said.

"Sounds like heaven itself," Kate added. "Apart from slavery."

They soon said their good-byes, agreeing to read Plato's *Symposium* for the following meeting. What no one except Kate knew was that, while she had shared her mother's secret, she had not shared her own.

That she had loved Johnny Boylston—Watkins, she now knew—almost from first sight had, for a long time, been an undeniable fact of her young existence. She loved his kinky hair and *warri* beads and even that vulgar ruby pinkie ring he insisted upon wearing. Or rather, the way he wore it so unapologetically until they forced him to remove it. She had not needed him to be handsome, but that he was, was no great demerit. Nor had she needed him to transcribe *Common Sense* from memory to appreciate his profound intellectual gifts.

But the revelation of Johnny's astonishing secret, that his father had once been a slave, and that he himself was perforce black—a "quadroon," some called it—illuminated her own feelings. Not because of what he had said, or even because of how proud she was of him, to always carry such a heavy burden, but because of how her own heart responded to this news. It beat on steadily, moved neither by revulsion nor fear.

Kate knew that Johnny did not love her back. Not in *that* way. Well, she consoled herself, heading up the stairs to her chamber, he may not love her now, but he was young yet. Sixteen. Feelings changed, did they not? She would wait. What choice had she, anyway? Love would not cease simply because it was unrequited, though such excellent reasoning gave her little comfort.

17

June 1795

MAY AND JUNE PASSED QUICKLY, WITH STILL no signs of Peter. Johnny demonstrated his proficiency to his tutors and was passed on to his sophomore year. Soon, it was time to say good-bye to Kate and Eliot for the summer. He felt slightly jealous at the news that Eliot would remain with the Lees over the summer, although this jealousy was eased by the knowledge that he would move in with Eliot that August. He promised them both he would write faithfully.

In his first days in Quincy, Johnny slept until his mother scolded him awake at around eight. The women found it nothing short of miraculous that he could sleep through dawn and the feeding of the animals, not to mention the children's shouts and their heavy treads upon the stairs. But Johnny had worked hard all year and had spent too many sleepless nights either studying or talking to Eliot. Now, though asleep in the parlor bed, he was miles away in his dreams.

After breakfast, there were chores for the children to do, but once dinner was finished, he allowed himself to be dragged in whatever direction the children chose—usually down to the beach. Or he walked with them to Houghs Neck, where they would row out to Noddle's or Grape Island. On these desolate islands, they would pretend to be shipwrecked explorers until the mosquitoes came out, it grew dark, and the prospect of food beckoned.

Some days were the province of men alone: one man, to be precise. Mr. Adams wished to raise a barn at the house where he was born, several miles away.

The barn building took place in the last weeks of July and the first week of August. Mr. Adams rose at six, enjoyed a leisurely breakfast, and then rode to Lizzie's cottage. On the second day of this routine, he was met by a fretful Miriam.

"Uncle John," Miriam scolded Mr. Adams, "can't you hurry up and finish that silly old barn? We want Johnny to play with *us*!"

"Miriam!" cried Eliza, who heard her niece from the kitchen. "Apologize to Mr. Adams at once!"

But Mr. Adams just laughed and said, "The girls shall always prefer to play with Johnny!"

"Yes, Mr. Adams," his mother agreed. "Yet that is no excuse."

Johnny smiled. The children did not yet know what he knew about his mother: that her tone was far sharper than her heart.

Riding east on the main road, Mr. Adams by his side, Johnny swelled with pride. As they passed through the center of town, people turned their heads at the familiar sight of their illustrious resident. Then they looked again to wonder, *Who was the hale young man by his side?*

Adams affected not to notice the stares. Instead, he fired at Johnny the usual fusillade of questions. How did his studies go? (Well.) What was his last oration upon? (Death.) What marks did he get on his exams? (Second. The devil take Eliot Mann.) Had he read Gibbon's *History of the Decline and Fall of the Roman Empire*? (He had.)

Johnny told Adams about his trip to Virginia and how impressive he found plantation life in *some* respects—the foxhunts, music, and sumptuous repasts. Then Johnny hazarded, "And I met Mr. Jefferson."

"Oh?" Adams feigned but mild interest. "What did you discuss?"

"To be honest, sir, I was too frightened to say a word. He wondered whether you had more success with your wheat crops than he did."

"Humph!" Adams smirked. "The great pretender adores his role of simple farmer—half believes it, too."

"Indeed, it's shameful." Johnny frowned. "Only compare how we ourselves are off to raise a barn of great diplomatic import."

Adams shot Johnny a look, and then laughed. Apart from Abigail, Johnny might have been the only person in the world who could speak to Adams in this way without risking an explosion. Adams was moved to ask, "Why do you have no such terror of me, child, though I am far more powerful than Mr. Jefferson?"

Johnny replied, "Sir, you have stated on several occasions that you find the job of vice president to be the most powerless one on earth. Naturally, I take you at your word."

At being hoist with his own petard, John Adams laughed so hard that he nearly fell off his saddle.

•   •   •

When not with Adams or playing with Lizzie's children, Johnny read and wrote letters. He wrote to Kate and Eliot, easy letters filled with news of ripening beans and cucumbers, suppers in the garden, and chases across the dunes with the children. That July, he also received two letters from abroad, one from Cassie and the other from Grand-mama:

> Dear grandson,
> I hope you are a diligent boy and doing well at school.
> I pass the days tolerably here, though the Lord knows
> Cassie can't be bothered with me. She has taken to
> selling her rabbits at market and has hired a girl to
> look after me. The girl does a *tolerable* job, I admit. I
> cannot deny she makes very nice jam cakes.

Grand-mama sounded very well, despite her complaints. Johnny then read Cassie's letter:

> My Dear Boy
> Cassie is so happe to receeve yor leter. I be obliged to hire
> a gurl for miss Margaret. She complain but is not unappy.
> My little bixness doz well. And big news! Isac get married
> next month! A sweet girl, mulatter, and most comely. But
> he say he will starve if I don't teach her to cooke.

After reading the letters from home, Johnny was seized with homesickness. Why was he not in Barbados? Why had he forsaken his father's shipyard? Why had it been so easy for him to forget them, when he remembered everything else down to its last detail?

He knew why, he reminded himself. He had made a choice, but it was easier to live with if he locked that door to his former life.

Meanwhile, Kate wrote Johnny nearly every day. She spoke of family matters, of what she read, and of the great pleasure of Eliot's company. Kate said that the dry sun, gentle breezes, and Bessie's good food had served to improve his health.

> Eliot says to tell you he feels strong and nearly well,
> and that he has not coughed blood in several weeks.

Johnny was heartened by Kate's letters. But in August, he received a letter from her that struck an ominous note. When Jay's Treaty was finally ratified by Congress and published that July, violence broke out in the streets of Boston. Kate wrote,

> Boys are returning to college early and many of
> them have joined those anti-Federalist clubs that are
> all the rage now. They sport the hats of the French

revolutionaries and put on Gallic airs. There have been
violent fights reported within our local taverns. I fear
these tensions shall grow worse.

Johnny replied,

I shall, I hope, remain above the fray. Fret not. I greatly
look forward to the reconvening of our little society. I
shall otherwise throw myself into solitary studies, and
the idiotic partisan fighting shall be as nothing to me.

Kate was not so sanguine. She was unsure whether Johnny could in
fact remain above the strife. He had an uncanny ability to recall the past
but could be woefully blind to all that stood in plain sight.

When the day of Johnny's departure arrived, Miriam was so despondent that she went into hiding and could not be found. As Martha's
chestnut mare had already been returned to her, Eliza spoke to Abigail,
who insisted that Johnny take their carriage. She also insisted that he
take four jars of beans and two of corn, raspberry jam for the Lees, and
all manner of biscuits and pies for himself. For Eliot, Lizzie had packed
a special cough tincture, a winter coat, and two blankets, though without, it was broiling and would remain so for another month at least.

It was easier for Johnny to take the carriage than to argue with
Lizzie or his mother. At the last moment, Miriam came out of hiding
and endeavored to climb into the carriage ahead of him. The younger
girls clamored and clung to his legs, exacting a solemn promise that he
would return soon. His mother hugged him for a long time, her head
on his chest. Johnny could swear she listened to the beating of his heart,
as if to confirm that he was alive and well.

Her own heart was so full that she managed only two words: "Be
careful."

Johnny sighed as he mounted the carriage. "I always am, Mama."

18

August 1795

THE SUN WAS A RED BALL UPON the Charles as the carriage made its way over the Great Bridge into Cambridge. The coachman brought Johnny to Harvard's main entrance and deposited his things upon the ground beside the walkway. It took many trips before all the items from Quincy had been transferred to his new lodgings on the third floor.

By the time Johnny made his last trip from the coach, the sky had darkened. Holding one parcel beneath each arm, he looked up and noticed that some students had placed candles in their windows. He wondered what they were for, until he saw a great flapping banner beneath one window: *Damn John Jay and damn all those who don't damn him!*

Johnny could not fathom how his fellow students could extol the virtues of the French Revolution when reports in the papers placed the death toll not in hundreds nor even in thousands, but in the tens of thousands. *That was carnage,* he thought, *not freedom.*

Worst of all were those Southern boys who returned to college wearing their tricolor hats in solidarity with France. The hypocrisy to cry for liberty whilst being fanned by slaves!

• • •

Eliot returned from the Lees' house the morning after Johnny had returned from Quincy. He joined his friend for breakfast in the commons, and Johnny was cheered to note that his friend did look much improved. His color was excellent, and he seemed to have gained flesh. Eliot's cane was conspicuously absent. They conversed for a few minutes about their summers. But eventually, Eliot asked the question they had both avoided.

"Is Fray returned?"

"Not that I can see."

"Ah, well. Perhaps that's the end of it."

The previous spring, Johnny had told Eliot the truth about Virginia, including Harriet's rape and his gift to her of his knife. Eliot had listened with careful attention, and when Johnny finished, had insisted that there was naught else Johnny could have done.

He was comforted by Eliot's words, yet he did not quite believe them. He could have challenged Frederick to a duel. But then he would likely have been unmasked, killed, or both.

After breakfast, Johnny returned to their chamber, leaving Eliot in the commons to finish his tea. He had just strolled out of Harvard Hall and approached his lodgings when he found Kate standing at the entrance, waiting for him.

She looked different, somehow. She had grown taller, and there was something about her face . . . Staring at her rudely, he tried to puzzle it out. Kate waited patiently for him to discover the change. Then she laughed. "So, you notice my new spectacles."

"I admit I did *not* notice them, though I do now. I noticed the amber color of your eyes."

Kate blushed. "Giles has long since been seeking a new project, and he found one. He discovered a means of ridding spectacles of their frames, all but the sides and bridge. See?" She removed her glasses and proffered them to Johnny. He held them gently in his hands. Two tiny bolts on each lens fastened to steel sidepieces and a simple bridge.

"How very ingenious."

"Yes, he really is. The body, though infirm, yet houses an inventive mind. Needless to say, I'm most grateful to him." Kate took her glasses back from Johnny and returned them to her face.

"Say—are you off to class just now?" she asked.

"I've half an hour—come." Johnny took her by the elbow and led her into the yard. He removed his calico gown and placed it on the ground for her. Though it was yet August, a number of yellow leaves had begun to float down from the trees. After they had inquired about the health of each other's families, Kate paused and stifled a smile.

"What is it, Kate? What are you hiding?"

"I had a suitor after you left for Quincy," she confessed.

"A suitor? *Who*, pray?" Johnny's heart thudded unexpectedly.

"Someone by the name of Pearce, a friend of my parents."

"Pearce," Johnny muttered. "Sounds old."

"He is not old." Kate smirked. "He's but thirty years of age, or perhaps a little younger."

"Humph," muttered Johnny, much as Mr. Adams did when dissatisfied.

"Why, cannot you imagine any young man taking an interest in me?"

"Of course I can!"

"You seem to think that because *you* do not find me attractive, no one will."

"That is not what I meant—"

Kate knew that was not what Johnny meant, but, affecting annoyance, she stood and brushed herself off. "I take my leave of you, Johnny Boylston."

Johnny stood as well, thoroughly confused. "Kate—what—?"

But Kate had already headed off toward home. She heard Johnny's call but continued walking as if she had not. She was smiling to herself, though. For she had gleaned something he had not. He was jealous! *Boys could be such fools sometimes,* she thought. Particularly Johnny Boylston.

19

IT WAS MID-SEPTEMBER NOW, AND JOHNNY believed that Peter was gone for good. The family must have arranged to send him somewhere closer to home. He was vastly relieved. There was unfinished business between them, but Johnny suspected that this business could never be resolved. It was best to let his experience of the Frays and of Virginia become swallowed up in the fullness of time.

During the day, Johnny and Eliot worked hard at their studies. At night, they talked, sometimes late into the night. If a coughing fit kept Eliot awake, Johnny would make him tea with Lizzie's tincture in it. Sometimes, to calm his friend's fears, Johnny would sing softly to him, songs that Cassie had sung to him when he was a child:

> Pack she back to she ma,
> Pack she back to she ma,
> Such a decent girl like Jessie Mahon,
> Pack she back to she ma.
>
> A pretty little girl named Jessie Mahon,
> She lazy since she born.
> De girl couldn' cook, she won' read a book,
> So pack she back to she ma.

"More verses!" Eliot always cried, for he knew there were more, and he didn't want Johnny to stop singing.

. . .

One morning toward the end of September, Johnny and Eliot walked into the commons and were about to sit at their usual table when Eliot halted. He stuck his thumb in the direction of Peter's old table.

"Regard. He's there."

Peter was sitting in his usual place among Farquez, Shattuck, Selfridge, and Wales, just as if he'd never left. The moment he saw Johnny, he rose from his chair, his eyes like blue stones. The other boys' glances, before merely indifferent, were now oddly cold as well. Peter approached Johnny, who bowed. Peter did not.

"Welcome back," Johnny said. "What happened to you? I thought you'd gone for good."

Peter said nothing.

Johnny continued, "As you must've noticed, I've moved in with Eliot. I thought you'd left the college and—"

"Meet me in the yard, in five minutes," Peter interrupted. He then returned to his friends and whispered something that made them all snicker.

Johnny sat down at his usual table, but he could not eat. As he took a sip of his coffee, he wondered what had happened.

Eliot asked, "I suppose he's angry that you've moved?"

Johnny shook his head. "Nay. It's something else."

"What else?"

"I know not. I'm meeting him in the yard. I suppose I shall find out."

"You don't need a second, do you? I should make a very bad one. You'll have to prop me up in a chair."

Johnny did not reply; his heart beat so quickly he could barely breathe.

Ten minutes later, having taken nothing for breakfast, Johnny strode out of Massachusetts Hall and into the yard.

Peter was waiting for him at the north end, on the playing field. The morning breeze was cool, but Johnny felt himself perspiring with fear. He recalled that very first day one year ago, when they wrestled in that field.

Seeing Johnny, Peter looked about to assure himself that they were alone. Then, staring directly at his old roommate, he said, "Frederick is dead."

For a moment, Johnny simply stood there. Shocked as he was, he could not feign sadness. He asked, "How?"

"He got into a fight with one of our slaves."

"When? What did they fight about?"

"February last. The nigger had noble ideas regarding his sister."

With slow horror, Johnny realized that Peter must be talking about Harriet.

"But it wasn't a fair fight. My brother was unarmed."

"What happened to the slave?"

"We hanged him—slowly. It took three days. In his last moments, he begged not for his own life, but for the safety of his family. We had promised no harm would come to them if he told us where he procured the knife."

Peter looked at Johnny with undisguised malice. He said, "You were concerned for Harriet, as I recall, though you endeavored to conceal it."

"I—"

"It was your knife, Johnny. I knew it the moment it was brought to me."

Johnny asked quietly, "Did you keep your promise to the man you hanged?"

"Of course not. Harriet was sold to a planter down in Mississippi. They were all sold, and good riddance, I say."

Peter hesitated, as if debating whether to share the rest with Johnny. Then he continued, "I know not whether I shall last the year here. It's doubtful whether my family can pay Frederick's creditors. I've spent the past months helping Papa to contact and pay them. If we can hang on to the plantation, it will be a miracle."

"I'm sorry," said Johnny.

Peter let out a raucous laugh. "You're sorry?"

"It was not my intention to make an enemy of you, or for anyone to be harmed." Johnny took a step toward his friend, but Peter sprang back.

He smiled coldly. "You *wanted* Fred dead and you gave Harriet the knife so she could do it."

"Nay, I—"

But before Johnny could finish, Peter turned and walked in the direction of the commons.

For several minutes, Johnny just stood there next to the field where boys played catch and wrestled. He imagined hands passing his knife in the night, the knife that he had hoped would kill Frederick Fray.

Eventually Johnny returned to his chamber, where he found Eliot resting on his cot. When Eliot heard Johnny enter, he sat up.

"So, what happened?" Eliot asked.

"A ghost from Virginia has returned to haunt me," Johnny said, his voice barely audible. Eliot moved toward his friend, anxious at how pale, how grave he appeared.

"Let me make us some tea—"

Johnny fell onto his bed and sobbed inconsolably. He hid his face in his hands.

Eliot said nothing, but his face wore a look of deep concern. He had lost his usual ironic demeanor.

"John, when you're ready, I'll be here to listen."

"Thank you." But Johnny did not take his hands from his face.

Eliot soon went off to class, and eventually Johnny rose and walked down to the river. On this autumn day, he allowed himself to feel a part of the wind that gusted and blew the loosening red and gold leaves from the trees. He wished to feel small, to disappear like a speck of dust upon the earth as it rotated around the sun.

Johnny returned to campus in time for dinner. He dreaded the moment he would see Peter again. But, to his great relief, neither Peter nor his gang was at the commons. After dinner, he studied in the library, then took a brief supper alone.

It was late in the evening when Johnny finally returned to his chamber. The bell for lights out had already rung. He glanced up at his building before entering it. In the windows, candles protesting the treaty with Britain had been lit. And there in the window of his former chamber stood Peter, staring balefully down at him. Upon his head he wore the tricolor hat of the Jacobins.

20

JOHNNY WATCHED PETER SPIRAL DOWN AND DOWN. There were times in the dead of night when, hearing a ruckus, he awoke to see Peter's drunken form stumbling across the yard, muttering curses about the British. It was as if he blamed his brother's death not just on Johnny but on Adams, the Federalists, and the political climate itself.

Meanwhile, from the moment Peter had told Johnny of Frederick's death, Johnny was never at ease. He found himself taking circuitous paths so as not to encounter his old roommate. He and Eliot entered the commons the moment it opened and returned to their lodgings while Peter and his friends were still within. He watched his back.

In December, a nor'easter hit the town, covering the college in more than two feet of snow. Classes were cancelled, and those students who could, left for home. Johnny worried that the road to Quincy would not be passable for some weeks. But after several days of unusually warm weather, the post stage got through to Cambridge, and Johnny received a letter from his mother. Although eager for his return, Eliza urged him not to attempt the roads. Instead, the boys would decamp to the Lees'.

"But say," Johnny asked Eliot, "do your parents not insist you come home? I know nothing about them, I realize, while you now know everything about mine."

"My parents. Ah." Eliot smiled, but it was not a happy smile. "I figured I would have to discuss them with you eventually. I was hoping to put that off. My parents, you see, find me a great disappointment."

"You? Why, you're first in our class."

"Yes, that may be. I write poetry, too. Did you know that?"

"I did not. Are you any good? I myself am dreadful at it."

"I'll let you judge sometime, John. But the fact that I'm a poet doesn't help my case."

"But they must care about your health, at least?"

Eliot shrugged. "I believe they think I'd be better off dead. But let's speak no more of this sad topic. I'm vastly happy to be adopted by your family, if only for a few weeks."

•　•　•

The old Brattle Street home was a welcome change from the dreary, tense atmosphere of Harvard College. Bessie had made sure that the floors shone. Indeed, they were so finely waxed that Eliot slipped and nearly broke his neck.

"Oh look, John," Eliot said once he'd righted himself. "It's enough to lift a weary scholar's heart."

"It is."

Holly boughs wound cheerfully about the banister. The dining table was dressed in its finest red damask cloth and bejeweled with silver candlesticks and crystal goblets.

Kate arrived to greet them. She said brightly, "Come, let me show you your chamber. Oh, isn't this wonderful! The Slotted Spoon together for two whole weeks!"

In the days leading up to Christmas, the roads improved, and letters flew back and forth from Quincy to Cambridge. Everyone felt so forlorn at being separated that, on Christmas Eve Day, eight souls from

Quincy squeezed into a carriage meant for six, which had the benefit of keeping them all warm.

By mid-afternoon, Abigail Adams, Lizzie and family, and Eliza all descended upon the Lees' doorstep. The winter sun was sinking down beyond the Charles. Johnny was just dressing for dinner when he heard a sudden commotion below. There were cries of delight and the rustle of coats and bonnets. Shirt unbuttoned, he raced downstairs.

Eliza was surprised to see her son in such a state of undress. "Button up, or you'll freeze," she said. As she glanced into the parlor, she saw a slender, pale youth rise up from the sofa to greet them. He coughed once and approached.

Hastening to button himself, Johnny said, "Mama, everyone, this is Eliot Mann, my marvelous friend, roommate, and poet extraordinaire."

"Poet?" Abigail exclaimed, her tiny form having been all but obscured by the crowd. "I'm *exceedingly* fond of poetry. Shall you do us the honor of reading?"

"Of course, madam." Eliot bowed. Proper introductions were made, and when Eliot learned to whom he had agreed to recite his poems, he sent Johnny a look of abject terror.

For dinner that night, Bessie made a fine dinner of creamed chicken and oysters.

"Oh! It's such a shame John cannot be here, for this is his very favorite dish," declared Mrs. Adams.

The table, surrounded by so many children, was very jolly. Throughout the meal, the children whispered conspiratorially, having planned some after-dinner entertainment.

After the meal, Ben and Elizabeth put on a puppet show. It was about two sailors who could not agree on a port and so were stuck in the ocean until a sea monster (played by Elizabeth) gobbled the stupid fellows up. Johnny thought the play a fitting allegory of their current political strife. The play made everyone laugh.

Finally, urged on by Mrs. Adams, Eliot read a poem. His bony knees fairly knocked together as he reached for his spectacles, pushed his thinning hair aside and read in a soft, tremulous voice:

> The Lord of light has journey'd down the sky,
> And bath'd his coursers in the foaming wave;
> The twinkling star of Even, too, hastes to lave
> Her silver form, and vanish from my eye.
> Now dusky twilight flings her sombre shade,
> O'er the bright beauties of the silent vale;
> The aspen trembles not, the verdant blade
> No longer nodding answers to the gale.
> Come, sweet Reflection! Hither, pensive friend!
> Direct thy wandering steps, and on this stone,
> Worn by no traveller's feet, with moss o'ergrown,
> Repose with me in solitude's deep shade.
> Then shall I know the height of human bliss,
> And taste the joy of other worlds in this.

When he had finished, everyone clapped enthusiastically, Abigail most of all. But Eliot's eyes rested tenderly upon his friend.

"I enjoyed that," Abigail said.

"Thank you, madam. It's an honor to make your acquaintance. It is only left for me to meet your esteemed husband."

Eliot had spoken in jest about meeting John Adams, who was then in Philadelphia. But Mrs. Adams had a sudden look Johnny knew well. It was the look of a woman who had made up her mind and would brook no opposition. She said, "We could sorely use a poet in Quincy, Mr. Mann. You must come visit this summer. The children are all grown up and fled the nest, alas, but the old fellow still putters about."

Eliot bowed deeply. "It would be a great honor, madam."

Then, from his bent posture, Eliot sent Johnny such a wide-eyed look that Johnny had to turn away to keep from laughing.

• • •

Eliot retired early, worn out by the excitement of the day. But Johnny remained awake after the others had bade one another good night. He paced the dark, silent parlor, occasionally looking out upon the white snow that shone faintly blue in the moonlight. Suddenly he heard a shuffle of small steps behind him.

It was Kate. She had changed into her nightshift and dressing gown, and her long, dark hair, always kept pulled back, fell in tendrils to the small of her back.

"Oh, goodness, Johnny. You're still here!" The reflection from her candle danced in her lenses.

"Kate. Why are you still up? Can't you sleep?"

"I brood upon too many things. It's often the case with me, I'm afraid."

"Ah. You're like me, then. What is it tonight?"

Kate hesitated. "You," she finally said. She took a step toward Johnny and looked up at him. "Something weighs upon you, but I can't puzzle it out. I've tried."

"Yes," he admitted.

"But you have no—you don't believe it would help to share it?"

"I don't believe so."

She paused. "I was also thinking of Eliot."

"What about him?"

"He is—attached to you."

"I know."

In the soft, flickering candlelight, with her dark hair flowing down around her bosom, Johnny thought Kate looked very beautiful.

"He's not the only one, I'm afraid. Do you know that as well?"

Johnny took another step forward. "I do now," he whispered. "I can be stupid, you know, so you must tell me things straight out."

Kate smiled. "I know."

He kissed her. Her lips were soft, her eyes closed. It was not his first kiss, but the others, with girls in Barbados, had meant little. The moment he and Kate parted, he was ready for another.

"Nay." Kate grinned. "We must go to bed before someone wakes."

Kate mounted the steps first. Johnny followed her after a few minutes. Once in bed, however, he could not sleep. He had greatly enjoyed that kiss. But what did it mean? Was he now obliged to court Kate? Did it mean they had an understanding? Johnny realized that he knew nothing of these matters, and his fear of treating Kate ill was very great. That he loved her was unquestioned. But it was not that breathless, exquisite torture he expected to feel for a girl, which he had felt for Marcia. Oh, why had he succumbed to such a fleeting temptation?

Johnny fell asleep at last around two and was awakened by the loud shouts of children as dawn broke.

He heard Martha cry from her chamber down the hall, "A moment, children! I arrive!"

Harry, in nightshirt and cap, followed his wife sleepily to the stairs. One hand rested on her shoulder as if to steady him. "Martha, why did we have all these children? Can you recall?"

"No, but I do recall that you were *there*." Mrs. Lee glanced slyly at him.

It was odd to think of this mild-mannered couple as the rebels they both had been in their youths. Someday, Johnny vowed, he would find out more about them.

Johnny was soon dressed. He emerged, bleary-eyed and grim. What must he say to Kate? He found his friends already seated at breakfast, locked in cheerful conversation. When Johnny entered looking like he was next in line for the guillotine, Kate cocked her head at him and said, placing a hand companionably upon Eliot's arm, "Regard our friend. Does he not have a faintly greenish cast?"

"He does. Nearly froglike. I believe you must kiss him and turn him back into a prince."

"Oh, shut up!" Kate slapped at him, and Eliot ducked his head. Then they both fell to laughing.

•　　•　　•

Kate was in excellent spirits that morning. For months now, she had dreamed of little else besides kissing John Boylston. And while she was not foolish enough to believe that one kiss from a confused boy meant anything, she reasoned that such a kiss made future ones slightly less improbable. That, she thought wryly, was enough to keep her in good spirits for a year at least.

When the family finished breakfast, the children ran from the table with shouts of glee. No gifts would be given until New Year's, but the tree had been decorated in the night, Bessie had made sweets for all the children, and Giles could not resist the chance to give Will and Harry the marbles he had made them for New Year's. He pitied the poor lads, to be so vastly outnumbered by women.

21

January 1796

IT WAS THE KIND OF BRIGHT WINTER day when ice melted off the branches and dripped down the windowpanes, when leafless trees, while not budding, seemed open to the possibility of doing so. Johnny walked slowly with Eliot through town, past the yellow octagonal courthouse, the meetinghouse, and the quiet market.

The Slotted Spoon Society would take up a new subject that day: whether a lie by omission could, under any circumstances, be considered a lesser evil or even no evil at all. Johnny had been assigned the topic by the university's Board of Overseers and would be presenting an oration to them that spring. He looked forward to hearing what his friends would have to say.

Eliot insisted on sitting in the kitchen, much to Bessie's dismay. There, he could enjoy the hearth's warmth and gaze out the window at the leafless apple trees. He watched as squirrels, moving in their herky-jerky, mechanical way, purloined the remains of apples unearthed by the snow's thaw.

Aunt Martha came in to kiss Johnny hello. For good measure, she kissed Eliot as well.

"But why do you sit in here, when we have a perfectly good sunny parlor?"

"I believe he likes the warmth, Mama," replied Kate, "though Johnny and I find it stifling." Kate turned to Eliot and made a choking gesture by sticking a finger into her chemisette.

Eliot stuck his tongue out at her.

Aunt Martha shrugged. "As you wish. But don't stay too long, or Bessie shall be vexed. I'm sure you're in her way."

Once she had gone, Eliot said, "Let's make haste, then. I declare that the people have no inalienable right to know things that do not affect them. For example, by what tenet, moral or legal, does the college have the right to know about Johnny?"

But Kate wanted clarification. "Does the college, or our state, have a law about the enrollment of Negroes?"

"Not written, certainly. But even if they did," Eliot added, "by what moral imperative are we bound by an unjust law? Even were Harvard to have such a law, it would be our obligation to ignore it."

Suddenly, Elizabeth and Hannah, who had been waiting, unseen, behind the door, leapt out.

"Pony ride, please. Oh, please, Johnny!"

"Not now, children." Kate waved them away.

"Soon," Johnny assured them with a smile. Once they had gone, Kate spoke. "But I should like to talk about the effect of the lie upon the liar, for it seems to me that there is a moral component there as well."

But the friends never got the chance to discuss Kate's question, for just then Bessie burst into the kitchen looking irate. She shooed them out of the kitchen, and the next thing Johnny knew, he was in the parlor, trotting about on all fours with a child upon his back.

•   •   •

Spring arrived, and Johnny gave his oration. He was not very satisfied with it. He argued that a lie by omission could be justified unless there existed a sound moral imperative to tell the truth, such as imminent harm to another party. The overseers seemed satisfied, but Johnny felt his argument was self-serving and ultimately incorrect. He had not yet discerned its precise flaw, however, and that irked him.

At home for spring vacation, Johnny endeavored to be cheerful for his family and for the children, but he was aware of its being an effort. He brooded almost constantly about the rash, impulsive act that, however well-meaning, had led to Frederick's death. He brooded upon Peter's final words to him, and his cold eyes.

Just before he returned to school, the Slotted Spoon Society held its final meeting of the year. The topic was whether the Constitution was in fact the perfection of the Revolution or the imperfect beginning of some future masterwork.

Eliot argued that there was yet a great deal to improve upon, and even more to interpret. "Why do you think we have these blasted partisan groups? The Constitution is to blame."

"It certainly is not!" Johnny objected. "The Constitution is perfectly clear on the balance of power between the three branches. How can you say such a thing, Eliot?"

Eliot shrugged. He was not intimidated by Johnny. "The document leaves too much unsaid. Its understanding of human nature is overly optimistic."

Here, Johnny stood up. "I would like to remind you," he said heatedly, "of that first sentence. 'We the people of the United States, in order to form a *more perfect union . . .' More perfect union.*" Johnny spat the words out, staccato. He thumped his hand upon a chair back for emphasis. "Not a league, not a confederacy, not a confederation or a compact. A *union*. The meaning is perfectly clear."

Johnny had thought they were merely engaged in a spirited conversation, but Kate burst into tears and was obliged to leave the study.

The boys stared at each other in amazement. Then Eliot said to Johnny, "I hate to see a perfectly intelligent female reduced to tears over me."

Johnny frowned. "I shall go after her. I have no idea why she cries."

"Yes. Console her for my loss as best you can."

Johnny caught up with Kate in the hallway.

"Cousin, dearest, why do you cry?"

"I *hate* crying!" Kate continued to sob into a delicately embroidered handkerchief.

"It does fog your glasses quite a lot," Johnny offered.

She smiled, removed her spectacles, and wiped them with the edge of her petticoat. "Do you know, Johnny, I'm not even sure *why* I'm crying. I have been so delighted—so very happy—these past few months in our little society. I fear . . ." She placed a hand on her heart. "I fear this is the end."

Johnny laughed at her. "It shan't be. Why should it? We'll reconvene upon our return in August. I promise."

She looked up at him gravely, her tears stanched:

"Do not make promises you can't keep, Johnny."

22

THE BOYS LEFT THE FOLLOWING MORNING, AFTER receiving word from the overseers that they had both been given commendations and would be moving on to their third year.

The family, hearing the carriage come down the lane, raced out to greet them. Miriam looked up at the carriage and, at the sight of Johnny's companion, frowned. "Who is *he*?" she asked.

"Not another word!" Eliza hissed.

Fortunately, Eliot had not heard this exchange, having turned to say something to Johnny. Lizzie, who had just emerged into the yard, wrapped an arm around her daughter's neck as if she might strangle her. She looked up and smiled at the boys.

"Miriam has grown very headstrong, Johnny. Don't let her order you about."

"I shan't."

Once they entered the cottage, Eliot said, "I fear I shall prove rather useless for children's games." He collapsed into Lizzie's wing chair.

"Nonsense," Johnny replied. "You can keep score. Be on your guard, though, for Miriam cheats."

"I do not!" Miriam objected. Feeling contrite for her previous rudeness, she now sidled up to Eliot and casually wrapped the fingers of her right hand around his cane. "What's this for?" she asked.

"To aid me in my decrepitude," he replied.

Miriam giggled.

"The winds grow strong by the water," Lizzie said. "It's best to play now, before they pick up."

Abby and Sara were drawing pictures at the kitchen table. Tom said a cursory hello, his bright eyes taking a curious glance at Eliot before he moved off into the fields.

Eliot coughed discreetly, and Lizzie, quick to observe the true state of things, said, "You must be exhausted. Do you wish to rest a while?"

Eliot looked up at her gratefully. "Yes, I am a bit tired."

She guided Eliot to her own and Thomas's chamber. Once the dairy, it was now a bright, pleasing room that looked out onto the dunes. Leaving Eliot to rest, Lizzie moved into the kitchen, where Eliza was just finishing the washing up.

"That poor boy," she sighed. "He's quite ill."

"Yes, I suspected as much," said Eliza.

"It is wearing him out to pretend."

"Are both boys to remove to the Adamses'?" Eliza asked dubiously. The Adamses had graciously extended an offer for Johnny and Eliot to lodge with them at Peacefield.

Lizzie replied, "I will recommend to Johnny that he go on to Peacefield, for a few weeks at least, and leave his friend here. John will be vastly happy, for you know he plans to build a wall this summer."

"I thought he was planning to chop down a cedar tree and build a fence."

Lizzie said, "I suppose Mr. Adams shall endeavor to accomplish all three." The women laughed.

That evening, Eliot finally met the object of the women's laughter, and the rapport between them was nearly instantaneous. It seemed they both had a streak of wickedness, and with great delight were soon finishing each other's malicious sentences.

"If only they could send Benjamin Bache out to sea—"

"—into a school of sharks."

Benjamin Franklin Bache, grandson of Benjamin Franklin, was the editor of the *Philadelphia Aurora*, a Republican newspaper highly critical of Washington and Adams.

"If only someone would publish—"

"Mr. Madison's execrable poetry."

"If only—"

"No more!" Abigail finally cried, placing her hands over her ears. "My head aches."

Later, when Johnny finally mounted the Adamses' carriage for the short ride to Peacefield, he leaned down and grasped his friend's hand.

"Eliot, I feel I'm abandoning you."

"Go on, Johnny," Eliot said. "Mr. Adams may make free to work you to death now, for he shall have no witnesses."

The man being spoken of heard nothing. He had already fallen asleep and snored loudly enough to drown out the crickets.

· · ·

There were posts to set for the new fence, and for the first week, Johnny helped with these. The weather grew hot and humid. Johnny worked so hard that, by the end of the day, he longed for nothing so much as a cool dip in the sea and solitude to read.

But one muggy, rainy afternoon, when Mr. Adams announced that he would work in his study, Johnny took himself off to the cottage, where he found Eliot sitting in the kitchen. His friend looked happy and rested, although on his cheeks sat two hectic spots of color that had not been there before. The women had gone to town with the children, and they were alone.

"Would you like some tea, John? I can make it."

"Not just yet, thank you. So, what have you been up to in my absence?"

Eliot tapped his spoon upon the table. "Oh, helping the ladies, mainly."

Johnny smiled. "How is it you help the ladies, pray?"

Eliot blushed. "Well, sometimes, Lizzie has me weighing and measuring herbs. Or I fold laundry off the line. When she is abroad, I converse with your mother."

Johnny nodded, and Eliot grinned sheepishly. "Don't worry, John. Mrs. Boylston and I do not speak about you. We have other things in common."

"Such as?"

Eliot struggled to think of something. Then he grinned and said, "All right. We talk constantly about you and interest ourselves in little else."

Johnny laughed. "I must keep better watch on you both, then."

That day, after tea and before returning to Peacefield, Johnny told the family stories about Barbados. The children had long been begging him to do so. He told of riding upside down on the windmills till Cassie was sure Johnny would break his neck. He told them of how he rode on the backs of the sea turtles, sometimes riding on them as they moved into the water and swam out to sea.

"Oh, did you drown?" asked Hannah, and everyone laughed.

He spoke of Mammy Apples as large as pumpkins, and of pomegranate trees from which the strange red fruit hung in profusion. "Oh, friends, if you only knew the pleasure of drinking a coconut's sweet ambrosia through a bamboo straw!"

The children's mouths hung open, and at the end of Johnny's narration, both he and his mother had tears of homesickness in their eyes.

•   •   •

As the time to return to Harvard approached, Johnny realized that this time he did not look forward to returning. In Quincy, he was able to forget about Peter, and his all-too-vivid memories of Virginia.

The day before he was to leave, Johnny and Mr. Adams worked on the wall at Penn's Hill. The old man asked him whether he had given any thought to his future.

"I have, somewhat," Johnny said.

"Well, what are your thoughts, child?"

"I should first of all like to be a lawyer, like you, sir."

"First of all?" Adams laughed. "What comes second, lad? The presidency?"

Johnny blushed. He had just confessed his ambitions to the man who most likely *would* be the next president.

Suddenly, Adams blurted, "Blast! My mind's going! Why, I know just the man. His name's Wilson. He resides in Philadelphia and has a mind like an encyclopedia. Personal friend of Washington's, too. What have you left at school? One year?"

"Two, sir."

"Two! Time creeps its petty pace. Well, hurry it up. Old Wilson's not getting any younger. Luckily, that's not true of me." Then Adams bent down and with a grunt heaved another rock upon the wall.

Johnny left work that day enchanted by the prospect of leaving Harvard early. Perhaps he *could* graduate in three years instead of four. He would inquire of President Willard the moment he returned to the college.

That evening, Johnny began to pack his things. When he was nearly finished, he walked over to the cottage to see how Eliot was getting on with it.

Johnny found him in the kitchen, chatting with Eliza. His friend's feet were raised upon a chair, and a cotton blanket was draped about his shoulders, though it was stiflingly hot within. He had not even begun to pack.

Johnny sat down across from Eliot at the table. "Say, you'd better get a move on," he said. "We leave rather early. By the way, I was thinking: What if we discussed the Bill of Rights at our next meeting of the Slotted Spoon?"

Eliot looked at his friend tenderly.

"I'm not going back with you, John."

"What's that?"

"I can't do it. It's no use my pretending."

At that moment, Lizzie entered the kitchen and moved quietly to the hearth. But her presence seemed to give Eliot the courage he sought to continue. "Mrs. Miller says that the effort of pretending robs me of energy."

Johnny stood up from the table and glanced accusingly at Lizzie.

"Pretending *what*, pray?"

Lizzie's shoulders flinched, but she did not turn from her task at the hearth.

"Pretending that I'm well enough to attend class and study till all hours, in a frigid chamber."

"It shan't be frigid."

"Not immediately, John, but think of December."

Johnny felt tears come to his eyes.

"I shall bring you your meals, Eliot. I shall purchase a mountain of firewood—"

"It's all arranged," Eliot replied with a forced lift in his voice. "My parents arrive next week. It seems the prospect of my imminent death has softened their stony hearts."

"They do not take you home with them?"

"Oh, no, that would be too much of a burden. Why should they, when I am so ably cared for here? Besides, I told them I had no wish to leave."

"Oh, Eliot—"

"Never mind. At least they arrive."

"That will be a comfort, I'm sure."

"A comfort?" Eliot laughed mirthlessly, then coughed into a handkerchief. "I doubt it. *Your* family is my comfort." He glanced over at Lizzie, now joined at the hearth by Eliza. They both smiled at Eliot.

Johnny said nothing, but he was seized by an unreasonable, crushing sense of betrayal. "But what about the Slotted Spoon Society? What about the Bill of Rights?"

Eliot saw Johnny's emotions for what they were and pitied him. In this business of mortality, he knew himself to be far better versed than his brilliant friend.

Johnny already understood that his outburst had been childish and selfish. He endeavored to strike a lighthearted note when he asked, "All right. What devil's bargain have the witches offered you?"

"Witches? Ha!" Lizzie blurted.

Eliot replied, happy to explain, "Well, I am to have my very own chamber overlooking the dunes, and the Millers, poor souls, shall go upstairs with the children. Your mother remains in the parlor. It was at their insistence, but I must admit it consoles me vastly to open my eyes to the sea and close them to the smiling moon. Your mama shall attend me when Lizzie is abroad."

"But surely you won't be content to while away your hours in gossip? Surely you'll continue to write?" Johnny knew he sounded petulant.

Eliot turned to the women. "Gossip, he says, Lizzie! That's how greatly he esteems you all!" He then turned back to Johnny. "Mr. Adams has told me I may borrow books from his library. I expect I shall see him rather often until he returns to Philadelphia in November. We are both very wicked and *enjoy* being so. Oh, don't look at me like that. I'm already slated for Hell. What harm can a little more wickedness do?"

Eliot coughed discreetly. Then he said, "There is but one thing I shall lack, apart from you, dear friend."

"What is that?" Johnny asked.

Eliot coughed again. There was blood on his handkerchief. "Time," he said.

23

August 1796

ON THE WAY BACK TO CAMBRIDGE, JOHNNY'S eyes blurred with tears. His chest felt tight, and he could not seem to catch his breath. By the time he reached Cambridge, he had perspired through his shirt, and his curly hair stuck to his neck. He wiped his brow and looked down at the Charles as they crossed the Great Bridge. The river was as languid and as picturesque as ever, with its small boats drifting by and strolling couples on the banks. Ladies twirled their parasols and children chased balls or fed the ducks. Johnny stared at the river, willing it to console him as it usually did. *I must prevail,* he thought. *I must. Eliot has not given in to despair, so what should be my excuse?*

•   •   •

It had been more than four weeks since Kate had seen Johnny, and she could not wait a moment longer. In previous summers, she had always delighted in reading by the river or playing with the children. Now these activities felt dull. She felt impatient, but for what she didn't know. She was fractious with the children and even got into an argument with her mother.

Martha had told her daughter that she had heard from Lizzie about Johnny's return. Kate wished to depart for the college at once. But at the door, her mother stopped her and asked, "Kate, dear, are you very sure it's wise to visit Johnny so soon upon his return?"

"Wise, Mama? How so?" Kate asked as she donned her bonnet.

"He has only just arrived. You would not wish to seem too eager, surely."

Kate faced her mother squarely. "What would you have me do, Mama? Remain a recluse, like an ancient Greek princess? I've hardly gone abroad all summer."

Kate had made it seem as if she were merely "taking the air," but Martha was not fooled. She laughed and said, "You can hardly blame your indolence on *me*. Twice I asked you whether you wished to join me at the Society of Friends and you declined."

Here, Kate rolled her eyes with exasperation. What did she want with a crusty old Quaker meeting?

"Besides," her mother continued, "a true Greek princess would not dare speak to her mother so, for fear of being set upon a broiling rock."

"Oh, but I'm going! I can't breathe!" Then, suddenly doubting herself, Kate asked, "Mama, do you really think I shall seem too eager?"

Martha gazed at her daughter with a stab of compassion. "Oh, well. What if you *do* seem eager? All I really meant to say was that boys are so easily frightened by a woman's feelings. Perhaps you could go armed with a ruse of some sort."

"A ruse, Mama?"

Here, Mrs. Lee reflected for a moment. "I know. There is to be a play at the Haymarket next month. Why do you not invite him along? You can say we wish to celebrate his birthday in town."

"Excellent idea!" Kate exclaimed. "Though probably not necessary. If I know Johnny, his fear of my 'womanly' feelings shall be mitigated by his failure to comprehend them."

At these words, Martha hugged her daughter to her, and they united in merry laughter.

• • •

Johnny had not been expecting anyone. He was sitting at his desk in his nightshirt, where he had been for several hours, poring over the pages of Saint Augustine's *City of God*. Immediately upon returning to college, he had asked President Willard to grant him leave to graduate in July. The president had approved Johnny's request. But he would need to fulfill all the requirements of the fourth year of study. These included advanced tutorials in Latin, Greek, and composition. Johnny was glad of the extra work. Without it, he should have gone mad with loneliness.

Suddenly he heard a light, irregular tapping against his window. It sounded like hail. He stood, stiff from sitting, and looked out. It was Kate, once more throwing pebbles at his chamber window. He opened the window and called down to her, "You shall break the window."

"Now that you've opened it, I shall break your head."

Johnny shut the window and threw on a dressing gown. He found Kate standing at the entrance to the building and was so unaccountably happy to see her that he nearly hugged her. But she pulled back slightly and curtsied, and so he bowed.

"Hello, Johnny."

Johnny brushed his hair off his face and felt about his chest as if to make certain he was not naked. "I was just reading and—"

"Don't speak." Kate laughed. "You look a fright. Run and dress."

Johnny nodded, ran up the stairs, threw on his shirt and breeches, extinguished his lamp, cleaned his teeth, and then ran back down the stairs and into the yard with Kate.

They sat beneath a maple tree, and Johnny was out of breath. Kate finally asked, "How was your summer?"

"Oh, excellent," he said. "I was only sorry to leave Eliot behind."

Kate looked stricken. "Leave Eliot? What mean you? Did he not return with you?"

"Oh, God, I thought you knew."

"Nay. Why has he not returned?"

"He grows weaker. He fears he can no longer manage at college. But take heart, Kate." Johnny grasped her hand. "He's happy. If only you could see him, you would be reassured."

Kate was silent. "I suppose this is the end of our little society."

"We can talk, Kate. Always. That is—" he was about to tell her he was leaving at the end of the year. Then, for some reason, he decided to wait.

"It's not the same though, is it?"

"No."

They sat in glum silence. Then Kate brightened. "But, oh, I nearly forgot. There was a particular reason I came to see you."

"There doesn't need to be, you know." He locked his blue eyes on her amber ones, and she blushed. She was no longer able to look Johnny in the eyes, she realized.

"Well, but as it happens, Mama—we—would like to go to a play at the new theater for your birthday. Would you like that?"

"Indeed, I would." Johnny grinned. He had hardly been to Boston since his arrival in America. What's more, Johnny had been contemplating joining one of the college's theatrical societies.

"Excellent!" Kate said. "But I fear I interrupted you before. Was there something you wished to tell me?"

"Oh, no. It was only about Eliot."

"I shall write to him at once." Kate stood, brushing the grass off her skirts. "Shall we see you on Sunday?"

"Of course."

She curtsied and left with a lift in her step. She even glanced over her shoulder and waved gaily. Seeing her good cheer, Johnny felt ashamed that he had not told her that his plans had changed and that he would leave Harvard in July.

•   •   •

Between September and the end of October, Johnny tried to make new friends. He auditioned for a part in a play, Marlowe's *Doctor Faustus*, winning a small role. And while none of the boys in the Hasty Pudding Club were very bookish, at least Johnny now had friends with whom he could sit at commons.

As October arrived, Johnny found himself looking forward to going to the theater. Perhaps, he thought, he could learn something from seeing how real actors performed their roles.

Meanwhile, the country at large was performing its own theatrics. As the citizens readied to vote for the second president of the United States, declamations of unprecedented grandiosity issued forth from both sides. Adams was dubbed a Monocrat, and the *Boston Chronicle* warned that if he were elected, heredity succession would be imposed upon Americans. And Thomas Paine, whom Johnny had once adulated, published a scathing article attacking the venerable Washington. "The world will be puzzled to decide whether you are an apostate or an impostor; whether you have abandoned good principles or whether you ever had any." But to Johnny, the most dramatic occurrence was the publication of Washington's Farewell Address, in which the old warrior begged his countrymen to eschew partisan fighting.

Alone in Philadelphia, Adams was glum and feared defeat. But by mid-December, unofficial word had begun to spread that he had won the presidency, with Jefferson coming in second. This news, though by no means official, made for great good cheer among Johnny's family, and it was with smiles and laughter that he and the Lees made their way to Boston.

"Oh," Kate exclaimed as the carriage moved off, "what fun we shall have!"

The new Haymarket Theatre was an enormous wooden building that towered over Common Street across from the Mall. That night's performance, *Bunker Hill: The Death of Joseph Warren*, promised to be well attended. Johnny was impressed by the opulent interior. Above their heads an enormous candelabra, already lit, swayed slightly, casting a dancing shadow against the theater's red walls.

As they settled into their seats, Johnny took the measure of the crowd: Though the building itself was bathed in elegance, the crowd was by no means so. Mechanics, sailors, and other workmen filled its seats and reeked of smoke. In the gallery above him, Johnny could already hear several voices emboldened by drink.

The sconces were lit, the curtains parted, and the play began. The subject of the play, those brave men who fought in the War of Independence, was honorable. But overlaid upon it was the insipid story of a Boston girl who falls in love with a British officer. Johnny disliked such sentimental treacle, but Kate seemed enraptured. Her eyes were fixed upon the stage, her posture erect and attentive.

The voices in the gallery grew louder.

"He's a bloody liar!"

"Says who?"

"Says me!"

"You and your bloody king-loving Federalists!"

People began to turn toward the gallery. The murmurs grew, someone threw a punch, and then came a piercing cry. The actors continued their declamations upon the stage, but Johnny knew they could not do so for much longer. At last, responding belatedly to the disturbance, the players fell silent and gazed into the audience to see who had cried out.

Johnny endeavored to ignore the drunkards. But as they continued their bitter rants, his anger grew.

Suddenly he stood up and turned to face the ruffians:

"Have you no shame?" he cried. "Have you neither eyes nor ears, that you heed not the call of our beloved Washington?"

Then something hard hit him on the side of the head. Johnny lurched back and lifted his hands to his face. Kate was on her feet at once, pulling him by the arm. The blow hurt so badly that for a moment, he swayed on his feet. They fled their seats, before the stunned drunkards could recover what wits they possessed. Once they were clear of the building, Kate and her parents hugged Johnny fiercely.

"Oh, Johnny. I was so frightened!" Kate cried. "I thought they would kill you."

"You were very brave," Aunt Martha added.

Johnny shook his head slowly. "I know not what came over me. Rarely am I moved to such anger. But for those idiots to sit on their haunches, enjoying peace and liberty, for them to disturb our citizens in such a way. Of what use is a government of the people if the people will not govern themselves?"

To this, no one had a ready reply.

It was a subdued ride home. But, since they had left the theater, a kind of excitement had begun to build within Johnny.

After a while, Kate said, "I'm afraid your birthday celebration was ruined."

"Yes, we're very sorry for that, lad," added Harry glumly.

"Don't be, sir. I do believe I've discovered something tonight."

"Pray, what is that?" Kate asked.

"My voice," said Johnny.

24

BENJAMIN RUSSELL, EDITOR OF THE COLUMBIAN CENTINEL, thought he heard something in the voice of the anonymous contributor whose short but compelling essay had just come across his desk. It was postmarked from Cambridge. *A Harvard tutor must have written it,* he thought. In its neat, even rows of handwriting, Russell could hear the kind of pure, idealistic voice that he'd not heard since the days of the Revolution.

> *As our great George Washington has said, the very idea of the power and the right of the people to establish government presupposes the duty of every individual to obey the established government. Those citizens who, regardless of the cause, refuse to obey the laws that they themselves have made, weaken the Union and make it prey to factional influences. Each man must uphold the Constitution and eschew such petty griev- ances as will tear the fabric of our society to shreds . . .*

The essay was called "What Tears Us Apart," and it was signed *Concordia Discors.* Out of discord comes harmony.

Johnny had not believed that Russell would publish his essay. But at Kate's the following Sunday, he noticed a copy of the *Centinel* on the parlor table and opened it to find the article on the second page.

"Kate! Come look!" he cried.

Kate approached. "What is it? What do you see?"

"Regard this article." Johnny pointed to his essay.

"This? Why, what is it? By *Concordia Discors*. Who's that?"

Johnny blushed. "At your service, madam." He bowed. "Oh, but I must tell Eliot! And Mama! May I borrow this paper, do you think?" he asked, wagging the broadside at her. "In case they don't have a copy."

"They?" she asked bewilderedly.

"I have a terrible urge to go to Quincy and boast of it. At once!" Johnny turned to depart but then said, "But, oh, I must return to get leave from a tutor or they shall fine me. Come to Quincy with me? Eliot shall be thrilled. If you agree, I'll return within the hour."

Kate, nearly as excited as Johnny at the prospect of going to Quincy, flew off to ask her mother if she could accompany him.

•   •   •

They left that same afternoon, taking the Lees' little one-horse curricle. As they rode through Cambridge and Brookline, and then across the bridge into Roxbury, the skies darkened and Johnny heard thunder. He hoped it wouldn't rain before they reached Quincy; that would slow them down considerably. Thankfully, the rain held off, and they felt the first drops and saw a flash of lightning just as they ran into the cottage, holding sacks above their heads.

Now in the third week of November, the farm had a vastly different feel from its summer aspect: without, the trees were gray sticks, and all the leaves lay about in piles, to be burned or used for mulch. There was not a soul in sight, and one heard no birds or crickets; there was only the roar of the waves.

Within, all was cozy and warm. Eliza ran to her son. "But we had no notion of your coming just now, and with Kate, too!"

Kate reddened. "I hope it's not inconvenient."

Lizzie said, "Oh, don't be silly. Eliot shall be very happy. He's just in here."

In the kitchen, they found Eliot in good spirits, though a shade or two paler than he had been when Johnny had last seen him. He was sitting in a wing chair by the hearth, beside a small worktable. Miriam sat across from him: they were playing a game of cards. When Miriam saw Johnny, she stood and curtsied.

"Hello, Johnny," she said, primly. Then she sat back down to finish the game.

"Johnny? Is it really you? And Kate, too?" Eliot turned to Miriam. "Miriam, allow me a few minutes with Johnny. We can finish the game later." Miriam rose reluctantly and left the kitchen. It seemed clear to Johnny that, having at first roundly rejected Eliot, Miriam had now transferred all her affections to him.

Eliot grinned at his friends. "But what brings you both here, and without so much as a whisper of warning? Come, man. Sit and tell me everything." Eliot patted the table.

"A truant disposition," Johnny joked.

"I would not hear your enemy say so," Eliot recited.

"We come for the night. I daren't stay much longer."

Once Johnny had sat down, Eliot reached across the table and pulled Johnny to him. "Oh, I've missed you!"

Kate stood quietly by the fire.

"And you, too." He nodded to Kate. "Come here!"

Kate installed herself beside them.

"Well, how've you been?" Johnny finally asked. "How's life among the womenfolk?"

Eliot gazed at the burning hearth. "I must say I've been vastly contented, Johnny."

Lizzie, who had come in to tend the fire, affected not to listen. But Will blurted, "He plays with us for hours and hours!"

"Will, let us leave the friends to talk." Lizzie ushered the ten-year-old out of the kitchen.

When they had gone, Eliot continued, "Yes, vastly contented, John. I live a life that is both more rewarding and more strenuous than you can imagine. Why, I've burned myself twice removing cakes from the fire."

"Removing cakes, Eliot?" asked Kate.

"Oh, yes," Eliot said with pride. "I've baked a goodly number by now. You shall have one this evening. I'm quite clever at it, you know."

"I should like to taste one," Kate said.

"You shall. Indeed, you shall, my dear!"

Johnny laughed. "Eliot the Baker!"

Eliot lost his smile and grew contemplative. "Why, but that's just it, John. This visit was meant to be my retirement from the world, but instead it has been my introduction to it. I admit it is a far cry from your world of books and ambitions."

"I don't know," Johnny mused. "I think I should grow weary of listening to women talk all day. Doing so reminds me too much of home. Cassie, Mama, Grand-mama. Talk, talk, talk, all day long. Enough to drive a man mad!"

Eliot and Kate exchanged a knowing look.

"Do you find time for your poetry?" Kate turned to Eliot. "I recall from your reading last Christmas that you're quite a good poet."

"Oh, yes," Eliot said. "I've simply forgotten to mention it." Suddenly, he grimaced and adjusted his position in the chair. He took a few moments to breathe. His breath made an odd sound, like wind against crumpled paper. When he had caught his breath, he continued, "I sleep in the afternoon and wake once everyone has gone to bed. Then I sit just here, in this kitchen, and write for several hours."

"Will you read us your latest masterpiece?" Johnny asked.

"Of course. But don't set your hopes too high, John. I wouldn't wish to disappoint you."

"You can never do that."

Johnny still had not told Eliot about the publication of his article.

Eliot looked at his friend. "There's something on your mind. What is it?"

As if suddenly remembering, Johnny blurted, "I wonder whether the rumors of Mr. Adams's victory are true? They've voted, you know."

"Of course I know," Eliot said.

Johnny heard hushed giggles. Then Lizzie called, "Would all friends of President Adams kindly come into the parlor? Dinner's ready."

"President Adams! So you've *heard*? Is it official?" Johnny asked.

Eliza stepped into the kitchen. "It's true." She grinned. "Abigail had the news from John just this morning, though there shan't be an official announcement till February, when Congress reconvenes. So you see, your timing is excellent."

In the parlor, the children had a surprise waiting for them: they had decorated the dining table with little American flags, one on each plate. They had used cattails for poles and painted the stars and stripes on scraps of linen.

"Charming, children!" cried Eliot. The children all grinned at him with unabashed affection.

Halfway through the meal, Will and Abby began to throw the flags across the table at one another. Lizzie grew cross and asked them to leave. They heeded her not, at which point Eliza stood and glared such hot fire that Johnny thought the children would shrivel from the heat. After they had skulked off, Eliza said with some annoyance to her friend, "You're too soft."

"One of us must be," Lizzie rejoindered, "or they shall grow up believing *all* women are harpies."

They were just rising from the table when a messenger boy arrived with a letter for Kate. Kate took it with trepidation. Messengers never brought good news.

"Who's it from?" Eliza asked anxiously.

"It's from Mama." Kate finally opened it and read:

> Ben has come down with a fever. I am very sorry, but
> as Papa is in town, I must ask for your help at once.

Miriam, overhearing, cried, "But you only just arrived! Don't go! Don't go, Aunt Kate!"

"I'm very sorry. I had hoped to stay till tomorrow."

"Write to me the moment you arrive home," Eliot said.

"I shall." Kate smiled cheerfully at him. "But say—has Johnny told you he's a published author?"

Johnny cast Kate a stern glance.

"What's that?" Eliot asked, pale brows furrowing. "Nay, what mean you?"

"Oh, he's quite famous now. Or would be, if people knew who he was. He had an article in the *Centinel* just last week!"

Eliot slowly turned to Johnny. "Why did you not tell me of this? What was the article?"

Johnny blushed.

The invalid looked up impatiently at his friend and extended his hand. "Well, give it here, man! Don't be shy!"

Johnny went to retrieve the paper from his sack. He handed it to Eliot, who read it and handed it back to his friend.

"This is wonderful, John. Truly. But why did you not wish to tell me?"

"I was going to."

A look of understanding came across Eliot's face. "You did not wish to rub the world in my face, while here I bake cakes alongside the women. Is that it?"

Johnny suddenly noticed the others' silence as they listened to the boys' exchange. A wave of loss rose up in his breast, and Johnny dared not reply.

Eliot perceived his friend's feelings. "But, my dear boy, you don't understand. I'm happy for you! Happy as only a truly contented man may be. But take care you don't anger anyone. I worry for your safety."

"Oh, I doubt five people have read my article," Johnny said lightly.

Eliot was not fooled. "Even if that's true, you know it shan't always be the case. If you don't wish to be read, then you should write poetry, like I do."

At this, Johnny could not help but laugh.

• • •

Kate left within the hour. Once she had gone, and the boys were alone at the kitchen table, Eliot asked, *"So?"*

"So what?" Johnny sipped his steaming tea.

"You and Kate."

"Oh, we're excellent friends."

"Four words, as false as they are brief." Eliot snorted.

Johnny said, "Must you always know my business?"

Eliot considered the question. "You know, I think I must, having no business of my own."

Johnny finally sighed and admitted, "I don't know. I feel not the pull of attraction. That fluttery feeling that makes one restless come the night." Johnny blushed.

"Such as you felt for the Marvelous Miss Burnes?" Eliot offered.

A plate crashed to the floor just behind them.

"Oh!"

The boys turned. The plate had not broken, but the cake upon it had become a crumble. Poor Lizzie stood over the mess, hands on hips. Johnny suspected she had edged too close in order to hear them and caught the plate on a chair back.

"Oh, tragic!" Eliot cried.

"Is there something I can do?" Johnny stood.

"Be a dear and help me pick this up," Lizzie replied. "I'd like to get Eliot back to bed."

Johnny moved to procure a brush and pan. As he cleaned the cake off the floor, he could hear Lizzie speaking softly to Eliot, asking him questions in a slow, concerned way. Eliot answered her in a lower register, almost as if he did not wish Johnny to overhear.

When Johnny had finished cleaning, he entered Eliot's chamber and found him already asleep, his head thrown back and his mouth open, his breath coming in shallow wheezes.

Johnny wrote his English tutor that same afternoon to say that an illness in the family delayed his return to school. He gave the letter to Lizzie to post when next she went to town.

The weather grew dismal, the winds fierce. Johnny and Eliot remained indoors for the next few days. They passed the hours playing cards, talking about philosophy or simply reading side by side. After a few days of such retiring existence, Johnny grew restless. He needed some pursuit. Yes, he would return to school, where he would write a new article and begin study for his senior dissertation.

When the time came to leave, however, it was difficult to say goodbye. Johnny held on to Eliot for several long moments. Pulling away at last, Eliot affected a cheerful laugh.

"Oh, Johnny. I'm not on death's door. I feel reasonably well. Do not grieve just yet."

"All right," Johnny said. "But you must promise me to remain well at least until spring break."

"I will do my utmost to oblige."

As Eliot's waving figure dwindled, Johnny's next article was already forming upon his lips. To have strength and health was a God-given gift, and so fleeting. He would write about the need for each citizen in a democracy to commit to meaningful action.

25

WINTER ARRIVED WITH A STORM THAT MADE the paths treacherous, and classes were suspended. Some days, Johnny would wake to a room so bitterly cold and dark that he would not leave his bed till near noon. The play they had meant to perform was cancelled, and as yet they had not rescheduled it. Johnny doubted they would. Only a letter from Eliot that December breathed life into his lonely existence:

> We are completely snowed in, and it is marvelous!
> We have excellent provisions, and what with keep-
> ing the fires going and fixing meals, we remain quite
> busy. I choose not to exert myself, of course, being
> inveterately lazy, and so spend my days in indolent
> comfort, writing poetry and being waited upon like
> King Solomon.

O, irony! thought Johnny. That one with so little time left upon this earth should be so cheerful; and the other, with everything to be thankful for, shrouded in such gloom!

When winter break arrived, many students left for home. This year, however, the college kept the commons open and the buttery supplied with firewood. The previous year, there had been many complaints from parents whose children had been forced out into treacherous conditions.

Johnny read and slept. He submitted his article to the *Centinel*. When that was finished, he began to research his senior dissertation. He spent Christmas at the Lees', but this one was far less festive than the previous year. Kate did not speak of Eliot, but she seemed anxious, and Johnny sensed their mutual friend was the cause. Nor did they resume the heady conversations of the Slotted Spoon Society. In this prediction, Kate had been prescient. The entire house felt as if it were waiting, somehow. When the first bluebells appeared beneath the snow, Johnny walked down to the Charles in search of other signs of spring.

There were a few clumps of snowdrops here and there, and more bluebells. Johnny watched the children play, heedless of the mud and wind. One child chased a red ball. Johnny was mesmerized by this child; for several moments, he thought he was the boy. He could feel the red ball in his hands. There were times when Johnny felt he had no skin at all, either black or white, and that he was one great ear, or eye, or heart.

The sun had descended behind the boathouse when Johnny finally made his way back to his chamber. There he found a letter from his mother beneath his door. It was the letter he knew would come:

> Dearest Son
>
> I wish I wrote with better news. Eliot is failing. He has put up a brave fight. But he finds the fresh stirrings of spring so inspiring that even now he writes until he can no longer hold his pen. He has no wish to leave us, but the body no longer heeds the soul. I fear it shall not be long before they are parted. Please come as soon as you can. He longs to see you.

Johnny stood immobile for several seconds before taking up his coat and hat. He left his chamber without bothering to lock it. On the way down the stairs, he met one of his tutors.

"Illness calls me away," he explained. "I know not when I shall return."

The tutor made some reply, but Johnny had already run down the stairs and did not hear him.

Aunt Martha answered the frantic knocking. Seeing Johnny, she called, "Kate! It's Johnny."

Kate appeared within moments, tucking a neckerchief into her bodice. Her hair was not pinned, and her cheeks were flushed. Perhaps she had been playing a game with her siblings when he had interrupted her.

Johnny looked at her; no words were needed. She allowed her eyes to rest upon his. Then she nodded, blinking tears.

"I should like to borrow a carriage, if I may. I must leave at once."

"Yes, at once," she said, turning. "Mama!"

Kate hesitated, then turned back to Johnny. "May I accompany you?"

"I would like that," he said.

Kate threw on her cape and, as her mother had not yet answered, said, "Would you tell Mama I go with you?" Without stopping, she ran to the stables to have the coachman ready the horses.

By the time Kate had returned, Aunt Martha had heard the news and prepared a small sack for her. She hugged her daughter, then Johnny, and placed her hands on their cheeks.

"Write me with news, if you have a spare moment."

"We shall," they said in unison. Kate kissed her mother once more and stepped abroad before the children could come running after her.

In the carriage, Johnny began to speak. "Kate, I've been a stranger."

"No need to apologize," she said. "You're a scholar with a great deal to do."

"I've been hard at work on my dissertation." Johnny fell silent, but Kate discerned his blunder at once. Her eyes stared shrewdly at him through her spectacles.

"Dissertation? That is for next year, is it not? You're in your third year."

"Kate, I know the moment is not opportune, but I must tell you, I cannot hold back."

"What is it? Oh, tell me at once, for I shan't bear it otherwise!" Kate leaned away from Johnny in the carriage, as if to avoid a physical blow.

"I'm leaving Harvard."

She looked back at him, confused. "What mean you? You have one more year."

Johnny shook his head. "I'll graduate this year. I applied to President Willard, and he has given his consent. Granted, I must work like a fiend for the next few months." He tried on an amused smile, but Kate did not return it.

"But *why?*" she cried. "Why do you wish to leave us? And why, of all possible times, do you tell me *now*, when my heart has no strength to bear another blow?" Tears ran unchecked down her cheeks.

"I've no wish to leave *you* or our families. But I stagnate here. Never have I felt so alone. I work and work, nothing more." He paused, then resumed with a more cheerful air, "Mr. Adams was good enough to find me a mentor in Philadelphia."

"Philadelphia! But that is so very far!" Suddenly, she grew red in the face. "Shall you have the courage to tell *him* of your plans?"

"I am thinking that—"

Suddenly, Kate inhaled and let it out almost violently. "Trask!" She called to the coachman. "Stop the carriage! At once!"

The carriage slowed and then came to a stop along the road to Roxbury. Kate rose and opened the door. She descended and began to walk back the way they'd come.

"Kate!" Johnny cried. "What are you doing?"

"Don't speak to me. Just don't speak. I can't believe you waited to tell me this when we were on our way to Quincy to visit our dying friend. Are you devoid of *all* sense?"

At first, Johnny just stared after her. Then he descended the carriage and ran after her. "Kate, please!" He grabbed her arm. "I'm so sorry. Forgive me. I figured . . . I figured we could not feel any *worse*."

Kate looked at him, astonished. Suddenly, she backed away from him and burst out laughing, part hopelessness and part incredulity.

"Excellent, John. Is there anything else you'd like to tell me whilst I 'cannot feel any worse'? Does Papa have a cancer, perhaps? Or maybe Mama has been arrested . . ." She wrapped her scarf about her neck so that her face was partly obscured. She shivered.

"The wind blows." Johnny begged. "Please return to the carriage. For Eliot's sake, if not for mine."

With a deep exhalation, Kate turned and walked back to the carriage. Johnny trailed after her.

"Trask, you may continue," she said.

The carriage resumed its pace. Johnny thought he saw the old coachman shake his head. Youth could be so volatile!

They crossed the bridge into Roxbury, then came to Boston Neck, where they turned onto the coast road. They were silent all the way to Milton.

Then Johnny hazarded, "Kate, I wish—"

"Say no more to me just now." Her amber eyes flashed a warning.

"Do you forgive me? I shan't rest until—"

"Oh, Johnny." She heaved a deep, miserable sigh.

"Do you? *Do* you?"

His voice was so abject, so pathetic, that she said, "Of course, I forgive you."

Kate's benediction loosened some great sadness buried within him. Whatever it was, he covered his face and sobbed. Kate moved next to Johnny and held his head in her lap, as one might a child.

26

LIZZIE HEARD THE CARRIAGE FIRST AND OPENED the door. Her eyes spoke the truth, but her voice cried cheerfully, "Hello, Johnny! And Kate, too! What a surprise!" A slow shake of the head warned them of what they would find within. "Eliot's just here, in the parlor!"

They entered. Eliot was sitting up in bed, and when his eyes lit upon Johnny, he grinned.

"Come here at once," he croaked, pointing to the foot of the bed. Johnny and Kate approached and hugged Eliot at the same time.

Although quite thin, Eliot looked better than Johnny had expected. Perhaps his mother had been precipitate in her urging him to come?

"You look well," he said.

"Looks can be deceiving, my friend," Eliot replied. He gave a hiccup of laughter, which sent him into a paroxysm of bloody coughing. Lizzie ushered them into the kitchen so that she could tend to him.

Johnny's mother appeared in the doorway, having been abovestairs. She hugged her son and Kate wordlessly. "Tea?" she finally asked.

"Oh, yes, please," Kate replied.

Johnny asked, "Was not Eliot's chamber just there, in the back?"

"It still is. But he likes to be at the center of our comings and goings during the day. He calls the parlor his New World, and us, its Pilgrims. But it is time to return him to his chamber. His parents visited this morning, but I sent them away so he could rest."

Johnny asked, "What are they like?"

Lizzie smiled. "The father is a minister of some kind and holds himself in great esteem; the poor mother appears cowed."

"I hope we didn't come at an inopportune moment?" Kate asked.

"Nay, Eliot is vastly contented to see you. But I fear the excitement has already worn him out."

The women came and went for some time in an effort to clean their patient and to bring him various medicines. At last they returned to the kitchen with grim expressions that they could not conceal.

"He sleeps," said Lizzie with a sigh, dropping heavily onto a kitchen chair.

Johnny, seeing the children standing about the parlor, asked her, "Do they know?"

"Oh, yes. They are none of them strangers to death. But I do believe Eliot has them all fooled by his high spirits."

When Johnny entered the parlor, little Sara cried petulantly, "We've been waiting and waiting!"

"I'm all yours," Johnny said.

"No—not you. Eliot!"

"He's resting, Sara. I will have to suffice." The little girl then dragged Johnny off to her chamber to play a game.

Just before Lizzie called everyone to supper, Johnny found the door to Eliot's room ajar. His friend was propped up in bed, dictating a sonnet to Kate, who held his diary in one hand and a pen in the other. His voice was hardly above a raspy whisper, and his face was slightly blue. Eliot saw Johnny enter but continued to recite until he finished the final sentence. Then he nodded to Kate, and she blew gently on her work to hasten its drying.

"My last masterpiece. Not to be confused with 'My Last Mistress,'" Eliot quipped. "Especially since one can hardly have a last without having had a first." Then, as if scolding himself, he added, "Oh, let's not be witty, friends, for Lizzie tells me I mustn't laugh."

"Johnny," Kate said cheerfully. "You must hear Eliot's new poem. It's astonishing." Here, she sent a warm glance in Eliot's direction. "May I?"

"Why not? You shall soon enough have a chance to read them all. I bequeath them to you, John. Do with them what you will. The college never does have enough newspaper in the necessaries."

"Eliot!" Kate frowned.

"I shall find them a publisher," said Johnny gravely.

Eliot waved this thought away, but Johnny could tell his friend was pleased by the idea.

"If you insist. A few might be worthy enough. Don't bother yourself overly. I feel proud to have refined my art these past months. I've no very great need of the posthumous adoration of the multitudes."

"Say what you will, Eliot, your work *should* be read by the multitudes," Kate replied sternly.

Eliot could not conceal a satisfied smile. "If you think so, dearest, that means a great deal to me."

But now he began to sink. His eyes fluttered closed, and the pillows that propped him up and made him look nearly well gave way beneath the downward inclination of his body. Eliot slumped to one side, nearly tumbling off the bed.

"Oh!" Kate exclaimed. Lizzie, who had been standing beyond the door, arrived just in time. She made her patient comfortable, then moved to pull the bed curtains closed.

"Time for him to rest."

Kate kissed Eliot on the cheek and said, "See you in the morning."

Johnny took his friend's hand. Eliot grasped it with surprising force.

"Good night, dear friend," Eliot said. "See you in the morning, God willing."

But instead of leaving, Johnny slipped fully clothed beneath the bolster. Eliot's eyes were closed, but he smiled. "At last, I get my wish. I had to die to get it, but it was worth it!" He shifted closer to Johnny and leaned his head upon his shoulder. Johnny's eyes looked blindly up at the ceiling. Tears burned them. There was silence for some time. He thought by Eliot's slow breathing that the boy was asleep. But suddenly Eliot asked, "Johnny, do you believe in the transmigration of souls?"

"I do," said Johnny. "But it's not merely belief; I have experienced it."

Eliot sought no explanation. He said, "I have, too. What has been your most recent sojourn?"

"A child, playing along the Charles River, holding a red ball."

Eliot nodded slightly, though his eyes were still closed.

"I have endeavored to enter you. I feel your body easily enough. Oh, how I envy you its vigor! But your mind is as dark as this room. It's heavy, impenetrable. Be happier, Johnny. I command it."

"All right." Johnny closed his eyes. "I shall try. Give me a moment." Johnny scanned the blackness behind his eyelids until a bright image emerged: Carlisle Bay.

It was his favorite time of day, early morning. The breezes were cool and gentle, and the aqua-blue water was still. His toes were buried in the soft sand beneath, and small fish swam about him; he could feel them slither between his legs like a thousand light kisses. Soon he would hear the bell of St. Michael's and the gathering clamor of children racing to a nearby schoolhouse.

"Ah, yes. Much better. Sunshine, and water. Do I lie on the sand?"

"Yes," Johnny replied, steadying his voice with difficulty. "Rest now. I shan't leave you."

He didn't. Instead, Johnny remained standing in the warm, blue water until he dozed and consciousness dissolved. He awoke to a soft, gentle hand upon his shoulder. His friend was turned away from him as if in sleep.

"He's gone," said Lizzie.

27

THE JOHN BOYLSTON THAT THE HARVARD OVERSEERS saw that spring was a tall, imposing young man who commanded every corner of the room. He recited his oration on the topic of the individual and democracy with stunning conviction. In it, he argued that democracy was not an idea but an act. It occurred when disparate men worked in tandem toward a common goal. A great nation, Johnny argued, needed the goodwill and effort of every citizen, no matter how small.

Afterward, convening to decide upon marks, the overseers agreed that they had not seen such a scholar since Joseph Warren. One overseer even made a gentleman's bet with another that John Boylston would be president someday.

Kate saw a different John Boylston. To her, the more successful Johnny became, the less happy he was. Kate knew that now Eliot was gone, he longed to flee Cambridge. He hoped and believed things would be different for him out in the world. Kate feared it was true: Things would be different. They would be more dangerous.

She recalled the previous year, when Johnny had argued that a lie by omission was justified when no moral imperative to reveal the truth existed. But, justified or no, she knew Johnny could not live with the lie forever. He was too honest. There was just too much Barbados in him, too much huckster and slave.

●   ●   ●

At that moment, Johnny did not feel very honest. He had been too cowardly to tell his mother that he was leaving and so had written a letter, explaining his position. She had replied tersely,

We shall talk about it when you return to Quincy.

Now, he lay on his bed, in the room he had shared with Eliot. Eliot's things were still there where he'd left them: his books, his blanket and pillow, the fine teapot and Turkey carpet. There was an old bloodied rag beneath his bed that the maid had missed.

Johnny had neither washed nor shaved since his oration. He had not attended classes. Then, one sunny morning at the end of April, he was pulled away from himself by a familiar tapping upon his window. He descended the stairs and saw Kate waiting impatiently just beyond the door.

"So this is how you honor the memory of our friend?" she asked. "Wallowing in the dark, and on such a very fine day as this? Come out, John. You're a fright to behold."

Johnny demurred, but Kate was not to be gainsaid. "How should your poor mother feel having left Cassie and her own failing mother, to bring you here, to enjoy the fruits of their labor, while—"

"Enough, I beg you."

Kate had no need to go on. One more harsh word would bring him to tears.

"Come on, John," she said more gently. "Let's walk by the river and enjoy the day, in honor of our dear lost friend. Eliot cannot do so, and we do him an injustice to mope about indoors."

"Yes, all right. Give me a moment." Johnny bounded up the stairs to his chamber, where he readied himself to walk among the living.

They spent the afternoon pleasurably, strolling the banks of the Charles, speaking of nothing in particular. Kate went directly home from the river. When Johnny returned to his chamber, he found a letter slipped under his door.

My Dear Boy

I find myself with an unusual moment of peace, during which I write to tell you of some distressing news. Philadelphia is not safe. The yellow fever rages there, and I fear it shall remain in this pestilential state for some time. Meanwhile, I have arranged for you to apprentice with another attorney by the name of Luther Martin. Though a Republican in all ways save his dislike of Jefferson, he is not odious like most of them and indeed is very well esteemed. He shall have much to teach you, I believe, regarding constitutional law. His offices are on Charles Street in Baltimore.

"Baltimore!" Johnny cried aloud. He had resolved never to go south again. If his mother was dismayed at the prospect of Philadelphia, only think what she would have to say about Baltimore. Johnny swore and threw the letter onto the floor.

Who was this Martin fellow, anyhow? Wilson had been an unsung hero of the drafting of the Constitution. But about Mr. Martin, Johnny knew very little.

It was not too late to search for information in the library. Before exiting his chamber, Johnny picked up Adams's letter, gently dusted it off, and placed it atop his chest of drawers.

According to one book, the city of Baltimore possessed a beautiful public garden between the town and the Lehigh River, a fine set of mills upon its banks, straight roads, and a number of theaters. Mr. Martin had been a delegate to the Constitutional Convention of

'87 but had refused to sign the Constitution, believing it to infringe upon states' rights.

This last fact did not sit well with Johnny. Unity was everything; Johnny didn't relish the prospect of going either to Mr. Martin's or to Baltimore. But if Philadelphia was unsafe, there was little to be done. He consoled himself with the thought that all those he hoped to meet in Philadelphia would need to evacuate until later that fall or even winter. Until then, Baltimore it would be. It was only left to tell his mother.

In the dead of night, just days before commencement, Johnny was awakened by the bell's shrill ring. He thought it signaled a fire and grabbed his dressing gown. He fled down the stairs and into the yard. There, other scholars already stood gaping at a hellish vision: John Adams, on fire.

The face, a stuffed sack, had been meticulously rendered. From a distance, it bore an uncanny resemblance to the living being. Huge flames danced out from its breeches and greatcoat, licking the air. But the body was far thinner than the man himself, having been half-devoured by flames.

Surrounding the burning effigy were five boys in black hooded robes with the word *Liberté* sewn upon them. They brandished burning torches.

"Unmask them!" someone cried.

A dozen scholars ran at once toward the robed boys. Two of them were caught, but three managed to escape. Tutors ran to procure buckets of water as others knocked down the effigy and stamped out the flames as best they could. President Willard, dressed only in a nightshirt, led the two guilty students away.

Johnny returned to his chamber, but he was too shaken to sleep. The hatred had been palpable; he could not help but feel that those boys might as easily have burned the man himself. He wondered why these Republican scholars had chosen that week to light their effigy. He thought it might have had to do with the publication, just the week before, of a letter from Thomas Jefferson to his former neighbor Philip Mazzei.

The letter had caused a great scandal. Written more than a year earlier, it was a scathing condemnation of the Federalists in general and President Washington in particular. The letter was an embarrassment to Jefferson, who never meant it to see the light of day. But somehow the Republican scholars took it as a legitimization of their Anti-Federalist cause.

At breakfast the following morning, a rumor spread that the two captured culprits had been expelled. But then another rumor made its way around that President Willard had commuted their sentence to six months' suspension in exchange for the names of the three escaped students. These were Selfridge, Shattuck, and Peter Fray.

By breakfast, Selfridge and Shattuck had already left the college. But as Johnny returned to his chamber from the commons, he came face-to-face with Peter Fray. The boy was dragging his heavy trunk down the stairs. Without speaking, Johnny took up one end and helped Peter down toward the street with his trunk.

"Thank you," said Peter.

"Quite a stunt last night," Johnny said, for lack of anything else to say.

"Yes. We thought so."

"Must have taken a lot of planning. I thought the face a particularly good likeness."

"You would know."

Johnny glanced at Peter with some alarm, for he had never told Peter that he knew Mr. Adams. How, then, did Peter know? What's more, Johnny could discern no anger in his former friend, neither anger nor the blame that he had felt so palpably after Frederick's death. Where had it all gone? Had Peter, in fact, forgiven him?

Bolstered by the thought, Johnny said, "Well, I'm sorry it's gotten you suspended."

Peter shrugged. "It doesn't matter. I needed to leave anyway—no money, old mole. Everything's gone. The tobacco, the servants. Even the foxes seem to have disappeared. It's all gone, or nearly. I have an uncle who for the moment supports us, but that cannot last."

"What do you plan to do?"

"I head to Richmond. Papa has connections there. Newspapers and such."

"Newspapers?" Johnny was surprised. "I never figured you for a reporter."

"Oh, I hear it doesn't take any particular gifts." Peter glanced insinuatingly at Johnny.

"Well, I wish you the best of luck." Johnny extended his hand.

Peter didn't take it. "I wish I could say the same, old mole. I really do."

28

July 19, 1797

AT LONG LAST, THREE YEARS ALMOST TO the day he arrived in Boston, Johnny found himself about to graduate Harvard University. Though only eight in the morning, it was already hot. His trunk was packed, and he was ready for his oration. It was the same one he had given to the overseers that April, though much abridged.

His palms were moist with anxiety. A great number of people would be in the audience: not only students and tutors but parents and town officials. The governor, Samuel Adams, would be in attendance, as would Johnny's entire family.

Without, tents and stalls had been erected and would soon be buzzing with activity. Johnny wondered whether he would see the fat baby, or the monkeys, whose captivity he had so pitied three years earlier. As he stood in the yard, he heard whoops and cries from the playing field. He walked toward the field and saw a crowd of people watching a contest of target shooting. On one side, crowded together, were a dozen Natick Indians; on the other, a dozen Harvard scholars. Johnny watched, mesmerized, until it became clear that the scholars had no chance against the Indians. For some reason, that made him smile.

Leaving the playing field, Johnny walked to the road. There, just at the entrance to the college, stood a baby elephant. It was tied to a thick rope, and its skin appeared unwholesomely dry and flaky, which made Johnny's heart contract with pity. Next he came upon a bizarre cabaret of people dressed as mermaids and mummies, followed by a display of live, braying two-headed calves.

The grotesque displays along the road had not changed, but he had. Three years earlier, Johnny had marveled at the strangeness of these commencement festivities. Now, he felt only disgust. There was no music, no dancing, no real joy. This was nothing like Crop Over. This was a pathetic show of dominance by small men over helpless creatures for monetary gain.

People were already coming and going from the meetinghouse. He peered in: extra benches had been installed, and all the doors were flung open. He looked at the freshly built platform from which he would give his oration, and his heart thudded once like the kick of a stubborn horse.

Continuing on, he walked toward the river, where he stood for a long time. He was ready to leave Harvard. And yet, some dark thought intruded just beneath his consciousness, and he wished to know what it was. He had been so filled with hope, so certain that his fellow scholars would be intelligent and honorable. But the only real intelligence he had found resided in a girl who lived down the road and had never attended school. And the only real honor had been in a sickly boy, now dead, reviled by all the pretenders.

When Johnny returned to the meetinghouse, the guests were gathered. Seated on the men's side were Mr. Lee and Mr. Miller. On the right, just across the aisle from them sat Kate, Lizzie, Martha, his mother, and the children. They greeted him with broad, proud smiles. He approached them and hugged each in turn, near tears at the sight of them.

Soon it was time to mount the platform, and the assembly fell silent. Only the whoosh-whoosh of the ladies' fans could be heard beating the hot air, like the wings of trapped birds.

Pastor John Pierce gave a sonorous welcome speech. A third-year student read a poem. Another boy gave an oration. After what seemed an eternity, Johnny finally heard his name being called. He wiped his forehead and gathered himself. Then, slowly, he stood.

His speech, a quiet plea for union, lasted a scant five minutes. When he had finished, he heard soft clapping and took a grateful step down the stairs, believing the ceremony to be over. But President Willard's hand stayed him and he returned to his chair.

Ten minutes later, it was all over. The inmates of the meetinghouse dispersed quickly, for it was now infernally hot within. When a cool breeze reached Johnny from the river, he inhaled deeply, gratefully. He shut his eyes and thought of his father. He would be so proud. Harvard had just graduated its first black man.

29

THE WOMEN WERE PACING LIZZIE'S KITCHEN. ABIGAIL had just returned from Philadelphia and had told them about the yellow fever.

"I would not let him go within one hundred miles of that city," said Lizzie.

"No, I agree. Something must be done," Abigail added.

"Oh, but it was all planned! He shall be vastly disappointed," Eliza said.

They spoke as if Johnny were not sitting right there, at one end of the kitchen table. He stared out the window at the boats drifting to and from Boston, seemingly indifferent to their conversation.

Finally, Johnny cleared his throat, then pulled a letter from his pocket.

"What is that, pray?" asked his mother.

"A letter."

"From whom?" Eliza's blue eyes flared.

"From President Adams."

"Why, what does *he* have to say?" Abigail asked suspiciously.

"I shall read it if you like."

"Yes, do!" they cried.

When Johnny had finished, his mother did not know whether to be relieved or dismayed.

"Baltimore! Oh, Johnny, why did you not say so?"

It seemed to Johnny that she would have preferred the threat of yellow fever to the prospect of his living in the South.

"I thought it best not to interrupt your convocation."

"You are too cruel, Johnny," said Lizzie. "We were very worried."

"And have you replied?" his mother asked.

Johnny recited his reply to Mr. Adams:

> Dear Mr. President
>
> I am disappointed not to be able to go to Philadelphia just now, but I thank you most sincerely for arranging my transfer to Mr. Martin in Baltimore. Perhaps my stay in Baltimore shall not be of very long duration. On a different note, I hear through unnamed sources that you are eager to move the dirt from the base of Penn's Hill to the top, for reasons that elude me. I would like to warn you against any ideas you might harbor about doing so by yourself, lest David prove no match for Goliath. Sullivan or Trask will be happy to help. Or, if you can be patient, I arrive on the 19th of this month, ready to serve.
>
> Yours most faithfully, etc. etc.

"The cheek, Johnny!" Lizzie cried.

"Ha!" said Abigail, delighted.

Eliza sucked on her lips as if to keep from smiling. But Abigail and Lizzie lost all restraint. They pinched and tickled Johnny and boxed his ears until at last he found an opening through which he dashed into the parlor and out the front door. The children were in the kitchen garden, playing catch. When they saw Johnny, they hugged him and cajoled him to play, for, in Eliot's absence, they loved him best once more.

When Johnny woke up the following morning, having slept in the parlor bed where he had been born, he felt his friend's spirit everywhere.

The spirit followed him into the kitchen and back into the parlor as he dressed for the day. The feeling was not unpleasant, exactly, but uncanny enough to propel Johnny out of doors without taking more than coffee for breakfast.

It promised to be a fine, hot day. The air had a fecund smell as he set off for Peacefield; he could hear the low ceaseless buzz of the crickets. He strode the scant mile and a half on foot and then down the path flanked by Abigail's exuberant flower beds. Johnny knocked upon the door, but no servant arrived to greet him. Perhaps the Adamses were out. But the door was open and, not wishing to have walked there in vain, he called, "Hallo! Mrs. Adams? Anyone?"

There was no answer.

Johnny looked about him. The house was utterly quiet. He mounted the stairs and knocked upon the president's study door. Then he walked in.

When Adams heard the door creak open, he woke from a doze and turned. Delight spread across his face at once. Johnny bowed, but Mr. Adams waved him over.

"Come here, lad."

He took Johnny's hands in his own.

"Well, hello, hello! Abigail told me that the graduate had arrived, and in more or less one piece, too."

"Indeed. It is very good to be home."

"I heard you gave a fine speech. Brief as well. The best kind. Well, but shall we head over to Penn's Hill?"

Instead of rising, however, Adams placed a hand on his forehead. It trembled slightly.

"Sir—are you ill?"

"Nay. But events do weigh upon me, and I have a sudden urge to feel the sea breeze. You know, Johnny, work can wait."

"Very well," Johnny replied. He had no great desire to climb Penn's Hill in the heat.

They strolled in silence down to the road and across it, toward the dunes. Once on the shore, Mr. Adams sat down upon the sand. It was rocky in places, and he moved about to find a smooth place to lie down. Johnny did the same. The president then proceeded to remove his shoes and stockings, revealing pale, swollen feet covered in spidery blue veins. He wriggled his toes with a grunt of pleasure, then stretched out upon his back and closed his eyes.

Johnny placed his arms beneath his head. He closed his eyes and listened to the gulls and squabbling crows. The rising sun shone orange behind his eyelids, and the breeze was warm. Johnny began to breathe more deeply and might have fallen asleep had not Mr. Adams said, "I suppose you've heard about Jefferson's letter to Mazzei, that former neighbor to whom he wrote a calumnious letter, and which the dastardly friend made free to publish?"

"Who has not?" Johnny replied.

"Can you recall it, child?"

"I think so. Some of it, at any rate."

Johnny, eyes still closed against the burning sun, recited,

> *The aspect of our politic has wonderfully changed since you left us . . .*

"Something, something . . ."

> *. . . timid men who prefer the calm of despotism to the boisterous sea of liberty . . . It would give you a fever were I to name to you the apostates who have gone over to these heresies, men who were Samsons in the field and Solomons in the counsel, but have had their heads shorn by the harlot England.*

When Johnny had finished, Adams mused, "Quite a condemnation, I should say."

"Indeed, sir."

"But of whom, exactly?"

"Hamilton, certainly, and Washington."

"And me?"

"The arrow points in your general direction, sir."

"And *this* is my vice president," Adams muttered. He pounded the sand with a fist. "Well, what must be done? What is the response to be? This has been the cause of my agitation all morning."

"None that I can think of."

"Why not?"

"It is what it appears to be. The people now know all. He has hoist with his own petard. Or quill, more like."

Adams lifted himself up onto one elbow and looked at Johnny with some surprise.

"That is precisely what Abigail said. Now, if only we had received that letter last autumn, he would not be my vice president."

They were silent for a while, enjoying the sun, sand, and sea breezes with their eyes closed. A traveler upon a boat would not have guessed that the old man lying on the beach with his belly jutting into the air and pale, bare feet squirming in the sand was the president of the United States.

Finally, Adams sat up with a sigh. "The truth I cannot seem to forget is that there are those who would sooner see a dissolution than to be denied their so-called rights. One of them happens to be my vice president. What kind of country is that, would you say?"

"A divided one, sir."

The president paused. Then he said, "Do me a favor while you're in Baltimore."

"Anything, sir."

"Keep those excellent eyes and ears of yours open."

"Of course, sir. I will."

"No doubt." Adams patted Johnny on the shoulder. Then he leaned on it to stand up. "C'mon. Let's go tackle that hill."

That afternoon, Johnny helped to move the dirt up the hill. Then, returning late in the afternoon as the light declined upon the water, he played with the children. He watched the canvas sails turn shades of yellow and orange.

Oh, gossamer summer days! Knowing they would soon end, Johnny loved them all the more.

• • •

His departure for Baltimore had been set for Monday, August 21. Just as he was enjoying his last Sunday dinner with the family and the Adamses, a messenger rode up to the cottage.

"It's from Kate," Lizzie said.

"What does it say?" Eliza asked.

Lizzie smiled reassuringly. "She wishes to say good-bye to Johnny. She arrives this evening."

Eliza turned to her son and gave him such a mournful look that he was prompted to ask, "Why do you look at me so, Mama? Are you not glad I go to make my mark? Was that not the purpose of our voyage?"

"Yes, of course. Only, I wonder: Would it not have been better to remain at Harvard another year? I fear the cities are dangerous at the moment, even Baltimore."

Johnny replied with some heat, "Surely you cannot wish me to remain here forever, Mama? To remain a child in the playground of Harvard Yard?"

"No, I—"

"Only think of it. I shall be out in the world at last, free! Surely you must know that a man can't be satisfied with mere talk all his life. There must be action as well."

"I want you to be safe, my love. The shadows may be dull, but one sees not so well in them. You have more to hide than most, remember."

"Remember?" Johnny erupted. "Remember? How could I forget?" He slammed his hand down upon the kitchen table, startling Eliza enough so that she backed away from him. Lizzie turned from her dishes to stare at Johnny. Thankfully, the children had gone abroad, although Thomas, who sat building a model ship in the parlor, heard them. He set down his work to listen.

"My dark secret. I'm so *tired* of it! I've a mind to shout it from the rooftops. Oh, let them know! Am I not still myself, this John Boylston everyone praises? Is not John Watson the very same being as John Boylston?"

His mother's eyes were wet with tears. When he saw them, his remorse was swift. "Mama, I didn't mean—"

Eliza was undaunted. She grasped her son's hands fiercely. "I know something of this place, Johnny. More than something. If you're found out, no one will care who you are."

Johnny's anger was spent, and he remarked wearily, "I'll try, Mama. I *have* tried and shall continue to do so."

"And I'm proud of you. But promise me you shall take care. Promise." She stared into his eyes.

Johnny sighed. "I promise." Suddenly he cocked his head and smiled: "I hear a voice."

"Whose, pray?"

"Eliot's."

"Oh?" Eliza smirked. "What does he say?"

"He scolds me for tormenting you so."

"You don't torment me. This conversation was inevitable, and I'm glad we had it." Eliza rose from the table. "Now, go pack."

Johnny went off to finish packing, sheepish and remorseful. Ten minutes later, he heard the snorting of horses released from their harnesses. There was a rap upon the door, and Kate entered without ceremony, followed by her mother.

Johnny thought that Kate looked flushed from the carriage ride; her hair had come partly out of its pins and tumbled down her back. Her step was lively, and she seemed filled with an almost effusive good cheer.

Lizzie prepared them all some tea and served it in the parlor.

"How long shall your journey take?" Kate asked as she sipped her tea.

"A week or so, if the roads are good."

All at once an unsavory vision rose up before Kate's eyes, one she hadn't previously considered. She saw Johnny at a provincial ball, where half a dozen beautiful Southern girls flocked about him like bees to honey.

"Kate?" he questioned, seeing her face sink. Just then, the church bell rang out nine o'clock.

"Oh, but regard the time!" she cried. "I must let you get ready. I know you leave for Boston this evening. Mama told me."

"Yes." Johnny stood up and moved over to her. The women scurried into the kitchen with the dishes to give them privacy. "Do not fear, Kate. I shall write so often that you will look upon yet another letter from me with disgust."

"Never."

Johnny turned away, and Kate had taken several steps toward the kitchen. Then, just as she thought she had broken free, she felt a stab in the heart that made her fling decorum to the winds.

"Oh, Johnny!" she cried and ran back to embrace him. He hugged her hard, lifting her off the floor. Then Kate ran off to join her mother before Johnny could see her tears.

30

HE LEFT AT TEN THIRTY THAT EVENING to catch the post coach from Boston, which would set off at two in the morning. He didn't relish the thought of traveling with strangers, of having to converse with them. He wished to be alone with his thoughts. The outburst at his mother still troubled him; and he was not entirely satisfied with the way he had left things with Kate.

The coach was not as uncomfortable as he had anticipated. It had springs, and the weather was dry. They reached Weston late that morning and stopped at a fine tavern. There, they were able to rest and take some refreshment. They arrived in Worcester that evening, where they stopped the night, setting off very early the following morning for Springfield.

On and on they rode, through Springfield and moving south on the post road until they reached Poughkeepsie, where they crossed the North River by means of a ferry.

The country was varied and beautiful. In one place, they were surrounded by forest; in another, they crossed a river. A third road gave them a breathtaking view of late-summer hills and rolling pastureland. But even such wonder and admiration were supplanted by Johnny's eagerness to get to Baltimore.

They stopped the night in New York and moved on toward Philadelphia the next morning. Skirting around the city the following day, Johnny and the other passengers saw a great number of tents housing refugees. His companions turned their faces away, as if somehow the wind might blow the contagion toward them.

They passed through Wilmington, which granted Johnny a fine view of the countryside and the Delaware River. Finally, on August 28, they arrived at the outskirts of Baltimore.

The city was built upon a hill descending to the Patapsco River. Looking down upon it, Johnny thought it quite beautiful. Some of the area was marshland, which, from a distance, looked nearly primordial in its pristine isolation.

The carriage came to a stop just past a large farm, and Johnny soon found himself on a narrow street with newly built brick row houses standing beside older timber-framed ones. He alighted at last before one of the row houses and waved good-bye to his traveling companions. A harried-looking woman of middle age came out to greet him. She wiped her brow with a sleeve and palmed his letter of introduction.

"Come on, then," she said, leading Johnny to the rear of the house. In the backyard stood a stone outbuilding, which might once have been a smokehouse or kitchen.

"Dinner's at two sharp," said his new landlady. She then left him to get on with her chores. "Oh, and there's a message for you, from a Mr. Martin." She left and returned a moment later with a folded paper, which he opened at once:

Dear Mr. Boylston

As it happens, I am having a little soiree on the night of August 28th, at 6 o'clock. If you arrive in time, please honor us with your attendance.

Yours sincerely, L. M., Esq.

Johnny tucked the letter into his waistcoat pocket and entered the hovel. As he looked about, his spirits sank. A low cot stood in the far corner of the room, and a desk stood opposite. It was a dark, close chamber, with but one grimy window that let in scant light. Johnny looked through it and calculated that, once cleaned, the window might let in a single ray of light between roughly three and three forty-five in the afternoon.

It would not do.

He needed little else, but Johnny could not live without light to read by. It would take wealth such as he did not possess to "make night, the day," as Homer said. Or, in this case, to make day the day. He dreaded complaining to Mr. Martin, but that is what he resolved to do. Not that night, of course, but within the week certainly.

Not bothering to unpack, Johnny went around to his landlady to ask for a bowl and pitcher. He was hot and dirty, and he needed to bathe before presenting himself to Mr. Martin.

It was now near two. The landlady, who called herself Mrs. Jennings, was apparently overwhelmed by dinner preparations for her several lodgers. But eventually she appeared with the requested items. Johnny bathed himself and then lay down upon the cot, forgoing dinner. At once, a large bug, disturbed after a long and entitled residence, crawled skittishly out. Johnny swore and leapt from the bed.

He found a bolster and laid it upon the mattress, stretched out on it with his feet sticking off the edge, and fell asleep. He awoke with a start sometime later, the room several shades darker than it had been. Johnny moved to the window and peered down at his watch: half past five!

He had brought a single good suit, which he now donned. It was abysmally creased, but Johnny did his best to smooth out the wrinkles. He rubbed a bit of pomade into his hair, suddenly wishing he had a looking glass. He rarely bothered to observe himself in this manner, but for some reason, on this occasion he wished to make a good impression.

Had Kate been there, she would have said he already did.

•   •   •

The attorney's stately home stood on the road to Philadelphia, just across from a large new hospital. It was precisely six when Johnny arrived. He cursed himself for having to always be on time. It was awkward to be the very first to arrive at a social gathering. He decided to wait ten minutes before presenting himself.

Johnny strode down the block, observing the solid-brick row houses in the golden light. It was still quite hot. Feeling absurd and direction-less, he sat impatiently for five minutes on the courthouse steps. This was a bizarre building. It seemed to be constructed on a pair of arches or stilts, allowing passage on the road below. But the view from behind it gave out upon beautiful rolling hills.

Johnny stood up and strolled back to Mr. Martin's house. He hesitated another few minutes on the stoop and finally knocked. A thin man of about fifty with a full gray head of hair answered. He looked at Johnny uncomprehendingly. Then he broke into an affable grin.

"Why, John Boylston, is it? Come in, come in. I've just sent the butler off on an errand."

Johnny followed as Mr. Martin led him up a flight of steps and into a capacious, well-appointed parlor. Everywhere Johnny looked there stood a sofa, or settee, or vase with fragrant flowers. *How lavish it is,* Johnny thought, *compared to the stark New England parlor.*

Mr. Martin was saying to him, "My daughters are here and a good friend. The rest of our party is not yet arrived. How was your journey? Not too tedious, I hope. The roads, I hear, are much improved from what they were—"

Johnny did not reply. For, at the end of the room, staring directly at him, stood Marcia Burnes.

Part III

31

JOHNNY MUMBLED SOMETHING APPROPRIATE, HE HOPED, TO Mr. Martin. He might have smiled, although at what words he knew not. Then he approached Miss Burnes, who curtsied.

She was as he remembered her: not tall, but with a proud bearing, her small shoulders rolled back and her long neck arching gracefully upward. Her face was still heart-shaped, and there was still a dimple in her chin. Her emerald eyes had that same ironic, bemused air that he found so confusing. She had gained flesh, but if anything, this made her appear more womanly.

After a long pause, Mr. Martin cried, "Oh, forgive me! Miss Burnes, this is Mr. Boylston. He is just arrived from—"

"We are already acquainted, thank you, Mr. Martin." She smiled.

"Oh, I see. Excellent!"

"Mr. Boylston and I met several years ago, at the home of a mutual acquaintance. It was . . ."

Miss Burnes paused to reflect when John said, "December 19, 1774, at approximately ten in the evening."

"Capital!" said Mr. Martin. "That's one less introduction I need to make this evening. Do allow me to present my daughters."

Johnny had no opportunity to ask Miss Burnes—or was she a Mrs. now?—what she did in Baltimore at this very house, because at that moment, identical twin girls approached and flanked her much as two dull stones might flank a diamond.

A sudden knocking below startled Mr. Martin into action. He flew on bowed legs across the parlor and down the stairs.

Between Rosa and Claire, as they were called, he could perceive no great difference. They were vivacious, bright girls who smiled most of the time. They had the same light-brown hair pulled into buns, the same receding chins, the same watery blue eyes. They were of identical height and build. Claire had a slightly longer neck, perhaps, but that may have been the effect of her gown's having a lower-cut bodice than her sister's. Fortunately these gowns were different colors, which was how Johnny would distinguish them for the rest of the evening.

"Your papa seems most affable," Johnny spoke at last.

"Our dear papa is kindness itself," said Rosa (blue gown), "but you will find him slightly—"

"Distractible," finished Claire (rose gown).

"Yes, a most excellent attorney but a rather pitiable—"

"—secretary."

They both laughed their identical laughs.

"But I suppose that's where you come in?" Rosa glanced up at Johnny and blushed.

"Secretary?" Johnny frowned. "Nay. Or, well, perhaps in part. I'm here to learn the practice of law." Johnny's words came out sounding more self-important than he'd intended.

"The practice of *copying*, I should say," joked Claire. "And I'm afraid you shall first have to *find* things before you copy them."

"You exaggerate, surely."

They began to giggle, but then someone entered whom the sisters felt obliged to greet, and Johnny was left alone with Miss Burnes. She led him to a table where he could take a glass of wine, but he shook his head. "I don't usually drink."

"Oh?" She looked surprised.

"I never acquired a taste for it. Besides," he said, and glanced down at his feet, blushing, "the world as it is renders me quite delirious enough at times."

Miss Burnes merely laughed. It was an easy, pleasing sound. "You're lucky. Many men waste their fortunes on the stuff."

"But what do you do here, if I may be so bold as to inquire?"

"Oh, of course. I suddenly realize my presence here must shock you."

"It does, a little," he admitted.

"Then allow me to explain. Last year, Claire and Rosa became good friends when we all attended Madame Latrobe's School for Ladies, in George Town."

Miss Burnes glanced at Johnny and continued, "We shared similar circumstances, being raised by our fathers, and our mothers having died when we were very young. I hardly remember my poor mama. Anyway, when they left, I felt so lonely, and I told them as much in my letters. They insisted I come stay with them. Papa refused at first, but I wore his objections down."

"Ah," said Johnny. That explained the matter sufficiently. But it didn't make him any less confused.

"And what do *you* do here? At Mr. Martin's, that is?" Miss Burnes asked.

"I was meant to be in Philadelphia, actually. But when news reached us of the fever, I"—here, Johnny hesitated, wondering whether he should mention Mr. Adams—"I procured a different position. Somewhere safer."

"Yes, I hear it's very bad there just now. But you know," she lowered her voice. "My own poor brother died of a fever just here in Baltimore two years ago."

"Yellow fever?" Johnny asked, uneasily.

"No. Potomac fever. I believe they call it typhus elsewhere." Miss Burnes returned to the subject of their reunion. "Uncanny, is it not?"

"Yes." Johnny blushed. "I thought—I thought I'd never see you again."

Miss Burnes grinned. "So you *did* think of me."

"Well, I—"

"That's all right." Her green eyes were warm when she moved closer to Johnny and whispered, "I thought of you, too. I thought I should never see you again. It made me sad."

He did not reply for some time but, seeing her take a sip from her glass, finally managed, "How's your wine?"

Miss Burnes giggled, sending the wine splattering directly upon Johnny's blue waistcoat.

"Oh, God!" She put her hand to her face. "I'm terribly sorry. Do let me call a servant. How awful!"

But Johnny looked down upon his now burgundy-spotted waistcoat and began to laugh. "Nay, never mind. I care nothing about it."

"You shall do, when the other guests think you a leper."

It wasn't true. Johnny easily forgot all about the dark stains on his waistcoat. Indeed, for the rest of the evening he noticed only the person who remained in the periphery of his vision, even as he spoke to the jovial Mr. Martin or his twin daughters. Always, when their eyes met, he saw that slightly bemused look, as if they both knew something others did not.

But Johnny had traveled all day, and by nine in the evening he was tired. He took his leave of Mr. Martin with a deep bow. Mr. Martin said, "Well, lad, stop by tomorrow morning bright and early. Say half past eight? There will be a great deal for you to do. You know where to find my offices?"

"On Charles Street, at the cross of Baltimore."

"Just so."

"I'll see you out," said Miss Burnes, who had come up behind him. As they walked down the steps, she asked, "And your lodgings, are they acceptable?"

"Abysmal." He laughed. "But fortunately not far. I was thinking of speaking to Mr. Martin, actually, in a few days' time."

"Really? What mean you?" Miss Burnes looked concerned.

"I have no wish to complain, but it's a dark hole. I believe it was once an old smokehouse, and has but one grimy window. I don't know how I shall see to study. All the lamps in the world will not brighten it."

"That won't do!" said Miss Burnes, and Johnny found even her pouty frown charming. "I must satisfy myself that you do not exaggerate."

"I never exaggerate."

"How do I know that this itself is not an exaggeration?"

"You don't."

"Well, then, I shall come around tomorrow, before dinner, to satisfy myself on this point. They do at least feed you, where you are?"

"In theory. We shall see what is meant by that tomorrow. I expect it shall be a dog's portion."

"Well, then, 'til noon. Where are you being smoked, by the way?"

"Gay Street, off of Pratt. A brick row house with a blue door, in a warren of similar houses."

"Until tomorrow, then. At your lodgings." She curtsied, glanced at his stained waistcoat, and fled up the stairs before she could laugh again.

* * *

Johnny knew not how he found his way back to his lodgings. It was a moonless night, and his thoughts whirled like leaves in a storm, driving his body will-he-nill-he through the darkness. Marcia Burnes! He had seen no husband; she had said something about spending a few months with her friends. He had hardly listened.

And how solicitous she had been of him! He thought he understood better now why she had lingered in his consciousness for so long. It was not merely her beauty, or even her charm, but how she made him feel when he was in her presence. It was as if they shared a thrilling, dangerous secret. And perhaps it was true, too. How shocking that she proposed to come unescorted to see his lodgings!

Johnny overshot the house and found himself at the edge of the river along Pratt Street. At the harbor, the road smelled like a sewer, but at the sight of the boats rocking gently on their moorings, oil lamps casting long lines of flickering light across the water, he felt a nearly ungovernable excitement. This, certainly, was a new chapter, though he could not guess what would be written there.

32

THE FOLLOWING MORNING, AFTER PROCURING A BISCUIT, a pat of butter, and a bowl of coffee, Johnny set off to his first day as an apprentice at the offices of Luther Martin, Attorney-at-Law. But first, he strolled to the water to watch the thick mist rise off Rowley's Wharf and the dockworkers loading and unloading heavy wooden crates. In the light of day, he noticed many Negroes. Whether these were freemen or slaves, he could not glean. That they were strong and used to hard work was obvious.

Once again, Johnny was assaulted by the harbor's appalling odor. He turned away, up past Baltimore and Market Streets, where old wooden houses vied for space alongside smarter shops and row houses. After five minutes, he turned onto New Church Street, where he passed the courthouse once more. Just beyond this building, he found Charles Street. He turned right and soon saw number fourteen. A dull brass plaque read "L. Martin, Attorney-at-Law."

The door was locked, and all was dark within. It was only eight in the morning; he was half an hour early. Johnny had dressed once more in his best and only suit, now stained by the wine Marcia had spilled on him. He returned to the courthouse and sat down on its steps. The air had already grown thick with rising humidity; and as the fog began to rise it left behind a mist that dampened his clothing and made his hair curl wildly about his head.

From the courthouse steps, Johnny gazed out over the city and the boats in the harbor. He saw a ferryboat arrive, pull close to the dock, and release half a dozen horses and their carriages from its deck.

The night before, Miss Burnes had made free to ask him whether he was married. He cringed now to think of his answer.

"Nay." He had smiled. "I am but nineteen—or very near it." The words were true enough, yet what volumes he had omitted! While he and Kate were by no means engaged, he could not deny that there was something unresolved between them. And yet, each time Johnny endeavored to puzzle out his feelings for Kate or hers for him, he found himself grasping at air.

"What a fool I am," he muttered aloud.

It would not do. Johnny vowed to correct the false impression he had given Miss Burnes the previous night. He stood up and dusted off the seat of his pants. Then he strolled in leisurely fashion around the corner to Mr. Martin's office.

Waiting for him was not Mr. Martin but Miss Burnes. She was dressed in a lovely lilac gown, a fetching broad-brimmed hat, and ivory kid gloves. Above her head she held a lilac parasol. She might have been the study of an enchanting painting. That she had already been painted by the greatest artists in the land, Johnny was blissfully unaware.

"It's you," he said.

"Obviously." She smiled. "I fear you shall get that inspection of your lodgings sooner than you anticipated. Mr. Martin has sent me to tell you he feels a cold coming on and shan't be in the office today. He sent Rosa along with me—" She did not finish the sentence. Johnny blushed at the thought that Miss Burnes had clearly contrived a way to come alone. "He bade us give you a key, however. Not that he expects you to know up from down."

Miss Burnes handed Johnny the key. Her gloved hand grazed his naked one. He turned his back to hide his confusion and opened the door.

"I'll just wait here," she said. "Shall you be long?"

"Oh, no. I mean simply to get the lay of the land." Johnny entered and looked about. The office contained a large double desk, four tall shelves, and half a dozen candleholders. Apart from that, it was hard to know where papers ceased and books began. He observed everything much as one observes a patchwork quilt: unfinished letters, banner headlines, and gold-leaf book titles assaulted his vision simultaneously. Cicero, Seneca, and Grotius were mingled with ink-smeared Republican broadsides. He shut his eyes, but the room's image remained: papers on the floor, on the shelves, the double desk, papers even resting upon the window ledges.

A door led to a small back chamber that housed a cot, a bowl and basin, and a chamber pot. As he left the office, Johnny saw a book he had wanted to read before leaving Harvard, Adam Smith's *Theory of Moral Sentiments*. He picked it up and placed it beneath his arm, exited, and locked the door.

"Already stealing from your employer?" Miss Burnes teased.

"A loan. I'll return it first thing tomorrow."

Miss Burnes lightly touched the thick tome.

"If you return it tomorrow, you shan't have finished it."

"I shall have."

"How can that be, Mr. Boylston?"

"I read quickly."

"You exaggerate."

"As I mentioned last night, I never exaggerate. I may be guilty of many things, but exaggeration isn't one of them. I find the world strange enough without embellishment."

Miss Burnes allowed herself a coy smile. "Well said. Now let us see if this holds true for your lodgings. If so, you'll have made a believer of me."

They strolled in silence down Market Street, now bustling with shopkeepers, workers driving loads to and from the harbor, and ladies going about their chores, shading themselves from the sun with color-ful parasols.

On the streets, just as at the harbor, many black faces mingled with the white ones, some in fine costumes. Never had Johnny seen Negroes so finely dressed in Boston. But then, one would not encounter a woman such as Marcia Burnes there, either.

As they walked, Miss Burnes told Johnny about Baltimore: "There is a new theater in town, just over there." She pointed to a building on Holliday Street. "And a marvelous library. It's round—imagine that! There are all manner of balls and parties, too. The Fountain Inn is charming. I don't doubt but that you shall be invited there within the week."

Johnny found Miss Burnes's lively approbation of the town touching.

"You're smiling," she said. "Why is that?"

"I was only thinking how you are hardly less a stranger to this city than I. Your delight is contagious."

"You think me unworldly." She frowned. "Admit it."

"Nay." Johnny grinned; his aqua-blue eyes seemed lit from within.

"You're a bad liar." Marcia swatted playfully at his arm.

"So my friends have told me. But I cannot believe that anyone acquainted with Mr. Washington can be accounted unworldly."

"*And* Hamilton, mind you. And Burr and Madison, too. Papa knows them all."

They had arrived at his lodgings. From where they stood, they could smell the fish from the wharves. Marcia covered her nose. Johnny led her around to the back of the house, where a few scabrous chickens were pecking at one another.

"It's just there," Johnny pointed. "Be quick. Here's the key."

Marcia took the key. She opened the door and ducked her head, placing a gloved hand above it to shield her from falling dirt.

"Goodness!" Johnny heard her cry.

After a scant minute, Miss Burnes emerged. The bright sunshine made her blink. Then she said, "Pack your bags at once."

"But where do I go?"

"I shall speak to Mr. Martin. He is a particular friend of Papa's." Miss Burnes then blushed. "Anyway, I believe he shall be more than happy to help you."

"I hate to impose."

"It would importune him more to have to find you other lodgings, I'm sure. But here—some letters for you." She proffered a packet of perhaps half a dozen letters, all tied neatly with string. His landlady must have placed them beneath his door. "You have a secret admirer, I see."

Johnny looked down at the letters with a jolt of horror. They were all from Kate.

33

HEARING MISS BURNES'S ACCOUNT OF JOHNNY'S LODGING, Mr. Martin offered his profuse apologies and called at once for his carriage. He sent two servants, and by mid-afternoon they had transported both Johnny and his belongings to Martin's own home.

The guest chamber down the hall was but a closet; there was room enough for a bed and desk. But it was as sunny and hot as the other had been dark and dank, and Johnny felt it to be a vast improvement. There was only one problem: now that he was beneath the same roof as Marcia Burnes, how would he ever concentrate?

That afternoon, Miss Burnes took herself off with the twins to the market, and he found himself alone at last. Sitting upon his comfortable, bug-free bed, he opened the first of Kate's letters. It was dated a few days after he had left.

> I returned to Quincy last night with Mama, who had an errand to do. The little ones are very glum with no one to play pony with. Miriam complains that she wants to go to Harvard University, too, and doesn't see why she can't. Poor Lizzie has had a time explaining things in a way that does not depress the child's naturally high spirits . . .

When he had finished reading the letters, Johnny felt as if his parched soul had been nourished by the news of home. He set them aside with a sigh, took up the book he had borrowed from Mr. Martin, and read for the rest of the afternoon. He fell asleep in his clothing and did not wake till morning.

He rose as dawn broke, descended, and sat in the parlor while the servants readied the buffet. These were free black servants, he learned. It seemed Mr. Martin owned no house slaves, which relieved Johnny immensely.

The parlor was bathed in morning light, illuminating the gemlike reds and blues of a thick Turkey carpet. A silver tea service adorned the center of the buffet, and the table was set with silver as well. Mr. Martin, a servant told him, had already left for the office, having missed the previous day. When Miss Burnes entered, Johnny rose and bowed. He had hoped that the shivery feeling he got in her presence would have abated after reading Kate's letters, but it had not. Miss Burnes espied the book he had been reading, which sat on the empty seat next to him.

"And, have you read it?" she challenged.

"I have."

"Mmm-hmm. Shall I test you?"

"If you like." Johnny shrugged. He had resolved to display neither warmth nor coldness to Miss Burnes. He carried his plate to the buffet, where he helped himself to ham, eggs, and a biscuit.

"Very well," she said, taking up the tome. She turned to a random page. "Describe, if you would, the second paragraph of the first page of chapter one, entitled 'Of the Sense of Propriety.'"

Johnny closed his eyes and saw one line, and then two. In the act of speaking, several more came into view:

Though our brother is on the rack, as long as we ourselves are at our ease, our senses will never inform us of what he suffers. They never did, and never can, carry us beyond our own

*person, and it is by the imagination only that we can form
any conception of what are his sensations.*

"Bravo!" Marcia exclaimed. She then added in a low, velvety voice, "So, you weren't exaggerating."

"I told you I don't exaggerate." Johnny grimly attacked his second helping of food and said he was late for work.

Work that day consisted mainly of organizing Mr. Martin's papers. The twins had been right: many court documents needed copying, but Johnny had first to find them. He did not return that day to the house for dinner, but strolled to a place called Kaminsky's around the corner, where he had a fine oyster stew in sherry and a mug of cider. Then he returned to the office, where he sorted through Mr. Martin's correspondence, making a list of all those letters in need of a reply.

That evening, as the heat of the day dissipated and the sun waned to the west, the twins proposed a walk. He and the three girls strolled up Capitol Hill, where he saw all of Baltimore, its brick buildings and pretty harbor glowing in the declining light. Cattle grazed in pastures at the ragged edges of town, and the outer harbor appeared before them like a blue bowl upon which canvas napkins, folded into triangles, rocked from side to side.

"This marvelous view reminds me of my home, Johnny," said Marcia. "Oh, I grow homesick."

"Where is home, exactly, Miss Burnes? You must forgive me. I'm a stranger in a strange land."

"Home is Maryland, by the Potomac. But it is changing so quickly I soon shall hardly recognize it. Our home is quite modest, but it sits upon the loveliest bank of a river, and from it, one has an excellent view of both the President's House and Alexandria."

"I should very much like to see it," Johnny said.

Miss Burnes glanced at him meaningfully. "Would you? Then by all means do."

The following day was a Sunday. After church and dinner, Johnny and Miss Burnes strolled down to Fell's Point, beyond the wharf and its fetid smells. The twins had meant to join them, but at the last moment, Mr. Martin had an errand he would have them do, and so Johnny found himself strolling alone with Miss Burnes.

At the Point, the air was fresh and slightly salty. There, the water was deeper and the boats larger. Johnny wondered why the founders of Baltimore had chosen a shallow spot for their harbor, when a much deeper one existed here. Yet the town flourished despite its shallow harbor.

There was a cool breeze and a touch of autumn in the air. Johnny was aware of Marcia Burnes's warmth as she stood beside him. A sudden gust off the water made her shiver, momentarily sanctioning their closeness.

As they made their way back toward town, Miss Burnes sighed.

"Why do you sigh?" he asked.

"You *do* have an admirer. Is that not true?"

Johnny stopped walking and turned to her.

"I have a—friend. A good friend, who is very nearly related to me. That is all."

But Miss Burnes continued cannily, "Were she to see us now, at this very moment, what would she say?"

"She would say nothing, for she is far too well-mannered," Johnny replied with some pique.

Still undaunted, Miss Burnes asked, "*Say* nothing, but feel . . . ?"

"She would feel—" Johnny noticed Miss Burnes's knowing smile, and it irritated him. "Miss Burnes, do not ask me to speak of this."

Offended, Miss Burnes did not reply but walked quickly ahead of him toward home. Johnny did not endeavor to keep up with her. For her part, Miss Burnes did not believe Johnny's words. Though hardly more experienced than he in such matters, she sensed that a boy with no feelings toward a girl should have no trouble speaking of her. And yet, Johnny did—a great deal of trouble. The question was, what should she do about it?

Johnny continued to walk behind her, having settled into the discomfort between them. Just before they reached the house, Miss Burnes stopped walking and turned around. She moved close to him and looked up expectantly, the complicit gleam in her eyes having returned. He bent down and kissed her. He held her close, feeling her chest rising and falling against him, pressing against his body.

She pulled away, smiling. "You feel it, too, at least."

"I do," he said miserably. "I always have."

34

HE TOLD HIMSELF NOTHING WOULD COME OF it, for several reasons. One, Miss Burnes would soon return to Washington, where she would be courted by the most powerful men in the land. Two, Johnny had nothing to offer her save his good nature and excellent prospects, and three, he believed Miss Burnes took their relationship for a pleasant dalliance, no more.

The temporary nature of their affair was given confirmation when, one morning at breakfast, Marcia said, "I've had a letter from Papa. He misses me greatly and hints at a weakening of his health. He asks that I return as soon as may be."

"When will that be?" Johnny asked.

"I'm not sure," she admitted. "I must make further inquiries."

Meanwhile, Johnny continued to receive cheerful, informative letters from Kate. Ben's front tooth fell out and, as he very much wished to keep it, he was upset to discover that someone had purloined it. He and Elizabeth got into a fight until Aunt Martha caught and scolded the *real* culprit, poor little Hannah.

Johnny replied with news of his own, sharing all that happened at the office: the miles and miles of writs to copy, letters in need of replies, and documents to file.

Mr. Martin is all affability though I learn little from him. Baltimore is a charming city and seems to be growing at a rapid rate.

To Johnny, his letter lied a great deal by omission, and he did not take his usual pleasure in writing it.

Miss Burnes went home to visit her father, and for Johnny, that time passed slowly. But when she finally returned, her wan face beamed with joy to see him.

"How's your father?" he asked as they shared a light supper with the Martin family.

"The doctor believes he has a cancer of the stomach."

"Oh, goodness. I'm very sorry."

"I shall have to return to see him frequently from now on. He says he doesn't wish to remove me from my current situation as I appear to him so contented." Marcia glanced at Johnny with tears in her eyes. "Oh, he is so good!"

Here, Miss Burnes began to cry. She wiped her eyes with her table napkin.

Johnny's resolve to show no affection to Miss Burnes vanished. He reached for her hand beneath the table and pressed it reassuringly.

• • •

As autumn moved into winter, the foursome took to walking westward in the afternoons, provided it wasn't too cold. They called the western edge of the city "the frontier," for it was here they could see the great covered wagons that stopped for the night along the densely forested road leading into Baltimore. One afternoon, as they strolled arm in arm to keep warm, Rosa remarked, "Marcia tells us you're from Barbados, but you don't have an accent. If anything, you sound British."

"I can sound quite Barbadian when I choose to." Johnny smiled. "Shall I give you a sample?"

"Yes, please!" the twins cried.

"All right, here is a lullaby my dear Cassie used to sing to me." And without needing further encouragement, Johnny began to sing:

> Da cocoa tea is a poison to me,
> Ev'ry time I drink it,
> I don't know where I be.
> If you want to find me
> You gotta look for me,
> For she got muh head up-sided down
> Wid a cup o' da cocoa tea.

> I was once engaged to a lady,
> Her love was all for me
> No matter the distance she did live
> It was no trouble to me.
> But another girl she did love me
> An tek me away from she
> An' the only t'ing dat bring me back
> Was a cup o' da cocoa tea.

This exotic recitation made the twins giggle with delight, but Marcia had covered her ears.

"It is too much! You sound like an absolute stranger."

"Then as a stranger give it welcome," Johnny said, bowing slightly.

It was a reference to *Hamlet* that Kate would have thoroughly enjoyed. But Marcia merely stared blankly at him for a moment and then turned to watch as snow began to fall on the wagons.

As they stood looking at the snow, Miss Burnes said brightly, "I've had a letter from Peter today."

"Peter?" Johnny frowned. "Fray?"

"Yes. He's in Richmond just now. You've not spoken of him, I notice. Are you no longer friends?"

"No." Johnny offered nothing else. Peevishly, he felt no inclination to apprise her of such a dark, unhappy story, when neither his childhood nor his mellifluous native tongue aroused her interest.

"That is too bad." She shrugged. Suddenly Miss Burnes turned to him. "But say, shouldn't you be in your fourth year now, as Peter would have been?"

"I received my degree in three years," he replied tersely. "So, what does Peter have to say?"

"His family, as you perhaps know, suffered a great tragedy. Fred was murdered."

"Yes, I know."

"Well, they nearly lost the plantation. Peter was certain they *would* lose it. But they have sold off a piece of land and by this means forestall disaster. Their debts, however, remain enormous." She lowered her voice. "He doesn't like to speak of it."

Johnny said, "Apparently he does."

He glanced at Marcia, at her unsuspecting face, and suddenly berated himself for his impatience with her. It was not the usual province of women to concern themselves with the relationships of men.

Marcia asked, "Have I offended you somehow? If I did, I apologize."

"No. *I'm* sorry. It's just—Peter and I parted ways. Our friendship fell victim to the current divisions that threaten our country." This at least was partly true.

Johnny thought Marcia would be thankful for his apology. But she drew herself up and said with a curl of her lip, "You think me ignorant and lacking in understanding."

"Nay, I did not—"

Her eyes flashed a warning. "It's not understanding I lack, Johnny. When I fail to see, it is rather because I close my eyes. There are simply things I don't wish to know. Relations between men can be so very ugly. Why should I torment myself with knowing when I can *do* nothing? As for my education, I have had a father to tend to, and it has been just the two of us. We didn't always have a vast fortune . . ."

Johnny, suddenly remorseful, touched her arm. As they descended the hill, a more cheerful mood seized her.

"Is Baltimore very different from Cambridge?" she asked.

"Oh, yes." He looked thoughtful.

"How so?"

"It is so much—warmer here."

Miss Burnes giggled.

"And how find you working for our dear papa?" Claire asked, relieved that the couple had resolved their argument.

"Oh, excellent. He keeps me quite busy."

The shrewd sisters heard the lie at once.

"Busy!" Claire objected. "I should say so. Come, come, Mr. Boylston. We know our father quite well. You cannot fool us. He's a dear soul. But we suspect his office is rather like the interior of his mind."

"A library—" began Rosa.

"—after a hurricane," finished Claire. At this, they all laughed.

"Well, perhaps you're right. There's a great deal of organizing to do." The truth was, Johnny had been with Martin nearly three months and was yet to learn anything from him.

They had reached Market Street and made their way toward the house a few blocks away. It was now nearly dark, and white snow-flakes shone upon their dark clothes and Johnny's hair. Marcia smiled maternally and wiped them off of him. At the house, Claire curtsied and said, "We take our leave." Rosa curtsied and followed her sister up the stoop, soon disappearing into the house. The couple was now alone, in the darkness, with the season's first snow falling gently upon them.

"Shall we go in?" asked Johnny. "I fear you freeze."

"Nay. You shall warm me." Marcia moved closer to him. She took his hand and led him beyond the house, away from curious eyes. She then wrapped her arms around him and held him tight.

"Well, well," he murmured. "What's this?" He held her close, feeling, in the press of her flesh, a painful, mysterious regret.

"I fear I'm not worthy of you, Johnny, that I fall short in your eyes."

"What mean you?"

"I know you've been among educated women. Boston, Cambridge—things are different there. Of all things on earth, I fear being *ornamental*. I know I am pretty, but I'm not ignorant enough to believe that beauty is a virtue. I may take no more credit for it than I can the fact of my sex."

"You are not pretty, Marcia," Johnny said, feeling a swell of tenderness for her. "You are beautiful. You're a feeling, intelligent being. Oh, I love you, Marcia Burnes!"

He bent down and kissed her. She kissed him back but then pulled away. Taking his hands, she said, "You should write your friend, if you haven't already."

It was a splash of cold water, roundly deserved. Marcia moved toward the house, and Johnny followed her. In the foyer, parting, he looked into her eyes and said, "I shall. I promise. Until tomorrow, my love."

Johnny retired, but, as was often the case, he could not sleep. Too many thoughts crowded his mind. Marcia had stood up for herself in the face of his critical judgment. She had been forthright with him, and displayed a keen understanding. He knew himself to be in love with her. Why, then, did he hesitate to write to Kate? Why did he feel ashamed to admit the truth? If there had been no definite understanding between himself and Kate, then there could be no breach. So why did he lie awake weighing and measuring, when he knew well that to do so was folly? It was around three in the morning when Johnny finally understood the answer: because he loved them both.

35

April 1798

THE WINTER HAD PASSED IN QUIET ENTERPRISE, but spring brought a sudden escalation of tension throughout the country. Adams released news that the peace mission to France, set in motion the year before, had been a catastrophic failure. The French foreign minister Talleyrand attempted to extract a bribe from the American ambassadors. Rather than barter for peace, the delegates turned around and came home. War with France seemed imminent. Irate mobs took to the streets in protest, exchanging their tricolor hats for good black American ones.

A letter from Kate to Johnny during this time seemed unreal to him in its contentment. She had moved to Quincy, she said, as the town had a "bumper crop" of babes. Aiding Lizzie and Johnny's mother seemed as good a use of her time as any. She wrote,

> Being close to Lizzie and your mother makes me feel close to you, just as being useful makes me feel close to God. I discover the pleasures of being a "farmer-ess," as Abigail likes to call herself. In spare moments, I even keep a journal. My greatest pleasure when not helping Lizzie is to reflect upon the current state of

womanhood. In my more confident moments I think I should like to devote myself to creating a magazine. Not one of those dreadful fashion rags, but something of real substance. It could be a refuge of sorts, a place for women to read about ideas and culture, to realize that they are not mad, not freaks of nature, not alone. I myself should have felt woefully alone had I not been surrounded by the best and bravest of women. How might I have challenged the great John Adams—or the great Eliot Mann and Johnny Boylston—were it not that I had seen Abby and Lizzie do the very same over the years? Anyway, what think you of my bright idea, John? Is it merely the fancy of an idle female mind?

Johnny replied that he thought it a most excellent idea. But his exchange of letters with Kate gave him little pleasure. His guilt at failing to mention Miss Burnes deepened the longer he put it off.

Just as he thought the political news could get no worse, word reached Johnny that Congress had passed several acts of dubious constitutionality. One made it difficult for foreigners to attain citizenship and allowed for deportation of immigrants deemed inimical to peace. Another, called the Sedition Act, criminalized the making of false or scandalous statements against the government or criticizing its leaders. The country had fallen victim to the gripping delusion of its having enemies everywhere, though Johnny had seen no evidence of such foreign enemies. Now, to watch their own government give credence to these absurd fears was more than he could bear. How could Mr. Adams have approved these acts? At once, Johnny wrote a letter to his mother:

As you know, I was meant to join Mr. Wilson in Philadelphia next month, but the yellow fever there is even worse than last summer. Many flee or have already fled, and many have died. I expect our esteemed friends have already left for home. News of the passage of the Alien and Sedition Acts has many here literally up in arms. My belief in the Old Man is shaken. Thank goodness you bore me in America, Mama, for I should otherwise have had to wait another decade to become a citizen! I know not what shall come of things. The senators attend their meetings armed with pistols and dirks. Never mind war with France. To me it feels like civil war.

Johnny considered cutting out this last paragraph to avoid alarming his mother, but then he chose to leave it in. She would hear it all from Abigail anyway.

After this, Johnny took special care to peruse the Republican papers for responses to the Alien and Sedition Acts. He knew there would be fervent condemnations, and that these would serve to broaden the rift between the parties. But he read every scrap of paper in Martin's office anyway, searching for particularly troubling news.

During his search, Johnny came across many papers written by Mr. Jefferson, going back to his days as governor of Virginia. One work was called *Notes on the State of Virginia* and had been published in England. Johnny perused its pages. He read quickly, and with growing horror. In this work, Jefferson posited a theory that whites were a superior race. While he believed it self-evident that whites were more beautiful, he also went on to argue the Negro's inferior judgment and imagination:

Comparing them by their faculties of memory, reason, and imagination, it appears to me, that in memory they are equal to the whites; in reason much inferior, as I think one [black] could scarcely be found capable of tracing and comprehending the investigations of Euclid; and that in imagination they are dull, tasteless, and anomalous.

Tears came to Johnny's eyes. As a child, Johnny had often heard his parents praise Jefferson for his courage in speaking up against slavery. His draft of the Declaration of Independence spoke of slavery as a "cruel war against human nature itself."

Oh, falling idols!

Johnny abruptly abandoned his search in Mr. Martin's office; he could not bear to continue for fear of what else he might discover. For the rest of that spring into summer, Johnny occupied himself with filing and copying, advancing neither his understanding of America nor of the law.

It was soon August, and Baltimore became infernally hot, well beyond ninety degrees most days. Johnny could do little either in or out of Mr. Martin's office. On the hottest days of that month and of early September, he eschewed the office altogether and joined the ladies beneath the shade of the willow trees down by the river. They played cards and told stories. Miss Burnes came and went, sharing with them news of her father's failing health. Of late, Johnny had heard less frequently from his mother, but in September he received a letter that contained grievous news:

> Abigail is perilously ill. I dare not express a shred of
> confidence that my beloved friend will survive.

Johnny started up from the grass where he had been reclining.

"Why, what is the matter?" Miss Burnes asked.

"I've had bad news from home. Mrs.—" he nearly said "Mrs. Adams," but stopped himself. "Mama's dearest friend is gravely ill. I must go home at once."

"But surely you shan't do any such thing? That cannot help her. You shall be obliged to pass by Philadelphia, and all those poor exiled inhabitants in their tents. Your mother shall have yet another thing to worry about."

In his haste to act, Johnny hadn't thought of that argument. The twins murmured their assent, and he sat back down on the grass with a sigh of frustration. "We shall see what else the post brings," he concluded.

A second letter from his mother arrived two days later. This one told him that Abigail was "a little better, yet gravely ill." His mother then relieved his mind by saying,

> I know you well enough to know that you consider
> returning home, but I beg you remain where you
> are. Abigail gets the best of care, and knowing you
> are traveling, and with the yellow fever all about,
> shall only fuel my anxiety.

"You see." Marcia nodded.

Johnny glanced at her. It annoyed him that Marcia had been right. But it annoyed him even more that he was glad of it.

It was not until the end of September that Eliza Boylston wrote with any confidence of Abigail's recovering. By then, she had also heard from Cassie that her mother had suffered a bad case of pneumonia but was slowly recovering. His mother ended her letter by saying,

> I shall need to return to Barbados before too long,
> John. I save my pennies to do so.

Johnny understood what his mother meant, that, henceforth, he could not rely on her for any loans or gifts of cash. But that was all right; Johnny had no intention of asking her. He would find a source of income.

In October, Marcia decided to host a party for Johnny's twentieth birthday. When she saw the suit he proposed to wear for the occasion, she wrinkled her nose.

"It's far too Bostonian," she said.

"What's wrong with a good Boston suit?" Johnny objected.

"It's so *grim*. Do save it, though. It's a perfect suit to be buried in."

Johnny laughed. Then he admitted, "Well, I daren't ask for money from Mama just now. She saves for her return to Barbados."

But Marcia was not to be contradicted. "Very well. I shall get Mr. Martin to waive his fee."

Most attorneys collected a fee from their protégés in exchange for mentoring them. As it happened, Mr. Martin's fee was the exact amount of a new suit. "Oh, do let me have my way on this point, Johnny. I should like to be proud of you at your party."

"You are not already so?" he asked, surprised.

"You know what I mean."

"I'm not sure I do," he replied. "Are appearances so very important to you?"

Her words brought to mind sickly, heron-like Eliot, whom the boys at college first teased and then cruelly shunned. He recalled the women slaves of Bridgetown, clothed in their one petticoat and blouse, both worn transparent with scrubbing, and the hucksters whose only possessions were the trinkets they fashioned. Some days, if they had nothing to give, then they gave Johnny a colorful smile and combed their strong fingers through his salt-soaked hair.

His eyes opened to look at Miss Burnes once more, and he felt a sudden pity for her. She could never know what that fine suit represented to him, or what joy it was to be loved by those who had nothing to give except themselves. What's more, since coming to America, Johnny had been spoiled living among such women as Kate, Aunt Martha, and Abigail Adams. By what impossible measure did he judge this lovely woman?

Marcia felt Johnny's pity. She turned away and left the chamber, her shoulders pulled back proudly. She moved down the hall, fighting tears. Johnny moved after her, his remorse as swift as his judgment had been.

"Marcia! I'm sorry. Forgive me, please. I'm a fool."

She waited for him to continue.

"It's just—we don't know each other well yet. You cannot know—that is, I see I must explain how, and among whom, I grew up. You can't understand my loyalties."

Marcia pursed her lips and replied, "I fear you are too good for me, Johnny. This has long been my fear."

He began to object, but she moved away from him with a tearful gesture that said, "Leave me be."

Johnny returned to his chamber and paced. He had no wish to ask his mother for the money. But neither did he relish the humiliation of having to ask Mr. Martin to waive his fee. Finally, he sat down and wrote a letter to Mr. Martin so that he could buy a new suit.

•　　•　　•

At the Fountain Inn, upon the arm of the stunning Miss Burnes and flanked by the two affable Martin daughters, Johnny felt like a foreign dignitary. He wore his new blue suit, the jacket of which chafed slightly beneath the arms. The wine flowed. There were toasts to Johnny's health and prosperity, and overall the party was so elegant, laden with delicacies, and hospitable, that it reminded him of Christmas at Moorcock.

On this night, Johnny met some of the luminaries of Baltimore, most notably the editor of the *Federal Gazette*. Johnny and this editor struck up a lively, forthright conversation, in which Johnny admitted that as a student he'd written several pieces for the *Columbian Centinel*.

"Indeed! Well, send me anything that strikes your fancy, Mr. Boylston. I'll read it with pleasure."

Johnny bowed and thanked him.

Marcia, who had been standing just behind Johnny, said, "You didn't tell me you wrote for the papers. That's a great accomplishment for one so young. Why did you not tell me?"

"My feelings about writing for the papers are—mixed," he admitted. "On the one hand, I wish to support the president; on the other, I feel that writing for one side or another serves only to broaden the rift between them. Then, to remain in the middle seems increasingly irrelevant. I would like to discuss my doubts with you sometime, Marcia."

"Oh, do!" Marcia replied, but already her eyes were wandering about the room to see whom Johnny should meet next.

36

THE WEATHER, WHICH HAD REMAINED UNUSUALLY TEMPERATE throughout the fall, finally turned wintry. Baltimore took on a self-protective air as tents were taken down, ships brought in from sea, and market stalls covered with canvas. People began to hunch against the wind as they made their way through the streets.

Philadelphia was finally declared fever-free, though this time the disease left more than three thousand dead. Mr. Wilson, Johnny learned, had also died, though not of the yellow fever, taking with him Johnny's hopes of living in Philadelphia.

Johnny had now lived in Baltimore for more than a year. He knew he stayed only for Miss Burnes. While Mr. Martin was forever producing fresh reams of paper for Johnny to sort, as yet there had been no systematic study of the law, no discussion of legal cases or history.

Johnny continued to read the broadsides. He had not forgotten Adams's request to "keep an eye out" for any information that might interest him. Johnny sometimes wished he would stumble upon something to share with Mr. Adams, but as yet, nothing had struck him as particularly important. There were the usual excoriations in the Republican press against the "monarchy-loving" Federalists, rants that Adams no doubt read himself.

Then, one morning that December, before Mr. Martin had arrived for the day, Johnny was reading through the broadsides as usual when his eyes lit upon something peculiar. In the *Albany Centinel* dated December 18, Johnny read an article reprinted from a June edition of the *Gazette of the United States*, which somehow he had failed to peruse that past summer. It was an article written by editor John Fenno, called "Fruits of the French Diplomatic Skill," in which Fenno both published the Kentucky Resolutions and railed against them. These resolutions, passed in the Kentucky legislature, essentially asserted Kentucky's right to ignore a federal law if the state deemed it unconstitutional. But behind the Resolutions was an even darker agenda: the threat of secession.

Now, Johnny read the article carefully. As he did so, he noticed something oddly familiar about it. When he realized what it was, he paced Mr. Martin's office in a paroxysm of indecision. Then Johnny took a pen and paper from Mr. Martin's desk and hastily wrote,

> Dear Mr. President
> Forgive, if you would, this hasty letter, but I find I shall be in Philadelphia this coming week and would be grateful for a brief audience with you on a matter of some urgency.

Johnny sealed his letter and walked the several blocks to the tiny shack that served as Baltimore's post office. As he walked back to Mr. Martin's residence, his agitation grew. Oh, if only he could tell someone what he knew! An hour later, at dinner, Johnny told Mr. Martin that urgent business called him away.

"Away? To where, pray?" asked the attorney. He had been reading upon a broadside and removed his spectacles, the better to look at Johnny from across the table.

"To Philadelphia."

At this pronouncement, the other girls, who had been engrossed in a discussion of a friend's coming-out party, stopped to listen.

"Philadelphia? Whatever for?" asked Marcia. "How long shall you be gone?"

"A week at least, perhaps longer. I'll do my best to resolve the business speedily."

"I don't know that I can do without you that long," Mr. Martin grumbled. Immediately, Johnny cringed with guilt. Mr. Martin had kindly agreed to waive his fee so that Johnny could buy a new suit, and now Johnny was asking him leave to go to Philadelphia. But the good man asked merely, "Well, but shall you take the carriage?"

"A good horse would serve, if you can spare one, sir," he said.

"Of course. You can take Betsy. Shan't it be too cold, though?"

"The cold shall spur my haste."

●　　●　　●

Johnny left very early the following morning, Marcia having bade him a cool good-bye the night before. The weather, much like Marcia, though cold, was not frozen, and the sun shone, promising a warmer afternoon. The roads were passable, although in places the clay soil made for slow going. Along the way, Johnny passed a bleak landscape of barren wheat fields and ruined fences. Several newly built settlements infused the air with the smell of pine sap.

Johnny traveled through the pretty, hilly town of Abingdon and then Havre de Grace, with its tranquil views of the Susquehanna. In late afternoon he arrived at Elkton, where he spent the night at an inn along the main road.

Finally, late the following morning, he found himself trotting down the road to the city of his childhood dreams: Philadelphia. Johnny stopped Betsy to take in the panoramic view from the hill above the Schuylkill River. It was a clear, bright day, and from this vantage point he could see all the way to the Delaware, wild forests giving way to a most rational grid of homes and shops. Here, stately brick buildings mixed with busy shops, and people of all classes strolled the cobbled streets. Johnny looked upon it with admiration. It was orderly yet industrious—nothing like chaotic Bridgetown or tightly buttoned Boston. How beautiful he found this city!

Johnny did not remain long on the hill, however, for the wind bit into his neck where a thin cravat did not fully cover his naked skin. As he made his way down the hill and onto the main road, the neat brick homes grew larger and more refined until he reached the State House and the President's House across from it. A moment later, he arrived at his destination.

John Francis's hotel, at 13 South Fourth Street, was a small yet elegant townhouse just off High Street. Johnny was shown to his room, from which he could look down upon the goings-on of the busy main street. A bowl and pitcher of fresh water stood in one corner, and Johnny gratefully washed and changed his dirty clothing. He was soon walking up High Street toward the President's House.

For several minutes, he simply stood before it and gaped. It was a tall, stately home with twelve windows fronting the street, all clean and glimmering in the bright wintry sunlight. Above the windows, triangular pediments lent an orderly air to the edifice.

Suddenly an unbidden doubt seized him, and he nearly turned back to his hotel. What delusion had allowed him to believe he had something of vital importance to tell the president? Surely Mr. Adams already knew whatever there was to know about the villainy surrounding him? Worse than his presumption was the nagging suspicion of his own motives. Perhaps this was no altruism but an ugly bid to ingratiate himself.

Johnny shook his head. He knew that such was not his motive. He believed he had discovered a deceit of the highest order. Despite disagreeing with Adams over the recent acts passed by Congress, Johnny's first impulse was to protect him. Taking a deep breath, he walked up the broad marble stoop and rang the bell.

He heard the rattle of heavy bolts, and an old butler appeared, stooped and bald. A few gray wisps of hair waved above his ears. Taking one look at Johnny, he said, "Parcels around back, lad." He pointed to the gate off to the left of the entranceway.

Johnny stood firm. "I have business with the president."

The butler pursed his lips. "Citizens' hours are on Monday. Today is Thursday."

Johnny contained his impatience. "Please tell Mr. Adams that Mr. Boylston calls from Baltimore on urgent business. Tell him I stay at the Francis Hotel and may return by and by, if now is not convenient."

The butler, ever dubious, shut the door in Johnny's face. He returned two minutes later wearing an officious smile.

"Come in, please," he said, granting Johnny a shallow bow. Johnny bowed shallowly in return and entered.

The first thing he noticed about the interior was its great height: thirty feet, he guessed. Next, he noticed its opulence: The ceiling contained three dramatic arches supported by fluted columns. A rich green carpet covered the wood floors. To the left, a finely carved mahogany staircase rose, bending twice on the way to an impressive gallery.

The butler led Johnny into a parlor at whose far end stood a massive fireplace. Three tall windows on the left of the fireplace looked out onto High Street.

"The president shall join you momentarily," the butler said. He bowed again and left Johnny alone in the parlor.

Johnny was just perusing a bookcase that stood to the right of the fireplace when he heard a cry:

"Johnny! Dear boy!"

The president moved toward him and did not stop until he had hugged Johnny warmly. Then he pulled back to stare at him.

"Why, I think you've grown since I last laid eyes upon you. You're nearly as tall as Washington!"

"And you, sir—" he began, indicating his admiration for Mr. Adams's silk costume.

"Quite presidential, eh?" said Adams, patting his chest. "Well, I can't very well strut about Philadelphia in my farmer's weeds, now can I? Though I should dearly like to." He stuck a pudgy finger beneath his vest, as if trying to pop a button. "This waistcoat is as tight as a corset, ha ha. But sit, do." Adams gestured to a wing chair by the fire. Then he fired off three questions: "Tell me, what brings you here? What news of home? How fare Mr. and Mrs. Miller, and all the children, and your dear mama?"

"They are all well, and the harvest, they say, was excellent this year."

"Oh, yes, yes. You've been in Baltimore—with Luther Martin, is it? Excellent." The president called for his butler. "Bartlett! Bring us some coffee. And a cake or two."

Adams looked at Johnny sheepishly. "My cook makes the most excellent cakes, which is perhaps not unrelated to the tightness of this waistcoat."

Bartlett brought the coffee and cakes and set them down upon a mahogany tea table. He then put a log on the fire before bowing deeply and leaving. Once Bartlett had left, Johnny sipped his coffee, took a bite of cake, and gathered himself for the topic he had come to broach.

"Sir, did you receive my letter?"

"I did. But I don't believe for a moment that you merely 'find yourself' in Philadelphia. Tell me truly why you're here."

"I've made a most unsettling discovery. I know not whether you spoke in jest when you told me to keep my eyes open, but I have, sir, and I think they've come across something you would wish to know."

Mr. Adams seemed more interested in his cake just then, of which he'd taken such an enormous bite. For one unsettling moment, Johnny feared the old man could not possibly swallow it. When he had, Johnny continued, "You've no doubt read the 'Kentucky Resolutions'?"

"I've heard tell of them but not yet read them."

"Well, I've just read them, and it is my studied opinion that there is a traitor in your midst."

"A traitor, you say?" Mr. Adams took a sip of his coffee.

Johnny removed from his waistcoat pocket a twice-folded page from the *Albany Centinel*.

"Read this, sir, if you would."

Johnny proffered the paper as Mr. Adams searched for his spectacles. Finding them, he read the heading:

"'Fruits of the French Diplomatic Skill.' Is that the one?"

"Yes, sir. That's it."

Mr. Adams read:

> Resolved, *That the several States composing, the United States of America, are not united on the principle of unlimited submission to their general government; but that, by a compact under the style and title of a Constitution for the United States, and of amendments thereto, they constituted a general government for special purposes* . . .

"And so on and so forth . . ." Adams trailed off and squeezed his tired eyes together with two fingers.

"Well, is it not treacherous to suggest that the Constitution is a mere 'compact' for 'special purposes'?" asked Johnny.

Adams was thoughtful. "I believe it to be, as you do, a treacherous interpretation."

Johnny had not expected this mild response.

"Sir," Johnny pressed, "do you not also recognize the voice?"

"Voice? Whose, pray? I don't know the Kentucky fellows very well."

They had come to the crux of the matter.

"Why, *Jefferson's!*"

Adams's eyes flickered toward Johnny. He said, "I cannot think him so low."

"Can't you? I can," Johnny replied hotly. "Besides, I have proof. Look just here." Johnny pointed. "Regard where it says that the Constitution,"

guarded against all abridgement by the United States of the freedom of religious opinions and exercises, and retained to themselves the right of protecting the same, as this state by a Law passed on the general demand of its Citizens, had already protected them from all human restraint or interference . . .

Johnny stopped there and waited.

Adams scratched his ear. "I hear the words, child, but know not what they signify." Adams peered down at the paper as if he might see the thing that eluded him.

"'This state' *cannot* mean Kentucky, sir. Kentucky never passed such a law. But *Virginia* did! Virginia passed the one Jefferson wrote in 1785, An Act for Establishing Religious Freedom. It is him, sir. I'd swear to it. Jefferson is the author of this foul document. He should be impeached!"

Johnny thought the old man would pump his hand and call for his cabinet. But Adams merely sighed.

"He should be, I agree. But I won't do it."

What had Johnny failed to understand? Adams's own vice president threatened the Union, yet the president himself seemed resigned. Had he grown senile? Johnny was just about to demand an explanation when Adams asked, "How do you find Baltimore and Mr. Martin?"

"I like Baltimore very well," replied Johnny, confused. "Mr. Martin is most amiable."

"But?" Adams heard the reservation in Johnny's voice.

"But I fear I am become more housekeeper than student of law. After all the chores, there's no time for study. And Mr. Martin hardly accomplishes his own work, let alone helps me accomplish mine."

Johnny had not meant to speak ill of his kind benefactor, nor did he mean to gain anything by it. But after a silence of perhaps a minute, Adams said, "Come to Philadelphia, Johnny."

Johnny hesitated. "To do what, sir?"

"I could use eyes like yours here in Gomorrah."

"To spy for you, you mean?"

"Nay, nay. To—report."

"What's the difference?"

Adams laughed. "You are far too clever. I don't ask you to cross the enemy line, only to stand near it. So near that, when they dine, you shall see their tonsils."

They spoke for a few moments more about how their families fared. All the while, Johnny's heart beat furiously as he thought, *I believe that Mr. Adams has just asked me to come to Philadelphia to be his spy. Oh, but what shall I tell Mr. Martin?*

As if hearing his thoughts, Adams concluded, "By the way. Should anyone ask, tell him that you are to be my legal protégé. It shall be true enough. I may even find a way to ignore you slightly less than does Mr. Martin, though it is doubtful."

37

SNOW THREATENED IN A HEAVY GRAY SKY as Johnny made his way back to Baltimore. He had spent an anxious night and set out before dawn, his body humming. *The president wants me in Philadelphia,* he repeated to himself. *And I shall earn a salary.* The prospect filled him with pride. This was what he had wanted all along, he realized. Not to mentor beneath Wilson or another surrogate attorney, but to serve *the* attorney. But what about Marcia? She would soon return to Washington City. There must first be some understanding between them. As Johnny traveled South, his soul flew to wild heights and depths until he finally resolved on a course of action. Pray she accepted him!

The Martins and Miss Burnes were all at supper when he finally arrived at the house, filthy and exhausted. The twins ran to the door to greet him. "Oh, Johnny! How are you? We were worried!"

Johnny glanced warmly at Miss Burnes.

"Was it a good meeting?" she asked. Her voice was cool.

"Oh, yes. That is, I think so."

Upon seeing him enter, one of the servants discreetly whispered to him that a bath was being prepared for him in his chamber.

"Excuse me, ladies. Let us continue this discussion in an hour. I'm hardly presentable like this."

The ladies curtsied and moved back to finish their supper. Once in his chamber, Johnny stripped off his filthy clothing and sank gratefully into a tub of hot water. After dressing, he ran down the stairs to find the family waiting for him in the parlor.

"There you are!" cried Mr. Martin. "Do tell us more about your impressions of Philadelphia. I was there many years ago. I imagine it's changed a great deal."

"It is the loveliest city I've ever seen," Johnny admitted.

"You should tell Mr. Martin whom you *saw* in Philadelphia," said Marcia, eyes sparkling with cold knowledge.

"Oh? Who was that, lad?"

Johnny sent Marcia a questioning glance. What did she know? And how did she know it?

"The president, Mr. Martin. Mr. *Adams*," supplied Miss Burnes.

"Is it true, Johnny?" the twins exclaimed in unison.

Miss Burnes addressed Mr. Martin with a knowing air: "Surely you recall how Mr. Boylston came to you in the first place."

"Yes, of course," replied the absentminded attorney.

To Johnny, this was all most strange. How did Marcia come to know so much about him? Then he felt a chill as he realized: someone must have told her. He looked at her with silent entreaty.

She went on blithely, "Oh, but Mr. Boylston and Mr. Adams are nearly family. Aren't you, Johnny? In fact, your mother is a distant relation to Abigail Adams, is she not?"

Johnny blushed. It was true. His grandfather had been a cousin of Abigail's mother. Yet Johnny had never meant for anyone to know these facts.

The conversation turned to other topics, but Johnny was thoroughly unsettled. From time to time, he glanced at Miss Burnes, but she avoided his eyes and affected great gaiety with her friends.

Johnny finally said, "Well, there is one thing you don't know, Miss Burnes. I was going to wait to tell you, but perhaps it's only fair to reveal all now. The president has invited me to Philadelphia, and I have accepted. I leave in two days' time."

"Accepted?" Miss Burnes rose from her chair. The lively, if mean-spirited, conversation died as her eyes immediately filled with tears.

Mr. Martin frowned. "I take it this is no insult to me personally, to leave in such a precipitate manner?"

"Nay, nay. My time here has been most, er, illuminating, sir. And your hospitality has been—well, you have treated me like one of your own. But it was Mr. Adams's particular request."

"Oh, in that case, of course." Martin brightened. "A young, ambitious boy like yourself can't very well turn down such an offer."

Johnny was moved to add, "There are some points of constitutional law upon which I believe Mr. Adams may further illuminate me."

"I'd say so!" enthused Mr. Martin, all affability now. "Well, we shall certainly miss you, Johnny. Won't we, girls?"

His daughters nodded miserably.

Now, near nine in the evening, the candles burned low, and Johnny felt a sudden delayed exhaustion. He needed to speak with Marcia, who had curtsied and excused herself, saying she was tired and wished to retire, giving him no chance of asking her to reveal her source of information.

•　•　•

It was early the following morning, not yet six, when Johnny rose. The house was quiet as a church. Johnny dressed and made his way softly downstairs, where a servant was already about, lighting fires. The girl asked Johnny did he want coffee or breakfast, but Johnny said he would first take a walk and would have breakfast with the others when he returned.

At the last moment, he could not find his cap and so grabbed one of Mr. Martin's scarves off the peg by the door. He wrapped it about his head like an old Barbadian woman and stepped abroad, into the whiteness. He had hoped the gently falling snow would steady his nerves, but as he walked, he hardly noticed the landscape.

He had already resolved to ask for her hand in marriage. But he needed to know: Why did he love Marcia Burnes? He could not fathom it fully, and this disturbed him. After fifteen minutes of walking the empty streets, Johnny turned back. He had no argument for loving Marcia except for how she made him feel: like the luckiest young man on earth. Well, perhaps it was true what they said, that love was a mystery. He was cold, and he wished to warm himself with a mug of coffee. Then, he believed, he would warm the chill in Marcia.

She was sitting in the parlor when Johnny returned from his walk, nibbling at a biscuit. She had just taken a sip of tea when she saw him enter.

"Oh, hello," she said. "Are you off to Philadelphia, then?"

"Marcia." He frowned. "Finish your breakfast and let us speak in private."

"But you haven't even sat down yet." She glanced at the seat across from her.

"I have little appetite."

"Well, I have." She lifted her chin and took another bite of her biscuit. He waited with barely concealed impatience as she chewed it and washed it down with a sip of tea. Did she mean to torment him? He thought so. Finally, Miss Burnes dabbed her mouth daintily and, placing the napkin with excruciating precision by the side of her plate, rose and said, "You have my undivided attention."

"Excellent. Come with me, if you would." He led her into Mr. Martin's study and shut the door. Unlike his office, Mr. Martin's study was tidy and elegant.

Once in the room, Johnny moved to embrace her, saying, "Oh, I missed you!"

But Miss Burnes stepped away. "Indeed?" she smiled coldly at him. To be alone with a man behind a closed door was most irregular. Was this why Miss Burnes behaved in such a cold manner?

"But Marcia, what has happened? How did you learn of my visit with Adams, and why has it upset you so? It was no great secret. I would have told you. But I feel—"

"You feel what, Johnny?"

"I didn't mean to keep my connection to the Adamses a secret. But I wasn't sure if—"

"Oh, I care little for politics." She shrugged, taking his meaning. "Though Papa abhors the man."

"So how *did* you know about my visit?"

"I had a letter," she said.

"From whom, for God's sake?" Johnny was losing patience, for this was not what he had meant to discuss with her.

"From our mutual friend."

"Peter?" Johnny took a step back, astonished. "What concern could my visit to Adams be of his?"

"He believed it to be a concern to *me*. He cares about me and has no wish to see me hurt."

"Hurt?" Johnny cried. "That is the last thing I would ever wish for. Miss Burnes, you must know why I asked for a private meeting with you. It was not to interrogate you. Nay, it was for another purpose entirely."

Johnny soldiered on, though he felt that somehow the mood had soured.

"What purpose was that, pray?"

Suddenly Johnny knelt down upon one knee. He was too nervous to notice the look of horror that had crept onto Miss Burnes's face.

"Marcia," he began. "Marcia, dearest, would you make me the happiest man on earth and agree to marry me?"

"Marry you!" She laughed in his face. It was a shrill, unpleasant sound.

"Why do you laugh at me?" Confused, Johnny looked up at her. He saw nothing but scorn.

"That's rich, indeed, to make *me* an offer of marriage when you are already betrothed to another."

The room wavered around him. "Betrothed? What mean you?"

Miss Burnes did not reply.

Johnny sighed; he believed he understood. "Do you mean Miss Lee? She's a dear friend. I've not seen her in more than a year. We are not betrothed, nor is there any understanding between us."

"That is not what Peter says." She looked at him balefully.

"Peter is mistaken. Do you not wonder why he wishes to harm me in this way?"

"No. Peter and I have known each other since childhood. He does not wish to harm you but rather to protect me."

Johnny's heart pounded. He reminded himself to say nothing that he would later regret. Then, at the same moment, he became too deflated to go on. He could never explain why he'd given his knife to a slave, could never admit to Miss Burnes that this knife had killed Peter's brother. Instead, he said, "I love you, Marcia. I wish to marry you. I wanted, I'd *hoped* to have an understanding before I left for Philadelphia."

"If that is true, then you must write Miss Lee at once. You must let her know about me in no uncertain terms. I take it you haven't already?" She cast him a shrewd glance.

"No," he agreed, blushing once more. In this, Miss Burnes was correct. Johnny bowed. "I shall do so. At once."

On the way to his chamber, a servant girl approached him. "The post has come, sir, and there's a letter for you." She handed Johnny the letter.

Johnny entered his room, sat down upon his bed, and placed his head in his hands. He now felt only the misery of Marcia's rejection. It had all gone horribly wrong; he hardly knew how. With a pained sigh he tore the letter open.

December 17th, 1798

Dearest Johnny

I have not heard from you in many weeks and hope this letter finds you well. All my grandiose plans for a lady's journal were put aside when Mama took ill in October. It was very like Abigail's own dreadful illness, with a fever that would not abate and a lingering exhaustion. We feared every day that we would lose her, but the Lord was merciful and she has recovered. Papa jokes, now that it is safe to do so, that the dear Lord wasn't ready for the likes of Mama!

Ben does well. He is learning to read but it goes slowly. He could use a good tutor to help him. In this regard, he takes after his papa, I fear, rather than our clever mother. Well, but he is a sweet boy, though he likes to pretend that he is hard as Quincy's granite.

Speaking of which, I was obliged to leave Quincy when news of Mama's illness reached me, but I have since had several letters from your mother and also Lizzie, who are both well and send their love. The crops were excellent this year, and though Mr. Miller travels a great deal, Lizzie and your mother manage to keep life and limb together. What they lack in material wealth they more than make up for in love, friendship, and the birthing of babes.

Johnny set the letter down and closed his eyes. His mother, Lizzie, the children, Kate, and Quincy all returned to him with perfect clarity. He suddenly felt such a longing for them all that he actually groaned. Why had no one told him of Aunt Martha's illness? What else did he not know?

But there was more, and he read on:

And now I come to that difficult part of my letter which I have dreaded to put to pen but fear I must: I have news of which I flatter myself may be of some importance to you. If I am mistaken, I beg your forgiveness. That we are friends goes undisputed, and I hope we shall remain so.

I have had a proposal of marriage. Imagine that! He is not a bad fellow as men go, though I can't help but hear Eliot telling me he's not nearly handsome or poetic enough. His name is William Pearce. Remember when we argued over his visit to me? He is some sort of importer of dried goods—or is it exporter? To speak honestly, I forget! He had a wife previously, but she died. He himself is perhaps thirty-five. I have met him now several times, and he is in a good position to take a poor wife. My parents, however, have assured me that I may do whatever will bring me happiness.

Happiness? I daren't raise the topic of my happiness with you. I do not wish to be a burden to my family forever. But the subject of marriage, as it shall be irrevocable, I raise now or you must forever hold your peace, as the parsons like to say.

I do not ask you to take my feelings into account, only to give you an opportunity to consult your own.

Yours ever, Katherine Lee

Johnny set the letter in his lap and finally exhaled, for he had been holding his breath. When he reached up to his face, he realized it was wet with tears.

38

HE HAD PROMISED MARCIA HE WOULD WRITE Kate at once, and now, with her letter before him, he had no excuse for delay.

Dearest Kate

I received your letter of December 17th just now, having last night returned to Baltimore from Philadelphia.

That it surprised me goes without saying. Not that I thought it inconceivable that someone should wish to claim you as their own, but that, upon reflection, I have long staked an unwitting claim upon your affection I could have no certainty of reciprocating. This, I understand now, was unfair.

My own circumstances include those you already know: my essential impoverishment and uncertain prospects. I had hoped to see you in person this Christmas and to be with all my beloved family, but I was called to Philadelphia upon short notice, where I hope soon to be of some real use to one known to both of us. Upon this topic I daren't say more. If you see my mother, please tell her I shall write her soon with all the news.

Then, because Marcia had insisted, he added,

> All this aside, I esteem you too greatly to be false, and must confess that while I shall always love you as a dear friend and "cousin," I have grown close to another, a woman whose name I might have mentioned to you years ago, having first met her at Peter's home in Virginia.

He finished.

> Not for a moment do I wish to stand in your way of attaining that happiness you so fully deserve, and I hope that we shall remain the best of friends.
> Yours ever, Johnny Boylston

As he sat by the fire in his small chamber, Johnny read over his letter. He was not very satisfied. He had told the truth, though not scrupulously so. For one, he knew full well that upon several occasions he had behaved as if he would court Kate. That Christmas Eve kiss, for example. Then he had omitted the fact that his impoverished state had not prevented him from proposing to Miss Burnes.

No, he was not proud of himself.

Johnny finally descended the stairs, letter in hand. He walked to the post and returned to Mr. Martin's in time for dinner.

Marcia was waiting for him.

"Is the deed done?"

"It is," Johnny confirmed bleakly. "I had a letter from her as well. She told me she had an offer of marriage, and that she has accepted it."

"An offer of marriage?" Marcia beamed. "Excellent news!"

Johnny frowned. This exchange darkened an already very bad mood. He excused himself curtly and went to his chamber, where he undressed and lay down upon his bed. He shut his eyes and dozed.

Johnny dreamed he was a child, walking home from the shipyard. His father held his small hand in his rough one. His father was laughing happily. John Watkins worked so hard, and they had only a few trusted friends. Yet every day his father seemed happy. Johnny always thought this was very mysterious, and in the dream he asked, "Why do you laugh, Papa?"

His father placed a large hand upon Johnny's small curly head. "I have everything I could wish for. I have the whole world right here, in my hand."

The dream had been so real that Johnny believed his father was alive, even after a quiet knocking upon his door woke him. It was Miss Burnes. As Johnny sat up and rubbed the image from his eyes, she boldly entered and took him by the hand. Her hand was soft, so unlike his father's.

"Come with me," she said. Johnny followed, still heavy with sleep.

Marcia led him down the servants' stairs at the back of the hallway. It was dark, and she clung to the railing, stepping carefully. Finally, finding the bend in the staircase, she motioned for Johnny to sit beside her.

"I've been hard on you, Johnny," she began in a soft voice. "I do love you, but I must be careful. You must understand that my marriage involves not only me but my dear papa, and he isn't well. I fear he hasn't long to live."

"I'm very sorry to hear it."

"I had a letter from him and, since your own departure is imminent, I've decided to return to Washington for good."

"Excellent timing," Johnny muttered bitterly.

Suddenly, in the stairwell's darkness, he felt Marcia's hand upon his face, felt her warm breath on his neck.

"I mean only that we should delay. If you truly love me and still wish to marry me, that is."

"I do," he said at once, though not very happily.

"Me, and no one else."

"Yes."

"Let us delay. A year, no more. By then Papa shall either have recovered or—or not. You shall probably be a member of Congress by then."

"I shall be one year closer to that dream, perhaps."

"Well, you are closer to *this* dream than you think, my love." Marcia took his hand and placed it upon her breast. She untied her bodice and wordlessly beckoned Johnny to undo her stays. He obliged her.

Marcia moved onto his lap, took his hands, and placed them beneath her loose stays. Heavens! He felt the soft mounds of her breasts, felt her nipples harden under his touch. His lips sought her mouth in the darkness, and she kissed him and pressed her body closer to his. After a few minutes, she guided Johnny's hand beneath her petticoats, placing it on her inner thigh. How incredibly warm her flesh was!

Marcia moaned and urged Johnny on to more and deeper caresses. His reason vanished at her sounds. He reeled with something akin to drunkenness. But, oh, how pleasurable it was!

Approaching footsteps from upstairs froze them in midcaress. Johnny stood up, and Marcia nearly fell back down the stairs, stays exposed. She hastily pulled her chemise across her breasts.

The footsteps paused. Then they retreated down the hallway in the other direction.

"That was too close," Johnny said gravely.

"Do my stays, would you?" Marcia asked. He tied them quickly. "Do you believe me now?" she whispered as they parted.

When Johnny arrived in the parlor, Claire and Rosa glanced at him and then giggled.

"What's so amusing, pray?"

"Your shirt is buttoned all wrong. You skipped a hole."

Marcia rose proprietarily to adjust his buttons, but he backed away from her. At once, her eyes flashed surprise and hurt.

"Very well, do as you wish."

Johnny felt sorry that he had bruised her feelings, but they needed to remain correct before the Martins.

Mr. Martin, engrossed in his paper, missed this exchange. Now he looked up and spoke: "You weren't at the office this morning, lad. Shall you come this afternoon?"

"No, sir. I apologize. I had letters to write, and then there is packing to do. You know I leave tomorrow?"

"Tomorrow?" Mr. Martin cried. "Certainly not. But, well, *did* I know this?" He looked beseechingly at his daughters.

"Papa," Rosa objected. "Johnny told you of his intentions two days ago."

"Indeed. But how quickly the time passes!"

"Oh!" cried Rosa suddenly. "Both of you gone at once? It won't do! How dull our lives shall be!"

"Yes," agreed Claire. "I know not how we lived before you came to us, Marcia. It's cruel to leave us. And Johnny flies the coop at the same time."

"I shan't be a stranger," Johnny muttered unconvincingly. "Philadelphia isn't so very far."

But the twins were glum. Never had they met a more intelligent, charming, or loveable boy. Indeed, Rosa had a mind to ask Miss Burnes whether they had an understanding. For if Marcia did not want him, well, she did! One of them, certainly, must have him.

Mr. Martin soon returned to his office, and Johnny spent the rest of that day writing letters, including one to his mother informing her of his move to Philadelphia. Abroad, it was windy; he could hear the wind's howling above the crackling embers.

The afternoon and night before his departure were long; Johnny thought the time would never pass. He was unable to sleep, and at one point nearly leapt out of bed to follow the post coach, thinking he would retrieve the letter he had sent to Kate. What if she did not truly love this Pearce or Putnam, whoever he was? It certainly did not sound like she was *very* in love with him. But then, he consoled himself, if Kate did not love the man, she would have no wish to marry him.

He fell asleep around four, and it was near nine in the morning when he finally made his appearance in the parlor and took his breakfast. Mr. Martin had already left for work, but the ladies were there. They had finished their breakfast and sat chatting over a final cup of coffee.

Seeing him, Miss Burnes glanced up briefly but took no special notice. She would be leaving later that day as well, and she gave the twins her full attention.

After he had breakfasted, Johnny called for the carriage and driver that Mr. Martin had agreed to lend him. Then he panicked to realize that he had not asked the attorney for a loan of cash. He would need it in order to pay for a night's lodgings and board.

Just then, Mr. Martin came noisily up the stairs. He was out of breath.

He approached Johnny and proffered eight silver dollars.

"Here are two pounds," he said, speaking in the language of the old currency. "You may pay it back when you're able. I'm glad one of us remembered. Why, you're near as absentminded as I, son, and not half my age!"

Johnny took the coins and bowed deeply.

"Thank you, sir. For everything." He put the money in his waistcoat pocket. "I think I must go before the roads become impassable."

Snow threatened. If it held off, Johnny would have a good chance of reaching Elkton before midnight. From there, setting off early, he could reach Philadelphia in time for dinner.

"Of course, of course. Off you go, son."

Just then, a servant descended the stairs with Johnny's trunk and another large sack containing the suit Marcia had insisted he buy.

Where was Miss Burnes, anyway? Would she not say good-bye? Suddenly a noise made him look up. There she was, at the top of the stairs, a goddess in blue satin with a black velvet ribbon beneath her breast, her dark hair in tight curls at the sides of her face, her green eyes grave but full of feeling.

Johnny was possessed of a sudden, wild hope that she would run down the stairs and fling herself into his arms. But she was composed, even stately as she descended the stairs. In the hall, she faced him squarely.

"Do write." She curtsied.

"Of course." Johnny bowed.

•   •   •

The wind blew fiercely, and the air had turned cold. He worried that they would not reach Elkton that night. As the coachman drove him silently northward, Johnny tried to understand what Marcia felt. Did she think the less of him for not consummating what they had begun on the servants' stairs? Was she angry with him for leaving her? When would he see her again? She had said she would accept his proposal in a year's time, but a great deal could happen in a year, Johnny knew.

Several hours later, their carriage finally pulled up to the Indian Queen Tavern, where they would stop the night. The carriage bumped to a halt before the rambling wood structure, and the coachman blew his horn. A stable boy came running out to greet them.

Johnny's mind had been taken up with unhappy thoughts about women, and his mood was low. But then he reminded himself, *I'm heading to Philadelphia to spy for the president of the United States.* Bolstered by such a thought, he descended, stomped the snow off himself, and entered the tavern, where he spent a restless night in a cold room with a stranger, for all the beds were full.

39

December 25, 1798

JOHNNY HEARD A CHURCH BELL STRIKE NINE. With a start, he realized he was meant to be at the President's House at that very moment. He rose, splashed some cold water upon his face, threw on his clothing, and sped down the stairs, where he very nearly knocked Mr. Thomas Jefferson over the railing.

Johnny shot one arm out to steady Jefferson, who had been mounting the stairs as he descended. "Oh, my sincere apologies!"

Jefferson glanced at the boy with a small gleam of recognition. But he said only, "Take care you don't break your own legs as well as mine, son."

"Yes, sir!" Johnny blushed, grabbed his cap from the hook, and ran out the door.

The encounter left him in a state of confusion. Was this gentle-mannered man who quipped about taking care not to break his legs the same as that pernicious author of the Kentucky Resolutions? And stayed he, too, at the Francis Hotel?

At the door to the President's House, Adams greeted Johnny cheerfully. "How are you, son? How was your journey?"

"Unremarkable, sir. But you'll never guess whom I nearly toppled over the stairs at my hotel just now."

"Mr. Jefferson," Adams said without hesitation. "So the viper returns to the pit. Took his time about it! And they say *I* stay away too long."

"How'd you know, sir?"

Adams shrugged. "He stays there when he's in town. I suppose he was very charming?"

"Oh, but he was, sir! He seems most affable."

"*Seems* indeed. Well, come. Let me show you about."

Mr. Adams led Johnny into the reception room that Washington had built at the back of the main floor. The Levee Room, as Adams called it, had three tall windows decorated in crimson damask. Johnny could well imagine the old general standing erect at the end of it, in his black velvet suit, waiting to greet his many callers.

There were several smaller reception rooms as well, everything appointed with the finest carpets, wallpaper, lamps, and silver. Johnny saw several servants scurry past, but otherwise the house was quiet.

"The library is just here—oh, but you know that already! If you've not yet been, you must go to Franklin's library around the block. It will astonish and perhaps devour you. Take care! But say, Johnny,"—the president abruptly ceased their tour—"I have plans to take a sleigh ride with my nephew today. Would you join us?"

At once, Johnny recalled that it was Christmas Day. In the tumult of his travels, he had entirely forgotten.

"I should love to join you," he replied.

"Then off you go. You'll need a warm scarf and mitts."

•   •   •

The day was clear, cold, and bright. Upon the fields, a foot of recently fallen snow lent Philadelphia a beautiful purity. Johnny was surprised to discover that Adams's nephew, Mr. Shaw, was the same Mr. Shaw who had sat with him and Peter Fray on their first morning at Harvard.

"Well, well!" Adams was delighted to learn of their previous acquaintance. "You must be thick as thieves."

"We hardly knew each other, Uncle," replied Shaw.

"Ah, well," Adams pronounced sadly.

Johnny thought Mr. Shaw was as charmless as ever. Indeed, after this exchange he had little conversation to offer and was soon asleep. They rode in silence over Gray's Ferry and around by Hamilton's Woodlands.

The sleigh sped away from the ferry and headed north before circling back to the city. Out of the silence, Mr. Adams said, "You know, Johnny, you yourself might well be president someday. What do you think of that prospect?"

At this moment, Mr. Shaw woke. Hearing his uncle's words, clearly not addressed to him, he frowned.

"I like it exceedingly well." Johnny grinned. Then he pretended to take Mr. Adams seriously. "Yes, indeed. I even know what my first order of business will be."

"Oh? What is that?" Mr. Adams repositioned himself in the sleigh, the better to enjoy the promised conversation.

"Free the slaves."

"Aha. And shall such a decree be legal by the writs of the Constitution?"

"I would have it no other way." Johnny could not contain a note of pride in his voice.

"How could it be?"

"Wartime decree. I suppose I shall first have to start a war and then declare the slaves necessary to the war effort."

Adams turned to look at the young man whose blue eyes shone in the darkening winter light. "I think I'll appoint you secretary of war. I've been having trouble with mine lately. What say you?"

Mr. Adams sounded amused, but his eyes looked at Johnny unsmilingly.

"I believe I need to be thirty-five years of age, sir. As I am but twenty, perhaps you could hold on to power another—sixteen years."

"God forbid!"

Adams slapped his thigh and the two settled back in the sleigh, chuckling. Mr. Shaw frowned, finding nothing amusing about the exchange.

• • •

They were now into the new year, and Johnny felt obliged to do the work he had been brought to Philadelphia to do: stand so close to the enemy that he could see their tonsils.

Each day, before heading over to the President's House, Johnny walked past the private residences of Adams's cabinet members McHenry, Pickering, and Wolcott. He rode out to Germantown, where Pickering retained an office, and to the State House on the corner of Sixth and Arch. He pressed his face to the window glass or pressed his ear to the crack beneath their front doors. Spying duly accomplished, he would head back to his hotel, stopping first at the library to read the day's papers.

After several weeks, Johnny had to admit that not only had he not found anything revealing about these men, but that what he had found made him sympathetic toward them. One had too many children to care for; another had recently lost his wife. A third seemed to have an unrelenting pain in his knee.

Johnny concluded that either one could not, in fact, "see into the hearts of men," or he was woefully inept at it. Too ashamed to face the old man, he wrote him a letter, which he delivered to Bartlett, the butler.

Dear Sir

You may wish to burn this letter at once and save yourself the time it takes to read. I must conclude that I lack that talent of reading men and fear I have come to Philadelphia on false pretenses. Here is what I learned in these past two weeks, for what little it's worth:

P. lives in a very plain house on Arch Street just off Sixth. He worships at the old Presbyterian Church, at the corner of Arch and 3rd. I espied five children at supper. I have also observed his comings and goings at the State House and at his office in Germantown. He has regular habits and usually goes to the City Tavern at around noon, where he eats a slice of ham with pickle on a thick slice of bread. He washes this all down with a single mug of cider. He still grieves for a son, who died suddenly in May. His grief appears very great.

I have seen no letter come or go addressed to B. (for Bonaparte, or Alexander Hamilton). Did you know that he was orphaned as a child and is also a passionate abolitionist? And does not that knowledge at least sweeten his poisonous breath somewhat?

As for the Scotsman, he lives in a plain house on the edge of town. He has a wife and one son. I have seen no letters to or from B. Did you know the Scotsman, too, is a confirmed abolitionist?

But this information cannot be helpful to you in pursuit of tonsils.

I must conclude, sir, that between the daily domestic life of these men and their destructive intent lies, for me at least, an unbreachable gulf. I must conclude that men's evil resides not in their persons but in the ideas they express and act upon. Alas, it seems the more I know a man, the more I pity him.

Apart from its vexing praise of Alexander Hamilton, Mr. Adams found this earnest letter from Johnny rather touching. The boy had many gifts, but clearly spying was not one of them. Taking up his pen, Adams replied,

> My dear boy
> Do not worry overly about your skills, or lack thereof, in this regard. I have others more adept. No, you are right: Read the papers, glean from them what you can. Reply when you are moved to. And you may as well keep an eye on the redhead, since you are neighbors. As for the rest, finish your studies so that I may have the pleasure of telling your mama that you have passed the bar.

Johnny felt a fresh resolve to scour every printed word and to reply in print where he saw he could be of help to Mr. Adams. He was relieved that his spying days were over, for pity was inimical to action.

Johnny had just finished breakfast and was preparing to head to the library when one of the servants handed him a letter. It was from Miss Burnes.

> January 14th, 1799
> Dear Johnny
> It is lonely here. Gone are the affable Martin sisters and the gay amusements of Baltimore. I shall dine in George Town tonight, however, and already I have received two invitations for sleigh rides. I have

purchased a pianoforte to while away the hours, but I play it very inexpertly. The President's House goes up slowly, as does the Capitol. I confess I can't imagine the day when it shall all be finished and Pennsylvania Avenue more than a marshy (frozen, now) swamp. The sun declines early; the day has hardly risen then a veil descends upon it. Papa, though sick and in need of warmth, adheres to his old ways and is quite frugal with the firewood. I find I shiver most of the day.

Poor girl! Johnny folded the letter and, after finishing breakfast, took up his pen:

Dearest One

Your letter of the 14th unsettled me for its despondent tone. I fear you do poorly without your Johnny. The roads are impassable at the moment, but I should like to visit as soon as is practicable, if you allow it. I long to see you . . .

Johnny felt better after posting his letter. Had the roads been clear, he would have set off that same day. But the temperatures had plummeted precipitously, and the roads were slick as a skating pond. Indeed, when Johnny later entered the President's House, he found Adams in his office behind his desk, jabbing viciously at his ink bottle.

"Blasted ink has frozen," he said. Smoke issued from his mouth as he spoke the words. "Briesler!" Adams called. "I can't even write a letter to my own wife! For all I know she has frozen to death!" Briesler, Adams's steward, was a man of middle age and deferent manner. He entered at once, but there was little he could do except to place the ink bottle by the fire.

Unable to write, Mr. Adams was fractious. "Well, son, give me a summary of the day's news. At least I'll have accomplished *that* much." This Johnny dutifully did. Then, after thanking him, Mr. Adams announced, "I shall take a nap. There is nothing else to be done. Briesler!"

Johnny bade the president good-bye, feeling useless. He weaved his way through the long crowded market and then watched the boats in the harbor. There, shipwrights sawed and fishmongers bartered from warehouse doors. Horses and oxen came and went, pulling carts that groaned with goods of every kind. And every living thing gave off a wispy, atmospheric smoke.

Johnny dared not remain long, for his feet had begun to freeze. On his way back to the hotel, he stopped at City Tavern to warm himself with a hot cider. While he sipped his cider, he attuned his ears to the other customers. Several rough-looking harbor workers were speaking of the threat of an imminent military coup on the part of "Bonaparte."

"He's just waitin' for the signal."

"Signal from who?"

"Washington, 'course."

"To do what?"

"Invade us and shoot Mr. Adams. Next morning we'll all have to bow down to 'im, like a regular king."

"G'won!"

"You don't think so? Why, he's already general for the sittin' army."

"Standing army, you eedjit."

"Not standing, neither—*temporary* army," another, slightly less inebriated man corrected them. "And Washington's the *commander in chief* while Hamilton's only c'mander gen'ral, and Washington won't be shootin' 'is old friend Adams!"

"Don't you recall, Bonaparte already took up an army against the whiskey fellows out west? Well, 'e'd do it again at the drop of a hat!"

As Johnny walked back to his lodgings, he thought over the conversation he had heard at the tavern. He had read about the Whiskey Tax, which Hamilton had instituted as Washington's treasury secretary in 1791. In 1794, a rebellion against the tax in western Pennsylvania had culminated in an armed insurrection, in which several men were killed. Washington amassed an army of nearly 13,000 men to put down the insurrection, a step for which many blamed Hamilton.

Johnny was moved by these men's fears. They were rough, uneducated men, but hardworking and honest. They had wives and children. Why should they live in fear for their families because their leaders could not work together?

Back in his lodgings, Johnny sat down at his desk and wrote for several hours. When he was finished, an essay was before him. He called it "Reflections Upon the New Year 1799: Ending or Beginning?"

> *So very much has happened "in the course of human events" since that fairest of documents came into being. A beleaguered people vanquished a great foe. Their new nation created a great Constitution. Now, stirrings of a dark and unhealthy nature have begun to rattle the peace like a snake beneath autumn leaves. One does not know whether to count one's blessings or batten the doors for yet another assault of man against men. Will 1800 mark the end of strife, or the end of honor?*

The article went on to discuss the challenges that faced the young nation, particularly the need to agree upon an interpretation of the Constitution. He ended it with something for Adams as well, urging dissenters to support "the heroic efforts of our government" in its spirit of unity, if not in its particulars. By "particulars," Johnny meant, disingenuously, the abhorred Alien and Sedition Acts.

When he was finished, Johnny felt satisfied. He gave the article to a servant at the hotel to deliver for him. It was addressed to Joseph Dennie, Editor, *Gazette of the United States*, 119 Chestnut Street.

Several days later, as he was sitting in Adams's study, prepared to read the day's Republican papers while Adams perused the *Gazette*, Adams suddenly frowned. "Well, would you look at this! Some idealistic fellow calls for peace abroad and peace at home. Does the daft man think I've got a magic wand? Is he from Mars and knows not how our citizens despise one another?"

Johnny, having gleaned that the article was in fact his own, was slowly turning an even whiter shade of white.

"Ah, well," Adams continued. "I suppose I can't fault a young fellow his idealism. I was once youthful and idealistic myself. But that was a long time ago."

Johnny mustered the courage to ask, "How do you like the last line, sir? The one about supporting the government?"

Adams stuck his nose back into the fold of the paper.

". . . even if not in its particulars. Hmm." All at once, Adams looked suspiciously at Johnny. "How know you this article? I only just received it."

Johnny paused. "It's mine, sir. I hope it meets with your approval. In some ways, if not in all."

"Nay, good work, good work, er," he said and looked down at the pen name, *Concordia Discors*. Adams had not meant to ridicule Johnny, and yet he was not satisfied, either. "But you *are* gentle, John. I fear that if you are to penetrate the tough American skull these days, you must use a verbal sledgehammer."

Then Adams seemed to remember something. He reached across his desk and proffered an ornately engraved invitation. "Here. I meant for you to have this."

Johnny took the invitation and read:

The Honor of President John Adams's Company is requested on February 22 at Oeller's Hotel . . . At a Birth-night Ball for George Washington

"But this invitation is addressed to you, sir."

"Yes, well, you may attend in my stead. I have no wish to go. I shall write back, civilly yet succinctly, that I decline the invitation."

Johnny set the invitation down on Adams's desk.

"Why decline it? Do you have a previous engagement?"

"No."

"Then do not decline it, sir."

"Why not?"

"You'll look peevish, and forgive me for asking, but why should you be so?"

"Why, indeed!" Adams slammed his hand down on his desk, making a dish of tea rattle precariously. "Why do I not get a ball on *my* birth night? I did not receive so much as an ice cream float. Why is *he* the one to get a birth-night ball?"

"Perhaps because he's—taller."

Adams frowned and cleared his throat. Then he suddenly burst out laughing. "Ha ha. Because he's taller! That's excellent!"

40

JOHNNY ATTENDED THE BIRTH-NIGHT BALL ALONG with Mr. Adams, although they arrived in separate carriages. Johnny used his small salary to buy a new waistcoat. It was bright red and went well with the suit Miss Burnes had prevailed upon him to buy in Baltimore. His overcoat, alas, bought in his second year at college, was in a sad state, but he could not afford another. Johnny hoped the weather would allow him to carry it across his arm.

On his way out that evening, he passed a looking glass nailed to the wall of the hotel foyer. The person in the mirror looked back at him dubiously. He was a hale young white man with slickly pomaded hair and an aristocratic bearing. Only a pale band of skin where Madame Pringle's pinky ring had been reminded Johnny of the kinky-haired child he once had been.

•   •   •

Oeller's Hotel, which stood in contrast to the absurd folly that was Rickett's Circus beside it, was the grandest building Johnny had ever seen. One entered into a hall that he estimated to be about 3,600 square feet, with a handsome music gallery at one end. It was papered after the French taste, with Pantheon figures in compartments, festoons, pillars, and groups of antique drawings. Many guests had already arrived and now milled about holding glasses of punch. Looking closer at his own beverage, Johnny noticed something floating in it. It appeared to be a translucent rock.

"It's ice," whispered a girl standing next to him. She was a pretty, slender person of perhaps sixteen or seventeen dressed in a simple white silk gown with a high waist. This new fashion, with its references to ancient Greece, appealed to Johnny. "Oeller's keeps a forty-foot block of frozen Delaware River in a store room. They sell chunks off to the neighbors and make a tidy profit, I should say."

Somehow, the idea of the Delaware River floating in his glass made Johnny even less inclined to drink it than he already had been. At around nine, the dancing began at Rickett's, and Johnny was dragged there by the girl who had told him about the ice, accompanied by several of her friends. The girl laughed gaily as she took his arm. "You appear to be the only man here under the age of two hundred."

"I'm afraid that means you shall be obliged to dance with all of us," said one of her friends, giggling.

Six months of dance lessons in Bridgetown, to which he had vigorously objected when he was a lad of ten, now saved him from abject humiliation.

At around eleven, from across the crowded dance floor, Johnny saw Mr. Jefferson. The vice president nodded to him in recognition. When the dancing had finished at around midnight, Johnny returned to Oeller's for a final toast to Washington. He was about to take his leave from the young ladies when a handsome man of perhaps sixty, tall and distinguished in bearing, approached him. The man's face was in keeping with the rest of him: aristocratic, with discerning blue eyes and a guarded expression that was not unkind.

This man came within two feet of Johnny and then extended his hand. "You must be John Watkins. You look a great deal like your father. I'm John Langdon. Senator Langdon, now."

"*Colonel* Langdon? *Sir!*" Johnny bowed deeply. He felt his knees tremble. "I never imagined I would meet you. You have been a figment of my imagination for so long. But how did you know I was here?"

"I didn't. But your mother wrote not long ago to tell me you were in Philadelphia. The moment I laid eyes upon you, I knew you were Watkins's son."

Johnny cringed at the mention of his real name. He moved closer to the man, "But you know, sir, we go by the name Boylston, now. Mama thought it prudent."

Langdon touched his forehead in self-reprobation. "Of course. Forgive me, Mr. Boylston." After a moment Langdon went on, "I hear you study law with . . . our friend."

"I do."

"But we can hardly talk freely here. I should very much like to see you." The senator added, "If you wish it."

"Oh, but I do!"

Langdon smiled, and Johnny had a glimpse of the dashing young rebel he must have been.

"I have stories of your father, ones even your mother does not know. If you'd be so kind as to meet me at my lodgings—are you free tomorrow?"

Johnny nodded. For John Langdon, he would be free at any hour.

"Excellent." Langdon gave Johnny the name of the boardinghouse. "Until then. I take my leave. I find all this"—he waved his hand—"more exhausting than a battlefield."

"I suspect it *is* a battlefield, sir."

"You learn quickly. Like your father." But Langdon was no longer smiling. He bowed. "Till tomorrow, then."

"Till tomorrow, sir." Johnny bowed deeply.

The next morning, as Johnny perused the day's newspapers in the president's library, Mr. Adams popped his face in the door. It was the quiet hour before the masses began to arrive. Thus far, Johnny had seen members of the Senate visit, singly and in large and small groups. There had been Indian chiefs, with whom Adams had dined, judges, lawyers, and the inevitable herd of job seekers. For the president, hours of peace and quiet were few and far between.

"Do I disturb?" asked Adams.

"Nay. Come in, sir."

"Oh, don't bother to stand, lad. I come merely to hear your impressions of the circus. Whom did you meet?"

"Hardly anyone, sir. The ladies kept me busy dancing."

"Ha—no surprise there."

"But I did happen to meet one whom I have greatly esteemed since I was very small."

"Who was that?" Adams said warily, jealous of anyone Johnny might esteem more than himself.

"Colonel Langdon, sir. Senator Langdon, now."

"Oh, my dear friend. How remiss of me not to have introduced you."

"That's all right, sir. I shall see him in an hour's time."

"Indeed. Well, send him my best."

Johnny soon found himself sitting across from Senator Langdon in his well-appointed study at a boardinghouse on North Fourth Street.

Langdon was curious to hear about John Watkins's life after fleeing America, and Johnny told him that, at the time of his death, his father owned a large shipyard with near fifty shipwrights in his employ.

"I don't doubt it," Langdon said. "He was the hardest worker I ever knew, and the most able." Langdon looked up into Johnny's eyes. "You have his eyes, you know."

Langdon was interested to know how Johnny's mother fared and how Johnny had enjoyed "the college at Cambridge." But Johnny, while endeavoring not to seem impatient, longed to hear the promised stories.

Langdon soon obliged him. He told Johnny how his father had risked his life to smuggle arms to Washington, and how he helped a young slave couple escape their masters, though he himself was yet enslaved. Then he told Johnny the story of John's meeting his infant son for the first time:

"Toward the end of the war, your uncle fared poorly. His house was confiscated, and he quickly sold all his property, including your father. Your mother begged me to help her find him. The moment I discovered his whereabouts, I sent for your mother. I arranged for Watkins to visit her and her infant son at their lodgings, stealing him away in the dead of night. But, though I was in great distress lest we be caught, he bade me wait while he put on a clean shirt. He had hidden it beneath his pallet for this unlikely moment. But he had not laid eyes upon your mother in more than a year and would not meet her in filthy rags. All the way to the tavern, he kept repeating, 'Is she really come? Is the child truly with her?' He did not cease his querying until your mother stood before him.

"Johnny, I shall ne'er forget how she stared at him as if she saw a ghost. And he nearly was, too. Worn down to nothing from grief and worry, the bones of one hand crushed—"

"Yes, I knew his hand had been broken, but Papa never told me the story. I assumed it happened at the shipyard."

"No. It was worse than a shipyard accident, I'm afraid. His master did that to him. I could tell he was in terrible pain that night, but the sight of you took all that away.

"He remained several hours, and when it was time to return to his prison, he was meek as a lamb. On the way back to his master's, he asked me, 'Did you see him, colonel? He's very fair, is he not?' I agreed that you were quite fair, if not white. 'He shall have a chance, then, thank God!'"

Suddenly, Johnny could no longer sit. He stood up as tears spilled from the rims of his eyes.

"But why could you not manage to free him then?" It came out as a reproach, which Johnny, in his anger, had partly meant it to be.

Langdon glanced at Johnny and understood. "Oh, you poor child. Yes, we were too slow. We had not the means just then. It took a great deal of work. But we did succeed—eventually. But never forget: those hours he spent with you and your mother were among the happiest of his life."

"Happy to learn that I would not suffer *his* fate," Johnny replied bitterly as he walked toward the door.

Langdon said, "I fear I've given you pain, rather than pleasure, as was my intention."

"You have given me both, and for both am I grateful. I hope we shall meet again soon. I am forever in your debt for the love you showed my parents."

Then, before he burst into tears, Johnny bowed and left.

Those angry tears were faithful companions as he walked back to Francis's hotel. It had begun to snow, and Philadelphia looked almost holy in its white mantle.

Back at the hotel, Johnny spent several feverish hours writing an article he knew he would never publish. He called it "My Life as a White Man." The longer he wrote, the angrier he grew. Having heard Langdon's story, Johnny regretted that his family had shielded him so well from the ugly truth of his father's life. Had he known, Johnny might never have left Barbados, never renounced the legacy his father had worked so hard to build. But perhaps that was the point. His father had no wish for Johnny to stay in Barbados out of a sense of guilt.

When he finished his essay, Johnny's anger was spent. He reminded himself that, above all, his parents had wanted him to be happy. But was he happy now? Johnny didn't dare to answer. He went to bed, snuffed out his candle, and slept fitfully.

The following morning, he wrote a letter to his mother about meeting Senator Langdon.

He is as great, kind, and noble a man as ever I met, Mama. Such stories as he told me of Papa I shall never forget. Nothing unworthy, I promise you. Quite the opposite. He sends his deepest regards and hopes to have the pleasure of seeing you again in this life.

That letter signed and sealed, Johnny was just on his way to the post when he came upon the postman, who took this letter in exchange for one from Miss Burnes. Eager to hear the news, Johnny raced back to his lodgings, slipping more than once on the ice that had frozen beneath the powdery snow. Heedless, he mounted the stairs two at a time. He was nearly at the top when, once again, he smashed directly into Mr. Jefferson. This time, the vice president was with his manservant.

"Easy there, my good man," said Jefferson. "Surely that letter is not worth killing us all for?"

"No, sir."

Jefferson smiled and patted Johnny on the arm before continuing down the steps. He noticed the powdery snow on Johnny's sleeve.

"But say, does it snow? Perhaps I should take my hat."

"Nay, sir," Johnny said, abashed. "I slipped and fell. The roads are icy."

"Worse and worse!" Jefferson laughed openly now. Then he looked at the letter Johnny gripped in one hand. "Well, she's a lucky woman to have a suitor so ardent that he is willing to break the neck of the vice president."

"No, sir—Mr. Jefferson."

All at once Jefferson stopped his descent and turned to face Johnny. His pale-blue eyes rested steadily on Johnny's face. "Have we not met before? I feel I've seen you somewhere or other."

"John Boylston, sir." He bowed deeply. "We met four years ago, at Moorcock Manor. I was with my roommate from Harvard, Mr. Fray. It was Christmas, sir."

"Ah, yes! I remember." Mr. Jefferson closed his eyes as if the memory were vivid. "We discussed Mr. Adams's crops, if I recall."

Johnny was astonished that the man remembered such an insignificant moment, so many years in the past.

"And what brings you to Gomorrah, Mr. Boylston?"

"I'm a student of law. I hope to pass the bar next fall."

"You have my condolences; now go read your letter."

Johnny nodded dumbly and continued his way up the stairs. He might have stopped to wonder at the easy banter he had exchanged with his former hero. But at that moment he sorely wished to know Miss Burnes's news.

Reaching his chamber, he tore the letter open at once. He skipped over accounts of parties and sleigh rides and came to the heart of the matter:

> Papa is not well. I fear he shall not survive till summer. I have told him about you. He wishes to meet you before he leaves this earth. Can you not find a way to come? I long to see you.
>
> Your everlasting,
> Marcia

Within moments, Johnny raced back to the President's House, this time checking to assure himself that Jefferson was not upon the stairs.

Mr. Adams was not happy to hear that he would need to do without Johnny for several weeks.

"I shan't be gone more than a fortnight."

"I hope not. We're in a bad way, Johnny." The president shook his head, ready to enumerate all the alarming turns the country had recently taken. Election fever had risen, and throughout the streets, cries of "King Adams!" and "Off with their heads!" could already be heard.

"My fiancée's father is unwell, sir."

"Fiancée? Did I know you were engaged?"

"Please don't tell Mama. I've told no one as yet. The engagement is—unusual."

"And who is this lucky young woman?"

Johnny told him.

"Miss Burnes, famed beauty and daughter of the obstinate David Burnes?"

"The same."

"Well!" Adams looked impressed, if not entirely surprised. "I sincerely hope he recovers. But if he does not"—Adams shrugged—"fathers are expendable. Ask my own children if you don't believe me."

41

FOUR DAYS LATER, JOHNNY ARRIVED IN THE new City of Washington. For the trip, Adams had offered one of his carriages, which, Johnny had to admit, was far more comfortable than the cramped stagecoach. The driver wished to skirt the city and go directly to George Town, but Johnny instructed him to enter the city from the north, which turned out to be a mistake.

The road from Baltimore to the new city had been dismal: a dark forest punctuated by the occasional mean, windowless hut. But when at last they reached Jenkins Hill, Johnny bade the driver to stop a moment. Just below stood the partially finished Capitol, standing as poignantly as a Greek ruin. Below it, Johnny counted seven or eight boardinghouses, a tailor shop, a shoemaker, a grocer's, and an oyster house. And that was all.

Below the hill was but a vast swamp. From it, stumps of trees protruded everywhere. Johnny knew not how the horses would manage, or how the wheels would avoid sinking into the mire.

The carriage descended slowly and carefully. Then the coachman, seeing higher ground on F Street, turned up this route to travel toward George Town. Everywhere Johnny looked, he saw timber and signs of construction but not a single soul.

How lonely, bleak, and isolated it was! His Excellency must have been mad to insist upon this place as the nation's new capital. As they turned onto Pennsylvania Avenue, Johnny could hear the suck of the horses' hooves and the coachman's angry mutterings. To his left, the forested land had been cleared, and an imposing white stucco house stood in splendid isolation. This was the new President's House.

Finally, beneath a canopy of leafless trees, a small derelict cottage appeared. Wooden outbuildings stood on either side of it, and a newer log cabin was perched close to the river. From this cottage Miss Burnes came flying out to greet him.

"Johnny!" she cried. "Oh, Johnny! I thought you'd never come."

"Oh, my love, I'm here!"

She ran into his arms. He held her close and felt her heart pound against his breast.

"Well, do come in. Billy!" Marcia called to an old Negro who stood by the stable door. "Take the horses and bring the driver around back."

The old man nodded. Billy limped toward the carriage to untie the horses. He must have been seventy if a day; his walnut skin had a waxen pallor, and gray stubble dotted his wrinkled chin. His shoes, held together by twine, were rotted through in several places, and his bare toes stuck through, exposing them to the cold.

Johnny frowned, but Marcia, overcome by joy at seeing him, did not notice.

"Come. Papa has been waiting anxiously."

She led Johnny by the hand through the low front door that opened directly onto a single great room. Within, it was cozy and warm. At the far end of the room a fire raged in a rubble stone fireplace. But the ceilings were low, and the small windows gave off little light. Several worn Turkey carpets lay upon a bare wood plank floor, and overall there was such a sense of frugality as seemed at odds with owning a fortune of $30,000. Had he not known better, Johnny would have said father and daughter lived on the edge of poverty.

The room was smoky, too. Not from the fire, which pulled a good draft, but from Mr. Burnes's pipe. It was fragrant and not displeasing.

Yet the overall effect was a dark, smoky, close room, and only the splendid view of the river beyond the windows saved it from feeling airless. Johnny could not imagine remaining there a day, much less the week he had promised.

An old man sat in a wing chair by the fire, a clay pipe in one hand. His face was pale, but there were two spots of color on his high cheekbones, and he retained a thick head of white hair. A large plaid blanket obscured his body. Johnny approached apprehensively.

"Go on, Johnny," Marcia encouraged him. "He won't bite. I'll fetch us some tea."

Johnny returned Marcia's smile and soldiered forth until he stood squarely before the sick man. They were alone; there wasn't a servant in sight.

"Come here, boy. Let me have a look at you."

The man nodded for Johnny to approach. When he had done so, he saw that Marcia's father was not so old as he at first appeared. He was a handsome man. The skin of his face, though pale and yellowish, was smooth. His blue eyes shone brightly, shrewdly. Now they combed Johnny like a harrow, and, overall, Johnny had the impression of someone about forty years of age with a formidable will.

"Sit down." Mr. Burnes nodded to a ladder-back chair. "Tell me about yourself. Ye know the president, I hear. Well, he's none so bad as the first, I suppose."

Johnny was taken aback. Was this fellow the same man who had fought during the Revolution and later negotiated land with George Washington?

"Why smilest thou, boy? Is Washington a friend, too?"

"Nay, I've never met him, sir."

"Very tall he is. And what airs and graces! Fancies himself a nobleman, I expect." Though Mr. Burnes's family had been in America for three generations, Marcia's father still rolled his *r*'s so luxuriantly that Johnny hardly understood him. "Well, but ye know, if it weren't for his

Martha—Mrs. Custis, as was—he'd 'ave been nobody of consequence. She came to him with two hundred niggers, she did. All tied in a bow!"

Thankfully, Marcia turned up with the tea at that moment, and Johnny rose to grab the tea table from the corner of the room. He lowered its top, locking it in place. Marcia set the tray down upon the table and began to pour the tea from a china pot.

"I don't know how you like it, Johnny. Imagine that!" Marcia giggled.

"One lump, a little milk, please." Johnny preferred coffee, actually, but was not so ill-mannered as to say so. He was still reeling from the boldness with which Mr. Burnes had shared his obnoxious opinions.

They drank their tea in silence. Then, staring suspiciously over his hairy dark eyebrows, Mr. Burnes asked, "And how is it that ye know Mr. Adams?"

"Oh, my mother lived not far from his family in Braintree. Quincy, it is called now, when I was born."

"Your mother, you say?" the invalid asked shrewdly. "And what about your father?"

"My father is dead. He was a master shipwright. Learned his trade from Colonel Langdon. Senator Langdon, that is," Johnny could not resist adding. But his boast had the opposite effect of the one he intended.

"Langdon!" Mr. Burnes scowled. "Well, I suppose a shipwright's an honest trade. But don't you know it was nigger-loving Langdon who helped Washington's own favorite wench escape a few years back?"

So this was a true Republican, unvarnished by city airs, Johnny thought. He was prepared to give a heated reply when Marcia intervened. "Papa, don't excite yourself," she said. But an insult against Senator Langdon was beyond Johnny's endurance.

He stood up. "Sir," he began, ignoring the flash of fear in Marcia's eyes. "Colonel Langdon is a very great patriot, and my family owes him a vast debt."

Marcia placed a forestalling hand upon Johnny's arm. But it was a slave girl who saved the day when she banged through the front door carrying a basket of eggs. She stopped when she saw the scene: a tall, curly-haired boy standing defiantly before the sickly tyrant.

The girl curtsied and removed her shawl. Marcia turned to address the girl. "Ginny, would you bring these dishes into the kitchen?" she asked.

"Yes, miss."

"Well," said Johnny once the girl had left them, "I should like to go to my chamber to wash up. The trip was long and muddy."

"Your chamber?" Marcia laughed. "You stay not *here*."

"Oh, I thought—"

Johnny flushed red at the misunderstanding. He had assumed he would stay at the cottage. Marcia had not mentioned otherwise.

"We have booked you excellent quarters at Suter's in George Town. It's not a mile down the road, and I dare say you'll be far more comfortable there."

"Your suitor stays at Suter's, then," he remarked. Miss Burnes smiled, and Johnny sighed with relief. Another five minutes with the invalid, and they should probably have come to blows.

42

AS HE WAITED FOR HIS COACH, JOHNNY stopped to listen to the conversation that had begun within. He moved toward an open window, the better to hear it.

"If you're thinking of marrying this fellow, think again, Marcia."

"Oh, Papa. Let's not argue. Johnny Boylston is an excellent young man with great prospects."

"Is there an understanding between you?"

"No, no. He is honorable, I am telling you. He could have no chance of success with me unless he asked you first."

"Well, tell him not to bother."

"Papa!" Her voice grew exasperated. "I'm not discussing this now. Be grateful for once for your good fortune."

"Good fortune, you say!" Mr. Burnes seemed to consider his daughter's words. "Well, I suppose I shall be dead soon, and then you'll do what you fancy with all my money anyway. That's my good fortune."

Miss Burnes sighed. "I must bid him good-bye."

Johnny heard her quick footsteps as she left the room, and he hastened to mount the carriage.

Out of the view of her father, Marcia smiled brilliantly at Johnny, stood on her tiptoes, and kissed him. Johnny lingered upon her lips; their warmth seemed the only antidote to the bad taste left by Mr. Burnes.

"Don't be bothered by Papa. He's not as hard as he seems. I have a feeling he shall like you, for he likes a good fight." As the carriage moved off, Marcia pouted in mock sorrow and waved till Johnny was out of sight.

Liked a good fight? Johnny shook his head. Within two minutes of meeting Mr. Burnes, Johnny had felt that the sickly figure in the wing chair embodied everything small-minded and hateful he'd heard about the South. Had the great Washington not needed a place to set down a government, Johnny thought, Mr. Burnes would have remained the mean, stingy man he had been born, and not the smug recipient of a vast fortune.

The sun had set and the air had grown quite cool. When they had made their way down the bumpy lane to Suter's, Johnny was pleasantly surprised at George Town's quaint, orderly appearance. The village, situated upon a rising hill to the northwest of the President's House, had cobbled streets flanked by stately brick homes. They passed a busy wharf, several fine-looking shops, and two churches before arriving at Suter's Tavern. Yes, far preferable to that Cyclops's lair!

As Johnny descended the carriage and walked toward the tavern's welcoming facade, he wondered, *Was Marcia not mortified by her father's vulgar manner? Was her affection for him sincere?* But these thoughts eased when he was shown to his chamber. It was clean and comfortable, and looked out onto busy M Street and the canal below.

Marcia visited him there the following day. They strolled arm in arm through George Town, across M Street and down to the canal, where they walked along the water. Although the ground was muddy, there was a path by which they were able to keep their feet somewhat dry.

Marcia stopped suddenly and pointed to the ground. "Oh, look, Johnny!"

Johnny let go her hand and bent down: she had spotted a purple crocus. He cupped the flower in his hand and held it up to her.

"Almost as beautiful as you, Marcia Burnes."

Marcia grinned happily and took her suitor's arm. They continued on their walk, following the canal for near a mile before turning back.

Later, Johnny was obliged to dine with Mr. Burnes, but Marcia had scheduled an event following their dinner so that they needn't linger. They met two friends of Miss Burnes's, Miss Bron and Miss Scott, at the Bunch of Grapes. It was a rustic place where local workers and elite society were thrown together in a smoky room. Miss Scott was older, perhaps in her late twenties, and unmarried. She was a small person with bright-red hair. A fever had left her with a weak heart, and she lived with her parents. But she had a lively personality and found Johnny vastly amusing.

Miss Bron, from a wealthy Maryland family, seemed haughty at first. She bragged of her dinner with the Madisons and the recent party she attended at Notley Young's, home of the wealthiest family in Washington. Then Marcia said, "Johnny is a protégé of President Adams."

Miss Bron ceased her bragging; in fact, she ceased speaking altogether, so mortified was she. Johnny thought it was cruel of Marcia to put her friend in her place so baldly.

Miss Scott asked Johnny how long he planned to stay in Washington.

"Not long at all. I must make my way to Quincy after returning to Philadelphia. I've not seen my family in near two years."

"And—Kate?" Marcia whispered to him.

"I know not," Johnny replied, annoyed. He had not heard a word from Kate since their exchange of letters back in December.

He assumed she was married by now, settled in to housekeeping somewhere, though his mother's most recent letter made no mention of it. The subject put Johnny in a bad mood.

Heedless of Miss Bron and Miss Scott on the other side of their table, Johnny added, "Marcia, have I not made my feelings obvious? Can you believe me so shallow as to replicate them with another?"

Marcia's friends, sensing the sudden tension between the lovers, engaged themselves in a separate conversation to give them privacy. Then Marcia placed her hand upon Johnny's and smiled winningly.

"Johnny, I do but tease."

"Please don't."

"Very well."

They were silent for quite some time, wherein Johnny endeavored to recover his good humor. Finally, he mastered himself and said, "As I was saying, Miss Scott, I shall spend the summer at home, studying mainly. I plan to leave in several weeks' time. I wish to be prepared to take—to *pass*—the bar in September."

"The Philadelphia bar?" asked Miss Burnes.

"Yes. Why?" Johnny was puzzled. She knew his interests full well. Was this yet more parading of his excellent prospects before her suitorless friends?

"Well, do they have a bar of that kind here?"

"There is a Maryland bar, I suppose." Johnny frowned. His mood had not yet fully recovered, and more teasing from Miss Burnes would not be welcome. "Marcia, do not toy with me," he said.

"I don't. I'm perfectly serious. How might you take, or pass, this Maryland bar?"

"I would first pass the Philadelphia one. Then I would need to study for the other. It would take another year at least." Johnny did not bother to tell her that three years was the usual period of study, because each state had its own laws.

"Why don't you plan to do that, then? That is, if you still *wish* to." Her voice trembled slightly on these last two words. Johnny's bad mood had made him slow-witted; he failed to grasp Marcia's meaning: that if he still wished to marry her, he would need to find employment in Maryland.

Meanwhile, the friends stared, mouths agape, having also lost the drift of this conversation.

"Marcia, what are you trying to say?" he asked moodily.

Marcia suddenly dropped her handkerchief upon the floor beneath the table. When Johnny stooped down to pick it up for her, she bent down and whispered, "Let us marry next June."

43

JOHNNY WORE HIS SMILE ALL THE WAY back to Philadelphia. *I'm to be married in June,* he thought, *and to the most beautiful, the most sought-after young lady in all of Maryland.*

Oh, how his heart sang with joy! It would not stop singing. In marriage to Marcia, Johnny saw not merely endless love and a happy domestic life, but the kind of meaningful engagement with others that would serve as a reward for all his hard work: a successful law practice; lively evenings with senators, congressmen, judges, and diplomats; and the warm and charming Marcia Burnes Boylston by his side.

There were a few obstacles, but none that Johnny believed to be insurmountable. For one, he would need to take the Maryland bar. For another, he would need to remain in the South for the foreseeable future. But such was Johnny's joy that neither of these obstacles could diminish it.

When next Johnny saw the president, about two days after his return from Washington, he found the man reading the *Philadelphia Aurora*, the most prominent Republican newspaper in Philadelphia. Adams was in one of his rages and did not greet Johnny.

He said, "In your absence I've been obliged to read everything myself. Why, look at *this!*" Mr. Adams fairly poked his finger through the paper, pointing to a recent editorial by James Callender. He was a slanderous rogue whom Adams abhorred, a conscienceless scandalmonger who, in 1796, had exposed Alexander Hamilton's adulterous affair with Maria Reynolds. This piece insinuated great evils on the part of Adams without supporting any of its claims.

"The storm shall pass," Johnny said dreamily, staring out the window at the stately Lombardy poplar trees lining the square.

"Political storms never simply 'pass,'" said Adams. Suspicious of his protégé's sudden equanimity, Adams asked, "How did you find Washington? I hear it is a veritable swamp."

"It has great potential, I believe."

Mr. Adams frowned. "I find you very unsatisfactory today, Johnny. Close-lipped as a clam and altogether too sanguine. I can't get a thing out of you."

"That, too, shall pass, I'm sure." Johnny turned from the window and flashed the president a broad smile.

"Humph!"

•   •   •

Mr. Adams left Philadelphia for Quincy soon after this conversation, to rumors of his having abdicated. He had offered Johnny transport, but the boy feared he could not bear six days of constant conversation, much less six nights in bed, with Mr. Adams. He thanked him but said he wished to remain a few weeks longer to study.

On April 23, Johnny set off in a hired coach bound for Quincy. The weather was cool but fine, the roads far better than when he'd traveled to Washington. The trip was uneventful until Trenton, where Johnny had to help push the carriage out of a ditch before they could continue. In New York, he posted a letter to his mother telling her of his imminent arrival. She could expect him, he said, on or around April 28.

But then in White Plains, his coachman took ill, and they were obliged to stop for several days. While there, Johnny wrote Marcia a letter filled with such sweet words that, had they been sweetmeats, they would have rendered the diner quite ill.

The coachman recovered from his indisposition and on April 27, they continued their journey, reaching Quincy on April 30. As they turned onto Lizzie's lane, Johnny's heart pounded with anticipation. He felt greatly changed from that boy who'd set off as a fresh college graduate in August of '97. He had met Marcia Burnes again, fallen in love, become engaged, learned the law (no thanks to Mr. Martin), and moved to Philadelphia. Twice he had nearly pushed Thomas Jefferson off a staircase.

Oh, he would need many hours to tell his stories!

Upon the sound of the carriage, Lizzie's children scrambled out of the cottage.

"Johnny! Johnny!" They were already pulling him out of it by his long arms. Indeed, they pulled so hard that for a moment Johnny thought he would fall out headfirst.

"John, dear John!" Eliza came flying out the door.

"Mama!"

"We were so worried!"

"The coachman took ill in White Plains. But all is well. Oh, all is most well!"

It was a tearful reunion, and everyone agreed that Johnny must never again be absent for so long. When he heard them pronounce this solemn pact, he felt sick at heart. He would not tell them about his plans to remain in the South—not yet.

The children had grown up since he'd last set eyes upon them. Tom was now a hale, taciturn young man. Little Sara was now an affable, outgoing girl of nine. Abby was the most ladylike one; she wore a pretty frock and constantly pet her neat auburn curls.

Miriam had changed most of all. Now seventeen, she had grown quite tall, slender, and proud. When Johnny suggested that they search for shells, she turned a shoulder and remarked, "Oh, that game is for the *children*."

That night, Johnny slept from ten to near noon the following day. In the delicious sleep of early morning, he could hear the bustle of the women; he saw the light beyond his closed eyelids and Tom's shadow pass across a window, off to feed the animals.

Johnny drifted in and out of sleep until the call of nature finally roused him. It was the first of May, a day of ancient celebration, and the farm looked fresh and well cared for. Neat rows of beans were just breaching the ground, and pale green-yellow buds appeared upon the fruit trees. Oh, it was good to be home at last!

His mother was in the kitchen waiting for him.

"Johnny, come sit a moment with your old mother," she said.

"You're not *very* old," he replied.

Eliza smiled, making the crows' feet around her eyes more visible. "Forty-three this December. How did that happen, I wonder?" But she laughed like a young girl now that she was with her child.

Eliza cocked her head at him. "You look different. You've no doubt had many new experiences. I should like to hear about one or two."

"I'll gladly tell you everything. Oh, Mama," he blurted, suddenly throwing his arms about her shoulders. "It's so good to be home. You know not how good."

She pulled away and looked at him. "Has something happened?"

"Oh, no, no. Don't take my words amiss. It's just—the world beyond Quincy is very different."

Eliza paused. "Abigail tells us that you visited the new city of Washington."

"I did."

"For what reason?"

"I—"

His mother drew him close and whispered, "Oh, do not waste your time thinking up a lie, Johnny. Not on my account. I can always tell. The reason is Miss Burnes, is it not?"

Johnny stared at his mother. "But how did you *know*?"

She shrugged.

Johnny frowned. "Mr. *Adams*. That incorrigible gossip! I *begged* him not to tell."

Eliza smiled. "As you lawyers say, I can neither confirm nor deny it."

But Johnny wasn't happy. "Well, since you already know, yes. We are engaged. It only just happened."

"You know Kate is to be married, too," Eliza said, watching her son carefully.

"I thought she already was."

"The wedding is to take place in October. She remains in Haverhill meanwhile, with Abby's sister, caring for the children. She has no plans to return to these parts until September at the earliest."

"Does she know I am come home for the summer?"

"I believe so."

There was an uncomfortable silence. Then Eliza asked, "Do you actually *love* her, this Marcia Burnes?"

"*Mama.*"

Eliza grasped her son's arm. "Look at me, Johnny."

He looked at her, and she read his eyes at once.

"You do," she said. But she did not sound very happy about it. "You're not twenty-one. That's young to marry, for a boy."

"I thought you said I was a man."

Eliza frowned as if the reason for her concern were self-evident. "You know it's never *you* that worries me."

At that moment, Lizzie came through the kitchen door carrying two pails of milk. She set them down.

"What's going on here? The room feels as if it is about to be struck by lightning."

"It already has been," replied Eliza.

Johnny said nothing. He rose, bowed to the women, and then removed himself to Peacefield. There, he was relieved to be away from his mother and her fears. He wrote a letter to Marcia, and in late afternoon finally sallied forth to help Mr. Adams with a few small chores.

And so began another Quincy summer: Once more, Johnny rose in darkness to take his coffee. As the sun came up, he walked to Peacefield. Then he studied in Mr. Adams's book room until the president appeared mid-morning, looking not very presidential in his farm clothing. Adams would say, "Ready, Johnny?" And Johnny, in his own calfskin breeches and linen shirt, would tackle the many tasks that awaited them. *I'm a hero of dirt and stone,* he thought, smiling to himself.

Each night, after hauling rocks or moving dirt, Johnny slept as if dead. He woke the following morning only to repeat the activities of the day before. By July, he was as fit and nimble as any young farmer in the parish. Indeed, he grew so dark that Miriam stared at him one evening and said, "Johnny, you look like a black boy."

"Miriam!" Lizzie cried, horrified.

But Johnny just laughed and taunted, "White girl!"

"Black boy! Black boy!"

Johnny lowered his voice and said, "Watch out I don't call you *lobster* girl, Miriam. Or rather lobster-*nose*, for the sun has turned *your* nose bright red."

"You shan't call me a lobster-nose, Johnny!" Miriam complained, placing a hand to her nose, whose burned skin had already begun to peel.

•   •   •

The summer moved apace, its days lazy yet full. There had been no repetition of that painful conversation with his mother, nor had Johnny, in telling his many stories, confessed his plans to remain in the South. But eventually Johnny found himself making preparations to return to Philadelphia. The thought put a metallic taste in his mouth, and

Miriam moped about, draping her long limbs along the furniture, a portrait of mourning.

"Well, but you knew I could not remain here forever," Johnny told her one afternoon.

"Why *not*?"

"Because, if I am to become president one day like your uncle John, I must first pass my exams and become a lawyer."

"What about *me*?" Miriam cried plaintively, sounding jarringly childish. All summer, she had posed so successfully as a woman that Johnny had nearly mistaken her for one.

"Your most excellent mama shall guide you."

Miriam wrinkled her nose with distaste. "But I shouldn't like to deliver babies. Ugh!"

Johnny laughed. "No? It is a beautiful thing, is it not, to bring a life into this world?"

Miriam frowned. "It is *not*. Mama took me once—it's disgusting!"

Johnny laughed. "Perhaps you shall feel differently someday."

"I won't. I wish to be like Cousin Kate."

"Cousin Kate?" Johnny was suddenly attentive. "Why, have you seen her? Do you know what she does at present?"

"Of course. Don't *you*?" she retorted. "She's made a magazine, and a very fine one, too."

"Have you a copy about? I should like to see it."

"Not yet, for it has just gone to the printer."

"Ah," Johnny nodded. "I see. Well, isn't that marvelous!"

And Johnny thought it was, although for some reason he felt tears start to his eyes.

44

September 1799

KATE TOLD HER MOTHER, WHO TOLD LIZZIE, who told Eliza, that she planned to arrive in Quincy in the first week of October. She wished to speak to Abigail about her new women's magazine. According to Johnny's mother, Kate had said not a word on the subject of her nuptials, and the general consensus was that Mr. Pearce was currently in Jamaica or possibly London. Johnny was set to leave for Philadelphia with Mr. Adams on September twenty-ninth. But news arrived of another virulent outbreak of yellow fever in that city, and the government made hasty preparations to go to Trenton instead. The outbreak of fever also meant the postponement of the Philadelphia bar exam, as the courts had all been disbanded.

Adams sent word to Johnny that he would depart on the thirtieth. This time, Johnny had no choice but to share a carriage and bed with the ever-conversational Mr. Adams.

The morning of September 30 was bright and sunny. Johnny's trunk was upon the stoop. He heard a dog bark on the main road and then carriage wheels creaking down the lane. Johnny stood, ready to hand his trunk over to the coachman. His mother, Lizzie, and the children all hurriedly exited the front door in expectation of greeting Mr. Adams and Briesler.

But it was not John Adams in the carriage; it was Katherine Lee. She wore a simple chemise and a calico petticoat, and her thick brown hair, though meant to be in a bun, mainly fell loose about her bosom. When she saw Johnny rise up off the stoop, her face blanched. Clearly, she thought he had already left.

"Kate!" he cried, approaching the carriage. It had been two years since he had seen her. Johnny moved to embrace her, but she stepped back, smiled wanly, and extended her gloved hand to him. The other women emerged from the cottage and flanked her protectively.

"What?" Johnny cried. "Is that all the greeting I am to receive? Why, do you not know me? You behave as if I were a stranger."

"Not so." She shielded her eyes from the rising sun. "I'd know you anywhere, though it has been two years since I've laid eyes upon you. You are John Boylston."

"*John*-ny," his mother drawled from the door, as if she had urgent business. "I would have a word with you!"

"*Ma*ma," Johnny turned and glowered.

"Come here, please."

Johnny moved toward the cottage. His mother whispered to him, "Can you not see the poor girl is fatigued from her trip? Allow her a moment to wash up and rest before pouncing upon her like one of the children."

"Oh, yes, of course." He looked abashed. "I shall offer her some refreshment."

Eliza sighed. Her son did not have the least idea of Kate's inner turmoil, though it was written plain as day on her face. Kate passed him by with a small smile as she mounted the stairs, and Johnny, having offered to make the tea, waited patiently for her to descend.

The tea was steaming hot, then cool, and then cold. Still Kate had not descended. Why did she not come to speak with him? He began to wonder whether she was angry with him for some reason.

Was it not she who had written him with news of Mr. Pearce's proposal? And was it not right to leave her free and unimpeded to accept it, if that was her wish? The mathematics had been right, but somehow he'd gotten the sum wrong.

Suddenly Kate appeared in the kitchen. She looked composed, though her eyes seemed overly bright behind her spectacles. She sat down and placed her hand around the dish of cold tea.

"Shall I make us a fresh pot?" Johnny stood, eager to do something.

"Nay." She stayed his arm and looked up at him. "I fear you have little time. You know Mr. Adams will be late and then wish to set off immediately, as if you delayed him. Your mother and I shall have ten buckets of tea once you leave."

Johnny nodded. Awkwardly, to fill the ensuing silence, he inquired after her family, and she said that as far as she knew, they were all well. She had not set eyes upon them in several weeks, having spent the summer in Haverhill.

"And how like you Philadelphia?"

"I like it very well, when it is not pestilential with fever. It seems particularly vulnerable to this yellow plague. Some say it is the miasma that rises from the canals."

"But surely you don't head there now?"

"Nay. We go to Trenton."

"Oh, that's good—although, is not Trenton very close to Philadelphia?"

"Far enough, I suppose," Johnny said dubiously. "But I hear the pest we truly have to fear is Hamilton. Adams tells me he's already there. You cannot know how much he detests Hamilton, and I believe the feeling is mutual."

Kate nodded. Then neither found anything to say. With a stab of nostalgia Johnny recalled those easy days of the Slotted Spoon Society, when they spoke for hours upon the subject of Hamilton, Jefferson, and even John Adams, sometimes laughing until tears came.

"How fare the preparations for your nuptials?" Johnny blurted. "I've failed to congratulate you. Hearty felicitations!" But some phlegm had gathered in Johnny's throat and the words came out sounding garbled.

Kate said, "Yes, well. It's a ways off yet."

"It's next month, is it not?"

"October," Kate admitted. "At the end of the month. But, oh, to be honest, I've been so busy with other things I sometimes forget all about it. Did you hear about the magazine? It's at the printer's now."

Johnny wondered how Kate could be so calm about her nuptials, when he spent every waking moment dreaming about his.

"Miriam told me. What splendid news. And have you subscribers?"

"Five." Kate smiled. "Well, it is but the first issue. Word will spread, I hope. Abigail's sister Betsy helps me just now. She's quite brilliant, and a fine writer, too. We're working on ways to raise capital. Advertising, I suppose you call it." Here, Kate let out a devastated laugh. "We're hopeless amateurs, I'm afraid. But if willing hearts and minds alone count for anything, we may yet succeed."

Johnny glanced at Kate and felt sad not to have been part of all her planning, not to have been there to help her with such a demanding and noble endeavor.

"I'm vastly proud of you, Kate."

She looked down. "Yes, well. And you—do you still write your clarion calls for peace?"

"I've had to choose sides, I'm afraid. The days of nonpartisanship are over. And yet to take sides goes against everything I believe in."

"Then don't do it," she said simply.

"Nothing is as clear as our leaders make it seem." Johnny hunched across the table and whispered, "Take Adams himself, for example. You know my love for him. But when he allowed those shameful acts to pass, he fell in my eyes. Then there's Jefferson, whom I once revered, and whose ideas on certain topics I fervently agree with, yet he has behaved treasonously. By rights, he should be impeached."

Kate considered what Johnny had told her. Then she replied, "Perhaps idolatry cannot be sustained. Love is easier, as it allows for faults."

She quickly added, "As you love Mr. Adams, for example."

"Oh, Kate," Johnny suddenly blurted, "how I've missed speaking my heart! How I miss speaking with *you*."

Suddenly, carriage wheels clattered upon the stony path to the cottage. The young people peered out the kitchen window. Mr. Adams and Briesler were in the carriage, Adams looking put upon.

"Where is that boy? He should be here."

Kate said, "You see."

Johnny smiled. "I must go." Suddenly he turned to Kate and kissed her on the cheek.

"Johnny!" his mother called from the garden. "Johnny! They're here!"

Johnny turned back as he ran toward the waiting carriage. "Write to me, promise?"

"I shall try," Kate said. In his haste, Johnny did not notice the tears flood Kate's eyes.

The women waved from the kitchen garden as the carriage turned around. Looking back over his shoulder, Johnny waved until he could no longer see them. Mr. Adams, who sat across from him and Briesler, placed a hand on Johnny's knee. He said, "Well, I fear I take you from the soft bosom of your family and drag you into the hard world of men."

"Sir, a man cannot remain forever among women."

"No," Mr. Adams said wistfully. "But I sometimes wish we could."

45

TRENTON WAS A PRETTY VILLAGE CONSISTING OF two main roads on the left bank of the Delaware. Johnny took the first possible opportunity to walk down to the river, where he could see the proud new statehouse, a grand stucco building crowned with a bell tower. Down by the wharf, a long tree-lined driveway led from William Trent's fine brick mansion to the water. There, sloops of varying sizes rocked back and forth in the wind.

Upon arriving in Trenton, Mr. Adams caught a bad cold, and Johnny found himself racing about the town to procure hyssop, sage, and balm, all of which, Adams insisted, were necessary to his continued survival.

Mr. Adams was a poor patient, fractious and unwilling to amend his daily routine. But from his bed he wished to discuss an issue with Johnny, over which he was in some anguish. He was about to send a convoy to France to negotiate a peace treaty. "The trouble is," he began, "I don't trust my cabinet. Pickering, McHenry, Wolcott, and especially that rogue Hamilton are against treating with France. I fear they'll endeavor to subvert the mission."

Johnny knew all this. "What is your question, sir?"

Adams glanced malignantly at Johnny. He was feverish and in a very bad mood. But Johnny didn't take his demeanor personally.

"The question is, Am I obliged to tell the secretaries when the convoy leaves?"

Johnny understood that Adams asked a moral question, not a legal one. But he replied, "They exist to give you advice, not permission. Is that not so?"

Adams was about to make a comment when a man burst noisily through the door and into Adams's chamber. He had auburn hair, and though he was of no great stature, his eyes flamed and his nostrils flared, making him look more lion than man.

"Adams! I've heard of your secret business, and I say I forbid it! Would you willingly lead us all to ruin?"

"Ruin, you say?" Adams replied, reaching for his handkerchief to blow his nose. He sat upright in his bed, surrounded by phlegm-sodden rags, looking feverish and miserable. "I fail to see how peace with France spells ruin. That's a savings of thousands of lives and millions of dollars. You will no doubt care most about the latter."

The argument continued, poor Adams coughing and croaking out his words. No one thought of making introductions, and Johnny was too spellbound to interrupt.

Finally Johnny was unable to bear the assault upon the sick president any longer. "Mr. Adams is unwell, as you can see. I suggest you return at a more auspicious time."

The man's eyes flashed at Johnny. "And who are you?"

"John Boylston," Johnny said defiantly.

The little man laughed. "Why, you're just a boy. Albeit quite tall."

Johnny moved closer, as if to take hold of the man's arm, but the fellow glanced malevolently at him and then at Adams. "I'll return in a few days. By then, you should be over your cold." He then fled the chamber without bowing to either of them.

Once the man had gone, Johnny turned to the president. "Is the man mad, to come bursting in here demanding an audience, without so much as a 'by your leave'?"

Adams nodded, then searched among the bed covers for a clean rag to blow his nose. He coughed, cleared his throat, and said, "The man may be mad, but he's shrewd as a fox. Take care you don't underestimate him. That, by the way, was Alexander Hamilton."

•   •   •

The government remained several weeks in Trenton before Philadelphia was declared free of the fever. On their return journey, both men were quiet, lost in their own private thoughts. Adams probably thought about his convoy and the farm. Johnny thought about Marcia Burnes. Arrived in Philadelphia, Adams's coachman dropped Johnny at the Francis Hotel, and Adams returned to the President's House.

After this, Johnny hardly saw the president. He studied every waking moment, hardly coming up to eat or dress. In early November, he felt ready to take the bar and did so, handily passing it just after celebrating his twenty-first birthday.

Briesler, on Adams's orders, held a dinner for Johnny at the City Tavern. A small crowd of Adams's friends was already jolly with wine when Senator Langdon entered, followed by another man. At the sight of these men, the company fell silent. The stranger was impressive for his regal bearing; he was a man in the prime of life, with a lofty forehead and dark eyebrows above piercing eyes.

Johnny believed this man was John Marshall. Mr. Marshall had a law practice in Richmond and also served in the House of Representatives. He was one of Adams's closest allies.

Johnny's guess was confirmed moments later when Senator Langdon shook Johnny's hand and then introduced his friend.

"John Boylston, this is Congressman John Marshall."

Johnny bowed. "Sir, to what do I owe this great honor?"

"I merely wished to meet you, having heard so much about you from Senator Langdon."

Johnny offered Mr. Marshall some refreshment, but he waved it off.

"Nay, I stay not long, but I should like to speak with you at your leisure. My lodgings are close by, if you would call upon me one afternoon this week. Wednesday, say?"

"Certainly, sir."

"Perhaps you've heard I have a very busy practice in Richmond."

"I have, sir."

"I find it difficult to manage everything given my current service in the House."

He bowed, handed Johnny a card, and was soon gone.

Johnny stared at the card in his hand disbelievingly. "What just happened?" he asked Langdon.

The senator smiled and nudged Johnny's arm. "If I'm not mistaken, you just received an offer of a position in Richmond."

●　　●　　●

That night, Johnny awoke and thought he had dreamed the meeting with John Marshall. But then he saw the attorney's card upon his desk glowing white in the half moonlight that shone through his window.

To Johnny, the idea of moving to Richmond was strangely alluring. In Richmond resided the most elite men of the South. There were many Republicans there, to be sure, but also staunch Federalists such as John Marshall. Johnny considered that even one year with Marshall's firm would assure his future. And the idea of living the Southern life, the life of Moorcock, though without slavery, was enormously alluring. But could he abandon Mr. Adams during an election year? Would his mother, hearing the news, die of heartbreak? Johnny fell back asleep before he could resolve it all in his mind.

The following day, Johnny told Adams what had transpired between himself and Marshall. Adams said, "If he makes you an offer, you would be a fool not to accept it."

"But I have no wish to abandon you during this critical year."

"Ah! You fancy yourself that essential to my survival, do you? Oh, well, perhaps you are—or shall be quite soon. I know not what the year shall bring, only that it will be a struggle to the death. Jefferson and I shall play the elderly gladiators. See if Marshall will keep it open for another year. Tell him I need you now, but shall release you from my grip in a year's time. By then"—he shrugged—"who knows."

On Wednesday, November 13, 1799, Johnny took a meal with Congressman Marshall at his lodgings. They spoke freely with each other on a number of topics. They had been discussing a point of moral philosophy when Johnny suddenly laughed and put a hand to his forehead.

"Why do you laugh?" Marshall smiled.

"When I was in school, a few of us formed a little society. We called it the Slotted Spoon Society, and we took it very seriously. As seriously as only those with no real experience of life can."

Marshall smiled warmly at Johnny. "I suppose like bright young men everywhere, you solved all the world's ills."

"Most of them," Johnny admitted. The two men laughed. Johnny could not bring himself to tell Marshall that one of the bright young men had been a woman.

They parted on warm terms, Marshall asserting that they would certainly meet again, and that his offer stood until such time as Johnny felt free to accept it. Johnny left the meeting humming with excitement. He could not wait to write Marcia. So exhilarated was he that he was halfway back to his hotel before he realized that he had failed to take his old coat. He had to race back to retrieve it, to his great embarrassment.

•   •   •

On December 17, 1799, a fire began at Rickett's Circus and quickly spread. Johnny heard the cries on the street below. He saw horses galloping by, and carts carrying water rumbled quickly up from the wharf. Johnny ran out into the street. He wished to help, but there was little to be done. By morning, the entire block was a smoking black pile of rubble. Oeller's, where he had seen his first cube of ice, was gone.

Later, people said that the fire was a bad omen, for that same night a lone rider galloped into the city to tell its citizens that George Washington, their great and unifying leader, was dead.

46

HE HAD DIED THREE DAYS PREVIOUS, AT his home at Mount Vernon. As the news spread, rumors abounded: The Federalists had killed him. The Republicans had killed him. He had killed himself in despair. Then, finally, on December 31, 1799, a story appeared in the *Virginia Gazette* that had the ring of truth, being written by the doctors who had attended Washington at the end.

> Some time in the night of Friday the 13th, having been exposed to rain on the preceding day, General Washington was attacked with an inflammatory infection of the upper part of the wind-pipe, called in technical language, *cynache tracheatis*. The disease commenced with a violent ague, accompanied with some pain in the upper and fore part of the throat, a sense of stricture in the same part, a cough, and a difficult rather than a painful deglutition, which were soon succeeded by fever and a quick and laborious respiration . . .

Some whispered that the Union would not hold without him; others whispered that the Federalists were finished. Jefferson did not attend

Washington's memorial service; the two had never spoken again after that business of the Mazzei letter.

Johnny did go, however. He followed the solemn procession behind the empty coffin and the riderless horse. Everyone in Philadelphia— dignitaries and common folk alike—wept together as the procession slowly made its way to the New Lutheran Church.

Like others across America, Johnny had half believed that Washington would live forever. He was their North Star. This light extinguished, all was darkness and greed below.

Now Johnny heard church bells tolling. Shopkeepers closed up shop, housewives held their children by the hand, and senators and congressmen all walked toward the church. Washington himself had been quietly interred at Mount Vernon in the family vault. But where his body lay mattered not. They came to honor his indomitable spirit.

When Johnny entered the church, the president and Mrs. Adams were already seated in the front row. Both wept at the sight before them: Washington's horse. In the stirrups, pointing backward, the general's worn Hessian boots.

Johnny sat directly behind the Adamses, for the front row was full. Adams, seeing Johnny, reached for his hand across the back of the bench. Soon, John Marshall would speak.

Oh, where was he? Gone! Gone! And what fateful timing, to leave them at this somber close of the eighteenth century. It felt much as Johnny had predicted in his editorial: like the death of honor itself. The noble white horse stood alone, very alone.

Johnny burst into tears and hid his face in his hands. When he finally looked up and cast about to see who might have noticed, there, across the aisle, sat Peter Fray.

By the time Johnny made his way through the crowd, Fray was already standing outside, beside a magnificent black stallion. Surrounding him were a group of acquaintances.

"Hello, Fray." Johnny bowed.

"Oh, hello," Peter replied. He then turned his back on Johnny and returned to his banter.

Nonetheless, Johnny asked, "What brings you to Philadelphia? I thought you'd gone to Richmond."

"Has Miss Burnes not told you? I've lately arrived to cover the news for the *Richmond Examiner*."

"James Callender's *Examiner*?"

"The same."

James Callender was the scoundrel who continued to calumniate the Federalists at every turn. But Johnny endeavored to hide his alarm when he asked, "You had no wish to return to Moorcock?"

"Impossible, old mole. Though, thanks in part to my employment, Moorcock yet belongs to us." Peter smiled, but his stone-blue eyes let Johnny know that nothing had been forgiven or forgotten.

"Apparently you are not too busy to correspond with Miss Burnes," Johnny said.

Peter paused only momentarily in his surprise. "Well, what of it?"

"You told her lies about me."

"Not so! I told her the absolute truth, though I may have omitted a few items. As we all do." Peter shrugged and grinned knowingly at his friends. These appeared to be slightly older, Southern versions of Shattuck, Farquez, Wales, and Selfridge.

"Truth? I was never engaged to Miss Lee and you know it."

"Semantics." Peter smiled. "Anyway, what do you do, Johnny? No, wait, I can guess. You write high-minded editorials about the death of honor whilst spying for the Monocrat."

Johnny reeled. How much did Peter know?

"Oh, and I hear congratulations are in order. You plan to marry and perhaps even move to Richmond?" Peter then said, with a disingenuous attempt at joviality, "The ladies always did love you."

"Some still do," replied Johnny.

Peter shrugged again. "Well, I'm off. A shame about Washington, eh? A real legend. I expect we shall soon have statues of him everywhere."

A Negro stable boy locked his fingers together, and Peter stepped on them to mount his horse. He waved to his friends.

Peter Fray in Philadelphia, and working for the *Examiner*. That was not good news.

• • •

After Washington's death, an embattled air fell upon Philadelphia. As spring of 1800 approached, attacks in the newspapers grew more bitter and violent. For the second time in his life, Johnny saw John Adams burned in effigy. In the middle of busy High Street, a band of masked men set a straw-stuffed doll afire with torches and then ran off before the constable arrived. Someone had placed dry ears of corn in Adams's head, and when the flames reached them, the head exploded.

Every afternoon, Republican floats rode down High Street with banners that read "Liberty Under Siege!" Federalist banners warned of Jefferson's "creed of atheism and revolution." He was "the greatest villain in America." Farther afield, in newspapers across the states, partisan editors warned of imminent disaster. In New York, one paper cried that if Jefferson were elected, "bibles would have to be hidden" and America would be overrun by the "refuse of Europe," meaning Irish and French immigrants.

Johnny did not see how either Mr. Adams or their fragile Union could weather another year of such violence, both verbal and, increasingly, physical.

The President's House took on a somber, battened-down air. Adams was irate and resigned in turns. At times, Johnny came upon the old man mumbling that he simply wanted to go home.

One afternoon, Johnny entered Adams's study in time to see him throw down the paper he'd been reading and exclaim, "Republicans! I have a mind to arrest the whole lot of 'em!"

Johnny said, "You would need to arrest half the country, sir."

"Oh, but it's all lies!"

"Perhaps. But the First Amendment does not say our citizens have the right to *truthful* speech alone."

Adams sent Johnny a withering glance.

"My only interest is to avoid war."

Johnny wanted to remain silent, but he could not help himself when he said, "You would avoid war abroad at the cost of inciting a civil war at home?"

"Incite! Incite?" He exploded, smashing his fist upon the desk. "You've no idea what it's like to be vilified, attacked by lies at every turn. It can't be borne!"

Johnny replied, "Mrs. Adams says that what cannot be avoided must be borne."

"Mrs. Adams! Dammit, Johnny, I've had enough of you both for a lifetime!"

•　•　•

Johnny decided then that the most helpful thing he could do for Adams was to keep track of the opposition press and counter it where he could. The invectives grew, both in violence and in quantity, and Johnny countered them word for word in nearly two dozen articles that winter. While Adams rarely mentioned Johnny's editorials, Johnny knew he wrote with Adams's silent consent.

One morning, as he perused Adams's mail while Adams sat writing a letter, Johnny found a pamphlet entitled *The Prospect Before Us*. The author was none other than James Callender. He read the pamphlet in its entirety and then looked up at the president.

"Listen to this, sir. The blackguard says that your administration is a 'tempest of malignant passions.'"

"Humph," Adams replied. "What else?" He continued to write his letter.

Johnny read:

> *As president, he has never opened his lips, or lifted his pen, without threatening and scolding. The grand object of his administration has been to exasperate the rage of contending parties, to calumniate and destroy every man who differs from his opinions . . .*

"I calumniate? I calumniate?" Adams, now beet-faced, set his pen down and rose from his chair. He stared at Johnny with something very akin to malignant passion.

"What else?"

"More of the same, sir."

"Read it! Go on!"

Johnny read:

> *Mr. Adams has laboured, and with melancholy success, to break up the bonds of social affection, and, under the ruins of confidence and friendship, to extinguish the only beam of happiness that glimmers through the dark and despicable farce of life.*

Adams sat back down and mastered himself with an effort. "A poisonous snake. One who, I must admit, can write."

He certainly can, Johnny thought.

Johnny left the President's House feeling he was, once more, on the scent of some treachery. All his senses told him that this pamphlet had been Jefferson's doing. And yet, he could not believe it. He did not think Jefferson would stoop to such personal vilification.

Finally arriving at his hotel, Johnny wearily mounted the stairs. He was ready to collapse onto his soft bed when, glancing in the direction of Jefferson's chamber, he noticed that the door was open.

Johnny slowed his steps and moved toward the open door. He peered inside. The room was large, with two windows fronting onto the street. There was yet some light to see by, and everywhere he looked, there were books and papers: on the floor, the bed, and especially the elegant writing desk at the other end of the room.

"Hello?" he called. No one answered. An overwhelming curiosity called him forward. He stepped inside and moved quickly to Jefferson's desk. At once, he found a plaintive letter to James Monroe and another to one of his slaves at Monticello regarding a purchase of iron for his nail manufactory.

On the left side of the desk sat a large account ledger, bound in worn brown leather. Johnny opened it and ran his finger down the most recent page: purchases of books from France and England, various bottles of French wine. Then, in the same neat, careful handwriting as the rest: "To James Callender, $50." This entry was repeated not once but several times, dating all the way back to the previous autumn.

This was bad; Johnny had not truly expected to find such confirmation of his worst fears. At the thought of telling Adams, he felt his stomach heave. Johnny hastily closed the ledger and, in so doing, dislodged a piece of paper that had been folded within its pages. The paper fell to the floor, and he picked it up. He was about to replace it unread when he heard people enter the hotel below. He stepped swiftly into the hall, leaving the door ajar.

The people now headed up the stairs, laughing and speaking in loud, cheerful voices, as if they'd just returned from a tavern. Johnny fled into his chamber and peered out the crack to see Jefferson and a Negro manservant engaged in lively conversation. When he noticed his door ajar, Jefferson stopped on the landing and said, "What? Was it you who left it so, Jupiter?"

"No, sir." The servant shook his head.

"I recall perfectly well that we left this locked. Blasted chambermaid!" Jefferson looked quickly about the hall. "I've asked her twice not to bother with my chamber. I shall have to speak to John Francis. Or better yet, it's high time we found our own house. I've ignored that onerous task for far too long."

They entered the chamber at last and shut the door, though Johnny could hear Jefferson's angry voice coming from within.

Johnny finally exhaled. He looked down and saw that one hand still gripped the letter. It was addressed to a Miss Sarah Hemings of Monticello. It had a line running through it, as if Jefferson had thought better of sending it. Or perhaps he had made a fair copy and meant to destroy this.

> My dearest one, I long to be home among my beloved
> family. I was grieved beyond words to hear of our little
> girl's death, but shall speak no more of it here and save
> my grief until I am in your arms once more. I am in
> a viper pit here and fear I shall be stung many times
> before finding my way out. If only I were there to place
> my weary head upon the breast of my beloved Sally!
>
> P.S. Please send love to your Mistress Martha from
> me. I pray you are able to console one another for
> the loss of our little one.

Martha, Johnny knew, was Jefferson's eldest child. But who was "Sally"? Suddenly, and with perfect clarity, Johnny recalled his painful parting from Moorcock years earlier. He then recalled Frederick's mocking words about Jefferson: "Yes, perhaps you'll even be so fortunate as to meet his favorite slave, Sally."

There had been rumors but never proof. The story of Jefferson and his slave was but one of the many vicious depredations that circulated at the time. Now, here was proof, or very near it. Johnny believed he had found something that, if made known, could change the course of the election.

47

THERE WOULD BE NO SLEEPING FOR HIM that night. It was past midnight when he finally dressed, pulled on his coat and hat, and left the hotel. He walked down Market Street to the river, where he watched the boats rocking in the moonlight and a lone dockworker lowering a crate from one of the ships onto a cart. He walked along the harbor, passing the shops on Front Street, now closed. Then he turned up Church Street toward Christ Church. The city was quiet, save for the constant chirp of tree toads.

Johnny considered what he knew and what he still needed to find out: He knew now with certainty that Jefferson was paying the scoundrel Callender to defame Adams. He sensed, but did not know absolutely, that Jefferson had helped to write that cruel, ugly pamphlet. Johnny knew that Jefferson loved a slave named Sally but not who she was or the exact nature of their relationship. This he would need to unearth.

He stood before the church a moment, feeling his heart thud against his ribs. Gently, he tried the latch. The church was open. He entered, though within was complete darkness save for the scant reflection of the moon through the windowpanes.

Now, in the vacant dark of this holy space, Johnny weighed the possibilities. He could reveal what he knew and win the election for Adams. He could tell Adams about both discoveries, or only one. Or, he could do nothing, tear up the letter, and pretend he'd never stepped across that threshold.

Johnny realized that he now held in his hands the "sledgehammer" Mr. Adams had spoken of. It would penetrate even the thick American skull.

To publish this information would be a dramatic and probably effective political decision. But would it be a moral one? How much did the public have a right to know? If Johnny were like Callender, he would use it at once, without a thought for the ethics of the thing.

Johnny wished he had his beloved Slotted Spoon Society before him. For more than an hour, sitting on the hard bench in the dark church, Johnny imagined a conversation of his little society in which they addressed several questions: One was, Might Johnny condemn an esteemed man to political death for the sake of the greater good? Was Jefferson's lie by omission—his relationship with this Negro woman—pardonable? And finally, if Johnny condemned Jefferson on this score, would he not have to condemn himself?

Jefferson's payments to Callender, on the other hand, *did* bear exposure. They were cowardly and backstabbing. Adams himself would think them seditious in the extreme. Then, once the information was made known, would Congress arrest the vice president for sedition?

Johnny remained in the dark church for some time. He wished God would speak to him; he wished his faith were stronger. He experienced God as a kind of silent space that allowed man to look into his own soul. But no guidance did he find. What religion on earth could untangle these uniquely American threads? As he finally rose from the pew at around four, his legs were stiff, his soul heavy.

He returned to his chamber and lay down on the bed fully clothed. He slept till six, then rose, procured a steaming mug of coffee, and sat down to his desk. He would administer to the public a hefty dose of the truth. Jefferson didn't deserve to lose the election because of a personal scandal. He deserved to lose because he was an underhanded traitor to the Union.

Behind the Mask of James Callender

The pen that accuses our president of monarchism and intolerance of dissent has, in the comfort of secrecy, been funding the most vicious and slanderous attacks against him. Unmask yourself, poison pen, and stand up for your beliefs in the light of day, so that all may judge whether loyalty to the Cause or base Treachery be your motive!

The moment Johnny finished his article at around ten that morning, he broke down and sobbed. Writing this piece had not ameliorated the doubt or the demons that swirled about his brain.

He walked up the high street to the offices of the *Gazette*, article in hand. As he walked, he realized he had yet to choose a new pen name, finally settling on *Littera Scripta Manet*. The written word endures. Johnny smiled bitterly. *For better or worse,* he thought. After placing the piece on his editor's desk, he walked directly to the President's House.

It was turning into a pleasant spring day. The market teemed with women wearing airy gowns and holding parasols. Dogs darted back and forth across the lawn. And behind them all, as in a silhouette, was only the blackened, empty space where the Fire of '99 had burned all the buildings to the ground.

Johnny ran up the steps and through the front door. He took the stairs two at a time and found Mr. Adams in his office, spectacles on his nose, peering intently at a document. When he heard Johnny cough, he looked up over his spectacles.

"Oh, hello. Just looking over McHenry's resignation. I fired 'im. About time, too. Lost my temper, though, which I regret. Why, *why* can I not control such a simple thing as my own temper?" Adams let out a long sigh. It was a rhetorical question, and Johnny did not answer it. "I find myself more and more alone, Johnny. I'm getting rid of Pickering as well. This is long overdue. I'm sorry for his son's death. But those who worship false gods must do so on their own time, not mine."

Johnny knew that by "false gods" Adams meant Hamilton. It was true that Adams had lost control of his cabinet. It was true he was entirely alone. But whether this was entirely Hamilton's doing, Johnny knew not. He found that explanation too easy, somehow. By now, half the nation had turned against Adams.

Johnny hesitated. Was this the time to share yet more bad news? He said, "I'm afraid, sir, the news I have to impart shan't help matters."

Adams closed his eyes and pinched the bridge of his nose. "I feel a dreadful headache coming on."

"I can return later, if you like, sir."

"Nay, sit and tell me your news. You look as weary as I feel."

Johnny sat, pulling his chair close to Mr. Adams.

"I have just now come from my editor's offices at the *Gazette*, having delivered an article that shall, I believe, be published Tuesday next."

"An article, you say?" Adams looked interested. He usually enjoyed hearing about Johnny's articles. "What, calling for my resignation? You won't be the first, ha ha!"

"Worse than that, sir. It's a reply to Callender."

"Oh, that scoundrel. Well, he's an easy target, I should say. You know I've put a warrant out for his arrest. We've got to find him first, though, the blackguard. No doubt he's fled to Virginia, where he won't be spotted as easily. There, Callenders are everywhere."

It was as good an opening as Johnny was likely to get. "Speaking of Virginians, sir, I have reason to believe your vice president had a hand in that poisonous pamphlet."

"A hand? What mean you?"

Johnny hesitated. "Editorially, I mean. You need not know the details."

Here, there ensued a dangerous silence. Then Adams slammed his fist down on his desk, rattling several old dishes of partially drunk tea.

"I'll know, dammit! I'll not suffer mere conjecture!"

Johnny wanted to say that he never merely conjectured but instead blurted, "I have proof."

"Proof? How, and where, did you acquire proof?"

"His door was wide open, sir, and I entered the chamber and saw his account book lying upon his desk."

Adams moved toward Johnny but then continued past him to shut the door to his study. He turned to the boy.

"Let me warn you before you go any further down this path: to speak against the vice president, to incite discontent among the people towards any of our leaders, is grounds for arrest."

"I know that, sir."

"You know, you know—and yet you know nothing!" Now Adams exploded. Johnny had witnessed many of Adams's fits of temper, but he'd never seen him in such a state as this: he looked like a madman as he began to pace his chamber in fury. "What if Jefferson chooses to arrest you? There is nothing I could do. *Nothing.* Why, you've gone stark raving mad—like the rest of us."

Johnny endeavored to calm him down. He said, "Jefferson won't arrest me."

"And why not? You think him above such hypocrisy? Then you know him not as I do!"

"He won't arrest me, for I know something about him that, were it generally known, could be the death of him. Politically speaking."

But instead of asking Johnny what this information was, Mr. Adams walked to the window and looked down onto the street below. His shoulders curled in, and he placed his hands upon the windowsill, as if in need of support. He was silent while the volcanic fury in him slowly cooled.

In a changed voice the old man said, "Son, I can recall first meeting Jefferson just here, in the room below us, as if it were yesterday. That was in 1775. Oh, he was so young, so young and tall. His hair was quite shockingly red, with not a trace of gray, you know. We were both young,

Johnny. Full of fire, like you. Fire to create something, too, not simply to destroy. I don't know how we got here. I really don't."

Johnny waited. Adams turned around. He had tears in his eyes.

"Washington was right to warn us," he continued. "I only hope—I do yet believe—that Jefferson acts against me from some fundamental idealism, not base ambition. Abigail says not, yet it is my fervent hope."

After a few moments, Johnny said, "I don't doubt the greatness in Jefferson, or his great gifts to this country. Even so, should he not be held accountable for his current treachery?"

But Adams had made up his mind. "Do not do it. Do not publish this piece on Jefferson and Callender. They'll go after you like wolves." Adams sighed. "Johnny, you've got courage beyond anything I've ever seen since the war. You've done your job. But I would not have you wade any further into the mire. No, I won't have that upon my conscience. To have to face your mother—"

"You mustn't worry about me."

"But I do! Naturally I do! Yet even were it not so, I admit that I fear the Union shall suffer a fatal blow. At the end of the day, I must choose the well-being of the country. For the country to lose complete faith in its government . . ." Adams shook his head. "People revere Jefferson almost as much as they did Washington."

"But the attacks upon Washington, upon you—"

Adams shook his head. "Jefferson wrote such words as future generations shall live by. You can't take that away from our citizens. Not now. Perhaps not ever."

It was an angle Johnny had not, for all his cold hours in the church, considered: what was good for the people of this country. And they called Adams a Monocrat!

Johnny was convinced by Adams's argument. But he suddenly realized that he needed to fly back to his editor's office to retrieve the essay from his desk before they closed for the day. He bade the president a hasty farewell and raced back to the *Gazette*.

The letter was not on the desk where he had left it. For several minutes, he looked through the piles of papers on the desk, becoming more frantic as the minutes wore on. He had left it in plain sight. But neither the essay nor Johnny's editor was anywhere to be found. Heart thumping, Johnny called out to a young boy who stood at the other end of the room. Johnny recognized this boy as the one he'd seen running back and forth from the printer's shop down the street.

"Say," Johnny called to him. "Do you happen to know what has become of my article? Has Dennie retrieved it?"

"Nay." The boy did not look at Johnny when he spoke but continued to gaze out the windows, as if he were waiting for someone to arrive "He's not been in. Gone to see about something up at the State House. His secretary was in, though. You just missed him."

Johnny thought that perhaps Dennie's secretary had taken the article for editing. He would have to return first thing in the morning to ask the editor himself about it.

When Johnny exited the building, he turned left and headed west on High Street. Two men who had been loitering before some shops slowly began to walk behind him. Johnny took no notice until he had turned onto Fourth. He had just reached his hotel when he thought he heard scuffling behind him. He turned to find four men holding rough wooden clubs.

"What? Who?" Johnny raised his arms defensively as they quickly surrounded him.

"Never mind who," said one of the men, inching closer. He was no child but more near forty, as were the rest of them. Johnny knew not who they were, but that they were not gentlemen was certain.

"Citizens, let us use our God-given powers of discourse!" Johnny cried. "Surely you are civilized men."

Another man laughed. "Discourse! he says. C'mon, let's give the boy his long-deserved discourse!"

They attacked him then with their clubs. They struck vicious blows upon him. Johnny's vision wavered, and then his world went black.

48

HE LAY IN THE STREET ALL NIGHT. Passersby must have thought he was drunk, for no one came to his aid. Toward morning, it began to rain. He felt the rain on his face. Rising into consciousness, Johnny knew he had been assaulted, but he seemed to have lost the will to pick himself up. Yes, it was a failure of will, a kind of indolence that had him lying there in the dirt, knees drawn up, spine twisted to the side, groin wet—not from rain but his own urine. His mind commanded him to rise, yet he continued to lie there.

Dawn broke, the rain ceased, and the street sweepers appeared. With one open eye, Johnny saw two of them upside down from a distance. One sweeper came quite close to where he lay, and he cried, "Help, please help. I've been attacked." But the cry came out a whisper. With preternatural will, Johnny managed to shift himself so that the sweeper saw he lived.

"Holy Mary, Mother of God!"

The sweeper whistled to a mate down High Street, who set down his broom and came running.

"Lord, what's this, Tommy? In his cups, what?"

"I don't think so."

"Help me up," Johnny said. "I've been attacked. I'm not drunk."

They bent down to look more closely at the boy, who did seem quite purple about the face. His hands were bruised and bloodied from his attempt to defend himself.

"Easy. Slowly," said Tommy.

"That's it," said the other. "Let's set him on the stoop." But the moment they shifted him, Johnny lurched forward and puked at their feet.

"He's sick—let's move it!"

"Nay." Tommy shook his head. "They've beat him about the head. I hear that can happen, afterwards. It makes a body powerful sick."

Wiping his mouth with his sleeve, Johnny slurred, "Mr. Francis, within. Tell him Mr. Boylston—"

Tommy entered the lodgings and returned with Mr. Francis, who was still in his nightcap and gown. The three of them managed to carry Johnny through the door and up the stairs to his chamber. Mr. Francis called for a doctor at once. At the feel of his soft bed beneath him, Johnny drifted into a welcome, painless darkness.

Two days later, he woke to find a large black, damp hand dabbing his forehead with a cool cloth. The poor woman had thought him all but dead, and the act of opening his eyes scared her half to death.

"Oh! You're alive. Goodness! I'll tell Mr. Francis." She set the rag aside and stood up. "I'll be right back."

She was as good as her promise and soon returned with a fresh pitcher of water and a letter for him. It was from Marcia.

"Would you kindly open this letter for me? That is—can you read?"

The woman smiled and opened the letter. She squinted at it. "It's got only one line, sir."

"What does it say?" Johnny endeavored to sit up but found his body unwilling to oblige.

"It says, 'My father went to his Maker Friday last. Please come!'"

Johnny needed little persuasion to quit Philadelphia, but it would be another three days before he could rise up from his bed and dress himself. As soon as he was able, he sent a note to Mr. Adams regarding Mr. Burnes's death and another to Miss Burnes, stating that he would arrive the following week. He said nothing to either of them about his beating.

The journey was not comfortable. Johnny's head pounded constantly, and he could not sit up without feeling he would puke. The carriage felt as if it had no springs at all. Each knock upon the ground cracked his already sore bones. Traveling this time, Johnny saw no lovely vistas, nor did he touch the food presented to him at the taverns where he stopped along the way.

Johnny's mood had grown as black as his eyes. He could not help but wonder who it was who had discovered his article, and he could not help but feel that somehow, his old friend Peter Fray had had a hand in it.

Before he quitted Philadelphia, Johnny sent word to his editor about what had happened to him. Dennie wrote back to say that the errand boy whom Johnny had spoken to never returned to work after that day. His whereabouts were unknown. They had to assume that the boy was a paid informant for the Republican press. Paid spies were everywhere, it seemed.

When Marcia Burnes opened the door to Johnny's carriage, she found him lying face down across one seat, swaddled in blankets.

"Why, Johnny," she cried, "what has happened?" Had his breath not been visible, she would have thought he was dead. Marcia and the coachman helped Johnny up to his chamber at Tunnicliff's Hotel, for he could not mount the stairs unaided. This was a newly built hotel that stood just east of the Capitol's north wing.

"Come, darling. Driver!"

"My head pounds," Johnny replied.

"I will get you some tea—would you care for something to eat?"

"No, my stomach heaves. The journey was abysmal."

They managed to get Johnny up to his chamber, a bright, new, and airy room that faced the partly built Capitol Building.

Ginny, the young slave girl whom Johnny had met on his prior trip to Washington, ran off to fetch tea. Marcia paced and fretted, waving a fan at her bosom all the while. "But who did this to you, pray? And *why*?"

Johnny shut his eyes. "Marcia, I shall explain everything by and by. I've not the energy now."

"But there can be no good or sensible explanation for it, of that I'm certain."

Johnny said only, "I wrote a piece for the newspapers that some fellows took issue with."

"What did it say? What could you possibly have said that would make people so violent?"

"*I* did not make them violent. They already were that. In fact, the article ne'er saw the light of day."

Miss Burnes looked confused, but then she asked, "Does your mother know? She must be worried sick about you."

"God, no," he said. "I would never frighten her so. All will soon be well. Thankfully, I may spare her suffering this time."

But Johnny's mind was on a different topic entirely. His head hurt, and his mood was mercurial. At that moment, he brooded about Ginny.

"Marcia," he asked, "does Ginny now gain a salary for her efforts? Is she a freewoman?"

"Ginny is a great help to me," she replied evasively. "And to you, now. How do you propose I manage a household and grounds all alone?"

"So you haven't freed your father's slaves?"

"Oh, Johnny." She smiled. "I fear you've been too long among those Northern idealists. Or perhaps it's your injury—"

"I am injured, it's true," he interrupted. "But my morality remains unscathed." Rather than finding her lightheartedness amusing, he was irritated by it.

"John," she said, her own patience wearing thin. "I now own slaves. They were a gift to me from my father. Oh, you must know I abhor the idea of slavery just as much as you do. But why should we spend all that money when they are *happy* to work for us—well-fed and lodged? Indeed, they've told me so."

He was not convinced by such a specious argument. In Barbados, he had seen many a slave grin and nod at their masters as blood dripped down their faces from a beating, to assure them that all was well. For them to suggest otherwise was to invite a further beating, or worse.

He had little strength to fight just then, but his injuries seemed to have simultaneously worn down his self-control and infused him with almost preternatural moral energy. "Marcia, you're a wealthy woman now. You can afford to pay for servants."

She looked down at him witheringly as he lay upon the bed. "Easy for *you* to instruct me as to what I should do with *my* money."

"Pardon?" Miss Burnes's mention of her own wealth was vulgar in the extreme, and her suggestion that he wished to control it even more so.

Marcia walked out of his chamber, signaling for Ginny to follow. She did not return the following day. It was just as well; Johnny would not have been very civil to her. On the third day she reappeared, her demeanor efficient and nurse-like. "Would you like some tea?" she asked.

"Please."

"Are you hungry?"

"A little."

After he had eaten, they both read books in silence.

But after several hours of this icy treatment, Johnny could take it no longer.

"Marcia, come. Sit here," Johnny said.

"I must arrange your medicines." She reached for the washstand beside the bed, but Johnny stayed her arm.

"Look at me."

She turned and looked at him with her green questioning eyes. "What, Johnny? What do you have to say to me?"

"I'm sorry. I love you very much." He looked at her tenderly, at her beautiful heart-shaped face.

"I love you, too," she said. Then, grudgingly, she added, "I don't believe you're merely interested in spending my money."

"Merely!" He laughed. "I am not interested in it at all. If you believe money to be my motive for anything, then you don't know me."

"I know you, Johnny." Finally she flashed him an affectionate smile. Oh, he had sorely missed it!

•   •   •

As the weather warmed and Johnny gained strength, Marcia was relieved to find that Johnny had no thought of writing again for the papers. When she broached the topic of the presidential elections, he actually yawned. He began to go abroad, walking a little farther down Pennsylvania Avenue each day. One day, he had walked nearly to the President's House before realizing that he should turn back.

By June, he was strong enough to attend the gay picnics Marcia arranged. Together, they sat beneath the willow trees by the side of Goose Creek. Marcia brought food, which she set out upon a blanket. Occasionally, Miss Bron and Miss Scott joined them. At night, they went on moonlit rides along the Potomac. Sometimes, depending on the liberality of the chaperone, Johnny was able to pull Marcia behind a tree and kiss her. She always responded with a reciprocity he had never imagined possible in a woman.

One night that June, when it had grown dark and there was no one about, Marcia urged Johnny to undo her chemise and place his hands on her breasts. She tossed her head back, shut her eyes, and said, "Oh, yes. Oh." Johnny stopped, and she looked at him with her eyes shining like a cat's.

"Marcia," he whispered, calling her back from wherever she had gone.

"Oh, very well," she said sulkily, drawing her chemise shut and tucking it back into her petticoat.

Johnny resolved that the next time Marcia complained about his being a gentleman, he would cease to be one.

•   •   •

On the gray afternoon of June 28, 1800, Miss Burnes was sitting in the dining room at Tunnicliff's when Johnny stepped abroad to see whether it rained. She noticed the *Gazette* on a neighboring table and picked it up. On the very front page, it read,

> To the Republican henchmen who beat me sense-
> less. You wished to rob me of my right to free
> speech. But you have failed. What's more, your
> acts shan't go unpunished. To resort to inflicting
> bodily harm is unacceptable In an advanced civi-
> lized society, such as we aim to be . . .

Johnny heard Marcia's cry and returned to their table. She waved the paper at him. "What is this? I thought you were done with this dirty business."

"I'm done telling *you* about it, for I know how it must fill you with apprehension. As for the business itself, I shall never be done with it. We are at war, and the stakes are the continued existence of our country."

Marcia ignored Johnny's high-minded words and sighed resignedly. "Oh, but you stir up such trouble this way!"

"*I* stir up? Must I remind you that I was beaten half to death?"

"Yes, and I fear they'll finish the job next time. I told Peter you had ceased writing for the papers."

Johnny froze. "Peter? Have you seen him? Is he *here*?" A hollow darkness invaded him at this thought.

"Nay. He writes me from Philadelphia."

"*Why?*"

Marcia shrugged. "We've always corresponded, since we were children, nearly. Do *you* not still write to Kate?"

This retort was more than Johnny could bear. He grasped her by the elbow. "Marcia, you must understand something."

She pulled out of his grasp and folded her arms defensively across her chest. "What must I understand, pray?"

"I believe that Peter played a part in my attack."

Miss Burnes burst into laughter. For the first time, Johnny found the sound ugly.

"Peter, attack you? That's ridiculous." She turned her thin shoulders away from him.

"Nay, it's true."

"Have you proof? I know he favors Jefferson, but many do. Papa did. And I must admit that I myself do not see the *greatness* in Adams that you do. Oh, perhaps, back in the day . . ."

Johnny cut her off. "It's more personal than that. I cannot say more."

"You *cannot*, or will not?"

"I beseech you, Marcia. Have no further contact with him. If you do, there are things I could no longer discuss with you."

"By your own admission, there is already a great deal you don't discuss with me." She rose. "I leave for home. The servants need my guidance this afternoon."

"The slaves, you mean."

She frowned deeply and left without further comment.

When she had gone, Johnny slammed his fist on the table in frustration, spilling his tea. A rebuttal to Johnny's condemnation appeared in the *Virginia Gazette* that week. It did not worry him particularly, for it said only,

> To our esteemed colleague *Littera Scripta Manet*:
> Whether it would be a tragedy were our nation to dissolve remains to be seen. But that the written word endures—we find ourselves in agreement at last!

Johnny spent his time making amends to Marcia. He reasoned that so long as he was with her, he might as well have a happy female as his companion, for an unhappy one was a miserable ordeal. Johnny even agreed to go to a dancing assembly with her. And, without apologizing, exactly, he let her know that he regretted their fight and that she was free to form or keep any friendship she chose. However, Johnny privately resolved never again to discuss his deepest concerns with this woman who was soon to be his wife.

49

July 1800

ON AN UNUSUALLY FAIR DAY TOWARD THE end of July, Washington's damp inhabitants were finally given a brief respite from the oppressive humidity. It almost felt like autumn when Johnny and Marcia toured the partially built Capitol's south side. Clustered about the buildings were half a dozen wooden houses, shacks containing the essentials of daily life for the city's masons, carpenters, and early arrivals from the government: a washerwoman, a printer, a dry goods store, a fishmonger, and a brewery. The latter establishment, Johnny thought mordantly, could hardly help to move the construction apace.

Looking down Pennsylvania Avenue, Johnny saw not a single soul for near a mile. He held Marcia's hand as they made their way, Marcia avoiding as best she could the sharp and dusty fragments of stone upon the uneven sidewalk.

They had gone perhaps half a mile when Johnny stopped and turned around. He was suddenly inspired by the perfect lines of the streets radiating out like spokes from a wheel.

"This shall be a beautiful city someday. An important city."

"If they ever finish it." Marcia laughed.

At last, they reached the President's House. It had been much improved since Johnny had first seen it the previous year.

"Shall we go in?" asked Marcia.

"Might we?" asked Johnny, spirits rising.

"Of course. I know all the workers. Ginny brings them refreshments nearly every day, and sometimes I accompany her."

What would eventually be the front of the mansion, as yet had no steps. Marcia led Johnny around to the back, where a wooden ramp led up to a pair of doors. They entered and found themselves standing in an elegant oval drawing room. Here, red flock paper with deep gilt borders had already been applied to the walls. Beyond the oval parlor, the couple walked between two columns and into a broad hall. To the left were the beginnings of a staircase.

"Perhaps we'll live here one day," Marcia said. Johnny looked up too late to know whether she teased him.

"I should be very content to live here," he replied. At Johnny's serious tone, Miss Burnes burst out laughing.

• • •

August in Washington was hot unlike anything Johnny had ever experienced. Barbados had breezes by the water and was never so oppressively humid. There was little he felt like doing; it was hard to move at all. He and Marcia either sat beneath a tree by the creek or rowed out to Notley Young's grand estate, where they were able to swim in his pond. Johnny could swim, but Marcia had never learned how. The first time they visited the pond, Marcia waded in, skirts and all. Johnny swam about in only his breeches. He swam in circles about Marcia, pretending to be a shark.

She laughed anxiously and said, "Stop it, Johnny! You frighten me!"

Some days, they planned their wedding. They were to be married in the Presbyterian Church in George Town, which Marcia had grown up attending. Afterward, guests would ride out to the Youngs', where there would be music and dancing in the ballroom, and everything fine and delicious to eat: crab, goose, boar, ham, sugared fruit pyramids, and cakes. All would be served in the great hall that opened onto a broad veranda overlooking the river.

Mr. Young placed his entire staff at the couple's disposal. Thus far, Johnny had gone along with the plan without a word. As they sat by the creek, Johnny looked up at Marcia, whose thoughts, he knew, were filled with seating arrangements and décor. But he could not prevent himself from saying, "You know, Marcia, I like not the idea of Mr. Young's slaves serving us on our wedding day."

"Who else would you have serve us?" she replied lightly.

"I don't know. Could you—could we not hire servants for the evening?"

Marcia looked puzzled. "Why should we hire servants at great cost, when Mr. Young has so graciously offered us his full staff? They might easily do it and are already familiar with his kitchens."

"I don't know—" He hesitated.

"Fine." Marcia shrugged and turned from him. "Let us be married at the Bunch of Grapes Tavern. My friends shall be delighted, I'm sure." Marcia then burst into tears and went running down to the river, away from Johnny. He followed her. A tearful bride would not do, and Johnny quickly relented. "All right, if we must. As Mr. Young has so graciously opened his home to us, we shall do what is most convenient for our host."

Employing slaves for his own wedding! Johnny didn't know how he'd arrived at this place. From Marcia's point of view, it all made perfect sense; indeed, it was easy for their host. Then why did Johnny not insist on being married elsewhere? He knew the answer: it would be scandalous to suggest the Bunch of Grapes Tavern when the Notley Youngs had opened their beautiful estate to them. How could the "Heiress of

Washington," as everyone called her, possibly attend such an event? She could not.

Johnny didn't dare imagine what his family would say when they saw the opulent feast served by slaves.

But Marcia was smiling. "Excellent! Let's go in the water—it's infernally hot!"

. . .

Johnny had sorely begun to miss his own family. He even missed the times he had spent lugging dirt or boulders up Penn's Hill, or how, returning home drenched in sweat, he would be bathed in a tin tub by women who treated him like the babe they had delivered. He missed chasing Miriam down to the shore to play catch or search for shells. But these memories seemed as distant as the ones from Barbados.

It had now been one year since he had seen his mother and friends, nearly six since he had said good-bye to Cassie and his grandmother. He had not heard from Kate, but then, she must be occupied with her new home and husband Pearce or Parson—why could he never remember the fellow's name?

Just as Johnny thought he could take the oppressive heat no longer, it broke, and the cooler air brought him its usual lift of hope. But from the dark close holes of editorial offices, tongues spewed poison. The truth no longer seemed to matter: Were Jefferson to be elected, "Murder, robbery, rape, adultery, and incest will all be openly taught and practiced," wrote a Connecticut newspaper that September. In October, the *Aurora* wrote, "The friend of peace will vote for Jefferson—the friends of war will vote for Adams or for Pinckney."

The newspapers were on fire, but Johnny would not touch that fire again. Spies were everywhere, and no pseudonym could protect him from retribution. He would have liked to warn Adams away from

Washington. But on the morning of October 22, Johnny received a letter from the old man dated the twelfth of that month, from Peacefield:

> The swampland of the Potomac awaits. Tomorrow, I leave my peaceful plot of earth and expect to arrive in Gomorrah 'round about the 1st.

So it was that, on November 1, Johnny once more found himself climbing the makeshift platform on the south side of the President's House. He entered into the oval parlor, where the old man greeted him with a warm embrace.

"You are a sight for these sore old eyes, lad."

"And you, sir."

"Ha ha! I dare say." Here, Adams grew somber. "But say, are you well? Are you fully recovered?"

At first, Johnny knew not to what the president referred. Then he stared at the old man. "You *knew*?" he asked. "But how?"

"You're not my only eyes and ears, lad," said Adams. "But are you? Recovered, that is? You gave us a fright."

"Yes, quite recovered now, thank you. Does Mama know?"

On this point Adams was evasive. "I might have told Abigail some thing about it."

"Oh." Johnny placed a hand to his head. He suffered to think that he'd given his mother unnecessary pain.

"She knows you are well now," Adams hastened to say. "And we are all very glad of it."

Johnny sighed. He should have known that Adams could not keep a secret from Abigail, and that Abigail would not keep such a secret from Eliza.

"But come, I'll show you around," Adams said cheerfully. "How like you my 'palace'?"

"It is coming along nicely."

"Why, you've already seen it? How can that be?"

"Miss Burnes took me through a few months ago."

"I should like to meet her."

"You will. Hopefully, you'll be in Washington in May and can attend our wedding."

Adams sighed. "I'd like nothing more, Johnny. But it doesn't look good. More and more, I find myself thinking that I would simply like to go home."

"There will be time to go home, sir. Now is the time to lead."

Mr. Adams nodded dejectedly. "I will lead if the people still wish me to."

Johnny cast the president a cynical smile. "Surely you know the evil machinations going on behind closed doors just now have naught to do with 'the people.'"

Adams glanced at Johnny and then waved him forward without comment. "Come," he said. "Let us leave that for another day. Come and see our beloved friend."

Adams led Johnny to a small parlor that served as his office. From the windows of this parlor, Johnny could see the wagon-rutted field beyond, strewn with stone and rubble.

"Look, Johnny. Just here." Johnny looked up to where Adams pointed. Before him hung the great Lansdowne portrait of George Washington by Gilbert Stuart, one of many the artist had painted. It was more than eight feet tall and dwarfed all else in the room. The general had been painted in his black velvet suit and, with his right hand reaching out, palm upward, he seemed to invite Adams, Johnny, and the future itself to carry on his mission.

"I miss him so," said Adams simply.

"A portrait of honor itself."

"I wonder," Adams muttered. "Was it all an illusion?"

"Was what an illusion, sir? Not Washington's honor, surely."

"Nay, not that. But all the rest. Our pride at victory. Our belief that we had achieved something extraordinary."

"But you *did*, sir," Johnny replied. "The question remains whether we can sustain that achievement."

Mr. Adams smiled.

"Why do you smile?"

"On days like today, I feel like a tired old man who wishes nothing more than to potter among his fields and leave solutions for the younger generation. But, say—perhaps you've not yet heard about France?" The old man's tired eyes brightened.

"What about it?"

"Follow me."

Adams returned to his desk and rummaged among his papers. He soon found what he was looking for and handed a paper to Johnny. "Read this."

Johnny read. He then set the paper down, and a powerful wave of emotion overcame him.

"A peace treaty has been signed with France. Sir, this is a very great accomplishment. You have campaigned on the promise of 'Peace and Neutrality' for many months. Now you've made good on that promise, sir." Johnny walked the length of the study to the window. "And yet I can easily predict the result of this great achievement. Why, it will be the nail in your coffin, Mr. Adams. Those who say they wanted peace with Britain will call you a warmonger. Those who wished for war with France will say you lacked courage."

Mr. Adams gazed calmly at the boy. "And so you finally grasp the fundamental experience of being president of the United States."

50

November 1800

IN THE SECOND WEEK OF NOVEMBER, A severe snowstorm fell across the East Coast and prevented the United States government from reaching Washington. When they finally arrived, on November 17, nobody turned out to greet them, the weather being too inclement for celebration.

That same day, Marcia had come to town to attend the parade, not knowing that it had been cancelled. "Well, now that I'm here, what shall we do?" she asked Johnny as they stood in the parlor at Tunnicliff's.

"We could stroll up to the Capitol and tour the north wing. I've not yet been inside."

"I've a better idea." Marcia smiled mischievously.

"What's that?"

She took his hand and whispered, "That we stroll to your chamber and have a tour, for I've not yet been inside."

"But you have." He frowned.

"As your nurse," she replied.

"But Marcia, what if someone sees you?"

"They won't."

She took his hand and led him up the stairs. She opened his chamber door, removed her cape, and then shut the door. She threw her arms about his neck, whispering, "Kiss me."

He did. She placed his hands upon her chemise. After Johnny caressed her beneath the thin muslin fabric, Marcia turned her back to him and said, "Undo my stays."

Hands trembling, Johnny did as she requested, though she could easily have undone them herself. These stays were quite short and did not take long to untie.

Johnny caressed her bare shoulders, marveling at the pale little freckles there. Turning back to him, she smiled and reached up to remove the pins from her hair. Her thick, nearly black tresses tumbled down her back and shoulders. Johnny placed his hands inside her stays against her bare flesh. It was warm, soft, and supple. He whispered, "Marcia," but she placed a finger to his lips and said, "Shh."

Then she pulled away and looked at him carefully. He stood before her, and, seeing the state of things in his trousers, Marcia laughed and began to unbutton his shirt.

"But if—" he began.

"We are soon to be married. So what if I become with child? Unless . . ." She looked pointedly at him, as if suddenly doubting him.

"I love you, Marcia. We shall be man and wife in six months' time."

"Well, then, let me sample what I shall soon be purchasing."

She pulled his shirt over his head. Johnny sat on the bed and removed his shoes and trousers. He crawled into bed and waited for her as she slowly revealed herself, emerging from her gown and undergarments like Botticelli's *Birth of Venus*. She stood before him, naked and unabashed, and Johnny thought, *When God created Eve, this was what she must have looked like.*

He reached for her.

Beneath him as he moved, Marcia maintained a mysterious smile upon her lips. Her eyes remained half-closed and unreadable. It was too much for him, and it was over too soon. Afterward, Marcia turned on her side, away from Johnny, and dozed. Johnny propped himself on one elbow and stared at her as she slept. At her white, soft skin, her small waist, large breasts, her long legs that had only recently wrapped themselves around his back . . .

Johnny lay back on his pillow and shut his eyes.

He wished . . . it seemed too brief. Should he say something? He had no idea. But somehow he thought it less than . . . the moving of the heavens.

He dozed and woke an hour later to find Marcia already dressed. She was gazing at herself in the small mirror by his dressing table.

Johnny asked, "What do you think about?"

"About the election, actually," she said, not turning around.

"The election?"

"Yes. I'm wondering who shall win. From what I hear, Jefferson shall edge Adams out. But it is close, is it not?"

Johnny smiled. "I see that if I wish to bring out the civic-minded in you, I need only to bring you to bed."

"I brought *you* to bed," she corrected him with a tiny smile. "And yes, I plan to *serve man* a great deal once we are married."

At this, Marcia laughed so gaily that Johnny had to remind her to keep her voice down.

"But tell me truly, Marcia, do you really wish for Jefferson to win?"

She shrugged. "It seems disloyal to support another fellow when Jefferson is a close friend of the Frays. I have met him and conversed with him on several occasions. I have found him to be everything affable and upstanding. He has even told Peter that, should he be elected, he might have a position for him."

Marcia continued to comb her hair.

Johnny replied with more mildness than he felt, not wishing to argue with her just then, "I agree that Adams may not *look* the part, but he is a thousand times more honorable than Jefferson. There are things you don't know on this score that, were you to know, would change your mind. Why, even on the subject of Negroes—"

Johnny shut his mouth in mid-sentence, literally closing his lips. Marcia turned to face him, her eyes hard and alert.

"What about the subject of Negroes?"

Johnny knew he needed to be silent, but his pride would not allow it. "I have knowledge as would topple Jefferson in a day, were it known."

The words were in the air, in Miss Burnes's ears, and they could not be retracted. Her eyes flashed. "What mean you?"

Johnny fumbled to cover his mistake. "It was just something I heard having to do with his finances."

"If you mean his debt"—she turned back to look at herself in the mirror—"well, everyone already knows about that. No one cares overmuch. Does not your Hamilton keep hammering on about how good debt is?"

"That's different, Marcia. Hamilton speaks of national, not personal debt. And he's not *my* Hamilton. I detest the man personally." Indeed, Johnny had only recently read Hamilton's letter published the previous month, "Concerning the Public Conduct and Character of John Adams, Esq., President of the United States," which assassinated the president's character at nearly interminable length. Fortunately, many considered this letter the ravings of a madman.

But Marcia, who was both quick and shrewd, remained unconvinced that this was what Johnny had meant.

"There's something you're not telling me, Mr. Boylston."

"There isn't." Johnny blushed.

She said nothing more on the subject. Instead, she yawned, stretched her arms above her head, and said, "I'm bored. Let's go abroad."

●   ●   ●

In the ensuing days, Marcia arrived at his lodgings just after dinner and remained with him till suppertime. Once more, but only once, she insisted on entering his chamber, where she laid herself next to him. Though he held her close, Johnny would have no repetition of that amorous interlude which had put him so off his guard.

One time, Johnny fell asleep briefly, and when he woke up he found Marcia sitting at his desk. A drawer was open, and she hastily shut it.

"What do you search for, Marcia?" he asked from the bed.

"Oh, nothing. You've been sleeping so long, I knew not what to do with myself."

After this occasion, Johnny no longer invited her to his chamber, and he moved Jefferson's letter to a trunk beneath his bed.

Marcia was not happy about being rejected in this manner. But one afternoon, after he steered her abroad, Johnny said gently, "Dearest, I think only of your honor."

"Honor, indeed." She glanced at him coolly.

Several times, Miss Burnes endeavored to engage him on the topic of Jefferson, but Johnny was now canny enough to change the topic. He didn't know absolutely whether she was merely curious or whether she wished to help her friend Mr. Fray. But he would err on the side of caution from now on.

Johnny knew he would never reveal the contents of that letter from Jefferson to Sally Hemings, not even to his wife. Then why had he not burned it already? He should have. Yet the letter confounded him: Repulsed as he was by Jefferson's hypocrisy, the letter moved him, connected him to Jefferson somehow. It even gave him a bizarre lift of hope.

He knew not what to do. What if Adams lost the election and Johnny could have prevented it? Over and over it he went. Finally, on the morning of November 28, Johnny strode down Pennsylvania Avenue toward the President's House bent on telling all. A second storm had blanketed Washington in a foot of snow, creating a haunting stillness. The snow masked the stumps and rubble, and Johnny kept tripping until he finally mounted F Street and walked along the smoother, higher ground.

From a distance, "the Palace" appeared like a portrait of lonely responsibility. Johnny walked up the south-side ramp and knocked. A black girl opened the door, and Johnny heard a feminine voice call from within: "She's a well-paid servant, Johnny."

Johnny grinned and ran to Mrs. Adams as if she were his own mother. She was standing on the other side of a large unpainted parlor. A fire raged within, and she was hanging laundry to dry. After a deep bow, during which he noticed the unfinished brick walls and hewn beams where a ceiling should have been, Johnny ran to hug her. But such was the force of his big body against hers that she was nearly knocked off her feet.

"Oh, sorry, ma'am!"

Mrs. Adams laughed. "Never mind. You've grown very strong. But there is snow yet clinging to you."

Johnny looked down at his feet and obligingly stomped some of the snow off.

"Goodness, not in *here*!" she cried.

"Oh, sorry!" Johnny bowed awkwardly and then moved toward Adams's office, where he saw Mr. Adams. Or rather, he saw the man's black silhouette against the white landscape beyond his study window. He was sitting with his spectacles on, reading something that seemed to puzzle him. He heard the door open, and when he saw Johnny, he set down his reading and removed his spectacles.

"Johnny! Torn yourself away from your beautiful lady to visit with an old man, ha ha? An old and depressed man, I might add." Johnny knew that Hamilton's scandalous pamphlet had hurt Adams, though the old man sought to make light of it. "To what do I owe the—but what is it, lad?" Adams suddenly noticed Johnny's expression. "What has happened?"

"Nothing, sir." Johnny glanced behind him and realized that the office had no door. He moved closer to the president and lowered his voice. "May I sit, sir?"

"Do." Adams pointed to a chair in a corner of the room.

Johnny pulled his chair close to Adams's desk, shifting his thoughts with the chair. "Since our last conversation on the topic, sir, I have considered what to do with certain information in my possession. For many months now, I've thought it right to burden no one with it, including you. But now, as election day nears, this knowledge weighs upon me. I have kept it locked inside for so long, it begins to burn me. I could not forgive myself if—"

"But what is this knowledge, child? Surely not that Callender business. That's old news."

Johnny inhaled. "Last winter, during that same event about which I in part told you, I happened upon a letter." Johnny whispered into Adams's ear, "It was from Mr. Jefferson to a certain 'Sally.' She's a slave at his estate, his daughter Martha's maid, I believe. I heard her spoken of years ago, in Fredericksburg, though I thought nothing of it at the time."

Adams held up a forestalling hand. "How did you 'happen upon' this letter?"

"It fell out of his account book."

"And why did you not return it to its place?"

"I heard footsteps—I ran. I didn't mean to take it."

"And what were the contents, exactly?"

Johnny recited the letter, long since etched in his memory:

My dearest one, I long to be home among my beloved family. I was grieved beyond words to hear of our little girl's death, but shall speak no more of it here and save my grief until I am in your arms once more. I am in a viper pit here and fear I shall be stung many times before finding my way out. If only

I were there to place my weary head upon the breast of my beloved Sally!

P.S. Please send love to your Mistress Martha from me. I pray you are able to console one another for the loss of our little one.

Adams was silent a long moment. He then quietly asked, "I can hardly believe it. But since you recite it so to the letter, it must be true. Where is this letter now?"

"I have it in my possession, sir. In a trunk at Tunnicliff's, beneath my bed. I was unable to return it, the rightful owner reappearing quite suddenly."

Mr. Adams turned away from Johnny and walked toward the window. He rested his arms on the newly planed windowsill and looked out.

"Such a beautiful dream we've created, Johnny."

"Yes, sir."

"I've known you a long time, lad. You are like one of my own children. You have greater gifts than my own sons, and a much gentler nature. But this was your first mistake, and a bad one."

Johnny didn't understand, but he nonetheless felt the swift sting of Mr. Adam's rebuke. "Sir?"

Mr. Adams began to pace about his office, avoiding Johnny. He said, almost to himself, "I suppose it's better you should make it with me than with anyone else."

At once, Johnny felt a lump of hurt pride rise in his throat. "What is that, sir?"

Pausing by the window, the old man looked across the lawn at the unfinished work, the dirt and stones, and the snow that continued to fall.

"Information is power. Think of your knowledge as a bomb: shall it explode in your hands or elsewhere? I, for one, have no intention of acting upon this news. Indeed, I would sooner discredit myself. Yet there are others, lad, very powerful others, who have no such scruples. They would reveal their own mother's secrets if it furthered their aims. That is this filthy business of governing."

"Do I understand your point correctly, sir?" Johnny's brain felt slow, sluggish. Tears threatened to replace all rational thought. "You would sacrifice your reelection for the public good?"

Adams looked at him pointedly. "That's precisely what I'm saying. Don't worry overly much about that. I've heard rumors of 'dusky Sally' before. But Jefferson, for all his faults, is a great patriot, father, and citizen. And this particular fault of which you speak, this unfortunate—*liaison*—I place not on Jefferson's head but on the evil institution of slavery itself. Know only this: the news you share with me today, Johnny, if true—it will explode. Mark my words. It is only a matter of time. But do not make a second mistake of revealing the weapon to anyone else."

"Yes, sir."

Johnny nodded, bowed, and left. But as he walked out into the deceiving whiteness, he knew he already had.

51

A LETTER GREETED HIM BACK AT TUNNICLIFF'S, having been slid beneath his door.

> Dear Son
> I shall not delay a single moment with news of any prosaic sort. Our dear Kate, who as you may already know, married Mr. Pearce in October and settled into housekeeping in Boston, has disappeared. I shouldn't blame you for being incredulous, and thus include a faithful copy of her letter, which Martha has kindly shared with me.

Johnny's mother had been clever to foresee her son's incredulity. Hardly breathing, he read the letter from Kate to her parents:

> Dear Mama and Papa
> I cannot give you details of my marriage, not yet, or its failure. Suffice to say I could not remain in it a moment longer. Circumstances require that I absent myself from society for a time. I have gone to New York, where I learn from someone with a great deal of experience. As you know, the first volume of my little endeavor,

published last fall, while a critical success, did not earn back the cost of making it. If I am to be successful and independent—which now, it will be obvious to all, circumstances require—I must learn how this magazine business is truly done. I find myself busy and useful, and this itself does me a great deal of good.

This letter sounded like Kate, and Johnny believed it was hers. But what she must have suffered to leave a marriage so! How much she must have omitted!

Marcia arrived at Johnny's soon after he read this news. Unable to conceal his distress, he blurted, "I've had bad news about my friend Kate."

He had expected solace and advice from his betrothed. But instead, Marcia looked at him pointedly as they stood in the hallway. "She's now a married woman, and yet you still care for her."

"Of course I care for her. She is like family to me."

"Is that all?" Her tone was insinuating. She set the letter down.

Johnny placed a hand upon Marcia's arm. "How can you doubt me?"

"Men are to be doubted, I've found." She shrugged.

"Indeed?" he asked heatedly. "Have I once given you reason to doubt?"

"Lower your voice, Johnny," she whispered. "People shall hear."

"What if they do?"

"All right." She turned to face him. "No. You've never given me reason to doubt you. Tell me, what is this bad news?"

"Never mind," he replied. "I thought you would understand." But Marcia proffered her hand, and he gave her the letter. As she perused it, Johnny found a place to sit in the bar.

Marcia set the letter down upon the table, then pulled up her own chair and sat down. "I *do* understand." She sighed. "But surely there are others who may get to the bottom of it?"

"*I* wish to get to the bottom of it," he said. "But now I take my leave of you, Marcia, for I have a letter to write, and I'm afraid it can't wait."

"Go on, then," she said, dismissing him with a wave of her hand. She ordered some refreshment and ate it alone.

•   •   •

Johnny wrote a letter to his mother in which he included a letter to Kate, in the event that they found her. But he had no illusions of their finding her, not if she did not wish to be found. New York was a large city.

In his letter, Johnny grieved for her suffering but was careful not to pass judgment. He ended his letter by saying,

> I pray you find peace, if not happiness, in your new
> and most worthy endeavor, my dearest Kate. And I
> hope I shall see you very soon. It has been far too long.

When he had finished, he returned to the dining room, where he expected to find Miss Burnes. But she had already left.

Throughout Washington, people's moods were grim, like Johnny's own. On December 3, the nation voted. Everyone settled in for the long wait, until Congress reconvened on February 11, 1801.

During this time, Johnny heard again from his mother.

> Dear Son
> Thank you for your last letter(s). We all miss you ter-
> ribly and doubt whether we can wait till May to see
> you. I know you cannot get away just now. Perhaps it
> would be wise for us to come to you? We have not yet
> located Kate but the men are working on it day and
> night. She is clever, and it seems she does not yet wish
> to be found. Martha is frantic, as you may imagine. I
> worry she will take sick over it . . .

Johnny wrote to dissuade his mother from making the arduous trip to Washington until they heard the election results. If Adams lost, Johnny would probably head to Richmond at once, to seek lodging for himself and his future wife. Mr. Adams had graciously extended Johnny's small salary through the election, but Johnny would not take advantage of such charity a day longer than necessary.

Marcia, meanwhile, returned to Tunnicliff's after a few days, just as if there had been no argument between them. She sought to distract Johnny from the election with an endless calendar of social events, beginning with a dancing assembly at the Bunch of Grapes Tavern.

Miss Bron and Miss Scott accompanied them to the event, and they all danced. The ladies were merry. Johnny smiled and bowed, as he knew he must. But as the evening wore on, he felt increasingly ill. He realized this was not due to indisposition but a kind of moral revulsion. A cataclysm was taking place, the conclusion of which would determine whether this America, this unity of diverse states, would hold or crumble to dust. And yet here were these people, dancing to the strains of ancient airs and minuets. It was as if they cared nothing for this grand experiment so long as the music played and the wine flowed!

At eleven, he bade good-bye to the ladies, choosing to walk back to his lodgings alone. Miss Bron and Miss Scott could accompany Marcia home.

Sometime after falling asleep, Johnny dreamed he was submerged in cold, dark water. He felt as if he were suffocating and sat straight up in bed, clasping his throat. He managed to fall back to sleep at around three but was awakened at dawn by shouting in the streets.

"It's a tie! It's a tie! Adams has lost!"

Johnny rose and dressed. He quickly descended the stairs and found a copy of the *National Intelligencer* upon one of the tavern tables. Adams had lost, but the race was not over. Jefferson and Burr were tied. According to the Constitution, a tied election would be placed in the hands of the outgoing House of Representatives. There was yet a small chance that Adams would win, but with many powerful men working behind the scenes to prevent the occurrence, neither Johnny nor Adams had any hope. The question was really whether Burr or Jefferson would be the next president of the United States. The waiting began.

It snowed. Marcia donned her fur-lined cape and hired a sleigh to ride out with friends. Johnny attended a New Year's ball at the President's House. The newspapers were eerily quiet, and conversations around dinner tables and in taverns reflected the city's tense, undecided mood.

John Adams, on the other hand, looked forward to going home. His last piece of business was to nominate John Marshall for chief justice of the United States. Though he would no doubt be criticized for it, Adams wished to make certain that the Federal cause was represented in the new government. Johnny heard of Marshall's nomination and had an uneasy feeling that his position in Richmond was no longer a certainty; but Marshall did not write him to say so.

Toward the end of January 1801, Marcia designed and ordered their wedding invitations. Together, they spoke to the minister regarding the details of the ceremony. Marcia wanted it to be flawless. She made Johnny practice what he would say, as if five simple lines and a single "I do" might prove too challenging for the boy who'd memorized *Common Sense* for Peter Fray.

Johnny purchased a wedding costume and spent an hour one morning at the tailor's having it fitted. Marcia looked on from a chair in the corner of the messy George Town shop.

"But the cuffs are far too broad. And those tucks at the back must lie *flat*."

The tailor, an old Scotsman, nodded silently, no doubt inured to overbearing fiancées. At the end of the fitting, Marcia clasped her hands together delightedly. "Oh, but it does bring out the astonishing blue of your eyes!"

Back at Tunnicliff's, Johnny found another letter from his mother.

Dear Son

I hope all is well with you and that you have not taken Adams's defeat too hard. Abigail says that she is positively jubilant. Meanwhile, I have had news from your aunt that Mr. Pearce has sold his house in Boston and sailed for England! Nothing is known, but the Lees are vastly relieved to learn that the man has no intention of bringing a suit against their daughter. Abby tells me that your nuptial preparations move apace. I cannot wait to meet the esteemed Miss Burnes and to call her Daughter ere long.

Johnny felt none of his usual joy upon receiving this letter from his mother. He could not help but imagine the scene in which his mother, Lizzie, Martha, and Abigail finally met Miss Burnes. He pictured Marcia standing there in her fine silks and ironic smile as Martha Lee, Quaker; Lizzie, the midwife; and Eliza, wife of a former slave, endeavored to converse with her. Was it possible? The thought of such a dissonant scene made him cringe. Fortunately, his imaginings were soon interrupted by a knock at the door. It was the servant girl, wishing to clean his chamber.

• • •

February 11, 1801. It was the day that Congress would reconvene to break the tie for the next president. Through a crippling snowstorm, delegates from every state of the Union made their way to the Capitol. They filled the cramped, dark Senate chamber in the half-built building, where the vice president himself tallied the votes.

Johnny was at his desk. He had just finished a brief editorial he meant to publish in the event of a deadlock. In it, he urged each delegate to vote his conscience and not to barter.

There is more than an election at stake. The question you vote on is no less than whether this democracy of ours can work.

He was just finishing when a knock at his door disturbed him. Annoyed, he rose and opened the door to find Mr. Tunnicliff.

"There are some men to see you, Mr. Boylston."

Johnny was puzzled. "Indeed? Who, pray? I'm not expecting anyone."

"No, but they're expecting an audience with you. A Mr. James Callender and one other, name of Fray. To see a man they call John Watkins."

52

WHEN JOHNNY ENTERED THE BARROOM, CALLENDER GLANCED at Peter, who nodded. Callender stood up. He was a short, almost deformedly ugly man of perhaps forty-five. His eyes were dark and observant; a long, pointed nose seemed to be their rudder as he gazed warily around the room.

Peter continued to sit at the table nursing his cider. "Hello, Johnny," he said, raising his mug.

Johnny did not greet either of them. He turned to Callender.

"Out of jail so soon, Callender? I thought Mr. Adams put you away for a long time." Callender had been tried and sentenced to nine months in jail for sedition the previous spring.

"Mr. Who?" Callender replied. "But to the subject of our visit. May I?" He sat back down, but Johnny remained standing. "It wasn't difficult to find out about you," Callender said. "I had merely to ask a friend in Portsmouth. Any old crone on the street will share the 'scandal of the era,' as they still call it there. Your family moved to Portsmouth after the death of your mother's brother. Your mother, but nineteen at the time, thought her uncle's slave Watkins most handsome. Yes, the slave's blue eyes are still whispered about among the pious old ladies at church."

Here, Callender looked into Johnny's own glaring blue eyes.

Fray finally stood. "And how coincidental that your mother left the country at almost the same time as Watkins escaped. But then, all I really needed to do was to write our friends in Barbados. The Cumberbatches and the Alleyns both knew John Watkins personally. Everyone there did."

Despite his steady demeanor, Johnny could feel himself giving way from within. It would not take much more to bring him to violence. The men in the tavern looked on with an eager air, as if a real Southern cockfight were about to begin.

Suddenly, in a last effort to repair their rift, Johnny addressed Peter, "Why is it you despise me so? I've told you before I meant no harm."

"That's just it, old mole. You *did* mean harm. Admit it. Deep down, you're all violent. Just waiting for the chance to cut our throats."

Johnny glanced down a moment. Upon a nearby table, a dinner knife lay poised. Johnny reached for it and slowly closed his fist around it.

"If you're right, Peter, then you are indeed in grave danger. You should leave."

"Now, now." Callender smiled and showed Johnny his palms. "You haven't heard our offer."

"I have no need of hearing any offer."

"Oh, I beg to differ. Tell me what you know about Jefferson, and who else knows, and the truth of your mongrel blood shall ne'er reach Miss Burnes's virgin ears." Peter sneered the word *virgin* as if he knew differently about that as well.

Johnny felt a click in his brain. He raised the knife to his hip and growled, "Get out of here before I can no longer account for my actions. A duel would be too good for you."

Peter took a step back and wound up falling backward onto the floor, taking the chair upon which he had been leaning with him. Several diners stopped eating, and two men who had been watching the scene now stood up as if they might join the fight. Johnny pointed the knife in their direction, and they backed off.

Callender grinned. "A death threat, too! Isn't that just grand! So much to write about these days."

"We're going," said Fray. He rose and dusted off his pale-green coat. Then he placed a forestalling hand on Callender's arm. "Please give my regards to Miss Burnes. It has been too long since I've seen her. Nearly five days."

The moment they had gone, Johnny dropped the knife back on the table. His palms were wet, and his hands shook. For several moments, he just stood there. Then he sprang into action. He raced up the stairs, grabbed his coat, and ran out of his lodgings. On Pennsylvania Avenue, he leapt over the snowy stumps and tripped over hidden holes, heading toward Marcia's house. He needed to tell her the truth before the *Examiner* did.

• • •

Johnny was covered in snow and out of breath when he arrived at her cottage. He could hear her at her pianoforte, playing a lovely ancient air. Hearing his frantic knock, she stopped midphrase and came to the door. The snow began to melt the moment Johnny stepped into the room.

"John, remove your coat and shoes at least, or my house shall become a lake."

"Oh, sorry."

In his stocking feet and wild hair that had curled from the melting snow, Johnny looked a fright.

"But what is the matter? What has happened?" She held on to his sleeve and gazed searchingly up at him.

"Let us sit," he said.

He trusted her; of course, he did. Had Marcia not, in giving her most intimate self to him, proven that she cared little for convention? But he needed to understand the precise manner in which she had been indiscreet, and with whom.

"Marcia, I've just now had a most unwelcome visit from Mr. Fray."

At Fray's name, Marcia frowned. "Peter? What did *he* want?"

"He wished to blackmail me."

Johnny told Marcia how the two men had arrived at his lodgings demanding to know what Johnny knew about Jefferson.

Johnny turned to Marcia entreatingly. "Marcia, know you how he could have known that I had information about Jefferson? You didn't happen to say anything, did you?"

"Of course not," she said, her eyes shifting evasively.

"This is important."

"Oh, well," she said irritably, "if you must know, Peter and I quarreled."

"He was here?"

"Why, yes. He's been in town these past several months, to follow the campaign."

"You *knew* he followed the campaign?"

"Of course."

"I only suspected it," Johnny muttered. "And you did not think to tell me? Do you not understand that Callender and Fray work together to destroy Mr. Adams?"

"As you would destroy Jefferson?" she replied.

Johnny bit his tongue to keep from saying anything he would later regret. He allowed several heartbeats to pass before asking, in a quieter tone, "What did you *tell* him?"

"All right!" she exclaimed. "If you'll not be so brutish as to interrupt me, I *shall* tell you! He stopped by, and we got on to the subject of the tie between Burr and Jefferson. I said it was perhaps not a certainty that Jefferson would win. My doubt seemed to annoy him."

By this point, Johnny's jaw was rigid. "You know not what blazing fires burn in the hearts of our men. Marcia, there is talk of invasion, of armies, even assassinations!"

"I simply recalled what you told me. I was flustered, and I told him that you knew something about Jefferson, the very whisper of which could destroy him."

Johnny put his head in his hands. He muttered, "You know not what you've done."

"Protected Jefferson's reputation, I imagine. But is not that good, now? You have often told me you prefer him to Burr, whom you call a madman. Is that not so?"

"It is. But the information they learned from you prompted them to unearth something about *me*. Something they would use to harm me, and by extension all those I hold dear."

Here, Marcia threw her head back and actually laughed. "Johnny, what could they possibly use against *you*? You are the most stainless man of my acquaintance. Why, everyone says so. The Youngs, the Carrolls, even Miss Bron and Miss Scott. They all believe you to be the most honorable, the most articulate, the most—"

"Marcia." He took her hands and looked beseechingly at her. "I'm a black man."

At that very moment, Ginny entered the parlor; she stopped moving so suddenly that Johnny thought she'd drop her tray.

Marcia turned abruptly. "Ginny, allow us a moment, please!"

"Sorry, miss. I thought you'd like some tea. Mr. Boylston looks wet through."

"Thank you," said Johnny. "In a few moments, Ginny."

Ginny curtsied and left the parlor. Once she had gone, Marcia whispered, "What mean you, *black*? Why, you're as white as I. Black how? Are you speaking in metaphors?"

Johnny took a deep breath. "Marcia, let us remove to the window." He pointed to the window overlooking the river, which had the advantage of being far removed from the kitchen and Ginny's ears. Johnny took Marcia's hands almost pleadingly. "My excellent father, John Watkins, was a slave. He was born of a young Antiguan slave girl and the royal governor of New Hampshire, a product of his rapine lust. Mama fell in love with Papa when she was living at her uncle's in Portsmouth. In '79, my father escaped, and together we fled to Barbados. I was but a babe."

Marcia was silent. After perhaps a minute, she asked, "And have you always known this?"

"I have. My parents never sought to hide it from me."

"Why then did you never tell me?"

"I knew not how."

"You thought I'd reject you out of hand." She looked at him gravely, for he had by now knelt down upon the carpet, almost as if he were proposing to her once more. And perhaps he was.

"I couldn't risk that. Not after I had met you again. It seemed that fate had brought you back to me."

"Fate." She sighed.

"But Marcia, can you still love me, knowing what you do?"

She looked almost puzzled by this statement. "Why, of course I can, Johnny. It matters not in the least. You are no different from who you were yesterday."

"Do you mean it?" He grasped her hand.

"Of course. But you must be eager to change out of those wet clothes. Would you like the coachman to drive you home?"

"No. I'll gladly walk. I could walk a hundred miles, now. Oh, Marcia!" Johnny embraced her.

Marcia walked him to the door. He moved to kiss her; she turned, alert to a noise behind her, and his kiss landed on her cheek.

"By the way, Johnny, who else knows? I am merely curious."

"Only my nearest family: Kate and her parents, and the Millers. Lizzie Miller is the midwife I told you about. And the Adamses, of course. They have known me since my birth."

Marcia nodded thoughtfully. "They—and Peter Fray and James Callender, now."

"Yes," he admitted. "But I don't see what they have to gain by sharing it. I made it clear to them I would never share what I knew about Jefferson. Indeed, I've resolved to burn the letter."

"You have an actual letter?" Her questioning eyes dilated slightly.

He suddenly recalled that he had never told her about the letter to Sally Hemings. He made no reply.

Marcia said, "Well, no matter. In the end, it's how one behaves that matters. You are white as ivory. We shall live in a fine home, and if we live as everyone else, our friends shall ignore the rumors." She smiled and touched his face tenderly. "You will let us keep my slaves, now, won't you?"

Johnny moved to kiss her. He was reeling from her declaration of undying love. But as she lifted her face to kiss him, his breath caught in his chest, and he pulled gently away from her.

"No," he said. "I cannot go as far as to own slaves."

He feared she would be annoyed, but she merely smiled. "Oh, well. There'll be time for us to discuss it. Won't there?"

Johnny bowed. Turning his thoughts to that one incontrovertible fact of her love, he fairly leapt out onto Pennsylvania Avenue, hardly caring about anything else. He saw not the snow or ice, he felt not the cold, now that he knew Marcia still loved him.

53

THE FOLLOWING MORNING, JOHNNY AWOKE EARLY, rose, and was about to descend for breakfast when he realized that he had not yet replied to his mother. He did so at once:

> February 16th, 1801
> Dear Mama
> Have you received any further word from Kate? I expect you will write to me the moment you do, for I shan't sleep soundly until I know she is well.
>
> By the time this letter reaches you, the election will have been decided one way or another. I find myself at the mouth of Charybdis, who sucks all combatants into the depths of her watery lair.
>
> I have only yesterday been approached by a certain blackguard of my acquaintance who has threatened to tell the world about me, that secret you well know. I did not think he would go to that length; he has no *reason* to do so. But as honor required, I told Miss Burnes. Oh, Mama! If you could have seen her. How brave my lady was! A model of fortitude and virtue! She said, "Are you not the same man you were yesterday?" You know not how my heart swells with

love! I long to see you, and for you to meet my soon-to-be wife.

Johnny then dashed off a message to Marcia asking did she wish to be present when the tailor made the final alterations on his wedding costume. A boy from the hotel, who had been running about with messages since sunrise, came to take the note for him.

"How fare things at Congress?" Johnny asked.

"I dunno, sir. But the fellows have been calling for their pillows and nightcaps."

Johnny frowned. That was not a good sign.

After breakfast, just as he headed to the post to mail his letter, Johnny saw a new edition of the *Aurora* on the hall table:

BALLOTS DEADLOCKED. THIRTY-FIVE AND COUNTING
RUMORS HAMILTON AMASSES SECRET ARMY

Thirty-five times the representatives had cast their votes, and thirty-five times they had returned the same result. When would it end? *How* would it end? Johnny wondered. He opened the paper. He half expected to find something calumnious about himself, but instead, the editors warned that Virginia and Pennsylvania had mobilized their militias. These states were prepared to fight their own countrymen in order to defend against "legislative usurpation." This news was quite alarming. But at least it was not about him.

Without, the air was frigid, the sky dark as coal, and the road beneath his feet icy. No one was about. The entire city, it seemed, remained indoors, awaiting announcement of the new president.

As he walked to the post office, Johnny became aware of feeling watched; willingly or no, he observed those around him for signs of imminent aggression. It was simple fear, nothing real, he told himself.

No one sought to kidnap or to harm him. Still, he felt that somehow he was in danger, his blackness exposed for all to see.

He mailed his letter at the post and took a meal at the Bunch of Grapes Tavern. There, everyone was talking about the election. Rumors flew that a senator from Delaware had offered to change his vote to Jefferson in exchange for certain Federalist compromises, and that Jefferson had accepted.

After his meal, Johnny returned to Tunnicliff's. There was as yet no reply from Marcia. The young chambermaid was just making his bed. She started when he entered and then whispered, "Good-bye, sir. You've been very kind." Then she curtsied and scurried from his room.

Johnny frowned. What had she meant? The chambermaid's words took on a more sinister cast late that afternoon when, descending for a mug of cider, Johnny was met by Mr. Tunnicliff. "Might we have a word?" he asked Johnny. "When you've a moment?"

"Of course," he replied.

Johnny gulped down a mug of cider and approached Tunnicliff's office. The owner was standing in the middle of the room, but when he saw Johnny, he moved behind his desk and sat down. He made a great show of opening his ledger, turning it around, and pointing to the current page. "I'm very sorry, Mr. Boylston, but as you can see, I'm expecting a large party from Virginia. I'm afraid . . . I'm afraid I shall need your chamber." Tunnicliff looked away.

Johnny could hardly reply. "But all the other boardinghouses are filled to bursting and shall be for several weeks, as you well know. Where am I to go?"

"I'm sorry," Tunnicliff said. "You may remain till the end of the week but no longer."

After he left Tunnicliff's office, a bizarre silence followed Johnny through the hotel's hallway and back into the tavern, where he ordered another cider. A few souls glanced up at him when he entered but then quickly looked away. Marcia had still not replied, and by the time he returned to his chamber, a dark mood had descended upon him. He read for a few hours but could not fall asleep. Then, no sooner had he succeeded than he was awakened by a great fanfare of church bells ringing and by shouting in the streets.

Jefferson had won.

Johnny heaved a sigh of relief. Now, he thought, it hardly mattered what he himself knew or did not know about the man. The battle had been lost and won.

* * *

Half an hour later, the sun rose upon a changed city, one half jubilant and the other miserable. In the taverns, men already argued about the legitimacy of Jefferson's victory. By nine, having still received no word from Marcia, Johnny decided to walk to her house. The sun was bright and the ice, while treacherous in patches, had begun to thaw.

At her cottage door, Johnny met Ginny, who curtsied but did not offer to see him in.

"I've come for Marcia. I have my tailor's appointment this afternoon."

"Oh, yes. But, well, the missus, she's not in just now."

"Not in? Do you know where she's gone?"

"No, sir." Ginny shook her head slowly.

"But she received my letter, did she not?"

"I believe she did, sir."

Ginny began to shut the door, but Johnny forestalled her.

"Kindly inform Miss Burnes that I stopped here, and that I shall be at Pringle's in George Town at three this afternoon."

"I will, sir."

Johnny walked to George Town, where he stopped at Suter's for some refreshment. He then moved on to the tailor, where he was fitted for his wedding suit.

Pringle chatted with Johnny, pins in his mouth. Standing erect in his fine blue silk suit with its brocade red waistcoat, white gloves, and impeccable trousers, Johnny could have passed for a king's courtier. The tailor made no mention of the election until the very end of the fitting, when he said, "Watch yourself heading home, lad. There's people gone mad out there. Stark raving mad." Then, looking at Johnny, he smiled proudly at his own excellent work.

When he arrived back at his hotel after a long, muddy walk, Johnny found a letter slipped beneath his chamber door.

> Dear Mr. Boylston
> As you must have been apprized, two weeks ago, the president did me the great honor of appointing me Chief Justice of the United States. I find this changes somewhat the prospect of my future needs. I shall be obliged to spend much of my time here in Washington and thus most regretfully must rescind my offer of employment in Richmond. I wish you the very best in finding a satisfactory situation elsewhere, and have no doubt that such an able young man as yourself will do so.
> Yours most respectfully, J. M.

Johnny stood there with the letter in his hands, bewildered. He did not doubt Marshall's word. This was a man of unimpeachable integrity. He had made Johnny an offer one year earlier and stood by it. But why then had he not written weeks ago, when Adams appointed him? Without the promise of that position, Johnny knew not how he could support a wife, much less continue to live in the South. The thought occurred to him that he might in fact need to return to Boston and prevail upon his friends. Perhaps an unscrupulous man could live off his wife's income, but Johnny would not consider it.

But, oh, how would he ever convince Marcia to leave her friends and head north? She had never evinced the least curiosity about New England. Now that her father was gone, Marcia delighted in those gay society events at the Notley Youngs' and the Carrolls' of Duddington. Without her circle, she was simply a woman with money but no great lineage or standing. Still, Johnny needed to tell her that the offer from Marshall had been rescinded.

Johnny sat down at his desk and wrote another letter to her. He read it over and was reasonably satisfied. He then took a new sheet of foolscap, over which his pen hovered until the ink on the tip was nearly dry. Finally, he dipped the nib in the bottle and wrote,

> Dearest Mama,
> There has been a turn of events since Jefferson's elec-
> tion, and I believe you shall find my news welcome.
> After the wedding, my bride and I shall have the joy
> of returning to Quincy with you.

Bolstered by his own hopeful words, Johnny sealed the letters, grabbed his coat, and descended. He gave the letters to one of the servants with instructions on their delivery, then stepped abroad. It was already near half past six, and the sky had grown dark. He thought he would head to the Bunch of Grapes. Apart from his refreshment at Suter's, Johnny had not eaten since breakfast, and he was hungry. At the Bunch of Grapes, he could have a meal and ask about lodging at the same time.

The tavern was quite crowded when Johnny arrived, but eventually he was seated in its smoky barroom and served an excellent meat stew with potatoes. His eyes and throat burned from the smoke, but the conviviality, even of those celebrating Jefferson's election, was better than the deep silence elsewhere. However, inquiring after lodging, he was disappointed to learn that they had not so much as a single bed to share.

When Johnny finally left the Bunch of Grapes, it had begun to snow. The snow came ever thicker as he trudged the mile back to his hotel. He had not worn his mitts, and his hands were stiff with cold by the time he pushed open the front door to his lodgings. Mounting the stairs, he thought he felt hostile eyes upon him from the other lodgers who were taking their supper in the public room. This must be his imagination, he told himself. *I am imagining enemies where I have none.*

As he moved to open his chamber door, he noticed a letter partially visible beneath it. His heart leapt—Marcia, at last! He would have to scold her for keeping him in such suspense as to her whereabouts. He stooped to retrieve the letter.

It was not a letter but rather a pamphlet, composed of several pages.

THE FEDERALIST MONGRELS

At first glance, he knew not what it meant. Then he clutched at his cravat and fled with the pamphlet back down the stairs. He sat down and ordered a pint of beer. But the server, a bent old man who might have been Tunnicliff's father, did not seem to hear his request. He ignored Johnny despite several loud calls. In a burst of frustration, Johnny cried, "Well, come on, man!"

The old man finally moved off and Johnny was able to open the pamphlet:

> *It is now an incontrovertible fact that certain men in the Monocratical Party, whom it delighteth the people to honor, keep, and have for several years kept, certain dusky boys to do their secret spying. What a sublime adherence to the Hyppocritic Oath for American ambassadors to place before the public eyes! Who doubts that, had he been King, they would have fanned him like a pasha . . .*

The article went on to name John Watkins in particular and several other men of Adams's "secret hoard of Federalist slaves."

Was this some joke? He knew it was not. Adams never kept a slave in his life, and never would. Many already knew this. But they had named him. Why? He thought there could be only one reason. Peter Fray.

Johnny's beer arrived; the old man set it roughly upon the table. He glanced at the pamphlet, then at Johnny, and was gone without a word. Johnny drank the pint and ordered another. It tasted sour; he frowned. He felt light-headed almost at once. Yet he drank it quickly as well, for the room appeared to have fallen silent all around him. Johnny stood, slightly unbalanced now. Did the old man know? Did the chambermaid know? Did the entire company in the bar know?

He cried to the scant crowd, "What cheerful fellows you all are!" and stumbled out of the hotel. He soon made his way to another tavern on Jenkins Hill. Here, Johnny drank a third and fourth tankard of beer. Then he stopped in at the new townhouses built by George Washington, which housed many of the arriving statesmen. To the butler and a small crowd behind him, Johnny angrily insisted that he was a personal friend of the president.

"Former president!" someone laughed and shoved him out by the shoulders. After this, things grew shadowy. Johnny recalled nothing until the following morning, when he found himself in his bed but knew not how he got there. He felt a stabbing pain behind his left eye.

February 20, 1801. It was the day he was meant to leave Tunnicliff's. But where to? In those remaining hours, he sent off another letter to Marcia. Johnny knew that the roads were slick, making for a treacherous journey down F Street. Perhaps the message had failed to reach her. Or maybe Ginny, out of a misplaced sense of loyalty to her mistress, was not passing his letters on to her. In his final letter to Marcia, Johnny let her know that he would be staying just near her, at the President's

House. The way he phrased it made it sound prearranged, when in fact Adams knew nothing about it.

Why had Marcia not responded? Had she not told him that his black blood did not matter to her? There had been no ambiguity, no dissembling on her part. Surely he would have seen it, felt it? Johnny resolved to confront her later that day. He would listen patiently to her explanation, for surely there would be one. After all, she still loved him. She had told him so.

The sun shone brightly, and it was with a lift in his spirits that Johnny went off to purchase a trunk. Since coming to Tunnicliff's that past May, he had acquired many books and clothing as would no longer fit in a single trunk.

Item purchased, he was just approaching his lodgings, dragging the new trunk behind him, for it had grown heavy, when he noticed a great pile of clothing and papers in front of Tunnicliff's. As he came closer, he saw with rising horror: his small clothes, several books that he'd purchased at great expense, even his wedding suit, had all been dumped onto the dirty road. Some of his papers had already blown far down the street. Johnny hurriedly set down his new trunk and began to chase after the rogue papers. One of them was Jefferson's letter to Sally Hemings. It went tumbling down Pennsylvania Avenue.

Johnny managed to retrieve most of the items, although several books and his one good hat had been purloined. He shoved everything he could into the trunks and began to drag them behind him down Pennsylvania Avenue. But the trunks were not locked and kept opening, spilling their contents onto the road.

The wind shifted and began blowing into his face. The sky suddenly grew black; frozen rain came down, light at first and then harder, slanting and painful as shards of glass upon his skin.

He felt like a vagrant as he dragged the trunks down the road. At some point, the sharpness of the glassy rain and the biting wind forced him to relinquish one of them. He hesitated only a moment before choosing to keep the case with the books. He donned his sad worn winter coat and left the rest of his clothing, including his wedding costume, by the side of the road, just across from the Bunch of Grapes Tavern. He suspected that it would all be gone when he returned to recover it the following day.

Tears sprang to Johnny's eyes, mixed with a growing, genuine fear. He was known now, ripe for the picking. Whether by Jefferson's men or bounty hunters hardly mattered. Fortunately, few men knew what he looked like.

If only I can make my way to Mr. Adams, he kept repeating to himself. *Mr. Adams shall take care of me.*

He came to a Negro lodging. Shadows stirred within; the sound of a violin wafted out of the front entry, along with drifting pipe smoke. He approached hesitantly, but the hostile stares that greeted him made him back away.

At last, Johnny reached the President's House. He was wet through and shivering. He mounted the icy ramp at the south end and rapped on the door. An old butler with a thick head of white hair answered.

The butler took a good look at Johnny and said, "The president is receiving no callers. It is too late in the day." He began to shut the door.

"I am a friend, and it's most urgent."

Johnny's hair was in a chaotic tangle. His hands trembled as if with drink and his coat was threadbare. He bent down and retrieved a piece of paper and quill from his trunk. Then he scratched out a hasty note and proffered it to the butler. The old man took it with two fingers of his gloved hand. As the frozen rain hit the ink, it began to stain his white glove blue.

"Tell him at once, if you will, that I am come. Tell him I—" Johnny hesitated. "I have nowhere else to go."

"That is most unfortunate." The old man frowned. He shut the door in Johnny's face.

Johnny paced for a while outside the door and then, unsure what to do, sat himself down upon the ramp. He removed his coat and used it as a blanket, then wrapped one arm protectively about his trunk. There he remained, until he could no longer feel his limbs. A deathly, indifferent drowse overcame him as he lay upon the ramp. This time, there were no dreams. No Bridgetown, Cassie, or Madame Pringle. No Quincy or Cambridge. His sleep was black, wordless, cold.

Johnny was awakened an unknown time later, while it was yet dark, by the sound of the door opening and a cry of "Dear Lord! Lowell! At once, you miserable cur!"

Johnny knew the voice—or did he merely dream it? He tried to sit up but found his limbs would not move. Ice had almost completely sheathed him.

"Sir," Johnny whispered, "I—"

"I arrive, I arrive!" cried Adams.

Mr. Adams, in stockings, dressing gown, and nightcap, stooped to help Johnny up. "Lowell" had finally materialized as well.

"Help me with him, Lowell. Why did I not know this boy was here?"

"You said to hold all seekers, sir, being indisposed."

Adams looked at the man balefully, and then he perceived the smudged letter in the servant's gloved hand. Lowell proffered it belatedly.

"So there was a message, too? Help me into a chamber with him. Then you may pack your bags and be gone from my sight."

"Sir—"

"Do it now, dammit!" Adams growled.

The two of them helped Johnny to his feet and took him into the First Lady's chamber. There, a young chambermaid soon appeared; she helped Johnny out of his stiff, frozen clothing and into an enormous nightshirt, no doubt belonging to Mr. Adams himself. She disappeared and returned five minutes later with hot tea, urging him to take a few sips. Johnny's fingers could scarcely hold the cup. They had gone from corpse white to a hot and painful red.

Adams came in holding Johnny's letter.

"I'm most grievously sorry, son. I have a terrible cold and have been imprisoned in my chamber near a week, or I should have known what Lowell was up to. Anyway, he is gone now and shan't bother us any longer. Come, Marie, dear," he said to the maid, "let him sleep."

Within Abigail's chamber, as in all the rooms, a good fire blazed. Johnny fell asleep at once and slept through the following day. He awoke at an unknown hour and stumbled to the chamber pot. He then returned to his bed and slept until the next morning. He did not want to think of the trunk he had left on the road or about Marcia's explanations. He knew now that there could be no good ones.

•   •   •

For the next two weeks, Adams's last two in office, Johnny lived in Abigail's sparse chamber. By day he slept, and by night, under cover of darkness, he trawled the seedy taverns where he was unknown. Adams had given him money, which he spent on drink. It dulled the pain.

When he could, Mr. Adams spoke gently to him. "I blame myself for believing that your secret could be kept," he said. He further spoke of the double-edged sword that was leadership, and of hard times and new beginnings. "That villainous pamphlet shall be but one assault among many."

For you, perhaps, Johnny thought. Not bitterly, but with a bluntness and clarity that reminded him of Eliot. *You shall move beyond the shame of my association. You shall retire to your farm and keep chickens. But how may I live with myself? What future have I?*

Mr. Adams soon gave up his attempts at consolation, for no words were forthcoming on Johnny's side. Concerned, he wrote a letter to Abigail expressing his fear for the boy. He wrote a more tempered one to Eliza, in which he said merely that he believed her son's engagement had been broken off.

Mr. Adams assumed that Johnny would travel with him by carriage back to Quincy, and on the afternoon of March 3, Adams said to him, "We leave tomorrow morning, John. And good riddance to Washington, I say."

But Johnny replied with a slow shake of his head. He spoke equally slowly when he said, "I thank you, sir, for your unforgettable kindness. But there are some things I would yet do." Adams thought at once that Johnny meant to drink himself into a stupor, alone. But then Johnny added, "I shall stay for the inauguration and then board a ship bound for Boston. One leaves tomorrow afternoon."

"The inauguration? What for?"

"My reasons are personal. Rest assured they're not disloyal to you in any way."

But Adams was only partly mollified.

"And a ship, you say? Have you enough—er—for your passage?"

"I believe so, sir."

The president fished about in his waistcoat until he found his billfold. From this he pulled out several bills and proffered them to Johnny.

"Fifty dollars?" Johnny was incredulous.

"A kingly sum, I agree. But don't argue. You may return what you don't spend. Better to have too much than too little. Keep it well hidden. Know you the name of the ship? We shall have a carriage waiting for you in Boston." This last was said in a peremptory tone, and Johnny accepted with a small nod. "Well, that's settled, then," said Adams. Johnny bowed and removed to Abigail's chamber.

In the First Lady's chamber, Johnny took up Mrs. Adams's looking glass, which lay upon the dresser. He looked at himself. Whose was that long face staring back at him? He didn't know. But for a terrifying moment, his mind played a cruel trick on him and he thought he saw the craggy face of James Callender. Johnny jumped, and the mirror fell to the floor, smashing to pieces.

Mr. Adams didn't care about the mirror; he now feared for Johnny's life. The child was not well. What's more, fights of all kinds broke out upon those rough cargo ships. Brawls, theft, drunkenness, illness. What if someone followed him on board in order to do him a harm? In his current condition, Johnny could not defend himself. Adams had never known the boy to drink before; now, he seemed inebriated most of the time. Adams had suffered the long, slow death from drink of his own son Charles. Youth, he understood, suffered far more sharply for its inexperience of pain. But this was not merely the ordinary pain of lost love. *Yes,* he thought, heading off to make his own final preparations, *perhaps they had all done Johnny a disservice to treat him like a white child, with every hope of a great American success.*

Johnny woke early on the morning of the fourth to find a note from Mr. Adams and several more dollars:

> Take care on that ship, Johnny. The fellows can be
> rough, and I fear that in your weakened state you
> shall succumb to their abuse.

Johnny had no worries about seamen; he knew seamen, understood them. He had no fear of bandits, either. His thoughts were what he feared. Thoughts, self-recriminations, doubts, and cruel visions: these attacked him relentlessly. Try as he might, he could not escape them. He should have stayed in Barbados. His family had warned him. He was unworthy of either love or success. A miserable liar and fraud! Only the drink succeeded, for a short while, in making him feel immune to attack from within, a stranger to himself. He had a powerful urge to stay that way forever.

Before quitting Washington, Johnny bathed and donned the same clothes he had slept in the night he spent on the president's ramp.

Someone had seen to cleaning them. He took nothing but the clothes on his back. No books, no mementos, but only those few items that had first gone to Baltimore, like his box of precious beads.

And Jefferson's letter to Sally Hemings.

Without, it was sunny, and a note of spring was in the air, though ice still glistened upon the road. It glazed the branches along Pennsylvania Avenue, forming a forest of translucent tubes.

It was just past noon when he reached Jenkins Hill and the Capitol Building. The inauguration was about to begin when Johnny pushed his way through the crowd to enter the Senate chamber. He had toured this chamber with Marcia once, but now he hardly recognized the place: It was crowded to bursting. People from the remotest areas of the Union were there—every planter, farmer, mechanic, and merchant that could squeeze himself in. Chief Justice John Marshall and Senator John Langdon sat in the back of the room, speaking softly to each other. He wondered if they had seen the pamphlet, too. No doubt they had. It hurt to think that Langdon had not yet written to him, though Johnny believed he would.

Finally, through a window, he saw Jefferson approach, alone and on horseback, looking the part of a simple citizen. But he was met by a detachment of Alexandria militia officers, swords drawn; they preceded him into the building. A discharge of the artillery was sounded, and as Jefferson entered, members of the House and Senate rose to their feet.

Mr. Jefferson made his way through the crowd. He turned and saw Johnny, and his eyes looked at him with keen emotions: recognition, surprise, fear, and knowledge. Johnny approached; he allowed himself to be swallowed up into the crowd, which pushed him inexorably toward the soon-to-be president. But it was Johnny's will that truly drove his feet, not the crowd. When he reached Jefferson, he removed the paper from his pocket. He groped for Jefferson's hand and felt Jefferson start at the sensation of something being placed there. The man blinked once, tucked the paper in his own pocket, and then moved to the front of the chamber, where he began his address.

After a few minutes, Johnny had heard enough. He turned to leave when he caught the profile of another familiar face. Marcia Burnes was sitting in the front row, among the men. She was dressed in a stunning black-and-white gown. As Jefferson spoke, she looked up at him with naked admiration. A blond, wasted youth in a pale-green silk suit sat beside her. Sensing eyes upon her, Marcia turned her head, at which movement Peter Fray placed a possessive hand upon her forearm. And though she looked directly at Johnny, it was as if she saw nothing at all.

Part IV

54

IN HIS MIND, HE WAS GOING HOME. Not to Quincy but to his real home, on the hill overlooking Carlisle Bay. To palm trees and trade winds. To Cassie and his complaining grandmother. They would scold him for riding the turtles or playing with the slave children on the windmills instead of going to Mrs. Husband's, where he was to school his mind. The older children would hit him hard with a cudgeling stick made of wild guava, turning his shins purple. But he didn't mind. Pain sharpened his reflexes. There was only the burning sun, the sand, and the children's cries. Later, he would walk in bare feet down to Madame Pringle's establishment, and women squatting at the side of the road would call to him, "Johnny! Where you goh? What you do?" Calling out for a child's sweet kiss in exchange for a few colorful beads.

His precious hoard was still in the box Aunt Martha had given him on the morning of his Harvard entrance exams. That was near six years ago. As Johnny walked to the ferry, he pulled out Aunt Martha's box and returned those beads to his wrists and neck. He returned the ruby ring to his finger. He removed the ribbon from his hair and let it spring loose around his head. He'd not pomaded it that morning.

When Johnny reached Lear's Wharf at the foot of M Street, the packet was already there, waiting to embark. But there was no wind, and it was near six in the evening before he was able to board. With him, tucked protectively beneath one arm, was a jug of spirits procured in a shop on the wharf.

Johnny cut a strange figure as he boarded the ship: a noble youth in a worn but finely tailored coat and trousers, with dogs' teeth and fish vertebrae about his neck and wrist, his hair wild. One could not tell if he were a gentleman who had gone native or a native who endeavored to pass for a gentleman. Nor could he have told you which he was.

They finally set sail at around eleven that night. Once on board, and snugly installed in his berth, Johnny drank. It rained all night, and in the darkness the bottle of spirits rained down his throat.

Johnny's destination gradually became indistinct. At times, he knew he was headed to Boston and dreamed that his mother would be waiting on the pier for him. But then, dead in the night, with the moon obscured by clouds and his mind obscured by drink, he thought he might be headed home to Bridgetown. His father lived, and the moment John Watkins saw the ship approach on the horizon, he would drop his adze and come running to meet his long-lost son. Johnny saw them: the tall Negro women in bare feet on the shore, monkey jars on their heads; and monkeys free in the trees, not caged and mad with worry as he had found them in Cambridge. As he drifted in and out of consciousness, Johnny thought he could hear the distant beat of the slaves' forbidden Coromantee drums, calling other slaves to action . . .

The ship made its way up the coast. It put in briefly at New York, and some passengers descended. In the harbor at Manhattan Island, Johnny thought he heard the sound of the drums once more, but it was only the halyards of moored ships hitting their masts in the wind.

Johnny was now feverish, in and out of delusion, part gin and part an ague that had traveled through the ship and laid all the passengers low. Was he at the good place? *Not yet,* he thought. *Not yet.* Coming to welcome him home were Abigail and his mother, Lizzie and Martha, and, of course, Kate. Surely Kate would come. But their white faces darkened in his dream and became Cassie and Madame Pringle and the hucksters by the side of the road. Well, they would all be there, white and black, to remind him that he truly existed.

At last, on the night of March 12, he heard the excited cry, "There it is! The North Church tower! Boston!"

Johnny was belowdecks in his berth, a large puddle of puke at his feet, so old and augmented over the days and nights that he no longer smelled it, though others, believing him to be deranged and near death, kept their distance. Several even chose to sleep on the poop deck to avoid him.

"Gather up your possessions, mates—we'll be in the harbor in an hour's time."

Johnny, still feverish but excited to be landing at last, stumbled up the narrow ladder to the deck and shot forward onto the ship's bow. He looked out across the dark sea, unlit by any light save the stars and a half-moon, and he believed himself to be already on land. He spread out his arms and grinned with joy. They were all waiting for him. He lifted his right foot as if he would step onto shore just as a sudden gust of wind came up from behind and pushed him forward, over the gunwales. With a weak cry, Johnny plunged into the icy waters of Boston Harbor.

"Man overboard!" someone shouted. But Johnny heard it not, for he was in a place of cold, calm silence, beneath the waves.

55

NO DREAMS, NO SENTIENCE OF ANY KIND, invaded the darkness. For three weeks, Johnny lay as if dead. When he did finally wake, he knew not who or where he was. Three concerned faces stared down at him.

"He's awake. He lives," one whispered, seeing the slit of a single eye. The slit shut tight once more, clamlike, to prevent the tears that threatened to leak from it. Was he truly alive, or was it merely those dreams that come? He felt bruised everywhere, as if he'd dropped from the sky. Then, Johnny fell back into the darkness before he could finish the thought.

Some time later, he felt a caress upon his face. He believed it might be real this time. The slit of one eye opened wider: The figure looked like a friend he once had, long ago. Her rich brown hair tumbled onto her bosom. Her amber eyes behind rimless spectacles filled with tears. She asked, grave-faced, "Can you tell us your name?"

Johnny shut his eyes. He was awake now, and conscious. Why did he suddenly feel like joking?

"George Washington," he said.

The girl frowned. "And what is four plus four?"

"Nine. A gluttonous sum."

A tiny smile crept to the corner of his mouth. One of the women whispered to another. It sounded like, "Did you hear him, Abby? That's Johnny. He hates it when others concern themselves for him."

At the mention of his name, Johnny knew that it was no dream. What's more, he knew where he was. He was in Quincy, in Lizzie's cottage, in the same bed in which his mother had given birth to him twenty-two years earlier. Eliza, seeing her son return from the dead, burst into tears. The others raced off to procure various remedies, eager to tend their patient now that they had one.

His lungs had been damaged in the near drowning. Lizzie prepared tinctures for his tea from precious mullein that she'd gathered, dried, and ground herself. She made him a fragrant plaister, too, one she often used on consumptives, lathering it so thick that Eliza was moved to remark, "You look as if you're making a cast of him, for a statue."

"Perhaps I am." Lizzie smiled down at her patient, who could do little more than breathe in and out.

And while Johnny was soon able to take a few steps, even walking across Lizzie's small parlor made him short of breath. He thought mordantly, *I shan't be helping the old man carry stones up Penn's Hill any time soon.*

When the weather finally warmed, everyone went to work in the fields. Thomas Miller, Tom, and Will worked the distant field. Johnny sat bundled to his chin just beyond the barn by the closer, smaller one. Although the air was brisk, yellow and purple crocuses had begun to spring up here and there. He watched in admiration as the women broke up the heavy winter ground. Each day it was as if he, and the earth, were born again. The fields began to come to life beneath the women's diligent prodding.

Johnny listened to the women as they conversed upon one subject or another:

"Oh, but I forgot to mention I procured some indigo for that petticoat you wished to dye," Lizzie said one day. They were placing dried beans in the neat rows of holes they had previously dug.

"Indeed," Johnny's mother replied. "We're so busy, I know not when I shall have the time. And that reminds me, Lizzie. We've had a letter from Martha. Did you see it on the kitchen table? She's invited us to attend her Friends meeting Tuesday next. They'll be discussing that couple from Georgia. You know, those poor souls I mentioned to you last week." Here, Eliza looked about her as if someone inimical to the abolitionist cause might be eavesdropping. But she saw only her son swaddled in his blanket. Johnny smiled at her, and she grinned back.

The endless talk of the women, which used to annoy him and for which he teased Eliot mercilessly, now had quite the opposite effect: he felt he could listen to them forever. The voices healed his wounded soul. They anchored him in time and place.

But Johnny was subject to moments of despair as well, especially when he came to realize that his mind had been affected. He could remember nothing from the moment he left the President's House until he woke up in Quincy. When he tried to read, his head ached, and the words vanished almost at once. Sometimes he asked a question and, several moments later, would ask it again. At these times he saw his mother exchange a look with Lizzie, but he knew not what it meant.

One evening, reading upon a book, Johnny's head ached so severely that he shut the book and clasped his head despairingly.

"Patience, Johnny," Lizzie said, placing her hands upon his shoulders.

Patience had never been one of Johnny's strengths. The moment he was able to walk abroad, he did so. One of the women always ran to his side, fearful he would topple; he walked like a drunken sailor. Often, Kate accompanied him. Johnny had only recently learned that upon hearing the news of his accident, Kate flew to Quincy from New York and remained there nearly a month. Now that he was out of danger, she had returned to Cambridge but visited him frequently.

At first, they strolled about the kitchen garden. Then they moved beyond the garden to the fields. They stopped to watch the men and boys working hard to make certain the harvest would be fruitful. But the sight of the men and boys working pained him. He felt so useless.

Reading his countenance, Kate said, "There will be years and years for work, Johnny. Have no fear."

They made their way down to the shore. Spring was in effulgence now; the trees had unfurled their tender fronds, and the sparrows had returned, infesting the bushes by the hundreds and making a great ruckus. Custard-yellow daffodils shivered in the breezes, and once more the sound of the blacksmith's hammer could be heard echoing across the village.

On one of their walks that June, a strange thing happened. As they made their way down to the water, two Negroes disembarked from a small boat. One of them was a short, slender woman of middle age. Another was a younger man, very dark-skinned. They looked familiar to Johnny. Suddenly he grinned and cried out to them. "Cassie? Cassie! Isaac!"

"Nay, Johnny," Kate said, "that's not Cassie or Isaac." She led him back to the cottage, but before they had reached it, he realized what his feelings toward those Negroes had been: they were those of a kinsman. He stopped before the cottage door and thought, *I'm no longer white. White Johnny is dead, drowned in Boston Harbor. I shan't ever be white Johnny again.* It was a good thing. But he began to cry for all his lost white dreams.

• • •

Slowly, Johnny healed. It was now July, and his mind began to assert its natural curiosity. One morning, after the others had gone into the fields, Kate remained behind to have breakfast with Johnny. He was quietly munching on a biscuit when, out of nowhere, he set it down and blurted, "But Kate—I simply *must* know. Why *did* your marriage fail?"

Kate laughed at his boldness, especially since he himself had not offered a single word on the topic of Miss Burnes. She took a moment to consider her reply. Finally she said, "There was nothing very wrong with Mr. Pearce, apart from the usual male vanity. But I felt—suffocated, Johnny. So suffocated I thought I would throw myself out a window just to breathe!"

"I'm glad you didn't," Johnny replied somberly.

Kate went on to say that Mr. Pearce did not approve of her work on the magazine. He wanted her to devote her energies to her new home and to start a family.

"But did you not know this about him previously?" Johnny inquired.

Kate looked at her hands in her lap, then fixed her amber eyes directly upon Johnny's. "We know things when we know them, not when we should know them. Don't you find that to be true?"

Johnny did find that to be true, but he did not say so. Instead, he asked, "And where is he now, this Mr. Pearce?"

Kate smirked. "You always did call him 'this Mr. Pearce.' I wonder why? Anyway, he's dead."

"Dead?"

Kate nodded. "Yes. His ship was attacked on its way to England, and he was killed in the skirmish. Poor man. We knew nothing of it for several months."

"I'm very sorry."

"I grieved for him as I grieve for any lost life. But as for the marriage, I must admit that I was not greatly wounded by its loss."

"Oh, I'm relieved," said Johnny.

Kate looked at him pointedly and added, "Shallow feelings are to thank for shallow wounds."

Although Johnny thought he caught her meaning, months passed before Kate was able to speak directly of the hurt Johnny had caused her. Johnny knew she waited for him to speak about himself and Miss Burnes. He knew he would need to share his story, if only to repay Kate's candor with his own. But he wasn't ready. Instead, as if testing his powers of narration on simpler topics, he began to speak of his travels.

As they all sat at dinner, Johnny described the rivers he had crossed, the forests he had traversed, and the great sea views he had enjoyed. He described New York's colorful harbor and genteel, sheltered Baltimore. He praised Philadelphia as the most beautiful city in the world. And at last, on a fine summer afternoon, as they sat having dinner in the kitchen garden, Johnny described Washington: "When you mount the crest of Jenkins Hill, the Capitol appears before you like a Greek ruin. *Delphi*, you think. *Or the Parthenon*. Below it, Pennsylvania Avenue carves a bold path through a marshland to the President's House. All the rest is but a frontier of clay pits, brick rubble, and toiling black bodies, slick with perspiration."

Everyone at the table grimaced. Then Johnny concluded, "Yes, there everything holds out the *promise* of greatness, like monuments to a dream. God grant they achieve it."

The company was just absorbing Johnny's somber verdict when little Abby broke the silence. "Johnny, do the Southern girls have pretty dresses?" she asked.

He laughed. "Yes, they do, Abby. Most beautiful dresses."

•   •   •

By late summer, Marcia had begun to fade in his memory. Or perhaps *fade* wasn't the right word, as he remembered her cleft chin, her green eyes, and her winning smile in perfect detail. But just as an Old Master portrait loses its greatness when exposed as a clever forgery, Johnny's image of Miss Burnes was forever ruined by his knowledge of her falsehood.

It was nearly September when Johnny finally spoke of her. He and Kate were on the shore, enjoying the last of the warm summer days. They had removed their shoes and buried their feet in the sand. They lay back with their eyes closed. Johnny recalled the time he had lain just so with President Adams, when the old man had asked Johnny's advice concerning the Mazzei letter. Kate reminded Johnny of the pink shells she had gathered those many years ago, and he replied that she had surprised him greatly by challenging Mr. Adams. Then they fell silent; Johnny seemed to doze.

After nearly an hour, he lifted himself on one elbow and turned to Kate.

"Kate? I'm ready to speak. But I'm afraid to—I've no wish to—hurt you."

Kate sat up at once, looking roiled. She had been Patience itself for months. Now she inquired pointedly, "Whose feelings do you consider, Johnny? Mine—or your own?"

"I—" he faltered. "You're right. It's my own feelings I fear. But come sit by me now, and I'll tell you what I know. I can do no more than that."

"Then I will listen."

Johnny helped Kate up and they moved off to a place nearer to the cottage, more protected from the wind.

"From the moment I saw Miss Burnes, I felt myself to be hopelessly in love. Why this was so, why it happened so swiftly, is still a puzzle to me. But I know it cannot have been because of her character, for I knew nothing of her character then. To me, she was a part of everything that I loved about Moorcock—the great good cheer, the wild foxhunts, Mr. Jefferson, and even the danger that seems to go hand in hand with all their sport. That life called out to me for its beauty and excitement. Oh, I wanted it desperately, the more so because I knew I could never have it.

"Miss Burnes was very beautiful," he continued. He thought he saw Kate flinch and hastily added, "Oh, not deeply so. I mistook a bauble for a diamond. But I was just a boy, pretending to know many things of which I was wholly ignorant."

Johnny grimaced and gripped his head as if struck by a sudden pain. But the pain soon eased and, wiping his eyes, he continued,

"I do believe she truly loved me for a time." He looked down at the sand, smoothing it with one hand as one might a blanket. "I should like to believe that, had I accepted her way of life, she would have accepted me."

At last, Kate spoke. In a soft voice she asked, "Do you really think so, Johnny? Would she have been willing to sacrifice the good opinion of all her peers, her friends, and even her country, as your mother did for your father?"

At the mention of his mother, Johnny's eyes widened. He pursed his lips. "No," he finally said. "One cannot compare them."

Kate thought she had worn down his last delusion when Johnny moaned, "Oh, Kate, I shall never be a senator or statesman. I shall never be a great man."

But Kate was smiling.

"For goodness' sake, why do you smile?"

"Because you are fortunate."

"Fortunate? How?"

"Great men are nearly impossible to love. They spend months and years away from home, and when they are home, they're restless. Their minds are often elsewhere, pondering the Eternal Questions. Ask Abigail if you don't believe me. Nay, a good man is far easier to love. And you *are* good, Johnny, though sometimes you can be quite stupid."

At this comment, Johnny laughed out loud, but Kate burst into tears, and Johnny held her to him. After the tears had been shed, they talked and talked. Kate confessed that she had loved him from his first day in America, that first morning, when his hair was wild about his head, his feet were bare, and his gaudy beads made a terrible racket as he and the children scampered across the floor.

Johnny told Kate that he'd loved her ever since that one kiss at Christmastime, which had so confused him.

"Yes," Kate laughed. "I pitied you greatly then, for I could see by the look of horror on your face that you thought you needed to propose to me then and there."

"I should have," he replied somberly.

. . .

In early October, Johnny was fitted for spectacles, which his doctor thought might ameliorate the headaches. Johnny joked that it was thanks to the glasses he could now appreciate Kate's every detail: the way her own spectacles misted when she felt emotion, the way she cocked her head when she was puzzled. When Johnny looked at Kate, he did not need to see all of her to know he loved her. A fingernail would suffice. The turn of a hip. The bare hollow of her neck. Any place, he thought, that beat with the pulse of her heart.

Autumn finally came, and Johnny was soon occupied with all the lively goings-on at the cottage. He enjoyed the smell of pies baking and the sight of the women as they sat together and darned their petticoats in companionable silence. Thinking all the while of Eliot, he watched as baskets of harvest bounty appeared about the house: apples and grapes, corn and wheat. *Here is so much bounty,* he thought. There was bounty, too, in watching Lizzie, his mother, and sometimes even Abigail from across the room, these extraordinary women, experts of the here and now.

56

ONE MORNING THAT OCTOBER, THE POSTMAN ARRIVED with a letter for Eliza. She took the letter, which, to judge by its besmirched appearance, had come a very long way.

"It's from Cassie," she said, closing the door upon the bracing air. Cassie did not often write, and Johnny's mother looked alarmed.

She tore open the letter. Her eyes scanned the page, and Johnny saw the tears come.

"What does she say?" Johnny asked. He was leaning over his mother's shoulder and straining to see the words on the page.

Your grandma is dead.

"Oh, poor unhappy thing!" Johnny cried. "Poor, poor Grandmama! We were not there! It's my fault you remained here so long."

"No," she said. "Not really." Eliza cried a little, but then she was seized with a thought that seemed to amuse her. "Mama insisted she was at death's door before you were born, Johnny. But once she laid eyes upon you, I do believe she lost her taste for illness." She smiled. "Well, in any case, I must return. It's high time. Do you wish to come with me? I don't recommend it, as you're only just recovered. But if you truly wish it, I could not deny you."

"Oh, I long to see Cassie!" he cried. Johnny thought about Cassie and Isaac and his old home. He recalled the hucksters, Madame Pringle, and Reverend Nicholls. He remembered the sandy beaches and how he used to ride on the backs of the turtles, though he was probably too big for that now. "Well, I'll think about it, Mama," he finally said.

The cottage remained somber that afternoon, when Lizzie and Thomas learned of Margaret Boylston's death. Not because they loved the old woman very much—they had seen firsthand the suffering she had caused their friend. No, it was because Eliza and possibly Johnny would leave them for many months, and sea travel was never safe.

When she learned the news, Kate returned to Quincy to say good-bye. Johnny saw her alight from the carriage through the parlor window. Her hair, as usual, had been pinned in haste and fell down about her shoulders. At the sight of her, his heart lifted with such joy that tears came to his eyes.

"Kate! Oh, Kate!" he called, but she didn't hear him, and so he ran to the door to meet her.

All that day, a great bustle of activity ensured that there would be no privacy for them. The women fretted about what Eliza needed to pack, what would be needed upon the ship, which departed from Boston the following week, and what she would take to give to others. It was a cold day, and everyone was within. The children seemed to be everywhere. It was only after everyone had taken supper and retired to bed that Kate and Johnny were able to sit alone in the kitchen. Kate had made them some coffee, for neither had any thought of sleeping.

Kate took a sip of her coffee and then began. "So, I expect you shall accompany your mother to Barbados? I'll miss you."

Johnny considered the question for a long moment. Then he reached across the table for Kate's hand, which she proffered. "Nay. I wish to stay just here, with you."

• • •

They were married the day before his mother's departure, in the North Parish meetinghouse. In attendance were John and Abigail Adams, Martha and Harry Lee and their children, Giles and Bessie, and, of course, the

entire Miller family. Miriam surprised everyone by tossing pink seashells at
them as they left the church, which had them all covering their heads, and
which turned Mr. Adams quite red in the face.

There was a little house for rent just down the road from Peacefield
that had belonged to one of Adams's gardeners. With the money they'd
been given as wedding gifts, they put a deposit on the house and settled
in easily. Almost at once, Johnny began to help Kate with the *Women's
Quarterly*, both of them hoping it would eventually turn a profit.

Miriam, now a young woman of nineteen, put aside all other pursuits to help Kate. She quickly distinguished herself as an able, intelligent partner in the magazine business.

When the headaches eased, Johnny began to write once more. One
day he handed Kate a small sheaf of paper, with neat lines of words
written upon them.

"What's this?" she asked him.

"My first essay," he said.

It was signed *John Watkins*.

"Oh, Johnny." Kate embraced him.

Kate published several of Eliot's poems, too, which were very well
received. And while it was so special printing him, they could afford to do
so, eventually they published a slender volume called *Dreams Before
Sleep: Poems by Eliot Mann*.

Just after the New Year, with some slight profits from the sales of the
journal and a loan from Mr. Adams, Johnny was able to rent a fine sunny
room on State Street in Boston. It had an excellent fireplace and a small
adjoining room where he could make himself a meal or a mug of coffee.

He amassed a goodly collection of legal texts, which he proudly displayed in a mahogany cabinet given to him by the Lees. Lizzie and Thomas
Miller donated a Turkey carpet, a desk, and a lamp. Finally, Kate painted
two fine watercolors, landscapes of their beloved Quincy, to adorn the walls.

He had easily passed the Massachusetts bar, aided behind the scenes
by a certain former president, who made it known to the judge that

he would "countenance no malignant excuses" to reject Johnny. None were forthcoming.

Johnny sat in his office all that winter and into the spring of '02. He entertained himself by reading the newspapers, and in this way learned that Callender, having been refused by Jefferson for an appointment as the postmaster of Richmond, had joined a Federalist paper and published the very same information regarding Sally Hemings that the blackguard once sought to suppress.

The news saddened him. Though he would never love Jefferson, Johnny yet believed that the man had a right to his privacy. Well, but he was out of all that now. His own life was here, in Boston. Johnny might have found out what had happened to Miss Burnes and Peter Fray, but he had no wish to know. *Not ever,* he thought. But several years later he learned that Peter Fray had died of the consumption, that Moorcock had finally been sold to another family, and that Miss Burnes had married a certain Benjamin Fairfield, another prominent Virginia planter.

Day after day all through that spring, impeccably dressed and having removed all his jewelry save Madame Pringle's ruby ring, Johnny sat in his office without anyone's entering it. By Easter, he thought he would have to close up. He was a black man in a town crawling with white lawyers. Everyone knew it now, thanks to the scandalous pamphlet that had spread ever northward like smallpox on the packets and by post.

No one would patronize him, although each day had brought its share of busybodies, those curious enough about the "Negro attorney" to peer into his office window. Some bold souls pressed their noses right up to the glass, the better to gaze at him. Their breath fogged the glass until he had a pattern of several dozen round marks upon his window, which he kept having to clean.

Then, one day just after Easter, an impressive coach pulled up before his shop. It was a barouche driven by a very long-limbed white coachman in a glowingly new costume replete with a tall black hat. Johnny was staring in awe at the sight, wondering who this person could possibly be, when who should descend but Abigail Adams, in a bright-orange gown. He had never known her to love ostentation, and he wondered at it.

Johnny hastened to the door, opened it, and bowed. But Mrs. Adams lingered oddly for a time in the doorway, as if she might have left a parcel behind in the carriage. This was, of course, the better to garner the attention of passersby.

Not a few people began to gather in the street to watch her. When a sufficient number had gathered, enough to draw yet more, as crowds inevitably do, she entered Johnny's office at last.

"Mr. Watkins." She curtsied.

"Mrs. Adams. To what do I owe this honor? But sit—do!"

She drew toward the young attorney's large desk and sat demurely upon the proffered chair.

"Well," she began, folding her gloved hands together, "I should like to conduct some business."

The nosier bystanders pressed their faces to the glass. Others edged their way in for a glimpse of the famous lady and the Negro attorney.

"Indeed. What business is that?"

"Well." She drew herself up, a tiny smile curling one edge of her mouth. "I've been most grievously wronged. I should like to bring a lawsuit."

"A lawsuit?"

"Yes, sir."

"Against whom, pray?" Johnny's heart pounded with sudden anxiety. He had never actually practiced the law, much less brought a lawsuit to bear.

"Oh, anyone will do, I should think."

As the crowd continued to shove and jostle their way close to the glass, Abigail grinned and glanced back toward the throng.

Johnny suddenly understood. "I see. Well, let us draw up some papers. I'll take the pertinent information regarding your suit against . . . Mr. Anyone, is it?"

"That will be fine." She nodded gravely. "I imagine it will take a long time."

"A very long time, I'm afraid, Mrs. Adams. Would you like a cup of tea while you wait?"

"Have you coffee?"

"I do. I dislike tea, always have."

Johnny moved to his little fireplace to put the kettle on, and in a few minutes they both sipped their coffee as Johnny prepared papers that no one would ever see.

The next day, his first real client walked through the door. And, soon after that, others did, too. After several months, a few other businesses owned by free black men opened up on State Street: a hairdresser, a grocer, and a flour merchant. Johnny befriended many of these men, just as his mother and father had befriended a number of free black families in Barbados.

Then, one day, after much private thought, Johnny walked into the Boston African Society on Beacon Hill. He told them he wished to join and to be of what use he could in the cause of abolition.

"Our membership is open to Negroes only," a young, well-dressed man told him. He began to show Johnny the door when, laughing heartily, Johnny disabused the fellow of his mistake.

Through his contacts in the society, Johnny became a member of Boston's first black Masonic Lodge. The lodge, which had been founded by a certain Mr. Hall, was a powerful presence in the growing abolitionist movement. Aunt Martha told Johnny that she knew Mr. Hall quite well. They often "collaborated," she said, by which Johnny knew they aided slaves escaping from the South.

It was a smaller life than he had once imagined, but a good one. A rich one. He practiced law, went to meetings at the African Society, helped the old man to carry stones up Penn's Hill, and loved his family, which soon included three healthy children. He grappled them all unto him like hoops of steel. It was enough.

He would leave it for future generations to do better.

Author's Note

THREE WEEKS BEFORE MY FATHER DIED, IN October of 2013, I received a phone call from him that began, "I'm reading about the 1800 election. Do you realize how contentious it was? I would think it would be important for you to know that."

"Of course I *know* that, Dad," I said. None of my siblings or I were ever comfortable admitting ignorance to a man of such encyclopedic gifts, even when he was ninety-six. Our father had always expected a lot from us. He assumed that others read as voraciously as he did, keeping up on history, politics, philosophy, religion, problems in the Middle East, and arguments for and against God's existence.

We did our best. But in the matter of the 1800 election, I had lied. Or, like Johnny, I had lied by omission. I knew *something* about the election, but I did not, in fact, understand the personal treachery, the emerging party system, or the radically bifurcated population that very nearly made the United States a brief, failed experiment.

I also did not understand how familiar this election would seem to a modern American: the way vicious partisan papers exaggerated or downright lied, the way so many people were terrified by a foreign presence in their midst. At the time, these unsavory "others" were French and Irish. The origins of the unsavory "foreigners" has since changed, but the hostility and paranoia toward them are much the same.

• • •

For a long time after my father died, I felt guilty about my little lie. Not so much consciously, but somehow, when I went to write the final novel in the Midwife series, I knew that it would be about a boy's involvement in the 1800 American presidential election.

Apart from being fascinating in its own right, the 1800 election seemed an excellent setting in which to place a brilliant young man seeking to change the world for the better, seeking the greatness theoretically possible in this new land. Heroic Johnny, partly black, holds out as long as possible for that promise of the American Dream. And in fact he has every chance at distinguishing himself, if only he can sustain the lie of his whiteness.

Readers who have read my other books know that, while my stories are entirely my own, many supporting historical characters get tangled up in them. As always, I have been careful to draw on many sources to determine the physical attributes, whereabouts, and personalities of the real people whose portraits I draw. Even though this is fiction, I am aware of the great responsibility I have to portray the lives and times as accurately as possible.

John and Abigail Adams should be familiar to my readers by now; I feel that I know them intimately, and their movements in this novel correspond to their movements in real life. For example, Adams really did catch cold upon his arrival in Trenton, New Jersey, in 1799, and an irate Alexander Hamilton did visit him there. The president's ink really did freeze in his Philadelphia study; and Abigail actually hung laundry in the East Room of the new President's House. Small facts like these help create a sense of realism. But more important, these details are the things that move me and inspire me to write.

A word about the novel's many letters and newspaper clippings. All of the letters are my own invention, with two exceptions: Adams's April '94 letter to Abigail, which Johnny quotes from the *Barbados Mercury*, and Jefferson's infamous letter to Philip Mazzei. The poem Eliot reads on Christmas of '95 derives from an anonymous poem of that period. Newspaper excerpts and articles are taken from genuine historical documents, except for Johnny's contributions. The vicious pamphlet called *The Federalist Mongrels* is also my fiction, though it is certainly in keeping with the tone of the times.

With the exception of a very few cases, the movements of my historical figures are accurate. For example, the Adamses' departures and arrivals—to and from Quincy, Philadelphia, and Washington—are usually correct to the day. When not at Monticello, Thomas Jefferson did in fact stay at Francis's hotel. Documents indicate that he lived there off and on from May of 1797 to May of 1800. Smaller events, such as the parties and balls that Johnny attends, are also real, though I've taken liberties with the attendees.

In two major places, however, fiction diverges from reality: James Callender was not released from prison until March of 1801, though his confrontation with Johnny occurs in February. And I recently discovered that Senator John Marshall stayed at Tunnicliff's for several months in 1800, while Johnny was there. But I decided to keep Marshall out of Johnny's hair at Tunnicliff's. Ultimately, a story must have the freedom to be true to itself as well as to history.

Johnny is based on no single real-life character, though if I had to name an inspiration it would be our forty-fourth president, Barack Obama. As I wrote the novel, I kept wondering how someone like a young Barack would fare in those treacherous times. I kept imagining a young man with prodigious intellectual gifts and a rare sense of justice having to hide his race as he moved toward his dream of greatness. In my original conception, Johnny didn't make it out alive. How could such a one live, if exposed?

Marcia Burnes did exist. She was very beautiful, as portraits of her from the time attest. Miss Burnes was heiress to the fortune her father, David Burnes, made when he sold his land along the Potomac to George Washington. The real Miss Burnes seems to have been a very good person and was later in life known for her philanthropy. My Marcia, on the other hand, is neither quite so good nor so philanthropic.

But perhaps my most ambitious undertaking was the portrait of Thomas Jefferson. To many, Jefferson remains an iconic figure of even larger proportions than Adams or Franklin. As the novel no doubt reveals, I am ambivalent about Jefferson. Johnny discovers that none of our Founding Fathers were quite the men they endeavored to seem, but this is especially true of Jefferson. Some would call Jefferson's covert attempts to destroy Adams the apotheosis of hypocrisy. But as Jefferson biographer Joseph Ellis astutely observes, "What his critics took to be hypocrisy was . . . an orchestration of his internal voices, to avoid conflict with himself." I'm inclined to believe that both observations are true.

The letter from Jefferson to Sarah Hemings is a fiction that I created. For a while, though, this letter was so real to me that, in fact checking the novel, I searched many hours for it before I recalled that it was my own fiction. The exposure of Jefferson's decades-long relationship with Sarah or "Sally" Hemings happened in 1802 by James Callender, as the novel describes. Adams's reaction to the letter in the novel is much as it was in real life: incredulity giving way to sadness. In the end, Adams placed the blame where it correctly belonged—not on Jefferson alone but on the institution of slavery itself.

Ultimately, I explored Jefferson's character not to pass judgment but to plumb his complexities. I suspected that Jefferson's complexity—his profound ideological vision coupled with profound personal contradictions—might provide a psychological road map of America during that time. In some important ways, I believe it still does.

If I've succeeded in portraying these people the way I wished to, a reader will judge less than question. Researching American history taught me not only about what has changed, but also what has remained stubbornly the same. Now as then, there is a great gulf between American promise and American achievement. And the question remains, What can be done about it?

I think even my father would admit that I now know a *little* something about the 1800 election. I'm sure he would have been proud. I wish he had another question for me.

Acknowledgments

FIRST AND FOREMOST, I WOULD LIKE TO thank my husband, Peter Hogan, for supporting me in so many ways. It's not easy being married to a writer: there are many hours each day when we are not physically present; and when we are, we can be mentally miles away. Peter is also my literary first responder, reading those cringeworthy early drafts and sometimes late ones as well, catching the worst of the bugs before they sneak their way into print.

Longtime friend Gloria Polizzotti Greis is another important reader, a brilliant historian who not only finds historical inaccuracies but also points out places in need of development or deeper authenticity. Of course, in a novel containing so many hundreds of historical facts, mistakes are bound to slip through, and I take responsibility for any that have.

Thank you to my team at Amazon, who always take my books to the next level: my superbly straightshooting developmental editor, Jenna Free; ever-supportive Senior Editor Jodi Warshaw; and the entire Lake Union author team. I feel very blessed to have all these talented people taking such tender care of my books.

Thanks also to my agent, Emma Patterson, of Brandt & Hochman Literary Agency. You are a voice of reason, grounded in good sense at just those times when I tend to lose mine.

Lynne Flexner, Donald Flexner, Matthew Daynard, and Nancy Daynard: you have always been there to support me in so many big and small ways.

Thanks also go to my friend Corrie Popp, who came up with the name of the "Slotted Spoon Society"; Annabel Truesdell Quisao, for her expert assistance with manuscript preparation; and to Barbados scholar Karl Watson, who graciously shared his encyclopedic knowledge of Barbadian history and race relations with me. Finally, I'd like to thank the archives at Harvard University and the Barbados Museum and Historical Society, where I was able to see and touch many period letters, diaries, and drawings. The Internet is a boon to researchers, but nothing can replace the unique aura of the objects that were actually there. To me, the way such objects can conjure their time and place is nothing short of magical.

About the Author

JODI DAYNARD IS THE AUTHOR OF THE best-selling novels *The Midwife's Revolt* and *Our Own Country*. Her stories and essays have appeared in numerous periodicals, including the *New York Times Book Review*, the *Village Voice*, the *Paris Review*, *AGNI*, *FICTION*, and the *New England Review*. She has taught writing at Harvard University, at MIT, and in the MFA program at Emerson College. These days she divides her time between the Yorkshire Dales in Northern England and her home outside Boston.